OUR LADY OF MUMBLES

Geoff Brookes

AN INSPECTOR RUMSEY BUCKE NOVEL

with my very best wishes

Geoff

Enjoy!

Copyright © Geoff Brookes

All rights reserved.

Print ISBN 978-1-8380752-9-3

The right of Geoff Brookes to be identified as the author of this work has been asserted by him in accordance with the Copyright Designs and Patents Act 1988

No part of this publication may be reproduced, stored in a retrieval system, or transmitted in any form or by any means without the prior permission in writing of the publisher. Nor be otherwise circulated in any form or binding or cover other than that in which it is published and without a similar condition being imposed on the subsequent purchaser.

All characters and events in this publication, other than those clearly in the public domain, are fictitious and any resemblance to real persons, living or dead, is purely coincidental.

Published by

Llyfrau Cambria Books, Wales, United Kingdom.

Cambria Books is a division of

Cambria Publishing.

Discover our other books at: www.cambriabooks.co.uk

To our children.

Laura, Catherine, Jennie and David.

Also by Geoff Brookes

In Knives We Trust (2018)

www.geoffbrookes.co.uk

CONTENTS

Prologue	1
Chapter 1	3
Chapter 2	18
Chapter 3	33
Chapter 4	47
Chapter 5	59
Chapter 6	76
Chapter 7	87
Chapter 8	101
Chapter 9	113
Chapter 10	125
Chapter 11	138
Chapter 12	148
Chapter 13	160
Chapter 14	169
Chapter 15	181
Chapter 16	192
Chapter 17	202
Chapter 18	212
Chapter 19	221
Chapter 20	229
Chapter 21	244
Chapter 22	254
Chapter 23	263

Chapter 24	274
Chapter 25	282
Chapter 26	297
Chapter 27	305
Chapter 28	316
Chapter 29	325
Chapter 30	340
Afterword	348

Prologue

Susannah did not know how far she had run or where she was. But then why should she? She had never been to Swansea before. Everything was strange, disorientating. She should have stopped when she crossed the railway line but she had wanted to get away and she was frightened that they might be chasing her. Now she was lost in the dark in this unfamiliar and threatening town.

Her mind was unable to process properly all that had happened to her. How could she have been so foolish? Had she picked up everything when she ran from them? She didn't know. She thought that she was wearing all her clothes, though it didn't seem to matter that much. She had to get away.

Tears came again, unbidden. They had dried up, as if stolen by the autumn winds. But now they had returned, blurring her vision. Not that there was much to see. The streets were poorly lit, without kerbs and their surface was uneven, with loose boulders and mud pools. There was faint but persistent rain. Susannah's best dress was now ruined, but she had to stumble on, as far away as possible from her shame. She was a teacher, for goodness sake. How could she have been tricked in this way? She heard a splash in one of the foul puddles behind her and so she ran, slipping and sliding and then falling full length. She managed to stand, then fell again, sobbing in terror and self-disgust.

Susannah crawled a short distance and then pulled herself up using an un-lit streetlamp and looked around. There was no one in sight but she was convinced she was being followed. So she stumbled on, because she was too frightened to turn around. A man outside a public house on the other side of the road shouted something at her and so she ran again – and found herself in Hell.

Through the open doors of the factories she could see furnaces and smoke and bright orange flames, with small dark figures silhouetted, carrying tools like devils. She had finally arrived; this was her fate. Eternal damnation. Susannah sat down on a mud bank above an unfenced canal and wept once more.

'A young man in business, aged 29,' the advertisement had said. 'Wishes to meet a Christian young lady with means, with view to early marriage.' She remembered thinking that this would teach Clifford a lesson. And now she was damned.

Who was that woman? Was it his mother? Was this sort of behaviour normal? Who could she ask? And what was the man wearing? Not one fleeting moment of what she had experienced made any sense at all. She hadn't felt right, distanced from herself, as if her body didn't belong to her. She knew that what was happening was wrong and she knew that it was happening to her but she could not stop it. No one had ever told her that this is what she had to do. She had a vague recollection of being in some way restrained and of someone muttering to her but she could not remember what any of it meant. Her chest and neck were sore, they felt bruised.

If only she could remember where the train line was, then she would be able to find the station – if, of course, they had trains in Hell. There was no one following her; that had been merely her imagination and she was relieved. The best thing she could do was to re-trace her steps. Be strong. Be sensible. Find a policeman. Speak to the landlord of a public house, anyone. Yes, that was it. Pull yourself together. She took a deep breath and stood up and immediately lost her footing on the mud. She slipped and skidded down the bank and fell into the filthy water of the canal.

Chapter 1

Inspector Rumsey Bucke travelled on an early morning train to Cardiff to witness the executions. He did not want to go but his official duties demanded that he should. After all, he was the officer who had detained Nancy Peters and John Rowlands in Swansea after the murder and the Chief Constable wanted him to attend the inevitable consequence of their arrest.

He looked out of the window, seeing nothing, and considered the cruel details of the case. John Rowlands was a quiet, unassuming insurance clerk who had lodged with Nancy following the unexpected death of his widowed mother. An only son, he had lived at home for all of his forty five years, sheltered from so much of the life that most people experienced. Alone and lonely in his simple room, he had fallen in love with his landlady, Nancy Peters. She was a small, dark and very attractive grocer's assistant, seventeen years younger than John, and trapped in an abusive relationship with her husband George, a violent man and a notorious drunk and petty criminal. She was more worldly than John and with her prompting, a relationship which began in stolen glances, soon blossomed into something more adult, bringing together two lonely and needy people.

Together, in the excitement and blindness of lovers, they plotted a unfeasible route to happiness, but the poison they administered to George in his tea did not work quickly enough for them, so emboldened by whisky, they pushed him downstairs and then beat him - eventually to death - with a poker. Nancy and John had then fled to Swansea where they took a room at the Gore House Hotel and went immediately to the Southern Seas Shipping Agency on Castle Street to book a passage to Australia in their own names, seemingly unaware until Dermot Murphy, the shipping agent, corrected them, that the route was served by no ships from Swansea. Bucke found them within an hour of receiving a telegraph message from Cardiff and the couple surrendered to him meekly.

Before their trial they both confessed separately to the murder in order to protect the other and Judge Frobisher, on the basis of those confessions freely offered, chose not to waste any court time determining precisely who had done what. They were both condemned to hanging and so now Rumsey Bucke had to watch them die.

At Cardiff Prison he made careful note of the arrangements and the specific duties of William Marwood the hangman and those of his assistant; he observed the two ropes hanging from a single beam above two tested traps and then stood to one side, with the scaffold looming above him, as the two separate processions brought Nancy and John to the gallows. She seemed insubstantial and bewildered; he was trying so hard to be brave but his eyes were dark holes of terror, in a face drained of all colour. Their arms were pinioned and on their heads were white hoods, sitting like caps, ready to be pulled down. Two chaplains were reading the service for the Burial of the Dead as the condemned couple mounted the steps and each was positioned below their noose. As the assistants quickly tied their legs together below the knees, John suddenly spoke.

'It is a cold morning, Mrs Peters.'

'I can't stop shivering, Mr Rowlands. Tell me it will be quick. Please tell me.'

Their hoods were lowered and the ropes adjusted around their necks.

John Rowlands raised his voice. 'I still love you, Nancy. I have no regrets.'

'I love you too, John. But I am so cold.'

The two traps sprang open with a clatter and the couple dropped from view. From one of them, Bucke couldn't tell which, came an audible snap. Then all was quiet. Justice had been served.

He thanked the governor of the prison for the permission he had granted to attend. There had not been an execution in Swansea for fourteen years and Captain Colquhoun wanted to make sure that someone in the town was acquainted with the necessary procedures, should the need arise.

Marwood was sitting at a desk in the office, eating a hearty breakfast. He smiled at Bucke as he mopped his eggs with a piece of bread. 'I have never attended to business in Swansea, Inspector. I am told it would prove to be a pleasant location to visit.'

'Long may that absence continue, Mr Marwood.'

He smiled. 'I administer to the immutable consequence of human behaviour, Inspector, as defined by the law. Sooner or later I shall be coming to call, never fear. The residents of Swansea are no different from people anywhere. Neither are those of the fair town of Nottingham where I must go later this morning.'

As Bucke travelled home, disgusted by the tragedy he had witnessed, he stared out of the window once more, this time into the sunshine, though he still registered little of what he saw. His mind was suddenly undisciplined, chaotic, full of disparate images. His wife Julia and their children Anna and Charles, the family he had lost to illness over a year ago now, were always with him, but today they were joined in his imagination by Constance White as she now was, his friendship with her a guilt-tinged joy and quite suddenly the most important thing in his life. There were vivid and haphazard memories of his military service in India on the North-West Frontier, which were suddenly replaced by the single memory of his nausea brought on by the unpleasant smell of a man with a cut throat in a Swansea privy. Then there was the image of the last man he had seen hanged, suspended from a water pipe in the police cells, murdered by someone more cunning than the constables. He saw bodies pulled from the docks, vagabond children with wet noses and no shoes – all jumbled with scenes from his morning in Cardiff prison. Nancy, slight and dark, a victim on whom the sun shone for such a very brief moment, marched in solemn procession by impassive men to her death, with her unexpected lover and murderer, John Rowlands, a man possessed by such surprising passion. Life-changing, life-ending. Ordinary people betrayed and trapped by the law. We are all ordinary people, he thought. And we deserve so much better. He stared blankly but could find no peace.

Had a stranger entered that empty compartment they would have first noticed the neat hair and beard of a youthful forty year old and deep brown eyes that had carefully catalogued the darker experiences which had shaped him. The scar along his jaw line, his souvenir from the North West Frontier, was now barely noticeable except for those who inspected him more closely than good manners allowed. It was more easily hidden beneath the beard he carefully shaped in his one concession to vanity and which also served to distract attention from his incomplete earlobe, a legacy of the same blow.

He left the train at High Street Station in Swansea and crossed the road to Tontine Street and the police station. It was a solid, reliable-looking building of attractive brick, with three curved steps leading up to a pair of fine mahogany doors with stained glass inserts. He always found it a comforting and re-assuring place, an oasis in the frequently chaotic world which surrounded it. The one unfortunate feature of the building, in his eyes, was the windows. Tall, arched, smart and the perfect target for the stone-throwing disgruntled. Today they were happily intact. He walked through the door, triggering the bell on the frame. He immediately smelt the polish, the daily legacy of three devoted and proud early-morning cleaners. Everything was clean, calm and ordered, the loudly ticking station clock marking out its measured tread. And it had ticked just so, all morning, whilst in Cardiff two ordinary people who loved each other had been executed.

'Good afternoon, Inspector,' said Sergeant Ball, who was standing, as always, behind the counter, ready to receive visitors anxious to be comforted by his generous smile and his avuncular manner. 'A grim business it must have been, I am sure.'

'Oh yes, Stanley. Most unpleasant.'

'Wouldn't like to see a woman hanged. Did Marwood do his job properly? She didn't suffer, did she? They say he can make mistakes.'

'Thankfully it was efficiently done.' Bucke shook his head slightly, remembering.

'At least that is some comfort. Her husband was a proper villain by all accounts, Inspector. Asking for it, I am told. My cousin is a constable in Cardiff, see. Glad to see the bugger gone.'

'But at a terrible price, Stan. And how are things here today?' Bucke looked around at the empty foyer.

Ball opened the ledger he kept on the counter and indicated that little had been added today. He turned to look at the clock. 'Calm all over today. You should go to Cardiff more often. There was a bit of a problem out at Glebe Colliery in Loughor last night. Someone has been damaging locks and chains, trying to get inside, they say. Goodness knows why.'

'Is it ours? Or is it one for Carmarthen?' asked Bucke hopefully.

'Ours, I regret. I have checked. The pit entrance is on our side of the river. I said you might go over there tomorrow but I do not believe that it is necessary. The local bobbies can deal with that, Inspector. Just youngsters, I'll be bound. Or tinkers. '

Bucke sighed. Those local constables, Stephens and Dennis, never filled him with confidence. 'Anything else, Stan?'

'Only that the Chief Constable called in, Inspector.'

'I am glad of it. He said he was hoping to call this morning.'

'If I might say, sir, it is good to see The Chief Constable out and about.'

'Yes it is, Stan. A welcome improvement in our arrangements.'

The new Chief Constable, Captain Colquhoun, had replaced the disgraced Chief Constable Allison and made an immediate impact. He stayed as close to his constables as he could, showing a proper concern for their welfare. He was eager to modernise the force and immediately upon his appointment replaced their old wooden rattles, unreliable and unwieldy, with loud whistles. Of course, the constables were immediately won over – whistles would leave them able to signal for help whilst keeping both hands free with which they could defend themselves. Colquhoun and Bucke had quickly become close colleagues, a relationship based upon mutual respect and one which made the Inspector feel much less isolated than he had previously.

'He used your office to have a word with Constable Plumley, Inspector.'

'I hope he has more success than I have had to date.'

Constable Herbert Plumley had been much troubled recently. He had never possessed the sunniest of dispositions, as Sergeant Ball frequently observed, but following the incident on the Strand during the recent failed assassination attempt, where he had confronted a group of drunk Italian seamen surrounding a disembowelled corpse and effected a swift and entirely inaccurate arrest, he had become bitter and morose. His new-found devotion to the church had done little to lift his mood. He was thirty two years old and many men of his age affected an interest in the church as the most acceptable way to advertise themselves in the marriage market and thus meet demure young ladies, but as far as Bucke was concerned, Plumley seemed only to have sought out God in order to immerse himself in retribution. There had been an incident the previous week when he had detained Oonagh O'Grady's boy Finn, who had stolen some carrots in the market and, with his police staff, had applied an extended punishment which was out of all proportion to the offence. It had taken a long and uncomfortable meeting with the family in their home on Jockey Street for Inspector Bucke, using all his diplomatic skills, to prevent the emergence of vendetta against Plumley by the Irish community as a whole.

'I am not sure that Captain Colquhoun found it an easy meeting,' said Sergeant Ball. 'Our Herbert doesn't say much these days. But I agreed that we would assign him to different duties. I've got him over in Llansamlet now. Quiet over there at the moment.'

'And are there any guests downstairs today, Stanley?'

'No, Inspector. Had a drunk French sailor in overnight, but when he had sobered up he started singing so I kicked him out. Cheeky bugger wanted breakfast. Thought we were a hotel. We were close to bringing someone else in this morning. Winnie the Washer was preaching in the market and telling all the stall holders they were sinners. Well, we know that, don't we? But they didn't like it, said it was keeping customers away. So I sent Constable Bingham down there to move her on but she had disappeared.'

'In which case, in view of the unaccustomed tranquillity here, I shall walk down to the Town Hall and appraise Captain Colquhoun of my morning's experiences. Fear not, I will report to you immediately should I see any signs of religious mania, Sergeant Ball.'

'You make sure you do, Inspector,' nodded the sergeant.

Inspector Bucke picked his way carefully between the dung and the debris on High Street on his way to the Chief Constable's office in the Town Hall, close to the South Dock. In front of him on Castle Street he could see that a small crowd had formed, with Constable Bingham hovering ineffectually around the edge.

In the middle of the street and clearly unwell, Winnie the Washer stood ranting. It seemed that she had beaten her tambourine so viciously that its skin was flailing about in tatters as she banged it against her head. It rattled comically, contrasting with the blazing insanity in her eyes. 'I have looked into the eye of God! He will never forgive me! I have looked at an empty socket in an empty skull!'

'Give us rest from all this, Winnie,' someone shouted. 'We have heard it before.'

'Did you not know? I am Jezebel. I am the wife of Ahab. Naboth shall be stoned to death and I shall be eaten by dogs!'

'I will go and fetch a couple then,' said a voice in the crowd to general amusement. 'Put us all out of our misery!'

'There shall be an altar of Baal in my dwelling place!' She threw out her arms and raised her head to the grey clouds, then slumped to the ground, her face wet with tears. The small crowd of angry shopkeepers jeered as Bucke slipped between them and bent down and gently took the broken tambourine from her. He placed her hands in his.

A voice shouted from the crowd. 'Shut her up, for God's sake Ramsey!'

Someone else laughed.

'It is for God's mercy that I am here,' she sobbed.

'Be calm, Winnie. Do not trouble yourself so. Here, let Constable Bingham care for you. He will take you to where you can rest.'

She looked at him imploringly, with tears streaming from her eyes. 'You must believe me, sir. I am Jezebel. I will be trampled by horses for what I have done. I know I will be eaten by dogs. I didn't want to do it. He made me do it, sir. And now I am damned.'

Bucke rubbed her hands gently. They were scabbed and scarred. Blood was seeping from cracked wounds. He spoke to her gently. 'Your hands are so rough, Winnie. The hands of a navvy.' He smiled at her. 'You haven't been working down the pit again, have you?' He moved one of his hands and touched the side of her face. 'Go with the constable, Winnie. Please. He is a good man and he will not harm you, I promise.' He helped her to her feet and she submitted herself quietly to Constable Bingham who led her away. The small crowd dispersed, their entertainment concluded.

No one could be sure who she was, for Swansea provided easy anonymity for those who lived in its slums. They knew Winnie merely as a washerwoman and occasional petty thief, who half-heartedly scrubbed the clothes of those no better off than herself, in a tub of water so filthy it was impossible to see how anything could ever be cleaned. People had stopped using her, seeing a connection between her and a short but vicious outbreak of cholera amongst her customers, their deaths, according to Baglow, a reporter for the *Cambrian* newspaper, 'bred in the squalor of a filthy alley.' Within days she was destitute and her mud-floored room in Regent's Court abandoned. She had re-appeared with a tambourine, singing hymns and occasionally raving outside the castle or outside St Mary's Church, abused by the people and ignored by the pigeons.

Bucke watched her stumble slowly up High Street with the constable and wondered what would become of her. Like Plumley, her religion seemed to be bringing her no comfort. He turned and headed towards Wind Street and down to the Town Hall.

Captain Colquhoun was waiting for him.

He was a generously proportioned man, his hair clipped short in a military style, a legacy of his service in Canada, with an expansive moustache dominating an intelligent face. His eyes made a careful assessment of everyone he met, piercing the guilty but soothing the innocent. He was a compassionate man and as the Inspector walked into his office, he handed him a tumbler.

'Good afternoon, Rumsey. I assumed that you would be prepared to share with me a small glass of brandy after your morning's work. It is a dirty business.'

'Most certainly it is, Isaac. Thank you.'

'There is little I can say to ease your trouble, Rumsey,' he said, resting a hand briefly upon his shoulder. 'It is a grim spectacle but one day we might need to know how to set such a thing in motion ourselves in Swansea.'

Bucke sat down, shaking his head. 'I have seen what the law demands but I did not think it was right. We have both seen some horrible things during our military service and in the police force, but I can think of little that is so deliberately cruel or so ill-judged. And no one stops to take responsibility for any of it. Everyone says they are merely doing their duty. It is something that they are obliged to do and so the machinery of death continues to work of its own volition and, as you say, one day it will come to us. But I hope fervently that I will never see it again.'

They sipped their brandy in silence. 'Hoped you paid the appropriate duty on this, Isaac,' said Bucke, trying to lift the mood.

Captain Colquhoun nodded. 'Naturally, despite the occasional advantages of working so close to the South Dock. But let me tell you about my meeting with Constable Plumley.' He sighed and then told Bucke he was sure that Plumley was a bomb that could explode at any moment; they must find him different duties as soon as they could. 'I need to tell you too,' he added, 'that I have had the reporter demanding an interview.'

Bucke was instantly defensive- and wary. 'Indeed?'

'Asked me why the Police Force was prepared to embrace immorality.'

'I see. This is about Constance, I assume.'

The Captain looked embarrassed. 'I am afraid so. Consorting with a married woman, that sort of thing. But I wanted you to know, Rumsey, not to warn you, but merely to inform you. You need to be aware that he is looking for something. And I wanted you to know that you and Miss White have not only my support, but also the blessing of Mrs Colquhoun. Sounds pompous I know, Rumsey, but it is true. And it matters to me.'

'Thank you, Isaac. I much appreciate it. There is no story for him to publish. She is my piano teacher.'

The Chief Constable smiled. 'Of course, Rumsey. Though a euphonium would be of more use to the Police band.'

*

Constance White sat on the stool with her back resting against the keyboard in what she liked to call her studio, but was really nothing more than a small sitting room with a small table, a pair of armchairs bought from Malachi Evans' Old Furniture Shop and, of course, the cottage piano, whose threadbare embroidery panels were the only adornment there, other than a small plaster bust of Bach on the window sill. She had been here most of the day teaching the piano to her pupils. She enjoyed her work, a liberation for her from a dismal and oppressed marriage, and she was developing quite a reputation for her patient and good – humoured teaching. But it was these moments with Rumsey that she looked forward to most of all. He called to see her every day and treated her with a respect that she had never experienced with her husband. Rumsey had regarded her from the very beginning as his equal and, in doing so, had given her the confidence to set herself free from her past.

He was a widower but she was still a married woman and they were careful to suppress, as much as they could anyway, any whiff of scandal which might prejudice her status as the Wronged Woman. They tried to disguise their friendship with the pretence that she was teaching him the piano and he did sometimes attempt to follow her instructions but so badly that they both ended up in fits of laughter, enjoying their only discordant moments.

She waited for Rumsey to speak, for she could sense that he had something to say. She understood his vulnerabilities and his compassion, so she put her head slightly to one side and waited patiently. Constance had an attractive face, with a neat up-turned nose which seemed to push her face into a permanent half-smile and encouraged people to talk to her. She was short and precise, with an engaging new-found confidence and the supple hands of a pianist. She was elegant in all that she did, although her long rich dark hair had an unwelcome capacity for ill-discipline which required frequent correction.

Rumsey sighed. 'Sometimes, Constance, my work overwhelms me with its relentless unhappiness and ..' he paused, looking for the right word. 'Injustice. Yes, that's it. Injustice. Everything I have seen today, in Swansea and in Cardiff, has filled me with unhappiness. How can what I have seen be right? Surely we can find a better way? We sanctify sorrow and pain instead of finding the means to end a brutal and unhappy marriage, which would have saved three lives. Instead we have to kill.'

She looked at him, recognising his anxieties, and tucked an irritating hair behind her ear. 'It could have been me you know, Rumsey. I could have killed my husband. It could have happened and then what would have become of me? But I had no one else to help me do it. If I had...well, who can say? But instead I found you and there was no murder. And that is so much better.' She reached across and put her hand on his knee.

He smiled and laid his hand on top of hers.

'I would not have wished to watch what you have seen.' She smiled in sympathy. 'Have you read the newspaper today?' She withdrew her hand, put her glasses on and read to him. '*What possible purpose could ever be served by stretching the necks of two sweethearts who have done Cardiff a public service by ending the career of George Peters, who had forever been a drain on the public purse and was certain to remain so.*' She put the newspaper down. 'My poor Rumsey. At least they are together in death.'

'And yet in life we are kept apart, Constance. It is wrong.'

She understood his frustration, for it was one she shared. 'We must be patient. Billy deserted me and soon I shall be able to seek a divorce. You know that, Rumsey.'

Her abusive husband, an egotistical head teacher, unexpectedly caught up in an international conspiracy, had abandoned her and, by fleeing in fear to America, had allowed her to begin a new life. Unexpectedly she had a lot to thank him for. Her life had changed so quickly and so radically in just a few months. Sometimes she worried that events were out of control, were happening far too quickly. But she also knew her marriage had effectively ended long before William Bristow had run out of school with his bag and away to the railway station. Rumsey had walked into her life as a result and she had known almost from the beginning that she did not want him to walk out of it. What he offered her was something she had never experienced before. Constance knew that it was pure, uncomplicated love. It was to be cherished, never sacrificed.

She had had a letter that morning, from her daughter Agnes, working as a governess far away in South Africa. They might not see each other for some considerable time but at least she had contact with her – something that Rumsey could never have with his own children. That loss, she knew, would always dwell within him.

'Let us have something to eat. Perhaps that will make you feel more relaxed. I cannot change what has happened to you today, Rumsey. You had to carry out your duty and you would not be the person you are, who is so important to the people of this town, if you could shrug it off as if it were nothing. Come, there has been a veal stew on the stove all afternoon.'

'That would explain the delicious smell,' he stood up. 'I still think you should obtain domestic help, Constance, now that you are respected music teacher. Your pupils would expect it.'

'My husband put an end to all that. After all, women across the town, many who you know, manage perfectly well without.'

'They might say it was not becoming.'

'And since when has that troubled me? Come and cut some bread for us, Rumsey.'

*

Later, as he walked home to his room on Fisher Street, he heard a sudden shout followed by loud drumming and chanting coming from inside the Agricultural Hall. He stopped, surprised by the intrusion.

'They call themselves The Church of Our Lady of Mumbles, Inspector,' said a voice out of the darkness. It was a voice he knew instantly. It was Sarah Rigby. Bucke had always liked her, for she was reliable and her refreshing honesty made her seem confident and sometimes amusingly cynical. She was bright-eyed and fearless, but her thin face, hidden beneath her habitual, battered straw bonnet which she decorated with trailing ribbons, was lined with cares and profound regret, for some years ago Sarah had become unexpectedly trapped in prostitution. She had fallen into it as a dog might fall through ice on a pond and then find it impossible to get out.

'Good evening, Sarah. Still with us I see. I am pleased to see you.'

Sarah was always on the edge of leaving Swansea to start a new and happier life. It was always the same. Just another few weeks and she would be gone – to Canada, to Australia, to New Zealand, even once to Denmark - but that was because of Olaf, a sailor she had met. Her destination always changed from month to month, yet she never went anywhere.

'I am here, of course I am, but not for much longer, Inspector. Of that I can assure you. And how will you then manage without me?' She laughed. 'They do a great deal of that sort of thing. There was a time when they were known as the League of Purity. Although how that woman could dare to use the word 'purity' is quite beyond me. I knew Ada before, when she had a very different life. All I can tell you, Inspector, is that these are not agreeable people.'

'You are always so well informed, Sarah, and always so enigmatic.'

'A person must always keep their wits about them if they chose to live on the streets. But you take heed of my words, Inspector Bucke.' Sarah adjusted her bonnet. 'Time for home, I think. It is a quiet night, apart from the noise. I bid you good evening.' She walked off along George Street.

Inspector Bucke watched her for a moment, re-assuring himself that the street was empty, but the evening, though dark, seemed safe enough. There was another moment of rapid drumming from the Hall, which drew his attention. Such unexpected fervour and excitement. Then a dog barked and snarled and pursued a rat down a passageway, returning Bucke instantly to the Swansea that he recognised.

Chapter 2

Sergeant Ball found Winnie the Washer dead in the police station early in the morning. Due to her distressed condition she had only received a cursory search on her arrival and had been put in a cell, to find the peace in which she could recover her senses. It appeared that she had choked herself after swallowing a battered metal cymbal that must have dropped from her tambourine, which they presumed had been trapped in her clothes.

It was a sorry sight. Her mouth and eyes were gaping and her body unnaturally contorted. Blood had oozed down her chin and on to her filthy blouse, her windpipe lacerated by a sharp edge of the battered metal which Sergeant Ball had seen when he looked in her mouth. Her emaciated body curled upon the floor had no more substance than the rags in which she was clothed. Inspector Bucke looked at her and wondered how she managed to stay alive, nourished only by her religious mania.

They would call for Dr Beynon and allow him to extract the cymbal; he would tell them nothing that they hadn't already identified for themselves and Winnie would be buried in an unmarked grave and everyone would forget about her. Then one day some drunk in a pub on a Saturday night would suddenly think of her and everyone would remember briefly how entertaining her mania had been. Her body was gathered up, weighing barely anything at all, and taken to the stables so not to disrupt the normal business of the day.

News was then delivered of another unexpected death, this one on the great Dillwyn Llewelyn estate at Penllergare to the north of the town. Bucke knew that the matter must be dealt with immediately and not by anyone with a rank below Inspector. The High Sheriff of Glamorgan must not be inconvenienced. There was nothing that he could do with Winnie so Bucke left immediately, but reluctantly, in the police gig, driven along Carmarthen Road with great ceremony by Constable Davies.

Evan Davies sat next to Bucke and chattered away quite happily with his schemes to improve the force. His ruddy complexion was accentuated by the wind as they bounced along. His face was clean of any hair, as if it was unwilling to grow on a face so anonymous.

'The way I see it, Inspector, velocipedes is what we need.'

'I see. In what way?' asked Bucke, finding himself drawn into the conversation against his better judgement.

Davies nodded wisely. 'Three-wheeled bicycles are the future. For a start they are easier to balance on than a two-wheeler and of course they don't make no noise. So, when you were on your beat, you could ride around and collar the villains when they weren't expecting it and if they ran, well we would be a lot faster, like. It will happen, you mark my words.'

'Perhaps the condition of our roads might make their employment less reliable than a horse,' observed Bucke, as the cart banged its way through a mud-filled pothole.

'Well think on, Inspector. We wouldn't have to pay no money on horse feed neither, would we? I think I might have a word with the Chief Constable when next I see him,' nodded Davies, sagely.

After four miles they turned onto the long approach to the house, past the Lower Lodge and on to Carriage Drive. Bucke had never visited the estate before. He had heard of it of course, but it wasn't a part of his world and he was prepared to be dismissive of its excess. But he could not fail to be impressed by what he saw. Who could not? This remarkable estate had been carved out of the wild countryside, a world deliberately shaped with the intention of improving upon nature.

The horse trotted along the long smooth drive which rose gently through the wooded hills on to a ridge, revealing beautiful views down the valley. The fast-flowing river Llan had been tamed, dammed to create two large lakes at different levels, where the gentlemen whipped the water in pursuit of trout and then shot the wildlife, whilst their ladies enjoyed carefully designed woodland walks. A waterfall had been created at the end of the top lake, restoring the flow of the river. It was, Bucke had to admit, a beautiful place. For those living in grinding poverty in Swansea, then this would truly be paradise.

The gig stopped just beyond the steps to the solid two-storey mansion. The area around it was laid with flower beds, still bright in the autumn sunshine, as a prosperous-looking gentleman with luxuriant side-whiskers and a fashionable double-breasted frock coat with a velvet collar came down from the house.

'Look, this won't do. It won't do at all. I expressly asked Colquhoun for no one less than an Inspector.'

'I am Inspector Rumsey Bucke of the Swansea Constabulary. And may I enquire to whom I am speaking?'

'I see,' he replied, completely ignoring his mistake. 'Llewelyn. J.T. Dillwyn-Llewelyn. High Sheriff of Glamorgan. I own this place. Well my father does really, but it comes to the same. What did you say your name was? Bucke? Well listen, Bucke. The whole thing is completely unacceptable. There are ladies staying here at present who would be most distressed. Outrageous, Bucke, that is what it is. I am expecting important guests and I find a body in my lake. Won't do at all. I would be obliged if you would put your cart behind the Observatory there, whilst you are about it.' He waved his walking cane around vaguely.

'The Observatory, Mr Llewleyn?'

'That building over there. With the telescope chamber on top. My father watches the moon from it. You see, found the blighter yesterday. Down by the waterfall. Consequences of charity, in my view. Told all this to the constable over there. Told Colquhoun quite distinctly I wanted an Inspector. Man from the newspaper is here, making a nuisance of himself. How come he was here before the police? That is what I want to know. And please get on and move your cart.' He looked around, surveying his property and signifying its extent with his casual cane. 'It is quite obvious the man fell into the river. I have already sent a message to the coroner. Mr Whittlestone will take you down to the body. He is the gardener, by the way – he is over there, busy at the peach wall. I'd be obliged, I have things to do,' he ended dismissively.

Bucke thanked his departing back and, leaving Mr Whittlestone untroubled, went to see the constable Llewelyn had referred to – who was not a constable at all, but his old friend Sergeant Flynn, now based at Gorseinon. He was a tall man, solidly built, quite imposing and with a natural authority. He was always clean shaven, always calm, always re-assuring. The best word to describe him, Bucke felt, was wise. He grasped Flynn's large hand with true affection and then they walked together down to the lake and along the side nearest to the house, which was fringed with water lilies, past stands of rhododendrons to the waterfall, whilst the Sergeant outlined what had happened.

'He left his haversack on the grass next to the falls and from what is written in the Bible we found inside, his name was Phillip Bowen and he was a clerk at the Swansea Bank. Lodged with Margaret Prosser on Nichol Street. Do you know her, Rumsey?'

'Don't think so, James. I will make a call when I get back. What happened?'

'If you want my opinion, I would say our Mr Bowen chucked himself in. The learned gentleman knows otherwise of course. He finds him yesterday sitting by the waterfall reading his Bible, trespassing. Never seen him before, he says, and Bowen asks if he can stay for a while because being here was like being in the Garden of Eden. It takes all sorts, I suppose. Anyway, our High Sheriff, thinking he looks like an unassuming sort, tells him he can stay for a while and off he goes to his fishing. Doesn't see him when he goes back up to the house and so thinks he has gone home, but early this morning they find his body, floating face down in five feet of water, just below the waterfall. Completely cold of course. He had been in the water for some time. He is down there.'

Phillip Bowen had been pulled over on to some rocks, his feet still immersed in the cold water. He hadn't fallen in accidentally. He had removed his watch and left it, with his wallet containing £5 and the Bible, in a haversack hanging from a tree some distance from the water, where they could be easily spotted.

'It looks like an act of self-destruction to me,' said Bucke. 'It is too neatly done to be an unfortunate accident.' He picked up the Bible and flicked through it. Bowen had left his personal details on the title page, beneath which he had written in capital letters, I AM ALPHA AND OMEGA, THE BEGINNING AND THE END, THE FIRST AND THE LAST. The rest of the book was free of commentary until the very end, the Book of Revelation, and then throughout it there was frenzied annotations, underlining and exclamation marks, interspersed with strange symbols that Bucke did not understand. In the margin of the very last page he had drawn a large spear. He put the Bible back in the haversack and took it with him when they walked back towards the house.

'I will come down to Swansea myself later on today, Rumsey. Had a problem overnight at Garngoch Pit. Someone trying to get in – it was all locked up. The night watchman called Constable Dennis and he arrested William Gammon. Denies it of course, but he was carrying a crowbar. Kept him overnight and I will bring him down to Swansea, see if we can frighten him into behaving. I doubt it though. They call him Billy Evil locally, and with good reason.'

'Billy Evil? Bucke was surprised. 'What had he done to deserve such an epithet?'

'By all accounts he had a particularly unpleasant way with cats when he was a boy.'

It had been a few weeks since they had seen each other and so they talked casually whilst Evan Davies, assisted by Mr Whittlestone, carried the sack containing Bowen's body back up the slope and placed it in the back of the gig. As Sergeant Flynn left for Gorseinon, promising to bring Billy Evil to Swansea in the afternoon, a young boy ran up breathlessly. He was perhaps thirteen and had been playing tennis. 'Are you taking him away? Did you see the body? I did. It was white. Do you think he killed himself? Can you tell?'

'It is very hard to say. All we can say for sure is that the poor man has passed away and will be mourned by his family,' replied Bucke.

'Do you think it hurt, drowning like that?'

'Perhaps to him at that moment it didn't matter a great deal whether it hurt or not,' said Bucke, gently.

The boy looked thoughtful. 'The skin was not broken, not properly anyway, and there was no blood. But he wouldn't have been able to breathe in the water, would he? I am sure it must have hurt. If I was going to do it I would use a gun. My father has some excellent guns we use for sport. He has promised to buy me a Westley shotgun when I am older.'

There was a shout from inside the house. 'Richard! Where are you?'

'Cripes, I had better be going. My brother's gone inside. Probably to complain that I beat him again. Not my fault he can't play tennis.' The boy turned and ran up the steps.

As the policemen were ready to pull away there was the scrunch of hasty footsteps on the gravel and they saw Baglow, the reporter from the Cambrian, waving at them with his brown tweed flat cap. He was in his late twenties, intelligent, devious and in possession of a permanent sneer, always prepared to trap people into saying unguarded things that he could use as a headline. 'Give us a lift back into town?' he asked, as he climbed on to the seat and squashed himself between the two policemen without waiting for an answer. 'Always room for a little'un. I can get in the back with your pal if you prefer,' he smiled, as Davies flicked the reins and the horse set off.

'Nice morning for it, though. Chance to see how the other half live, eh? Tell me something, Inspector. Do you think your pal here did himself in? What is your thinking at the moment? Are you in a position to offer the High Sheriff additional police patrols to guarantee his estate is free of intruders. Do you think he came to spy on the ladies in the house, watching them at their toilet?'

Bucke sighed. 'Please, Mr Baglow. You know very well that it is your job to speculate, not mine. My job is to determine the truth.'

Baglow ploughed on, regardless, enjoying the privilege of uninterrupted police attention. 'Bit of a Bible-basher they say. They are the worst. Is that fair comment? There is a lot of it about. Didn't Winnie have a turn in Castle Square yesterday? What, in your opinion, is behind this phenomenon? Would you say that the epidemic of religious mania in Swansea is out of control? In your opinion?'

'Please, Mr Baglow. I offered you a journey back into town. I did not offer you an interview. If you would rather walk...'

'Of course, Inspector. I understand. Just trying to save a bit of time, find out which direction the investigation is likely to take, whether the High Sheriff of Glamorgan is in mortal danger, that sort of thing.' There was a brief pause as they descended the drive to towards the Lower Lodge.

'And how is Miss White, Inspector?' he asked suddenly. 'Very comely woman by all accounts. Discerning gentlemen are most complimentary.'

Inspector Bucke held on to the side of the gig tightly. 'Mr Baglow, this is entirely inappropriate and I would be obliged if you admired the scenery.'

'I mean to say, Inspector, you are a widower, are you not? Is Miss White – or Mrs Bristow as I suppose we must properly call her – is she the most attractive woman you have ever met? Or would you describe her as the second best? I am just asking.'

Bucke looked straight ahead. 'Constable Davies, stop the gig, please.'

He pulled up the horse and applied the brake. They had only just reached Cadle Mill.

'Mr Baglow. I should be grateful if you would dismount from the gig.'

'Inspector. Don't be hasty. I am just trying to fill in a bit of background for my readers. You know, *Widowed Inspector finds solace as crime threatens respectable families.*' That sort of thing. The human element.'

'I am not going to spend the rest of this journey listening to your ridiculous questions. I think a brisk walk might be advisable. Now.' Bucke was angry for letting the reporter get under his skin, but he had gone too far to back down now.

Baglow smirked as he pulled himself out of the gig. 'As you please.' He stood by the side of the road, smiled and raised his cap. 'Good day to you, sir.'

A small but significant victory. He had rattled Inspector Bucke.

'Persistent bugger wasn't he, like?' said Davies as the horse trotted away.

On their return to Swansea Bucke reported immediately to Captain Colquhoun, whilst Davies took the body to the police station to await the attentions of Doctor Beynon. Since the death had occurred on the land belonging to the High Sheriff, it was vital that Colquhoun was kept properly informed. He did not, however, mention the incident with Mr Baglow.

*

Billy Evil was a squat figure of muscle, power and simmering hatred. He was generally feared – and with good reason. His lack of height had never inconvenienced him in the violent world he frequented; he made up for it in instant and unexpected aggression. His dark jacket and waist coat were stained with mud and what may have been rust. His dirty beard made his face dark and his eyes brooded always over imaginary sleights and insults. He didn't appear to have a proper job and he was always available for those who knew him, if something was to be done. His head was permanently thrown back and not just because he was often looking up at the rest of a taller world. It was an act of defiance. He had not enjoyed a comfortable night in the single cell in Gorseinon but he was determined to offer the police as little as possible.

'Same as I told you last night. I was taking it to my sister. She asked for a crowbar, didn't she? Not my place to ask my sister what she wanted it for. Nothing to do with me. Might want to take out her husband's teeth. Wouldn't blame her.'

'And what is her name?' asked Inspector Bucke.

'Ada Gammon.'

'Where does she live then?' Flynn did not believe him. 'Tell me again, Billy.'

'In Swansea. In Pier Street. Unless she has moved since last night, Mr Flynn.'

'Please excuse me, Mr Gammon. I don't know Gorseinon very well. Why were you going that way, through the colliery?' Bucke smiled, trying to appear reasonable.

'Taking a short cut. The quickest way. Until the constable got involved.'

'And that is the colliery where those men died in July?' asked Bucke.

Billy shrugged. 'Might be. Dangerous job down the pit.'

'Only just re-opened,' added Flynn. 'Plenty of new equipment around.'

'And you were carrying a crowbar?' asked Bucke.

'Yes, I told your friend here, Sergeant Flynn. I thought I had just explained why. Must be mistaken.'

'It was for your sister?'

'Yes, Inspector. As I said. Might have wanted to hit a constable with it. What's it to do with me?' Billy stared back at them. Bucke could see that Billy was sure that they couldn't find a charge that would stick.

'You see, Billy, someone tried to break into the Garngoch Pit last night,' said Flynn.

'Well bugger me. There's a surprise. And?' He picked dismissively at a scab on his arm. It started to bleed.

'Why did you do it? What were you looking for? Tools?' Flynn looked at him closely.

Billy sighed. 'What are you talking about?'

'Someone tried to break into the pit. Marks all over the gate. Marks on your crowbar too.'

'Of course there are. It has been used before. It isn't new. And it is good enough to get a man through the gates, if he had a mind to. These thieves of yours need a better crowbar.' There was a long, deliberate pause until he spat out the word, 'Sergeant,' as if it were blasphemous. Bucke was not surprised by his insolence. 'Let me go, Inspector. We all know you haven't got nothing on me.'

Bucke knew it was time for him to intervene. 'My advice, Mr Gammon, is that you need to be very careful about where you find yourself in the hours of darkness, if you wish to avoid giving people the wrong impression,' he said, with exaggerated concern.

Billy looked at him defiantly, pushing his head forward very slightly, holding his gaze. 'Can I have my crowbar back now?'

'Collect it from the police station in Gorseinon, lad. Tomorrow. When I am back,' Flynn conceded, knowing that he had to let him go.

Billy smiled. 'Best be off to visit my sister then.' He stood up and pushed his chair back with his thighs. He looked at them both. 'Been a pleasure,' he said, as he slowly and carefully replaced the chair under the desk.

Bucke looked at Flynn as Billy strode confidently down the station steps towards the habitual pile of ashes at the corner of Ebenezer Street.

'Not seen the last of him. Something about him I don't like,' commented Bucke.

'Don't forget, Rumsey. Billy Evil they call him. With good reason. We have made our point, but he is not likely to heed it.'

They soon followed him on to the streets, though they turned in the opposite direction. They walked between the Pottery and the slaughterhouses, where terrified calves were crying, and down Orchard Street to Phillip Bowen's lodgings on Nicholl Street, talking as they went of the old times, of arrests and incidents they remembered.

The house was in the middle of the terrace, neat, clean and unassuming. Margaret Prosser, the land lady, maternal and rotund, had already received the news of Phillip Bowen's death and she was clearly still distressed. She took them upstairs to his room.

'I said to him. You are studying too much. Always reading, you are. Always in your room. I told him, get out more. Go to the Music Hall, I said, but he wouldn't listen. Mr Prosser will tell you, sir. I told him. All that reading, affecting your mind, I said to him.' She dabbed at her eyes with the corner of her apron, distressed that her wisdom should have been so foolishly neglected.

His room was sparse but clean and extremely neat, with everything ordered and precise. The bed neatly made, his books stacked carefully by size on the small table, with the largest at the bottom. All of them had a religious content; they were either collections of sermons or Bible commentaries. They waited for him importantly, in the centre of the table directly in front of the chair, his life's obsession. Bucke flicked through the top one casually and then realised that it was a small diary. The last entry was written three days ago, on Sunday night. 'Our Lady says I must fast to purify my soul. I shall begin tomorrow, for forty days and forty nights, unless I am called before.' The Inspector put the diary into his pocket.

'What were your impressions of Mr Bowen?' asked Flynn, as he looked in the wardrobe and found nothing.

'He was a very proper young man, sir. Very quiet and no trouble. Very clean. I was so shocked to learn about what happened. He was very studious in his disposition, sir, always speaking to Mr Prosser on religious subjects. Always very regular in his hours. I won't find another lodger like him, I am sure.' She wiped at her eyes again, regretting most perhaps, thought Bucke, the loss of his rental regularity.

Bucke opened the single drawer beneath the table top. There was nothing in it. 'Would you say he was particularly troubled of late? Anything bothering him, that you knew of?'

'He was not a young man to say, sir. But I did notice that when he come back from church on Sunday he sat up all night. I heard him praying. When I saw him in the morning I remarked that his fire had not gone out and he said he had not been to bed.' She started to cry. 'And then he went out yesterday morning without his breakfast and I will never see him again.'

'Do not blame yourself, Mrs Prosser. It is a great shock but you have done your very best. Perhaps if you had not taken such care for him he may have taken his own life sooner. I was aware of that from the moment I came into the house. Go downstairs and take tea with Mr Prosser. The sergeant and I will not be here for much longer.'

She nodded and blew her nose into her apron, leaving the policeman looking at the empty, sterile room. 'Not much here, Rumsey. The coroner can decide that he fell into the water if he wants to, there is no one else involved. Seems to have been a rather solitary young man.'

'Yes, James. This book of his shows his mind.' The Inspector produced the diary and flicked through it. 'Just full of symbols that I don't understand . And it says that he had started to fast.' He glanced across at the simple bed and, for the first time, noticed something odd about the shape of the heavy blanket across it. 'What's that? In the bed?'

Sergeant Flynn shrugged and then pulled back the blanket. There beneath it was a layer of brambles, spikey and dry. The sheet on which they rested was stained with spots of blood and blackberry juice.

'Oh dear,' said Bucke. 'I wonder which church he went to?'

They asked Mrs Prosser if she knew, but she wasn't sure. 'I have a feeling, sir, that it might have been Our Lady of Mumbles. Talked about that a great deal. Never been myself. I am a Baptist.'

When they returned to Tontine Street, Doctor Beynon was waiting for him, ready to tell the Inspector about the terrible state of Bowen's back revealed in the examination. He was rather surprised that Bucke already knew about it. 'He was sleeping on brambles, David. His back will be full of thorns.'

*

Billy Evil didn't go to see his sister at all. Once he knew that he wasn't being watched, he doubled back and walked out to Llansamlet. He needed to see Herbert Plumley, for he had a message for him.

He found him leaning against a wall behind the Plough and Harrow, staring at the grave yard and tapping his police staff on the ground.

'Where have you been? You are late. It is cold waiting here.' He was trying to be assertive but it was wasted on Billy Evil.

'You must blame your pals then. They pulled me in.'

'Constables?' Plumley was alarmed.

'Nah. Sergeant and an Inspector.' He enjoyed seeing the colour drain from Plumley's face. 'They accused me of breaking into Garngoch pit but they had nothing on me and anyway the place isn't suitable for our needs. It is what the police do, or had you not noticed?'

'Only with justification, Billy.'

'Justification? Don't be stupid.' He moved closer to Plumley, staring up threateningly into his face. 'Listen up, sonny. I have a message. Our Lady wants you to get hold of the keys to Calvary. Do you understand? Do you know it?'

'It is abandoned. There is no one at Calvary Pit anymore.'

'Just do it. There's a good boy. You have been told.'

'I always do what I am asked, don't I?'

'Yes, Constable, and Our Lady is delighted. But you have this to do, now.'

'And will Our Lady see me again, if I do?' asked Plumley, feeling threatened.

'She will be very grateful, constable. She has told me. She will grant you all that you desire. And more. But you have to get the keys to Calvary. You understand, don't you? Calvary Pit. Get the keys. And you must do whatever it takes to get them. And she needs them now.'

Chapter 3

It was going to be an exciting evening. For the first time since her husband had disappeared Constance was going out for the evening with a new acquaintance, Mathilde, the wife of Louis Barree, another, more established, music teacher in Swansea. Of course they were professional rivals, but in truth they were operating at different ends of the spectrum. Louis Barree was an accomplished pianist and was involved in most of the musical activity in the town; however, he was a poor teacher, with little interest in pupils who would never match his talents, which was most of them. It was something that never troubled Constance. She sat patiently at her cottage piano whilst her inexperienced pupils cheerfully punished the keyboard and then guided them gently in the direction of melody.

Mathilde was tall and severe, her forehead forever elevated in haughty superiority, and Constance did not find her particularly stimulating company but perhaps, she thought, that was a consequence of living with her husband. This new friendship was, when she reflected on it, a strange one for Mathilde to foster. Perhaps it made her feel superior, for Constance was not financially comfortable. But it might, in fact, be entirely the opposite. Perhaps she envied the freedom that Constance had discovered. After all, Mathilde had to deal with the irascible Louis on a daily basis. But whatever the reasons, tonight it felt as if she was being re-admitted to society, no longer a spectator, and Constance was not going to miss it.

She had one properly formal dress left and it was not difficult to find in an empty wardrobe. It was the one which Rumsey had told her, wisely, that she should keep, rather than pawn at the Old

Clothes Shop, along with the few others she had. It was bright red and had a high standing collar. Constance believed that it made her look taller and made her walk more elegantly. It was also pleasingly long enough to hide her shabby boots from disapproving stares. The last time she had worn it, there had been a shooting in the lobby of the Mackworth Hotel; she could not hope for similar excitement tonight. Mathilde sat patiently on the piano stool, occasionally passing her finger along different surfaces and looking with distaste at the kind of dust that inevitably accumulated when you didn't have proper staff, waiting for Constance to get ready. She walked into the room trying to pin up her hair, which was misbehaving again.

'The colour of your dress suits you, Constance. It is so very, how do you say? Vibrant?'

'Why thank you, Mathilde. You are very kind. I am so looking forward to this evening. They say he is an exciting speaker. His meetings are always extremely popular.'

'This is what many people say, Constance. For myself, I would think perhaps that a religious man should not seek out popularity, always. This does not provide an opportunity for reflection and his use of the Agricultural Hall lacks a certain reverence, I fear.'

'Oh well,' said Constance cheerfully, 'it is his message that people go to listen to, I imagine. But Mrs Brown at the bakers said that he has moved now. Tonight he is using the old chapel on Oxford Street, just behind the Agricultural Hall. It has been renamed. The Chapel of Our Lady of Mumbles. That is where he is tonight. For the first time too. It has been empty for a long time. He puts on quite a show, they say.'

'This is not the Star Theatre, Constance. This is devotional, not a cheap entertainment. You must bring some coins, for I understand that he collects money. He has, it is said, abandoned all worldly goods to better represent the Lord. But a man must eat, even a prophet.'

Constance pulled a face that Mathilde could not see. She had been admonished. She really must try to take her salvation seriously. Perhaps next time they went out it would be her chance to choose and she could persuade Mathilde to go to a séance.

Rumsey was later than she had expected and when he eventually arrived, Constance and Mathilde were just about to leave. She saw the disappointment in his eyes and wished he was going with her. When Mathilde wasn't looking, Constance surprised Rumsey by giving him a surreptitious kiss on his cheek. She saw him blush faintly and then watched him quickly adopt the role of a senior police officer.

'I must, of course, in these circumstances, escort you both to your destination and, perhaps more importantly, home once more. Some of our residents can often be a little over-excitable in the dark.'

'Thank you so much, Inspector Bucke. I am happy to accept your kind offer of protection,' said Mathilde stiffly.

He took the outside of the narrow pavement as they walked the short distance towards the church, passing the entrance to the Agricultural Hall and onwards, towards the growing noise of a crowd.

'I last attended the hall when I purchased a Magnetaire belt,' announced Mathilde, unexpectedly. 'It employs the curative powers of magnetism to soothe my sciatica. Very invigorating.'

'I am sure Monsieur Barree is most appreciative,' replied Constance. She sensed Rumsey suppress a laugh in the darkness between gas lamps.

They saw that the Oxford Street Chapel, once neglected and over-looked, appeared tonight to be full, with the congregation spilling on to the street. It was a very noisy crowd, with a scarcely controlled air of hysteria. As the two women moved away from their escort, Constance turned to speak to Rumsey and saw him step backwards in the crowd to allow an old lady through. He appeared to knock into a small and filthy girl pushing a child's toy pram. As he began to offer an apology, the girl looked up at Bucke and asked him, 'Are you evil, mister?' Constance was surprised by the unexpected nature of the question but was unable to resist the press of the crowd that drove her and Mathilde inside and she quickly lost sight of Bucke and the little girl.

It was merely the first of a number of strange things that would come to dominate her memories of the evening. Her most over-riding memory, however, was that, from the very first moment, she felt completely out of place. No one else had dressed for the occasion in the same way, generally because most of them would have been unable to do so even if they had wanted, and she felt that Mathilde and herself were too conspicuous. The congregation was drawn largely from the poorer parts of town and included a disproportionate number of the forceful elderly, who pushed their way through in their single-minded determination to secure the best seats. Constance, however, managed to snake a path for the two of them which led upstairs to the back of the gallery where she could, between the shifting figures in front to them, look down on the pulpit.

'It is very busy tonight, isn't it?'

'I believe that his services are busy most nights, Constance. There are many people in our town seeking salvation.'

'So it would appear.'

Mathilde leaned forward. 'Look there, just below. I see Enid Wharton.'

'She doesn't look as I would have expected,' replied Constance. 'I think we are over-dressed.' She was right. Enid Wharton, the wife of a ship's chandler, was noted for her fashionable appearance. But tonight, she was dressed in brown and shabby working clothes, with a woollen shawl.

Mathilde snorted. 'She looks like a cockle woman. At least she has brought her maid with her.'

Constance looked at their own clothes. 'Perhaps she prefers to remain unnoticed.'

She looked around her. The chapel was remarkably small and the pall of incense hanging heavily in the air made her feel both claustrophobic and excited at the same time. There was a growing hum of expectation. There were mirrors all around the chapel, magnifying the light from the paraffin lamps, and in one of them she saw the unexpected reflection of a striking teenage girl, but the mirrors were disorientating and she couldn't see where she was seated.

Then the lamps suddenly began to dim, inspiring instant and absolute silence. It was unnerving. Then a single voice called out, softly but clearly, 'Father Milo.' Then someone else repeated it and then others joined in and the lights seemed to dim still further, as a whispered chant – 'Father Milo…Father Milo' - spread through the chapel, an unstoppable tension rising as a drum joined in, four syllables, four beats, softly at first but quickly increasing in volume and speed. Constance found it completely hypnotic.

There was a sudden flash of light in the ceiling which drew everyone's eyes and the crash of a cymbal. The frenzied drumming stopped and the lights were raised and there in the pulpit, arms outstretched, eyes wide, was Father Milo. A woman screamed and suddenly there was uncontrollable shouting and cheering. Milo did not move.

Constance was enthralled by the drama of it all and by the limitless devotion Milo was being offered by his adoring congregation. Mathilde was already caught up in the thrill of it all, clapping vigorously then holding her face in her hands, then clapping again. Perhaps, thought Constance, she should go along with it, but she could not suspend her disbelief and until she could do that, she realised she would continue to find all that was happening just as she had when it had started, choreographed and calculated. She was an observer, not a participant.

She examined Father Milo carefully, a still presence amongst the swaying and restless adulation and the unquestioning love which rose like steam from the pews. He was tall and thin, with large, extraordinarily intense eyes. His hair was unfashionably long, swept back from his forehead, curling at his collar, and his beard completed the frame around his face intensifying, if that were possible, the brightness of his eyes. He was wearing a simple sackcloth robe, as a man might if he were to renounce all worldly possessions, like a Biblical figure suddenly transported to late nineteenth century Swansea.

He slowly brought his hands together into his chest and crossed them over his heart, then spoke in a deep resonant voice. 'I have looked into the Eye of God!'

'Hallelujah!' The response came from somewhere unseen beneath the gallery.

'I am the Alpha and the Omega. I am the beginning and I am the End. I am the First and the Last.' He paused, then cried loudly, 'Hallelujah!'

There were shouts and imploring hands reached out towards his multiple reflections. He stood motionless, impassive. There was silence from a congregation, desperately seeking guidance.

'My friends. You shall dream dreams tonight, but they will be merely the twisted images of an impure life. But I shall see visions once more, for assuredly Almighty God will speak to me again. He has accepted today two new apostles, who have shed the tainted shell of the body and already drink the waters that spring from crystal fountains beneath his sapphire throne! They are honoured members of the Militia of Jesus. They are waiting for us, even now.'

His sermon was long and sometimes rambling to Constance's mind, but there was no doubt that he was a mesmerising and dramatic speaker. In the intense heady atmosphere of the chapel, the mirrors reflecting the flickering lights suggested that Milo was moving around amongst them, and each member of the congregation believed he was speaking to them alone. His mission, he reminded them, was to create a home for the love of God within the pure hearts of his followers. He repeatedly said, 'No matter your station in life, you have been chosen by the Lord. He has chosen you for the field of Armageddon. You have been blessed by God, for you are The Chosen Ones.' His speech became more insistent, more frenzied.

'God has spoken to me. The passion for the Lord in your heart is a sign of the Divine Will and those who do not believe this are at war with the Will of God. And those who oppose the Will of God are at war with good, for God is, and must, be good. It is written that those who oppose you and ridicule you must be evil, they must be the instruments of Satan!'

Constance was aware of a thin feather of smoke rising from behind the pulpit which very quickly became thicker and, as it did so, the drums seemed to start once again, beginning faintly in the veins of the congregation and soon consuming them entirely.

Father Milo threw his arms out once more. 'Bring me my spear!'

Suddenly Constance was aware of a figure which appeared unexpectedly in the middle of the acrid smoke, a woman dressed in white robes, outlined dramatically in the disorientating gloom. She stood beneath the pulpit with a large spear in her hand, with which she amplified the slow heavy rhythm of the drums by beating it upon the floor. She was a larger woman than many, but she had striking features –a broad face, full lips, a mass of long black hair which hung even further down her back as she threw her head backwards.

'Deborah! Our Lady of Mumbles! Almighty God has chosen us as his warriors in the final battle that surely approaches. And it will be Deborah, who once led the armies of the Israelites into battle, who will now inspire us to certain victory!' Milo reached up his hands to heaven.

The drums became louder and the mesmerising rhythm was augmented by stamping feet which seemed to Constance to shake the gallery. An overwhelming chant emerged within the chapel, this time with three syllables, 'Deb-Or-Ah. Deb-Or-Ah.' As it became louder Deborah herself lifted the spear in both hands and held it horizontally above her with her eyes closed in ecstasy, her long hair sliding down over her white robes. Constance heard a scream close by and realised that it was Mathilde, completely immersed in the whole experience, shaking, tears rolling down her face.

The drumming became manic and uncontrolled until the lights went out and everything stopped. Then the lamps were relit and Deborah and Milo were gone and the thick acrid smoke which had collected against the plastered ceiling swirled in thinning clouds as the chapel doors were opened. Everything had been so carefully orchestrated, made so dramatic and sensual in comparison with the daily lives of most of the congregation, but when the doors to the outside world were opened, the illusion dissipated and, as the insubstantial wisps of smoke disappeared, the mundane returned.

Members moved amongst the rest of the congregation with buckets and battered saucepans, collecting small donations, whilst Constance and Mathilde waited for a route to open up down the stairs. Suddenly, Constance was aware of a short man with a twisted face that leered up at them, who pushed himself pleasurably up against a horrified Mathilde.

'Nice clothes,' he said. 'Toffs, eh? Listen to me, my ladies, to follow Father Milo and be saved then you must renounce everything. Give me your money.' They threw their small coins into the bucket he held before them and Constance led Mathilde past him to the exit. 'Plenty more where that comes from, I'll be bound,' Billy Evil shouted after them. 'The Lord knows you! And I knows you, too.' Don't you forget!'

Constance looked around anxiously and was relieved to see Rumsey waiting for them, a little apart from the crush around the door, bowing his head in welcome before escorting the two women, both silent, both lost in their thoughts, along Oxford Street towards the Barree house on Cradock Street.

As they turned left along Union Street, Constance saw Mrs Wharton continuing purposefully down Oxford Street, with her maid scurrying along in her wake. Mathilde suddenly blurted out.

'You must understand, Inspector Bucke, that everything was quite miraculous. How did Father Milo appear so suddenly? At the beginning? Where did he come from? We were in the presence of the Divine, of that I have no doubt.'

'Mathilde you mustn't allow yourself to be deceived,' said Constance. 'There is a door behind the pulpit. We were made to look away by the noise and the light, and whilst we were doing that, he slipped out of the door, that is all. I was watching.'

'It was God's work,' said Mathilde, shaking her head. 'We were in the presence of the Lord, who spoke to us through Father Milo. I know that it is true. I would be grateful, Constance, if you would accompany me on another occasion to see Father Milo. I feel that he is a great man.'

'Of course I will come with you, Mathilde. I would be delighted. But perhaps next time we should not dress so well.'

Mathilde smiled and knocked at her door. 'Good night, Constance. Good night, Inspector. I should like to thank you both for your company.' Elodie, her maid servant opened the door, curtseyed and Mathilde Barree slipped inside.

Constance and Rumsey retraced their steps through the empty streets. It was a still, dark evening, one side of the sky sprinkled with stars, the other side obscured by a rain cloud. She felt as if they were the last people living in an abandoned town. It was Rumsey who broke the silence.

'Tell me, how was your evening, Constance?' he asked.

'It was a wonderful evening, Rumsey. Thrilling and exciting and entirely silly. Mathilde, however, got completely carried away. It seems that she believes it all. She was enraptured, I would say. She let herself go in a way I think she has not done in a very long time. It was a strange thing to see, indeed.'

'And what is there to believe, would you say?' asked Bucke.

She thought about her answer carefully before she spoke. 'That Father Milo is our salvation. That he will protect his followers in the cataclysm that will surely come, that those who do not hear his message are damned. And the message was clear enough. We can only be saved if we give everything to him. Everyone in the chapel was entranced, believing everything he said. And he is very persuasive, very absorbing. What he says is familiar to those who go frequently. They know what to expect and they wait for it. And it is exciting for those like Mathilde who have not been before. He spoke about salvation to poor people who have very little and who have difficult lives. Then they give him everything they have. He takes their money and in return offers them an empty dream, an invitation to a world in which they will have everything.' She paused. 'But I think it is a sham. I did not like him and I do not like the things that he is doing.'

She went through the details of the evening, though she realised that there was little substance to what had happened, and then remembered suddenly that Father Milo had mentioned two fortunate apostles who were waiting for them somewhere, whatever that meant.

'Two, you said?' The Inspector said nothing more for a while, until they arrived outside the door to Constance's rooms. He rested his hand upon the door handle. 'I was outside of course, but it seemed to me to be a very strange place, unlike any other in Swansea.'

'I think you are right. But I have had a very interesting evening, Rumsey. Quite unexpected in parts. My only regret is that you were not there to share it with me. It would have been much more fun. So please, come inside for a moment for a cup of tea, before you go home. I have missed an opportunity to talk to you tonight.'

'The hour is late, and it might not be considered seemly, Constance.'

She was exasperated. 'For goodness sake, Rumsey! A cup of tea surely would not harm,' She put her head on one side. 'Unless of course, you don't want to.'

Rumsey smiled. 'Walking the streets, as I have done tonight, is thirsty work, Constance.'

'Then please come in, Inspector. It is the least that I can do after you have escorted me safely to my home along such dangerous streets.' She pushed the door open. 'Common courtesy is more important than rumour, Rumsey. Please remember.'

On the other side of St Helen's Road, from the darkness of a doorway, Baglow the reporter watched them go inside. He'd been waiting there for a while, and his patience had delivered to him the evidence he sought. He made an entry in his notebook. A good night's work.

*

The atmosphere was less measured on Cambrian Place. Enid Wharton had hurried home after the thrills of the chapel to their rooms behind her husband's chandlery, next door to the Custom's House and conveniently situated for the docks and the timber yard. She was anxious. Jeremiah had abandoned his usual hostility and had been unusually eager for her to go to the meeting tonight, which was totally out of character. He even gave her some money for the collection. Enid had brooded about it all night and it had rather detracted from the mesmeric experience that drew her to see Milo as often as she could. She just couldn't get Jeremiah out of her head.

As she walked at speed through the door, she saw a bonnet circled by grubby ribbons on the kitchen table. It wasn't hers. Then, she saw a woman she did not recognise, coming down the stairs and fastening her blouse.

If truth be told, Enid was not surprised, but she was shocked by the sight of another woman inhabiting the house as if it was her own. There was the briefest moment, during which the two women exchanged glances of anger and defiance. Then Enid shouted out, 'Get out of my house! I demand it! Get out now!'

'Of course, Mrs Wharton, that is my intention. I am very happy to leave, for my business is concluded,' said Sarah Rigby as calmly as such circumstances would allow. 'Naturally, I hardly need tell you that I am here by invitation.'

'This is my home and I do not need a pinchcock parading through my house as if it belonged to her!'

Sarah tried to retain her composure. 'Your issues, madam, must be with your husband, with whom I reached an arrangement, but they are none of my concern. I have been involved in a transaction with the man who invited me here. He asked me to come to him, tonight. I had no reason to refuse. You might wish to consider why he was driven to enter into an agreement with me.' She had always known that such a confrontation was possible, inevitable even, given the nature of her employment, but she knew she had to stay calm and get out of the house as soon as she could.

Jeremiah Wharton peered around the door at the top of the stairs, not ready to intervene, but rather, cursing an inconveniently short sermon by Father Milo.

'And my husband paid you?' Enid was shocked, bewildered, horrified.

'Of course he paid me. Do you think I would be here if he hadn't?'

'Get out of my house! You bunter! You hedge creeper! Get out of my house!'

'With pleasure.'

'Pinchcock!' Enid grabbed a large earthenware meat dish and waved it frantically in her direction. Sarah was frightened and tried vainly to calm the betrayed woman.

'Please, Mrs Wharton. Compose yourself. I am leaving, as you can see.' She grabbed her hat and backed out of the kitchen.

Enid threw the dish at her and missed. It struck her maid, Violet Lee, on the forehead, and fragments broke off, cutting her forehead open. She fell to the floor, stunned and insensible. In the resulting silence and shock, Sarah seized the opportunity to leave, glancing scornfully at Jeremiah as she did so.

Jeremiah went to close the door that Sarah had left open and then came nervously into the kitchen, looking at Enid, who by now was holding Violet gently, her rage subsiding in the face of her guilt at injuring her so badly. She cradled her head in her lap, bathing Violet's forehead with warm water from the kettle and watching her carefully.

'You best not have killed her. It would not go well for you,' said Jeremiah, grateful for the chance to turn attention away from himself.

'And if her condition is serious then you shall be to blame.'

He snorted derisively. 'You threw it. What did I do?'

'You invited that woman into our house, into our bed. That is what you did. Go from me now. I have no wish to see you.' Enid stroked Violet's cheek gently with the back of her fingers.

'And what's a man to do when you spend all your time with that god whisperer, that infernal bible beater? Answer me that.'

'He talks more sense than you will ever know.' She saw that Violet was starting to stir. 'Do not think that for a moment I am coming to bed tonight. Not with you, Jeremiah.'

'Please yourself,' he shrugged. As far as he was concerned, the only thing he had done that was wrong was getting caught. He certainly hadn't hurt anyone.

'And I will tell you this too,' Enid said coldly. 'If something like this should ever happen again, then it will not be poor Violet lying here in my arms. You will be lying on the floor and I will be on a train. To freedom.'

'An interesting offer, Enid. An offer worth considering. A price worth paying.' He nodded as if he was considering a genuine offer that she had made.

'Leave me be. I have no time for you, wretch.' She watched him leave and winced slightly as he slammed the kitchen door.

'Poor Violet. I am so sorry. I was in a temper. I never meant to harm you. It was a terrible mistake.'

'My head hurts. I thought I had gone to join the Militia.'

'No, Violet .You are quite safe, I promise you. You are here in our home and you will be fine.'

Chapter 4

Inspector Bucke lay awake on his narrow bed into the early hours, listening to the wind rattling the window, studying Phillip Bowen's diary. He was concerned by what Constance had told him of Father Milo and also by what he had seen for himself. He had stepped quickly back into the shadows when he saw Herbert Plumley going into the Chapel and even further into the darkness when he saw Billy Evil just behind him —an unexpected and worrying combination, though he had not mentioned it to Constance. He had a feeling, that familiar unexplainable feeling of alarm, that someone more fanciful might call a policeman's instinct. Something here was wrong. He wondered how Milo had secured use of the Oxford Street Chapel. How had it come into his possession? Could you just rename a chapel as you saw fit? Didn't you need to ask someone?

As far as the diaries were concerned, there was a great deal that he could not understand, though he did wonder if anyone could ever pretend to understand any of it. The book was nothing more than a window into a frustrated and unhappy life. Pages of carefully drawn symbols were interspersed with what Bucke assumed were Biblical quotations. 'Remember therefore from whence thou art fallen,' was written neatly in the middle of a page and then, on the next, a little more untidily, 'Fear none of those things which thou shalt suffer.' One of the last entries read, in capitals, 'LEARN GREEK!!!' It was all obviously highly important to Bowen, but it would always prove impossible to unpick how his mind had been working or to understand the forces which had been driving him. He was a lonely young man seeking solace in religion, receiving easy solutions to his anxieties and encouraged to believe that he had achieved an understanding that was denied ordinary people. The inevitable conclusion was that his religious interests seemed to have inspired what appeared to be an act of suicide. The possibility that Milo might have referred to his death and that of Winnie in a positive way in his sermon last night troubled Rumsey greatly.

There was an interesting echo too of something that Winnie had said. On one of the pages, surrounded by elaborate symbols, he had written 'Looking into the Eye of God,' a phrase Constance had reported. Bucke was sure that there was a connection between Bowen and Father Milo, it seemed obvious. Mrs Prosser had said he had attended the church of Our Lady of Mumbles and the diary showed Bucke that there was a great deal here that he needed to understand.

He slept very little, worrying away at the scant information he had until dawn, when he fell into a deep sleep from which even the bells of St Mary's struggled to wake him, so he was walking briskly up the High Street, later than he would have wished, when the police wagon drew up alongside him.

'Morning, Inspector. Me? I am busy already. They sent me out, didn't they? To fetch the rats from down St Mary's.' Constable Davies, who had rather enjoyed his day riding around in the gig yesterday, had obviously volunteered to take the wagon out and was now returning to the police station.

'Rats, Constable Davies?'

'Too true. Mind you, it were not a pretty site. Looks like some dogs got into a couple of rat nests in the graveyard at St Mary's. The little buggers were spread everywhere. Vicar was quite upset. A right mess. Surprised you didn't hear it on account of where you live. So I have been there and collected up as many of them as I could find and it is now my official duty to take this sack of rats up to the station for burning. And I would have to say that this would have been the perfect job for a constable on a velocipede.' He twitched the reins and the horse walked off, leaving Bucke behind on the edge of the pavement, avoiding the animal's legacy which was steaming in the gutter on this chilly autumn morning. It would be a day to get out of the police station. It was bad enough with the stink of the slaughterhouse at the end of the street but the aroma from a bonfire of dead rats was not what the police station required.

When he got there he could see that Sergeant Ball was rather preoccupied, dealing not with a plague of rats but with a plague of criminal damage. There had been a steady stream of complaints from the more prosperous side of town. There had been an explosion of vandalism on Westbury Street and angry residents were demanding action. Door knockers had been removed and someone seemed to have used a stolen brace to bore round holes through the front doors. It was almost certainly the work of the strangely-named Hat Stand gang, a group of young boys who were constantly in trouble around the town. They lived on Miers Street in St Thomas and had the unquestioning support of their parents, to the extent that seemed to believe that they were untouchable. They had stolen door knockers before, which had been found a few days later buried on the beach, but now they were suspected of selling them for scrap. Last week two members of the gang had broken open the contribution box at the Blind Institution and stolen two penny pieces, for which they each received four strokes with the birch, which Bucke regarded as a pointless punishment since it was accepted by the boys as both an unfortunate occupational hazard and as a badge of honour. He heard Sergeant Ball trying to calm frayed nerves and hoped fervently that he was not to be encumbered with such issues in addition to two dead bodies in the last 48 hours. What concerned him was, that as a force, they were reacting to events, unable to understand or prevent the arrival of a corpse at the police station or to keep alive someone they had detained for her own safety. It was usually the way things were but he never felt that it was a good position to be in. Constable Morris was dispatched to Miers Street and Bucke hoped that the ex-seaman would be able to keep his temper in the face of the inevitable contempt he would face.

It was just after midday when they found the body in the Swansea Canal, trapped in the sluices of the Maliphant Lock. It had been in the water for a few days and was in such a terrible condition that the bargeman, who had initially freed the body whilst trying to unblock the sluices with a hook, wouldn't pull it out. He allowed it to remain there for the constables to handle and sent a young lad, who had been watching the barges, racing off to the police station.

When he arrived with constables Davies and Bingham and the police wagon, Bucke could understand why the bargeman wouldn't touch it, for the head had been mashed to a pulp. They dragged it from the water and loaded it on to the wagon. It was clearly a young woman's body, though almost completely unidentifiable, and was taken in a dripping cortege back to Tontine Street, followed by a respectful group of ragged children, for a post-mortem.

They had no idea at all who she was and when Doctor Beynon arrived, he put his bag down and sighed heavily. 'You must really stop finding bodies, Rumsey. You must have other duties to which you can devote yourself. The police station is in danger of becoming a charnel house.'

He proceeded to examine the corpse carefully. 'It is one of the steam launches that has done this, Rumsey, I am sure of it. They pull the barges and they need to be rather powerful to drag them along the canal. Have you seen them? One of the engineers told me about them last week. He broke a couple of fingers in a gate. Those launches have two propellers. Three blades each? Four? I don't know, he didn't say. But it looks to me as if her head was caught between them, as if it was in a mincer. Horrible. I have seen some things in the course of my work for you, Inspector, but this is one of the very worst.' The Doctor shook his head. 'She drowned, by the way. Her lungs are full of water so I would imagine that she was dead when the barges did their work. Been there a few days I would say. Three? Four? What else can I tell you? I would say she was in her middle twenties. An attractive woman I would imagine. Her hair, from what little remains, might have had a reddish tinge – Flora would probably say auburn. I cannot say whether the Cardiff train ticket I have found in her garments was hers. It might have attached itself to her in the canal.'

Bucke picked up the corner of her embroidered jacket. 'Her clothes seem to be of good quality, David.'

'Yes they do seem to be. They might not be hers, of course. But someone must once have spent a tidy sum on this dress and it is not what you would wear for cavorting alongside a Swansea canal. But what I do not understand is why she was wearing no undergarments. None at all. It is hardly likely that the fish ate them – even if any fish could ever survive in that stinking ditch.' He paused. 'Of course there are these marks all over her torso and neck. She has been bitten and it did not happen in the water.' He looked at Bucke and raised his eyebrows.

'No, it didn't. Is there any suggestion of outrage, do you think?'

'I should not speculate in these circumstances, Rumsey. You know that. But if I was to offer you my opinion, I would say that there has been. She was not innocent, I can tell you that, though I cannot tell you how recently that innocence was lost. There is no sign that she has ever been delivered of a child.'

'So we have a nameless woman who may have been raped and then died in the canal.'

'I hand over such matters to you, Rumsey. It was an accident, it was deliberate self-destruction or she was murdered. You must tell me. Doesn't help very much, does it? Reminds me of that woman who threw herself under a train about a month ago. You never found out who she was, did you?'

Bucke shook his head. 'This one does not appear to me to be one of our night-time ladies, and no one, so far anyway, has been reported to me as missing.' Bucke shook his head, sadly. 'Rather like the woman beneath the train.'

'I would suspect, said Beynon sorrowfully, 'that there may be a family somewhere which is missing her. They will tell you eventually and then you will have to explain all this.' He gestured at her body. 'I do not envy you that, Rumsey.'

'Remind me about my other bodies, David.' Bucke looked intently at the bite marks that covered the woman's shoulders and her breasts.

'I think you have had two suicides. Thought you would have worked that out for yourself, Rumsey. The young man yesterday? There are no marks upon his body apart from the scratches you tell me were caused by brambles in his bed. He went to his death willingly. His arrangements don't seem to me to be those of someone overtaken by an accident. And our Winnie? As I told you yesterday, she choked on the cymbal from her tambourine. Was it deliberate? I cannot say, though I would suggest that she had no idea what she was doing. But how and why did the cymbal get into her mouth? Don't suppose that matters much, but if she swallowed it deliberately, which must be the only logical explanation, it was a shocking thing to do. Ripped open her throat from the inside.'

The Doctor paused and Bucke considered the misery that daily they both faced, in a town where most of the inhabitants lived precarious lives. He waited for David Beynon to speak. He seemed nervous and uncomfortable and then appeared to make a sudden decision. 'Perhaps you and Constance would like to come to dinner? Flora would be thrilled to meet Miss White. The whole town speaks highly of her, a hidden secret of Swansea it seems, suddenly revealed.' He smiled, pleased that he had said it, ignoring the terrible incongruity of offering such an invitation beside a mangled body.

'I would be thrilled too. I cannot speak for Constance, of course, but I am sure she would be very happy to accept. It has been a long time since I have seen your delightful wife. Instead of withdrawing for cigars and stinking out your home as fashion demands, perhaps Flora and I could exchange examples of how difficult you can be.'

'It would be an opportunity I am sure she would be anxious not to miss, though I suspect it more likely that Flora and Constance would devote their time to a discussion of the perfidy of the male. It could prove to be a difficult evening for us and, whilst I agree about the cigars, it may be an opportunity to raid my wealthy father in law's valuable brandy store. He owes me a favour. I married his daughter after all.'

Bucke was, quietly, relieved. He recognised it as a significant moment. Dinner with a respected and devoted couple like the Beynons would be a sign of the social acceptance of his relationship with Constance.

David Beynon picked up his bag and was about to leave when he paused with an afterthought. 'I wonder, does Miss White speak French at all? Our Emily has been unable to practise her language skills since Professor Axmeyer disappeared, and I fear that her skills are beginning to wither. Thought I would ask. Needs something to occupy herself with, I think.'

The conversation was one of the few highpoints of an unrelentingly grim day, one suddenly defined by a new addition to the death toll and by the inevitable impression that the town was running completely out of control. Bucke needed to find a way into the puzzle that might unite these deaths and the only plausible clue that he had was religion, or religious mania. The death of his children had wiped away any beliefs he might once have held himself and he required help to make sense of something with which he had no sympathy, help from someone who would not condemn him for his lack of faith.

Bucke needed to think. Three bodies wasn't a happy news item and he knew he had to discover whether they were linked before others, with no evidence at all, told him that they were. In the past he had always found his greatest inspiration in watching other people. By imagining their lives and their thoughts and their emotions he had always found unexpected clues to strange and peculiar motivations. These days, he preferred to talk to Constance. But he still took pleasure in spending quiet moments observing the place that it was his duty to protect.

He walked down High Street, and watched the town preparing itself for Friday night. The men installing the wires for this new telephone invention were taking down their ladders, calling to each other in relief at the end of another week. They had already managed to festoon Swansea in untidy strings radiating from a central office in Castle Buildings, the heart of a web for this fantastical idea of speaking through wires. It was impossible to believe it would ever be real, but if it did work it would make communications between police stations so much easier. Officers would be able to intercept suspects, exchange information quickly and to talk to each other, no longer relying upon messengers. That is what his job was, finding things out and then interpreting them, turning fragmentary sentences into a story. It is just what he had to do now, with pieces like Winnie and Bowen that he was sure fitted together, somehow. But what about the Girl in the Canal? And if they were all linked, then what was this strange religious cult doing? And if they were not, then an evil spirit of disorder was stalking the town.

He leaned against the closed door of Mr Williams's Hair-Cutting and Bath Rooms on Wind Street and watched black smuts falling from the sky, accelerating the autumnal dusk. He regretted once more the heavy staining of black smoke on the otherwise elegant buildings around him. Swansea lived beneath a shadow, he decided. The acrid taste of the sulphurous air that always caught at the back of his throat was so familiar as to be unremarkable.

A gang of foreign seamen was proceeding raucously up from the docks, a night-time of dubious pleasure beckoning to them. '*Où sont les street rats?*' one of them cried and the rest of them cheered. There were a couple of girls outside the George Hotel who pulled up their skirts in anticipation, but it might well be too early. Food first, thought Bucke. Dai Potato was setting up the oven on his cart at the end of Green Dragon Street. Bucke knew that he shouldn't really be there but he had encouraged his constables to turn a blind eye to his unlicensed trading. He persuaded himself that Dai's baked potatoes helped to soak up the alcohol. He realised that he might be deluding himself but he felt that at least he was doing something which might, in some unquantifiable way, reduce the conflict between constables and sailors.

Reverend Blyth from the Seaman's Chapel on Adelaide Street gave him a cheery wave and continued with his search for those who might prefer quiet moments of Christian reflection, rather than the dubious thrills of the public houses. Bucke watched him place a comforting arm around the shoulder of those who seemed apprehensive of the dangerous pleasures their more experienced friends were eager to enjoy. After all, this was an unfamiliar town, one with unscrupulous citizens, eager to separate visitors from their money with practised ease.

Bucke admired Blyth for his work and his persistence. He had once told him that their mission was to eliminate the spiritual destitution which existed among seamen and as far as Bucke was concerned, they had set themselves an impossible task. Blyth was an old, avuncular, gentleman, who gave hope and support without prejudice. To Bucke it all seemed so carefully done. He admired the way in which Blyth seemed to know instinctively who was vulnerable and unhappy and offer them an escape from those unwelcome obligations into which the rest of their crew might pressure them. With practised kindness he directed sailors, when he could, to the Public Coffee House on Oxford Street, a Temperance Inn with the noble, but probably vain, hope of confronting the scourge of alcohol.

This was a valuable support to those who did their work at sea in order to provide for their families still at home in coastal towns and cities across Europe. And did the Chapel of Our Lady of Mumbles operate in the same way? Bucke knew little about them but he was sure that their purpose was entirely different. Until very recently he had barely aware of their existence. Other sects and cults had occasionally sprung up in the town like those hideous toadstools that suddenly appeared in open sewers. And they had faded away just as quickly. But this one? They seemed to be everywhere all at once and they troubled him. He needed more information. He was nothing without it. And, as he moved off towards St Helen's Road, he realised how he might be able to get it.

*

Bucke sat at the table drinking tea opposite Constance, who studied him carefully, enjoying his company. The curtains were closed and the lamps were lit, a small fire glowed in the grate. This week's edition of the Cambrian newspaper was folded neatly on the piano stool and all was comfortable, peaceful, re-assuring.

'Constance, will you help me?' he asked. 'With my investigations? It is this church you went to with Mathilde Barree. It troubles me greatly.'

'Of course I will. Need you ask?' She was pleased, for his request was another welcome opportunity to be part of his life.

'I have to tell you that I feel it might be dangerous, though I am not sure why I think that at the moment. But it has potential to be so, I fear.'

'How exciting!'

'No, Constance. Listen carefully. I am uncomfortable about these religious meetings and I need you to go to more of them and take careful note of what is said and what is done. I dare not go – I would be far too conspicuous. But there is something wrong there. You tell me that Milo seemed to talk about self-destruction. You told me that he appeared to welcome it, perhaps even to encourage it. He talked about the Field of Armageddon, you say. So I need to know what this is all about. And I worry too, that this might be dangerous, because they seem to me to revel in death. As I say, I cannot go there. I would not be welcome, you can be sure of that, and I would discover nothing. But you can. So if you watch them, I will watch you. Please do not tell anyone that you are going to these services. Become part of the congregation, but say nothing. It would be too easy to trace it back to me.' He paused and looked at her carefully. 'You do not have to agree, Constance. You can say no and that would be an end to the matter. I do not lie when I say I think that it might be dangerous, so please consider what you say very carefully.' He sat back in his chair. 'You can tell me tomorrow, if you wish.'

'Rumsey. It would be – almost – my greatest pleasure,' she replied, raising her eyebrows. 'And if it should be dangerous? Well, I have been locked away for too long.'

'It is great deal to ask of you, I know,' Bucke added.

'But you have asked already and I have agreed. You must not trouble yourself about it. I want to do it. I may be able to help you prevent misfortune falling upon another. And so really, Rumsey, it is my civic duty to do so.'

Rumsey smiled and nodded his thanks. 'But there is also something else that I need. I would also ask you to find out about Jezebel too, about what she did in the Bible, if it is not too much trouble.'

'She had lots of male companions, as far as I know. After that, I know nothing.'

'It is what I know of her, too. But you see, Winnie saw herself as the new Jezebel. What had she done that led her to believe this? The poor woman was clearly deranged. But why did she believe she was Jezebel? Perhaps it was a fantasy, the product of her over-heated brain. After all, who else chokes themselves with a cymbal?'

'How unpleasant. It must take such a very troubled mind to do such a thing. Brave, almost. Or so guilty of something she had done that a horrible death was a more acceptable alternative than life.' Constance shuddered.

'But why Jezebel? That is my point, Constance. I am sure there is something else here and I do not know the Bible well enough. Can you look for me? I need to understand, if indeed there is anything to understand.'

Constance interrupted him. 'Rumsey, you have given me a task. Perhaps you should allow me to complete it, in my own way.'

He bowed his head in apology. 'I am so sorry, Constance. I have confidence that you will do it in your own way, and successfully too.'

'I should hope so too, Rumsey Bucke. Naturally I will not tell Mathilde of my mission but I think it might help me to collect the information you need if we continue to attend together.' Constance leaned forward and placed her hand gently upon his. 'Have you seen the newspaper, Rumsey? I think that you should look at it.'

'No I haven't seen it. But you have seen it? So soon?'

'Oh yes. It has always been my habit to read it immediately and quickly, too. In my other life I was forbidden. My husband required that he should always read it first, as if in some way I could wear out the ink. So I would look at it quickly before he saw it. It was important to me that I should defy his wishes, even in such an insignificant way. Often it was the most important thing that I ever did in a day and it became a pointless game that I was determined to win. But I do think that you should read it.'

'Later, Constance, when I shall be able to give it my full attention. Tell me, would there be more tea, do you think, for a thirsty police inspector who must return all too soon to learn what his constables have found out for him?'

Chapter 5

Salvationist Condemns Sinful Swansea.

'An epidemic of suicides sweeps the town, one of them in police custody, and yet our police officers seem too wrapped up in their own licentiousness to respond. Surely the Watch Committee should be asking what we are paying for? Death stalks the streets but senior police officers show more concern for their own appetites than they do for the safety of ordinary citizens.'

Bucke had lived with the Cambrian newspaper report through the weekend. He had not been on duty on Saturday and he and Constance had gone down to Mumbles to walk in the thin but pleasant sunshine and to enjoy the freshness of the sea breeze. But he believed that all those they passed knew who he was and agreed with the barbs that had been directed at him. It was a shadow neither he nor Constance could shake from them. So, on Monday morning he had gone to the Town Hall to see the Chief Constable, before he went to the police station.

'It is a dangerous moment for us,' said Captain Colquhoun. 'Daily deaths. The Press hounding us. The Watch Committee is extremely concerned. Civic disorder. Town out of control. We have all seen it before. How our newspaper men love a drama.' He ran his hand though his previously neat hair. 'It doesn't matter if it is true; all that concerns them is that they can persuade their readers that it is true. I will speak to the Watch Committee again tonight. But I am glad you are here because I wanted you to know that I will be asking them to approve my intention to bring James Flynn over here from Gorseinon. We need more officers here in Swansea who we can trust.'

'I am very pleased to hear it. James is a good man.' Flynn had once been based in the town but had been moved in order to facilitate a disastrous moment of nepotism by the previous, disgraced, chief constable. 'Will he be returning as a sergeant?'

'No, Rumsey. He will be acting as an inspector. Such is my intention and I think it unlikely that the Watch Committee will disagree. He will assume responsibility for general duties and that should give you more of an opportunity to investigate the issues surrounding these suicides.'

Bucke nodded in agreement. 'I will be glad to see James back in town – and as an inspector. We will be stronger when he is with us. I think that we need to be.' He was uncomfortable. 'The nature of the report in the paper seems, well, rather pointed, Captain.'

'Yes it is, Rumsey. The Watch Committee has every faith in you and no trust at all in Mr Baglow. But some progress and an arrest would not do us any harm at all. By their very nature, the majority of suicides are impossible to predict. And, of course, if they are suicides, then who can we possibly arrest to placate the press?'

'I can speculate, Isaac, however. I can look for links which might not exist but I can look for them. And I do, because there is something not quite right about what has happened. Religious mania seems to have played a part. But I can tell you nothing at all about the Canal Girl. She seems to be beyond recognition.'

Captain Colquhoun rested his chin on his two thumbs, fingers interlocked, his elbows on the table. 'None of our own ladies of the night have been reported missing – although that in itself means very little. But we have had no news and usually, in my limited experience, they will tell you very promptly if there is a problem.' Captain Colquhoun smiled. 'So we have an unidentified – almost unidentifiable - body that has spent a few days in the canal. You will understand that I have a concern that this might be another example of what our friend Mr Baglow calls '*An epidemic of self-destruction in Swansea.*' He sighed. 'It would be so much easier if we knew who she was. It will not be easy, as you know, since there is almost nothing left to identify. But why would a woman be alongside the canal with no undergarments? Was she there at night? Because then the evidence is pointing in one direction only, towards her profession. And so, particularly with those bite marks all over her, to those two possibilities of accident or suicide, we can add a third - murder. It is the old problem, Rumsey, isn't it? On the basis of no evidence at all we start to connect things to tell a story which may, in fact, have no substance at all. The evidence we have could be entirely unconnected.'

Bucke sighed. 'The constables have found little so far. A copperman standing outside the Villiers Arms can remember a young woman running up from the Strand in the dark, looking distracted. He shouted after her but she didn't stop. So he said. But only one other person I trust seems to have seen her. And if she had previously been on the Strand, then why should anyone take notice of her? It is not as if she would have been the only single woman there.' Bucke scratched his head aggressively with both hands. 'But you see, Isaac. Some of the women think they might have seen her – and Eliza Keast is, for me, the only reliable witness. She remembers a distressed young woman running past The Troubadour. She thinks she remembers some superior quality clothing. If this is true, I believe she was running away from someone. But that is all we know at the moment. And I think about this a great deal, Captain. Why does this death, amongst so many that we have had in Swansea, trouble me so? I don't know. Undeserved? But then so many are.'

'She is important to someone, Rumsey and they will miss her, I am sure of it. Let Baglow report it. See if anyone comes to us with information.'

Colquhoun sat back in his chair and offered him some information of his own. Bucke was not surprised to hear that a large amount of money had disappeared from the Swansea Metropolitan Bank – where Phillip Bowen had been a quiet, rather solitary, clerk.

The manager had come hurriedly to see Captain Colquhoun. £666 had been taken from the safe and there was clear evidence that Bowen had been involved. There was note in the safe in place of the money, in Bowen's handwriting, which he passed over to Bucke.

He read it carefully. *'Here is wisdom. Let him that hath understanding count the number of the beast: for it is the number of a man; and his number is Six hundred threescore and six.'* The nature of the note held no surprises for Bucke. 'It is entirely in character, at least as far as his personal notebook is concerned, anyway. These words are from the Bible, are they not?'

'Yes, Rumsey. From the Book of Revelation.'

He nodded. 'There was no trace of this money either in his room or anywhere on his person. So I must ask myself, where did he hide it? Why would someone about to take their own life hide away a large sum of money? Unless, of course, he gave it to someone else.'

'Did he have debts, do you think?'

'Not that I am aware of, Isaac. But it is hard to know very much about him.'

'Apart from his mania,' added the Captain.

Bucke nodded. 'The Bible is important to so many people and yet everyone seems to see it in their own way. It is hard to know what Phillip Bowen was thinking.'

When Bucke returned to the police station, he sent Constable Morris up to the Penllergare Estate to ask whether any ground had been disturbed where Bowen had been seen. Were there any signs of digging? Any rocks moved or piled up in an unusual fashion? Large piles of money hanging in trees? Morris found nothing and returned only with a strongly worded complaint from Mr Whittlestone that someone had been stealing frogs from the lakes. Once Mr Dillwyn Llewelyn found out he would be especially agitated and would demand an additional and immediate police presence.

Of course, amongst all this insanity, normal villainy continued – theft, drunkenness, violence. The police station was a busy place; at times Bucke thought that the insistent clock was merely counting every felon that Sergeant Ball and the constables were dealing with after a busy weekend. There had been a robbery on Saturday from a Llanelly cattle dealer by two unidentified women who got him drunk in the Adelphi and had taken his wallet containing a considerable sum of money. Of course, he had no idea who they were and, quite naturally enough, no one remembered the man being there at all. He was an angry man, for he had lost over £50, but he could never hope to penetrate the Swansea Wall of Silence. He ranted in Welsh at the villainous English in the town, but there was nothing that could be done. He had paid a heavy price for his foolishness. Two sailors from Newcastle were refusing to get back on their ship because they said they had been badly treated and so had been locked in the cells and a woman leaning against the counter sobbed loudly because her suitcase had been stolen at the station. The arrival of the newly promoted Inspector Flynn was welcomed by everyone.

The first case Flynn had to deal with was a break-in at Malachi Evans's Old Furniture Shop on the Strand. A carpenter staying at Beth Griffith's Lodging House and on his way to work at the saw mill, noticed that the front door was open. He told Constable Gill as he passed him at the bottom of King Street, who at that moment was feeling fresh and attentive at the start of his shift. It was such a pleasant morning, he thought, and he inhaled the air fresh from the sea through his long broad nose, reddening his pox-marked cheeks. The information from the carpenter didn't seem to be the sort of thing that would complicate a pleasant day. Not at first, anyway.

Gill walked down to the shop but Malachi wasn't there and so he asked after him at the Foundry on the opposite side of the road, but no one had seen him for a while. The shop had been locked up.

If someone had tried to get in during the night, well, it could have been anyone; it was the Strand after all. Perhaps Malachi had gone away. Gill looked around the shop, picking his way carefully between haphazardly stored pieces of furniture. It was never a place that smelt good. It was musty and stale, and, in the corners where the roof was unreliable, damp wood decayed, peacefully and untroubled. Nevertheless, some of the pieces were serviceable, if you looked carefully, and Gill decided he would come back for a solid-looking washstand when he'd been paid. So much of the rest though was nothing more than tomorrow's firewood. As far as he could see nothing had been taken although, given the nature of the shop, there was no way of knowing. Malachi, however, would know. He was always very careful. There could be no chance that he would ever have left money in the shop overnight. There was no till or cashbox, for Malachi put his unswerving faith in his money belt. There was some damage to the door, of course, but whatever dream it was that had led intruders into the dark and untidy building, they would have left sadly disappointed.

Everyone knew Malachi. His was an important business, one that people from across the whole breadth of the town visited, either to buy or to sell. Most of Swansea's residents had never found themselves troubled by the luxury of new furniture.

The shop felt strangely abandoned and neglected. It wasn't like Malachi Evans to be absent. He was always there and Gill had a growing sense of alarm about it. It was unexpected, out of character. However he knew where he lived, so he decided to go to his house on Pier Street to tell him about the break-in and to ask him to attend, to check if anything had been stolen. But, as he later reported to Inspector Flynn, he seemed to have wandered into a puzzle.

'Very strange it is, Inspector, I have to say. Because you see, he wasn't there. Someone else was living in his house, like. No idea who they are, but what I can tell you is that when I knocked on the door, it were answered by Billy Evil.'

'Truly?' Flynn was suddenly alarmed.

'I thought you would want to know. That is why I come straight back here. Billy said that Malachi Evans had moved out. I didn't know. No one told me. As far as I knew Malachi owned it, it weren't rented. He had it from his father. I haven't heard that he has sold it. Wouldn't let me in, not one for being cooperative is that bugger Billy, as you know.'

'Never once, in all the years it has been my misfortune to have dealt with him,' agreed Flynn.

'I had a look round the back but I couldn't see anything. Shocking smell though. Must be drifting up from the docks. Either that or there's a bunch of dead rats under the privy.'

'And you have asked around?' asked Flynn, looking thoughtful.

'Certainly, Inspector.' Gill always tried to do his job properly and when he was a sergeant, Flynn had once told him that he was 'dependable,' which always made him feel proud. 'No one has seen him or heard anything of him for nearly two weeks now. It is like he has disappeared. Never done it before, so they say.'

'I wonder what that baggage of trouble Billy Evil is doing there,' reflected Inspector Flynn.

Gill scratched his head 'Well, Inspector Flynn. I went back and asked him. Not happy with me knocking on the door, was he? What you doing here? I asked. And he told me that Malachi had given his house to a preacher, seen the light or something. He had signed papers and everything had been done proper. Said that Malachi had gone now, didn't know where.'

'I wonder if they are aware of this unlikely conversion at the synagogue?' mused Inspector Flynn, a frown deepening across his face. 'I tell you what, Harry. You don't do things by halves, do you? A right little mystery you have brought us this morning.'

'It is that,' said Constable Gill, scratching the length of his nose wisely.

'You stay here for a minute Harry, rest your legs. Let me go and have a word with Inspector Bucke.'

Bucke had just returned from the funeral of the Canal Girl. They had no other name for her and she had been buried promptly because they could never have shown her body to grieving relatives, even if they ever found any. Best to say, they decided, that she was now at peace. Bucke always felt obliged to go; he had every reason to fear funerals for the memories that rose within him unbidden, but, at the same time, he hated the idea of the lost and the poor buried alone, even if they had been forgotten by those who might once have loved them. Canal Girl was now in a pauper's grave in St Margaret's Churchyard, where other recent Swansea victims now rested. He wondered if anyone would ever come looking for her.

A quick word from Inspector Flynn and soon they were out on the streets once again, this time led by Constable Gill towards the sea and Pier Street. The three policemen stopped and examined the Old Furniture Shop briefly. Gill showed the Inspectors the door which he had temporarily secured. It seemed to Flynn that those who had broken open the door had never previously visited the store and had imagined treasures within that it could never hope to provide.

They walked on to Pier Street, amongst the shipping agents and the bonded stores. Bucke's attention was drawn by a large wooded cross planted in a small weedy front garden and which appeared, rather gruesomely he thought, to be stained with what must be animal blood. Their destination was the adjoining house of three storeys, built from red brick. The windows were narrow and the door was large and heavy. Rather smart, thought Bucke, for a seller of old furniture.

Gill seemed to read his mind. 'Inherited it from his father. Made candles and furniture polish. Never short of a bob or two.'

The door opened and a young girl stood before them. Bucke was surprised by what he saw though, as always, he tried to keep his reactions under control. But it was completely unexpected for all of them. It was as if they had been suddenly immersed in an illustration from a child's Bible. The girl was wearing what seemed to be a coarsely woven tunic in brown, worn without a belt, over which there was a long, almost floor-length, open gown, beneath which dirty sandaled feet appeared, with a deep hood that covered her head. The strands of her hair that they could see were pure white. Her face was similarly hypnotic, for it was twisted by a hare-lip and an unsightly crooked nose. Her eyes were crossed.

'Good day, miss,' asked Bucke. 'We are here to make enquiries about William Gammon and would be pleased if you could offer us a few short moments. We are very eager to speak to him. Do you live here, miss?'

'I am Delilah. I am the Godly servant of Our Lady of Mumbles and I once helped to destroy Samson.'

'I see,' said Bucke. 'So many of the lives lived in our town are unexpected, Delilah. You are a servant, you say. Is your master available? Or your mistress, perhaps?'

'My master will be carrying out his daily devotions and must under no circumstances be disturbed. I will ask my Lady if she is available. Please wait here.'

'Our names are Inspectors Flynn and Bucke...'

'I have no interest in who you are.' She closed the door.

'Do you think she is mad, sir?' asked Constable Gill.

'She does seem rather unexpected. Perhaps the house is involved in some kind of theatrical production and this morning is a rehearsal,' Bucke said hopefully. He looked again at the cross next door and noted that he had failed to convince himself.

'It is a possibility, Rumsey,' said Flynn. 'Christmas is coming. Tell me, Harry. Who lives next door? With the cross. Do you know?'

'William Rosser, sir. You must have heard of him. Claims to be the oldest teetotaller in Swansea. Nigh on 60 years since he last touched a drop, he says.'

'Never been a policeman then. Is he the one who writes to the paper about the drinking in the Somerset Hotel? Must be at the back of his garden. A right den of villains that one is.'

The door opened the door and Delilah was there once more. She bowed deeply, with her right hand stretching out towards them, like a supplicant.

'Our Lady will see you briefly. Please follow me,' she said and then turned and took them along the small, shabby hallway with its stained wooden panels. The house was much larger than the entrance suggested. Their boots made a heavy sound on the black and white tiled floor and Delilah turned sharply and put a finger to her lips but said nothing. There was a staircase on the left with a narrow threadbare carpet running down the middle, inlaid with grime. Beyond it there was a door which Delilah opened and showed them into a small room at the back of the house. It was a barely furnished room, with just a small table and a simple chair and with a rough crucifix on the wall, fashioned, it seemed, from the branches of a tree. There was nothing in it to distract them from the impressive and intimidating figure of a woman standing before them, framed by the bright sunlight from a window behind her. She was dressed entirely in white robes with long black hair, one of the most striking women Bucke had ever seen. Her features were precisely defined – a perfectly symmetrical mouth, a straight full nose and naturally arched eyebrows. There was an authority about her, an inner belief that fuelled an unassailable self-confidence.

The three policemen stood uncomfortably in front of her as she looked at them intently in silence. She folded her hands and rested them on the silken cord that ran around her waist and, by raising her eyebrows, silently asked them what they were doing in her house.

'Good day, madam. I am Inspector Bucke of the Swansea Constabulary and these are my colleagues. Thank you for seeing us. We would like to speak to you about Malachi Evans.' He paused, but the woman remained impassive. 'No one knows where he is and we believed, like many others did, that this was his home. We also wanted to speak to William Gammon about why he was inside this property and you may be able to help us with that too.'

'And such a conversation with William requires three police officers? Is he really such an entertaining speaker?'

'You are William Gammon's sister, is that correct?' asked Bucke.

'That is what so many have believed. I must tell you, with regret, he is not here now, as far as I know.'

'He was here earlier, I believe.'

'I believe so too, but he appears to have left. He has many tasks to perform. As must we all, Inspector,' she added.

'We are speaking to Ada Gammon, are we not?' asked Inspector Flynn, who was already feeling impatient. 'I ran you in, didn't I? Mumbles. About four years ago, I'd say.'

'That is what once I was called,' she said with condescension. 'But that was before the truth had been revealed to me. I am now Deborah, the Prophetess, and I promise my followers salvation.'

'I see. From what, may I ask?'

'But of course, you do not know. At Armageddon, where the armies will gather for the Final Battle, those who follow the Spear of Jehovah will triumph and so be saved. It has been revealed to Father Milo that here in Swansea is where we will find Armageddon.'

'It doesn't feature on any of the beats that the constables patrol, Ada. Not at the moment,' sighed Flynn.

'We need to speak to you about Malachi Evans,' said Bucke, eager to move the interview away from her beliefs. 'He has disappeared, even, it would seem, from his own home.'

'It is his home no longer, Inspector. Malachi is a man whose soul was saved and so brought word from God to grant this house to Father Milo. He is the true representative of God on Earth and of this there can be no dispute. Malachi, once before, was a prophet who foretold the coming of Christ and has now been walking amongst us once again. He is a messenger from God, sent to warn us of the terror that shall fall upon Swansea for its corruption and for its love of Satan. Malachi knew too, that in the corruption in which you wallow, the word of God is seemingly not sufficient and so he took the precaution of signing a paper which can be shown to you when Father Milo is ready to do so. The house is ours.'

'And where, may I ask, were you living before?'

'We were offered rooms next door by one of Father Milo's most fervent disciples, who in Swansea goes by the name of William Rosser, a man for whom devotion to the Lord God is his only reason to live and for which he will be justly rewarded in the afterlife. Our preparations for the field of Armageddon necessitated larger premises and the Lord, through Malachi Evans, saw our need, and so we are here.'

'I would like to speak to Milo about this …' Bucke wasn't sure what to call her or of the nature of her relationship with him.

'Father Milo is unavailable, I must tell you. He is in meditation, as he is most frequently at this time of the day. He looks directly into the Eye of God and is thus directed by God alone,' she spoke as if everything she said was beyond contradiction.

Her words triggered a memory in Bucke's mind. He had heard this before. 'And when will he be available, do you think?'

'When God's will has been done. Surely you can see that this is not for me to say?'

'I see. And where is Malachi now, do you think? We would like to speak to him, too,' asked Inspector Flynn.

She casually dismissed the question. 'This has not been revealed to me. I am unable to help you any further.' She moved away from the window towards the door, presumably to call for Delilah, allowing Bucke to see into the garden.

It adjoined the gardens of the houses on Somerset Place and gave an illusion of open space at the rear of the house, in which stood a brick privy and what initially appeared to be, from a distance, a large shallow water butt which might be collecting rainwater, its lid askew. It seemed to be full, and the ground around appeared to be saturated. That's Winnie's washtub, he thought.

Suddenly Constable Gill spoke. He could contain himself no longer. 'Please, Mrs Gammon, can you answer me a question. What is that smell in your garden?'

She smiled thinly. 'It is the stink of evil. I am surprised you do not recognise it. It is the rank corruption that must be wiped from the face of the earth. You, gentlemen, must make your own choice, though I fear that your presence here to question me in my home, indicates that you are agents of Satan. But you cannot reach me, of this I know most well. I am beyond your authority. To oppose me is to oppose the Lord God and condemns you to eternal damnation.' She opened her hands towards them. 'We all have choices to make. I have made mine. I will be interested to discover the choice that you will make, now that the truth has been revealed to you. If you will excuse me? Good afternoon, officers. Delilah will show you to the door.'

They stood outside looking back at the house. It seemed abandoned. There was no sign of life in any of the windows.

'I shall be going back for Mr Milo, never you fear,' said Flynn in exasperation. 'And Billy Bloody Evil, don't you worry.'

Constable Gill was agitated, trying to understand what he had seen. 'Do you think she is harmless, like? A bit of a lunatic, but harmless?'

'I hope you are right,' said Bucke. 'She seems to think that she has an answer for everything, except of course for the questions that we ask her.'

*

'Thank you Constance. This is very nice indeed. You have been busy,' said Bucke with appreciation.

Constance was pleased that he liked what she had prepared. 'Here we are, two English people, eating the famous Welsh cawl.'

'It is very good, though hardly different from stew. But on a day like today, so very welcome.'

'Possibly so, Rumsey, but here it is called cawl and we are all obliged to accept that it has magical qualities to revive and restore. Everyone in Swansea knows that. It cures everything. Amputated limbs regrow after a bowl of cawl.'

'And I thought it was just a stew.'

'What little you know of the Welsh. Their finest delicacy. Certainly more palatable than their other.'

'Cockles?' he asked.

'No, I can tolerate cockles. Laver bread is something I cannot bear. It is little wonder that the people of Swansea are fractious and troublesome if fate has decreed that they must eat laver bread.'

'I find it quite palatable, Constance, though I am not aware of any secret powers that may have. But your cawl is a triumph. When did you find time to make it?'

'My pupil this morning, Letitia, was unwell so I made use of the time I had gained by cooking, something I enjoy when the mood is upon me – if I am cooking for you at any rate. And I found some fresh parsley in the market and so I felt quite pleased with myself.'

'You must allow me to pay for the ingredients.'

She smiled her thanks, happy to accept his offer. 'But, you see I have some news. Before I went into the town I called at a bookshop. I didn't want to be blundering around the shelves with a heavy basket full of vegetables, so I went to Mr Mallam's second-hand book shop in Calvert Street. I found that Mr Mallam was a very obliging gentleman.'

'I am quite sure he was eager to help you,' he smiled knowingly. 'I wonder why that always seems to happen?'

'Rumsey. Please. He found for me this book. She held up a small red volume. 'Stories from the Bible. Moral Instruction for Young People.' It was written by Reverend Robert Rogers, Vicar of Llangyfelach Parish Church. In Swansea, Rumsey. How very convenient, I thought. Published in 1876. It is a fine piece of work and, since it is written for children, even a policeman should be able to understand it.'

'I do hope so, Constance. And so what does it have to say? You must summarise it for me since, as a mere police inspector, I will find it so hard to read it for myself.'

She opened the book and Bucke watched her eyes skip down the page. 'I shall do my best to help and I shall try not to over-complicate the story for you. Now pay close attention, for Reverend Rogers knows everything about our interesting friend, Jezebel. She was the Queen of Israel and the wife of Ahab. She tried to get him to worship pagan gods and persecuted the prophets of Israel. I think she was always so busy doing evil that she had hardly a spare moment to consort with men, whatever other people might say. The other thing she did, when Ahab wanted a vineyard next door belonging to Naboth and he wouldn't give it to him, she arranged to have him stoned to death. Eventually she was thrown out of a window and eaten by dogs.' She closed the book for emphasis. 'I would have to say that I find it remarkable how people can believe such things, spending all their precious time lost in such a ridiculous story.'

He tore off a piece of bread and dropped it into his bowl and then stirred it around thoughtfully. 'This really is very good, Constance. And thank you for the work you have done today.' He held her gaze for a moment. 'It means more to me than I can say. This is especially helpful.' He ate his well-soaked bread. 'You see, Jezebel is important but in a way that neither of us realised.' He put his spoon down. 'Winnie knew the story well. She told me about horses but also about the dogs. And do you know what is especially interesting? She told me about Naboth too.'

'The man with the vineyard?'

'Yes, the man with the property next door that Ahab wanted. It just happened to be a vineyard in the story. And you will know that we have no vineyards in Swansea. But we have other property. Such as houses.' He took a drink of tea and then put his cup down decisively. 'I think, Constance, that she was telling everyone, in her own way, about Malachi Evans. He lived next door to your preacher, Milo. And Milo has now acquired the house and Winnie, a disciple of Milo, felt very guilty about it. She did something or saw something which happened to Malachi that turned her mind.'

'Oh my goodness, you don't think he has been stoned do you? Like Naboth?' She was fascinated by the way these stories unfolded, fascinated by the way in which Rumsey made it seem so obvious and logical.

'I do not know, but I fear for Malachi, and Winnie's story gives me cause to return and have a closer look at the house, which has already been taken away from him. These are very strange times that we are living in, Constance, and I have no idea what I might find.'

'There was something else too. In the service I attended, Milo referred to Deborah as the leader of the Israelite army or something. But she wasn't, according to Roger's book anyway. She might have offered advice and guidance but she wasn't up there waving her spear and stabbing people. Not at all.'

'And so Milo got it wrong, did he? Why am I not surprised?' He paused and shook his head. 'Tell me something, Constance. Is there any more of this delicious parsley- flavoured cawl of yours?'

It was dark when he reluctantly began his walk home, leaving his heart behind. He found his feelings hard to manage whenever he was with Constance. He always felt so guilty. He did not see himself building a new life, rather he felt as if he was rejecting his old one. He would never have involved Julia in his work as he had already involved Constance. Did that mean he somehow loved her less? Julia would not have had that naïve enthusiasm that Constance displayed, which seemed to be able to unlock mysteries. She would never have shared Constance's discovery that life was an adventure. Julia would have been more measured, more distant, more ready to separate home and work. But all it showed was that they were very different people and he had loved Julia and had known he would have loved her forever. And then that forever had gone. And now, unexpectedly, he loved again.

His family had left him almost without warning and he still grieved for them, especially in the nights when sleep would not come. He knew it was time to rebuild his life, he knew beyond any doubt that he loved Constance, but he could not escape the idea of betrayal.

Chapter 6

Bucke and the constables arrived at Pier Street early in the morning as the rain finally cleared away and, whilst Bucke went to the front door, Bingham and Davies were sent to climb into Malachi's garden from those adjoining in Somerset Place. There was something wrong out there, he knew it.

Delilah answered the door, slightly bowed, her faced obscured by her hood. She said nothing in greeting.

'Good morning, Delilah. We are here to search this property.'

'I do not think my mistress will allow it, sir.'

'I am not here to ask permission, Delilah. I am here to tell you that it is happening. I have decided to begin my investigations in the garden.'

'You will have to wait, Inspector. Our lady is carrying out her devotional duties and must not be interrupted.'

Bucke tried to catch her eyes but they remained hidden beneath the hood. 'It is a crime to obstruct police enquiries, Delilah, particularly in a case of murder.'

Delilah remained impassive. 'I am required not to admit anyone to the house during these sacred moments. It is Father Milo's strict rule.'

Bucke decided not to make life difficult for her by demanding immediate access through the house. 'You may tell Miss Gammon that I am in the garden.'

'There is no one here of that name, Inspector.'

Bucke sighed. 'I shall be in the garden, Delilah.'

He went next door to William Rosser's house and climbed over the low wall into Malachi's garden. The smell was shocking. He watched the constables search the sour ground. Little enough would grow here at the best of times, but Winnie's tub, leaking its foul water, had turned it into a swamp. It had an ill-fitting wooden lid that was lifted in one corner. The tub was ancient, an abandoned barrel perhaps from the copper works or a brewery which had, for many years, served time in the prison laundry. It was three feet deep and about six feet across. By what circuitous route it had come into her possession no one could be sure but someone, surely, must have brought it into Malachi's garden for her. Her dolly stood close by, leaning against the privy wall.

The loathsome smell hung over them and their first inclination had been to search the privy but it revealed nothing to them that was out of the ordinary. No bodies, no rat colony, no blockages.

'It is right stinky here, Inspector, If you don't mind me saying,' said Constable Davies.

'I imagine he has noticed,' grumbled Constable Bingham, shaking his head.

Two men attracted by the police activity leaned over the wall from the Somerset Hotel. 'Oi! Copper! Sort it out! Been like this for a week now. It is getting worse, mun.'

Bucke knew where the smell was coming from. He had no doubt at all. And he also knew what they would find. He looked at the tub, at its size, at its malevolent presence, and directed the constables towards it. He looked back towards the house and saw a Christ-like figure watching them impassively from the window.

The three of them together lifted off the lid and the smell intensified. Bingham looked distinctly pale. Winnie's Washing Tub had been filled with stones and rubble and Bucke was irritated that he had not anticipated this, because what was before him was suddenly becoming obvious in all its insanity. He stood there in the water weeping from the warped staves, watching the constables as they lifted and grumbled, paddling in mud and removing the rocks one at a time, complaining about the staining on their uniforms. The stinking water started to seep from a hole and then the flow slowed down and stopped. Bingham bent down and removed a plug of debris from it. The water started to flow again, rank and stained. He looked at what he had in his hand and knew immediately what it was. Human hair.

Soon enough, as they created space in the tub, they found Malachi Evan's bloated corpse revealing itself in the foul water, wedged amongst the rubble. Stoned, thought Bucke. Just as Winnie had said.

Bucke ensured that they allowed the water to drain from the tub before they attempted to move the body. It was in a poor condition and very likely to fall apart. So they removed the staves to avoid having to lift him up and managed to ease Malachi out on to a canvas sheet. Bingham vomited but he seemed to have been planning to do this for a while. Bucke was relieved to see that he seemed a little better afterwards and so sent him off to collect Doctor Beynon. He decided it was too early to speak to either Ada or Milo. Let them wait, let them stew, until the body had been examined. He dispatched Constable Davies to ensure they didn't leave.

Doctor Beynon gave Bucke one of his special looks when he arrived. 'Thank you, Rumsey. This is one of your particular triumphs I see.'

'I like to bring you interesting corpses when I can. What can you tell me?'

Beynon carefully moved Malachi's head to one side. 'My God it stinks. Quite simple, Inspector. He took a heavy blow to the back of the head – the mark is still there. With a rock? Who knows? Then he drowned.'

'He was stoned then, David?'

'You could say that.'

'Oh yes, he was stoned to death. I think I can tell you what happened too. He bent over the washtub for some reason. Might have been looking for his socks? Possibly. He was hit on the head with a rock. Pushed into the tub, the stones were piled in and then it was filled with water and was topped up by the rain.'

'As a theory that is quite impressive, Rumsey. Nothing you say is not possible.'

'And I think I know who did it too, David. He was murdered by Winnie the Washer.

'My cymbal woman?'

'Whether alone I cannot say. But she confessed, I think, in her own way. And she was undoubtedly incited to do so.'

'Inspector,' shouted Davies. 'Live and learn around here, don't you? Man next door. Rosser he's called. Do you know what? He tells me that when he was alive the first time around he was called Enoch and he lived until he was 365. Still smiling, like. But to be honest I don't think the old boy is right in the head. Still, at least it isn't raining. Terrible night. Mam's roof was leaking.'

Bucke's heart sank. Why was Davies not guarding Ada and Milo? Why had he been gossiping with a confused old man? And, of course, when he went to the house he discovered that they had gone. Called away by God, said Delilah blankly. She didn't know where. It was unfortunate but he would be patient. He knew they would return. He told the constables to watch out for them and report any sightings. He was sure that one day he would be able to find a job that Constable Davies could perform effectively. He did wonder though, how long that would take.

*

He walked away from the Star Inn. A free pot of beer was always welcome, always made his beat a little more acceptable. Herbert Plumley knew that he wasn't the best policeman ever to walk the streets of Swansea - or as it turned out, the streets of Llansamlet. He had accepted some time ago that he didn't really care that much about other people. They were an inconvenience, generally. He knew he wasn't as corrupt as some of his colleagues had once been, though he longed for the return of those good old days, even though they were not that long ago, when, in his mind, everything had been much more free and easy. He sighed as he strolled slowly past the church, all new but already showing signs of staining from the smoke. He was thirty two years old and he could not accept the prospect of the rest of his life as a policeman.

Plumley was squat and unattractive. His thick neck, broad nose, fat lips and a permanent scowl meant that children took every opportunity to mock him but, more significantly, his appearance reflected a brooding unhappiness that consumed him from within. Thin strands of hair crossed his scalp like threads and neither they nor his untidy beard offered the distraction he craved from his baldness. His disposition did not make him a winning companion in the eyes of his colleagues who had not been disappointed to see him posted to Llansamlet.

Warmed slightly by the free beer, he reflected on his employment. He would have taken particular objection if anyone had called him a criminal, but he was not averse to accepting a little gift here and there – a couple of chops perhaps or a small consideration to turn a blind eye. He saw nothing wrong with something that, in his view, oiled the wheels of life. It was the idea of being accountable for his actions that troubled him. Surely the inspectors and the sergeants should leave the constables alone to do their job as they saw fit? It was hard work patrolling the streets, chasing off dogs and tramps, distributing punishment. Why did they need to know where he was all the time? Why did they insist on giving him jobs that he didn't really want to do?

It was the time he spent with Ada that he liked best. She often called herself Deborah now but she would always be Ada to him, just as she had been when he had tried to arrest her in Mumbles. Was it really ten years ago? He hadn't arrested her though; they had come to an arrangement, which had established the pattern for their occasional relationship. But she hadn't let him visit her for a while, now she had gone all fancy in the church. He wasn't sure what had changed. Plumley knew that he was not the only visitor Ada entertained; after all, he had once almost arrested her. But he was very keen to please her so that he could be granted another visit. Or two. Or more, he hoped. The message she had sent him had been very straightforward. He had to get the keys first. Why did she want the keys to an abandoned mine, he wondered? It was probably too deep for him, he thought, and then smiled at the invention of his own wit. He had heard the things Ada now spoke about, now that she was Deborah, Our Lady of Mumbles. He listened to Milo preaching, too. It sounded like a lot of nonsense, but it couldn't do any harm, could it? Just get the keys.

Old man Fowler had the keys. He was a night-watchman who kept his eye on a few of the premises in this black industrial area which all mined the same four-foot seam of coal. Fowler was meticulous in his duties and followed a habitual route checking on his responsibilities in order. There was the Gwern Colliery, the engine house of Scott's Pit which was no longer worked but served to ventilate and drain the next one along, the Cae Pridd Pit, and then the old Calvary workings which had been abandoned some time ago and were now blocked by a rusting and locked iron gate across the entrance.

Plumley didn't like Fowler, finding him difficult and contemptuous. The older man was eager to show him that he knew the area better than a recently imported constable. Plumley was tired of hearing how Fowler had been in Llansamlet all his life, he had watched the place for twenty years, not like a fat constable sent out there just a few days ago, with no idea of what was what. The old man had tried to unsettle him by only speaking Welsh but Plumley had learnt it from his mother, a small triumph which appeared only to irritate Fowler even further.

He didn't have much of a plan for getting hold of the keys. Perhaps he should start by simply asking for them, he thought. But he would refuse and after that he wasn't sure what he would do. He should have a plan, he knew that, and so he walked on towards Peniel Green thinking hard, but try as he did, nothing came to him.

When he returned along his beat a couple of hours later he found Thomas Fowler alone, sitting on a stool in the occasional sunshine outside his cottage with its well-kept garden, between the main road that went to Skewen and the brickworks. He was a tough old man, his skin wrinkled by long hours of hard work outside in all weathers and at all times of the day, but he remained wiry and strong and appeared to Plumley to be quite relaxed, enjoying the unexpected sunshine that so rarely broke through the poisonous clouds that hung over Llansamlet. It seemed to be as good a time as any, so Plumley asked him quite politely if he could have the keys to the Calvary pit.

Fowler laughed and slapped his thighs, as if enjoying a comic song in the Music Hall. 'Don't be stupid. Why should I give 'em to you? My job is to hold the keys. Not yours. I don't need to do nothing that a copper says to me. Not obliged too. So go and swing.'

'Listen Fowler. Give me the keys. There is something I need to check. Inspector Flynn told me.'

'Go to hell. Why should I give you the keys? I told you. Not obliged.'

'Because I have asked you. You would be helping the police with their inquiries.' Plumley was quickly becoming irritated.

Fowler spat exultantly, deliberately just missing Plumley's boot. 'Not got a mind to give you the keys. But I will tell you what I will do. I will come with you and open it up. Then you can have a look for whatever it is you think you are looking for and then I can lock up. That's what I call helping the police, Bertie, but I ain't giving you no keys.' He stood up and rattled them in his face, insolently, taunting him.

Plumley punched him in the nose.

Fowler stepped backwards, knocking the stool over, which tangled his legs and his hands flew up and the keys caught Plumley on the side of the face. It was a sharp pain, as if he had been cut. He became suddenly enraged, consumed by all his different frustrations, and fell upon the old man and beat him first with his fists and then he stood up and hit him repeatedly with the stool until Fowler's face was a messy pulp and the pool of blood in which he now lay started to expand very quickly.

Plumley suddenly stopped and realised what he had done. It had happened so quickly but there could be no going back now. He pulled the keys out of Fowler's hand and put them in his pocket. His mind was racing. Then there was a noise. Fowler might have groaned, he wasn't sure, but he thought it best to hit him once again.

As he raised the stool to bring it down on Fowler's head for the last time, a woman came around the corner of the cottage.

'Tommy,' she began and then stopped, in bewilderment and horror.

'He hit me first,' Plumley blurted out desperately. 'Here. Cut my face, the bastard did.'

It was Mrs Fowler and she ran screaming to the Star Inn.

*

It was a terrible and apparently senseless thing to have done but Plumley stuck solidly to his story, but then it was the only one he had and he knew that it was best not to change it, no matter how unlikely it sounded. He needed to be consistent. Fowler had gone mad, had assaulted him. He had struck the first blow and Plumley had defended himself. He introduced what he considered to be convincing detail by telling how the old man had got so tangled up in the legs of his stool that he had fallen heavily to the ground and banged his head. But he knew that the watchful Inspector Flynn regarded his story as feeble. He told Plumley that, whilst the shock of seeing her husband in that condition might suggest that she was not the most reliable of witnesses, Mrs Fowler was adamant that the constable had been hitting her husband with the stool. It was clearly covered in blood.

Inspector Flynn, as he always did, took Plumley through his story once again, pointing out gently that, if he had been struck first by an old man, his response was completely out of proportion.

There was a bang on the window and angry voices were shouting outside from the crowd which had gathered, once news of Fowler's death had spread through the district. The landlord of the Star Inn and a delivery man from the brewery had made a citizen's arrest on the basis of what Mrs Fowler said, sent for an inspector and detained Plumley in the saloon bar.

'It is a difficult circumstance you have got yourself in, Bertie. No mistake about that. Tell me again. Why did you do it?' he asked.

'Look, Inspector. I have told you. See this mark here on my face? It proves the stupid old man started it. Hit me with his keys and came at me again so I blocked him and defended myself and then he fell over and hit the ground with a bang. You can see the blood.'

Flynn looked at him intently and slowly shook his head. He could see that Plumley himself knew that his defence was hardly convincing. Flynn knew that one of them had gone mad but he was sure it wasn't Fowler. He had other worries too. He had to get Plumley back to Tontine Street unscathed and Llansamlet was in an ugly mood. One of their own, an old defenceless man, had been beaten to a bloody mess by a Swansea constable and a threatening crush had gathered around the door. Amongst them, pushing, muttering quiet incitement into every ear, was Billy Evil.

When a handcuffed Plumley was taken out of the Star Inn and escorted towards the police wagon, the angry crowd surged forward and there was a brief moment of confusion. Billy Evil slipped next to the disgraced constable as his colleagues tried to force back the vengeful mob.

'Have you got them?' he asked.

'In my pocket. The left one. Ada will see me alright, won't she?'

'Don't you worry, Bertie. You have done well.'

'She will rescue me. From prison. Won't she? I won't be in gaol for long, will I?'

'Ada will be very pleased to see these keys.' He put them in his pocket. ' Everything will be just dandy. Don't you worry, Bertie.'

'Our Lady will come to me. Won't she?'

'Never doubt it.'

And then the constables restored some order. The hissing crowd were pushed back sufficiently to allow Plumley to be bundled, head bowed, into the wagon.

Billy Evil slipped away into the evening gloom before any of the policemen realised that he was there.

Inspector Flynn sat opposite Plumley on the way back to the station. Plumley said nothing at all. They negotiated occasional jeering groups of youths who gathered to hurl mud, stones and threats at the murderous constable. Flynn knew better than to confront them unnecessarily. Let them have their moment. But he found Plumley's behaviour entirely inexplicable. He had a good idea of what would happen to him. There was not enough evidence to condemn him of murder and there could be no way of contradicting his defence of self-defence, no matter how unlikely it seemed. But he would be found guilty of manslaughter and would be imprisoned for a considerable period of time. Why?

'Funny how things turn out, isn't it, Bertie? Wouldn't have thought my day was going end like this,' he said, trying to persuade him to talk about what he had done. He remained resolutely silent, staring down at the floor.

His concerns changed in a moment as they turned into Tontine Street. It was chaotic and the police wagon had to stop. It was impossible for it to pass through the large crowd which had gathered outside the police station, chanting, blocking the road, in some cases wailing. There were people carrying flaming torches, beating tambourines, singing hymns.

Flynn considered ushering the handcuffed Plumley through the crowd but knew he would be unable to get access to the police station because the door was locked. There was the sound of breaking glass as someone smashed the lamp above it. Prudently, they backed the wagon out on to High Street and took his prisoner to the Town Hall to avoid exciting passions even further. There were cells which served the courts and Plumley could be housed there until the morning.

And all this because Father Milo had been brought into the police station for questioning.

Chapter 7

The police wagon had been out in Llansamlet all evening and so Davies and Gill brought him to the police station in a cart, rather like a tumbril, with people lining the street and with Milo dispensing a benediction as he passed through them.

An excited congregation had gathered on Oxford Street outside The Chapel of Our Lady of Mumbles for Milo's latest service and so there was a ready crowd who heard of his unexpected journey to the police station, their expectation of his mystical stories of the eternal conflict of good and evil cruelly snatched away from them. Constance and Mathilde had been amongst those waiting and had felt the mood of the devotees shift quickly from bewilderment to anger as the service was cancelled and, for a brief moment, they were swept along in the crowd, unable to escape, until they could slip into a doorway and watch the mob flow past them, an unexpected mix of disciples, and a swelling number of the curious, looking for the police cart and shouting aggressively. It didn't seem safe to be part of the anger or the unpredictable way that it might be expressed – though it did not seem to trouble the filthy little girl pushing the pram, who scurried along at the rear. Mathilde was especially irritated that her night of voluptuous immersion in the mesmerising words of Father Milo had been stolen from her and so stalked off home in a temper, refusing Constance's offer to accompany her. No footpad would dare to intercept Mathilde tonight, given the mood she was in. Constance for her part, concerned for Rumsey's safety but unable to do anything to guarantee it, returned to her rooms where she sat in the window and anxiously tried to complete a meaningless piece of embroidery whilst watching the road outside.

*

In the police station Bucke sat back in his chair, his arms folded, looking at Milo. He was such an incongruous figure in his robes and sandals and with that Biblical hair. He appeared indifferent, bored perhaps, and it was clear that he was determined not to be intimidated in any way. He had placed a collection of papers on the desk, bound in a scroll by a simple cord, and looked at Bucke and raised his eyebrows quizzically.

This was not what Bucke had wanted at all. Davies and Gill had used the cart to go out to Morriston to look for signs of illegal horse dealing and on their way back had picked up Milo and Ada as they were finishing an impromptu prayer meeting by the side of Neath Road. Bucke was horrified at the thought of Milo parading through the town as if in some sort of holy procession. He had wanted something quiet and effective, but the constables were eager to please and soon the journey to the police station had run completely out of control and, as always, Milo was able to take the moral high ground. He had been out to Llansamlet, he told the crowd loudly, to examine the field where the Battle of Armageddon was to take place, but had been called to pray with the devout and god-fearing Mrs Fowler, her husband cruelly murdered by the police. Bucke knew this was a fantasy, but the damage had been done.

Milo was a tall angular man, his hair smoothed back carefully from his forehead and his face framed by that crafted beard. He might have been forty, perhaps older, but well-preserved, so it was hard to be certain. His most dominant feature was his eyes – pale, blue and intense. They were his greatest weapon and they seemed to contract and expand at will, drawing people into them. Bucke regarded him carefully, seeing before him a very calculating man, one who assessed everyone and everything around him, probing for weaknesses. He looked back at the world down his long nose, his expressive head moved backwards and to one side when he listened and then pushed forward when he spoke, always, it seemed, with confidence and insistence. Bucke saw him as devious in private and could understand why in public he appeared mesmeric with a susceptible audience.

'What have I done, Inspector? Please tell me why you have disrupted our evening of devotion with such orchestrated drama. I had a message from God to deliver to my followers and instead your constables have brought me here. What was it that could not have waited a little longer?'

'You have incited others to commit crimes and I would like to know why.' Bucke felt there was no point in being cautious, particularly since he guessed how evasive the man in front of him would be.

'And so this is why I am here, is it? Because of what other people have done? Please do me the courtesy of considering what you have said. You must realise that it is entirely absurd. You may as well arrest yourself because a cab driver in Cardiff has attacked a young woman in the street and committed an outrage. What are any of these absurd things dwelling inside your head to do with me?' Milo spread his arms wide, in innocence.

To Bucke's developing irritation Milo was confident, untouched, superior. He knew that detaining him on the street and then bringing him to the police station on a night when his followers were waiting to hear from him, had been an unfortunate miscalculation.

'Some of your followers have committed crimes – serious crimes – suicide and probably murder, after listening to you. And I believe that if it wasn't for what you said, they would not have done the things that they did.'

They considered each other in silence for a brief moment. They both knew there was nothing that Bucke could do, no case here that he could prove, no crime for which Milo could be punished. Milo hadn't killed Malachi and so he was emboldened, assured, not intimidated at all.

He laughed. 'I speak the truth to my congregation. You should come and listen. How can the truth be incitement? I show them that the world they live in is mired in corruption and I bring them messages from God, as his ordained representative. You tell me now that this, somehow, implicates me in crime. Please, Inspector, you yourself must realise how ridiculous this is. You have detained me and I have been transported in procession through the town to the general scorn, not because of something I have done, but because of something someone else has done. Whatever that thing might be.'

'If you had not said what you said, then these people might still be alive.' Bucke was not prepared to be distracted. He wanted to provoke Milo, to see how he would respond.

'You can only say these things if you are ready to doubt the words that God has given to me, alone, amongst all men. Everything I do is authorised by God. And who are you to question that?'

'I want to talk to you about Malachi, found dead in a Winnie's tub in the garden of a house that you apparently now say is yours.'

'I have these papers,' he said, pushing them dismissively across the desk, 'that show Malachi bequeathed his house to me. And the furniture warehouse. You, who are so obsessed with worldly goods, can surely see that this is true. His possessions became mine before God as a witness, for I am the one true representative of God on earth. Malachi must have fallen into the barrel when God selected him to do so. We should rejoice. He has truly died by the visitation of God. How we must all envy him.'

'And you knew the washer woman? Winnie?'

'A disciple, Inspector, and a good one. Loyal, devoted, distressed by the corruption that surrounded her.' He gestured dismissively at the room. 'Troubled by demons from Satan, of course. But, as we now know, she has triumphed over them and God will reward her. Now she is fighting a different battle, Inspector Bucke. She is following the Spear of Jehovah in the Militia of Jesus.'

'And why do you think that she believed that she was Jezebel? Did someone tell her?'

Milo smiled indulgently. 'Her spirit was anxious to atone for her earlier sins. People display this anxiety in different ways, Inspector. They bring so much with them from an earlier life which still troubles them.' He paused. 'I form the impression, Rumsey, that you do not believe me.'

Bucke changed the focus of his questions. 'I ask myself why Malachi would give the house and the shop to you, a stranger. Is this signature a forgery, I wonder? Did you persuade him to do it? Or did you kill him? Or did you incite Winnie to do it? That's your style, isn't it?'

'He gave me his house because he is a believer, Inspector. Because he believes in God and in salvation. May I call you Rumsey?'

Bucke looked at Milo with scorn, showing, he hoped, that he was aware of the games he was playing. 'Malachi was a regular and popular member of the Synagogue. Did you know that?'

'An even greater reason to celebrate then, Rumsey, for Malachi finally found his way to God. As perhaps you should, too.'

'And how, may I ask, did you come into possession of the chapel?'

'A foolish question, Rumsey. God gave it to me. You don't mind me calling you, Rumsey, do you?'

'I must presume then that God did not provide you with any papers authorising this transfer.'

'Oh how droll, Rumsey. How very amusing. I hope very much that you do not burn in hell for eternity as a result of what you said. Will Constance Bristow burn also, do you think? Just a question.' He smiled once again.

Bucke stared at him, controlling, as much as he could, the dislike he felt for the manipulative man in front of him. Milo smiled at him in return but he persisted. 'The chapel. How is it that you now possess it?'

'Because it is God's will that I do so, Rumsey. I have the keys.'

'And how did you get the keys?'

'God sent old man Rosser to me. He knew that he should give them to me.'

Bucke gave the documents on the desk a cursory glance. He changed his emphasis again, trying to unsettle Milo. 'Did you know that Winnie had murdered Malachi?'

He smiled and shook his head. 'How is it murder? Perhaps Malachi was called, for he had done his task on earth? Perhaps Winnie was told what to do? We do not know, because both of these loyal disciples have been called to share in the certain triumph of the Lord God, against the forces of darkness. May I ask, Rumsey, which side will you be on in the final conflict, soon to be upon us? Surely, since there could only ever be one rational choice to be made, then your indecision betrays you as an agent of Satan. You might not have realised this until now, for Satan and his familiars have seated themselves in your soul. But I know that I can set you free. Follow me, Rumsey. Follow me to certain salvation.' His eyes appeared to be expanding, trying to draw Bucke in.

'Perhaps you need to concern yourself more with more mundane issues, Mr...' Bucke realised that wasn't quite sure what to call him.

'Please call me Milo. Father Milo. I am your salvation, if only you would permit me.'

Bucke ignored him. 'Whatever the nature of your religious beliefs, I have some serious crimes to investigate and you have a civic duty to assist me.'

'Of course, Rumsey. And that is what I am trying to do. I can offer you no information about an incident which you regard as so important. I had no involvement in it.' He leaned forward and dropped his voice and his bright eyes burned themselves into Bucke's face. 'I do not kill people, Inspector Bucke. Neither do I raise the dead. I am a messenger bringing news from God, that is all. He speaks to me and he speaks to me alone. The end is coming, that much is made known to me. Only those who follow me will survive and will live to build a better world, once what you see about you has been wiped clean. Why do you choose to remain faithful to this poisoned world? To live in dung like a beetle or a fly in the rank garden of earthly depravity? Let me help you, Rumsey.'

Bucke returned his stare, unwilling to blink. 'And so how else do you explain that body, drowned in a barrel, trapped beneath the water by a pile of stones? He did not pile the stones on top of himself. Did Winnie do it all on her own?'

'I do not understand your question. You are mired in Satan's world of senseless death and cruelty and you ask me how can I explain it? I could not do such a thing as murder. Look at my hands. These are not the hands of a murderer. It is not the kind of thing that God would call upon me to do. You need urgent help, Rumsey. The Devil is abroad in Swansea, for we have entered the End of Times. He knows me as his greatest enemy and will do everything he can to destroy me and he is using you to try and achieve that. Can't you see it, Rumsey? A diabolic conspiracy. And you must make a decision about what you are going to do. If you are still free enough to decide.'

Bucke looked at window as something crashed against it. Outside the chanting seemed to have been augmented by a drum. It was theatre and it was orchestrated. He could hear a woman's voice, strident and angry. Probably Ada. Someone banged on the door. The demonstrators could not get in – but then the police officers couldn't get out either. Milo saw it too.

'And this is how you lead your life, is it, Inspector? Hiding away from the righteous? You bring me here but you have no reason, you have no evidence. And so you will have to let me go. We both know that. I find it interesting that you, a police inspector, have committed incitement.' He smiled. 'You will have incited my followers and disciples outside this police station to righteous anger. I cannot know what the consequences of that might be.'

Bucke saw that bringing him in for questioning might prove to be counterproductive and he was angry with himself for not preventing it. Had he created a common, single enemy for Milo's congregation, who might now be united in opposing the police? He was sure that Milo would now present the police as the instruments of Satan and award himself the celebrity of a martyr. It would not make the job of the police any easier.

'You have unwittingly become involved in a struggle which is beyond your understanding, Rumsey. I can help you. I can set you free. You must understand that if Winnie helped Malachi to pass over, then she did so under God's instruction. He needed Malachi by his side at that moment and so he was called. Who are you to question this?'

Despite himself, his temper was rising. 'If that is the case, then why did not God speak to him directly? Why was it necessary to involve Winnie? If it was Winnie, of course.'

'Such are the mysteries of God. Who are we to question him? I did not kill Malachi and you have no evidence that would indicate that it was me. If you continue to challenge me, it must be because you have been sent by Satan to oppose me, even if you do not know this yourself. You have unwittingly become his instrument and you will suffer horribly for this. I have looked in the eye of God today and I have nothing to fear.'

'What can you tell me about Phillip Bowen?'

'Another hero who has been called to bring about our victory at Armageddon. Another hero who has chosen an Eternal Life.'

'He attended your chapel, didn't he?'

'Of course he did. The Lord provided him with the answers to the questions that troubled him most.'

'And he was so pleased with the answers that he took his own life? Is that what you are saying?'

'But, Rumsey…'

'I have heard enough. Did he give you money? A large sum of money?'

'Many of my followers make donations that allow us to continue with our work. They are all ready to divest themselves of the illusion of possessions, so that they can better serve the Lord.'

Bucke was not prepared to allow himself to be distracted. 'And did he give you a large amount of money? In cash?'

'I do not know what you are talking about. What is a large sum of money? I believe that policemen are not very well paid and so….

'£666.'

'Ah! The Number of the Beast.'

'Did Phillip Bowen give you £666, in cash?'

'What an interesting number.'

'Did he?'

Milo was dismissive. 'I do not recollect that he did but these are details that do not trouble me. I do not deal in trifles. I am a simple man, I lead a simple life. I live my life in God's hands and I do his bidding.'

'Was William Gammon in the house today, Mr…'

He smiled. 'Please. Call me Father Milo.'

Bucke tried another approach. 'Why was William Gammon in the house?'

'To visit his sister.'

'And his sister is Ada Gammon?'

'She was once known by that name, yes, Rumsey. A wonderful servant of God.'

'And where is he now?'

'Doing God's work, Inspector. He does not tell me where he goes and he has no reason to do so.' Bucke leaned back in his chair, put his hand over his mouth and pinched his nose, then waited for Milo to speak. 'It seems to me that you are so enmeshed in your sin that you do not believe that I speak with the authority of God. But I do and I am concerned for the condition of your soul. If only you would let me help you.'

There was an anger boiling within Bucke now. He could feel that he was being provoked but was unwilling to ignore the provocation. 'I can respect no god who kills innocent children,' he said bitterly, and immediately regretted it.

'And how do you know they were innocent?'

'Because they were mine!' and he banged his hand upon the desk in anger, knowing he had allowed himself to be goaded.

'I shall pray for you, Rumsey. There is so much that you do not understand.'

Bucke tried to compose himself. 'I think there is a great deal you do not understand, either. And a great deal that you are not telling me. It makes me think that we will have to resume this conversation on another occasion, I am sure of that.'

Milo suddenly threw up his hands. 'Listen! Do you hear it? We have a visitation!' There were two sharp raps upon the table. Milo was knocking on it but Bucke could not see how he was doing it, for his hands were visible. 'Speak to us, oh spirit!' he called. There were two more loud knocks. 'It must be the manifestation of the spirit of your deceased wife and she has arrived here, through my instrumentality! Speak to us, Julia!'

Bucke was shaking in horror of this moment, appalled at the way in which Julia's memory was being debased by such a deliberately vicious trick. It was calculated and he knew that he should not respond.

'Have you brought the children with you? Speak to us, Julia!' There were two more loud raps. 'You see, Rumsey! Rejoice! We are not alone! She is here! Your children are here!' He shook his head and rolled his eyes, as if entering a trance.

'Enough of this nonsense!' said Bucke, who was also shaking, but with horror at this unspeakable cruelty.

'They speak through me to you. What is it you say, Julia?' Milo adopted a high pitched whisper. 'I live to bless you, my precious darling.' He shook his head, his eyes open wide.

'Stop this ridiculous performance!'

'Wait! One of your children wants to speak to you now. It is a boy. Charles, is it? Speak to us Charles.' Again Milo used his high pitched voice. 'I am with you always.' He went on, 'Another voice now. A girl! Hannah? No. Anna, that's right. What does she say?' He squeaked again. 'I love, love, love you as I always did.'

Bucke stood up and banged on the table. 'No! I order you to stop!'

'Don't go! Please stay a little longer, your father wishes to speak to you.' Milo shrugged. 'Too late. I can hear nothing.' He cupped his ear with his hand, as if listening to a distant sound, and then laughed loudly. He had distressed Bucke and was proud of it.

Bucke stared down at him, refusing to speak and shaking with emotion. The whole interview had been a test, a challenge, and he wasn't very sure how successful he had been. The final performance was contemptuous and provocative. He knew he should not have responded, that he had no chance of extracting a confession from Milo about anything.

Tonight was merely a skirmish, nothing more than that. They had been testing each other out, ready for bigger battles to come. They both knew it. And of course the inspector had no evidence, either, with which to detain him. They both knew that, too.

Milo stopped laughing but said nothing.

'Allow me to show you to the door. Look around. Make yourself familiar with it all. My only regret is that I haven't had time to show you the cells. But I am reassured, since I am sure you will see them soon.' Bucke opened the door of the police station and a silence fell upon the crowd outside. It was much bigger than Bucke had anticipated.

Milo nodded at him. 'I shall pray for you,' then he stepped outside. The crowd was lit by blazing torches, fuelled by oil-soaked rags. There was an unsettling infernal atmosphere in the street, at odds with an ostensibly religious unity which had brought all these people together. Ada was standing on an upturned barrel, beating it with the end of her spear. When they saw Milo there was a huge cheer. He stood on the steps with his arms outstretched and as the crowd quietened itself he said. 'Let us pray to the Lord to protect us from Satan, for his forces surround us. But soon they all will perish. Of this there can be no doubt.'

*

Bucke was contrite when he reported to Captain Colquhoun the next morning about the nature of his meeting with Milo. It had not gone very well, though the Captain seemed less exercised by it. 'You have made a point with him, Rumsey. He knows we are watching him. It may make him more cautious – or it may drive him to recklessness and then we shall have him. Your alternative was not interviewing him at all, which in these circumstances would not have been acceptable, once the constables had brought him into the station so publicly. Yes, he managed to stage a performance but that is what he does, as I understand it.'

'He is a difficult man to deal with.' Bucke pulled at his damaged ear and sighed. 'Slippery and a manipulator. He has the same answer for everything, which becomes tiresome. He is a messenger from God and to doubt him indicates you are in league with the devil. It allows him to control every conversation, because nothing you say has any significance. I need more facts if I am to confront him properly. Otherwise I am playing a game and he is setting the rules. So much of what he says make no sense and if Satan is truly abroad, licking the gutters of Swansea and spitting into the eye of God or whatever it is that he is supposed to have done, why does The Prince of Darkness bother employing people as his agents, whilst waiting for the final battle which he is apparently destined to lose?'

Captain Colquhoun shrugged. 'And you do not think that he killed Malachi?'

'Milo didn't do it. Not directly. There was no need for him to get his hands dirty. He incites others to do his work. I know that he told Winnie what to do, told her that she was Jezebel and she believed him. He told Phillip Bowen to take the money from the bank and to kill himself. I know that he did these things and I am sure he knows that I do. But he also knows that I have no evidence.'

'But you have warned him and perhaps that may require him to be more careful. Do we know anything about him? Where he came from? What he is doing in Swansea?'

'I will make enquiries, Isaac. I need to know more about him.'

'Try not to let this man agitate you. He is doing it deliberately to cloud your judgement.'

'I know that, Isaac. But he is a very provocative man. He is clever and he is devious. But that link with Billy Evil troubles me.'

'And the girl in the canal? Do we know any more?'

'It is not proving easy. No one has been reported missing in Swansea these past few weeks. And if she came from somewhere else, then where from and why?'

'Let's hope we can find out who she is and what happened to her before the world ends. You can do it, Rumsey. I know you can.'

Chapter 8

Edie the housemaid had been busy all day. Glasses washed, the very best china arranged, the cutlery polished. Flora Beynon fussed around, anxious to ensure that every item on the table was precisely positioned. It had taken a long time, especially since Flora kept changing her mind, worried that her guests might not find her hospitality satisfactory. At least she did not have to worry about the cooking. That was in the hands of the housekeeper, the formidable Mrs Morley.

She was, without question, a legend in Swansea for the quality of her cooking and the precision of her domestic arrangements. His more observant patients had noted some time ago that Dr Beynon had taken to occasionally walking the longer way between appointments and declining the kind offer of cake. Good living had settled upon him and he realised that he needed to be careful. Mrs Morley was a cook who was much in demand, regularly receiving offers of employment, with improved terms, from every part of Swansea, but she was fiercely loyal to the family. She could not be bought; Eaton Crescent was the Beynon home and it was hers too.

The Beynons were a comfortable couple, though Flora was a great worrier about everything. David was more relaxed, the unpleasantness of the tasks he sometimes had to perform convincing him that his home should never be anything other than a sanctuary of well-ordered tranquillity.

In fact, tonight Flora didn't have to worry much about her guests or their expectations. She would not be ridiculed across Swansea for an ill-positioned tea spoon by either Constance White or Rumsey Bucke. The occasion would be beyond criticism, since the evening had enormous significance for both of them. Rumsey and Constance were, for the first time, out together in Swansea society with people who expected to see them together and accepted them as they were.

David and Rumsey had been friends for many years and the recent and disturbing decline in standards of law and order had brought them too frequently into professional contact, though this would the first time they had met socially.

They came in to the house nervously, a little hesitant with handing their coats over to Edie, both of them unused to the presence of domestic servants. Constance smiled brightly, though Bucke could imagine her feelings within as he stood with his hands behind his back, moulding them together, unseen. He realised that Flora was trying her very best to create a relaxed occasion, despite her own quite obvious tensions.

'I am sure the men have plenty to talk about. What is it so excites them this week ? Arguments at Council meetings? General Roberts and the Afghan War? Who in all conscience should care about such things? Let us leave them to it. Come with me, Constance. There is someone I would like you to meet.'

The two men watched Flora usher her into David's study which was at the back of the house, overlooking the garden. Their only daughter, Emily, was sitting at the desk, making a deliberate show of concentration to avoid eye contact and so did not look up as they entered.

Flora appeared nervous of her. 'Hello, Emily. I have Miss White here. I told you about her earlier. She might be able to help you with your French studies. I am sure that with her you would make tremendous progress....' Her words faded away.

Emily said nothing.

'I am hardly fluent,' said Constance, trying to ease the tension in the room. It didn't work.

Flora suddenly lost her nerve.' Oh well. Must get back.' she said with forced cheerfulness. 'Make sure Mrs Morley doesn't need me,' laughing uncomfortably.

Emily finally spoke. 'She never does, mamma. You know that.'

Flora laughed again, rather too readily. 'Oh, but we have guests, Emily! I must dash.' Flora looked flustered. 'Miss White is here to help you and I am sure…Gracious me, is that the time? I shall leave you for five minutes or so, get to know each other…' She hurried out of the room, as if she could not get out quickly enough.

There was silence. Constance put her head on one side and tried to get a proper look at Emily's face. She was sure she had seen her somewhere but she couldn't quite remember where. She was a very pretty girl, sixteen, slight, very dark and destined for beauty as a woman. She had a sketch book in front of her and what looked like green threads with which she was creating a picture.

'Bonjour, Emily. Comment ca va?' Constance sighed. 'I fear your mother may have exaggerated my language skills, I am afraid. It might be a while before we can move on to something even slightly more interesting. To be honest it's more likely that you will be teaching me.'

'I am busy,' she said, frowning in concentration at her picture, refusing to look at her.

'I can see that, Emily. Concentration is essential for all artists, I believe.' Constance watched her using what she now recognised as scraps of seaweed to decorate one of her own pencil sketches. It was meticulous work, teasing out threads of algae and manoeuvring them delicately into place on thin strands of glue that she had previously applied with the tiny brush that rested on a stained sheet of blotting paper. She was creating realistic-looking trees which stood to the side of a church that she had previously swamped with a representation of ivy. She had made a grassed area in front of the church, with a crooked gravestone seemingly rising from unkempt grass. It was precise and effective.

'I haven't seen this sort of work before. It is a clever thing to do. Where do you obtain the seaweed?'

'I scrape it off the rocks at Mumbles Head,' she said quietly, manoeuvring another piece gently into place, using a pair of tweezers.

'Are you often so absorbed in your art, Emily?'

'Sometimes.' She refused to offer Constance the encouragement of eye contact.

'Do you do much of this work?' Constance persisted, although she could see that Emily was wilfully refusing to start a conversation.

'When it takes my fancy. It is something to do to pass the time.'

'It does look very interesting,' Constance said cheerfully. 'Very impressive. But rather too intricate for me, I am afraid.'

She looked up from her work suddenly, her dark eyes appraising her coolly. 'Is the Inspector your lover? Everyone says he is. All the girls at school. Everyone.' She smirked faintly, thinking that she might have shocked her with her bravery by being so outspoken.

If she was trying to provoke her, then Constance was not going to respond. 'No he is not, Emily. He is my most special friend, the most important person in my world, but he is not my lover.'

Emily picked up her pencil and made an imperceptible alteration to the church steeple. She frowned and Constance waited, knowing that there was more to come.

'Do you love him, Miss White?'

'Yes I do, Emily. He is the most wonderful person that I have ever met and the sun only shines when we are together.'

'I thought so.' She nodded wisely as if she was an expert in relationships. 'But you are married to someone else, are you not, Miss White?'

'Yes, Emily. I am. Never imagine that life always runs smoothly; it does not. I wish for more, but sometimes you have to accept what you have. Because it might be all that you will ever have. And keeping it, however slight it might be, is preferable to losing it altogether.'

Emily was looking at her now. She seemed impressed and surprised by Constance's unexpected honesty. Constance raised her eyebrows, inviting her to continue.

'And life is difficult for everyone, would you say? I mean, do you really think that?'

'In its own way, yes. At different times and for different reasons. Happiness is a very fragile thing and in my experience you should do whatever you can to preserve it. Bit like my hair, I suppose. No matter how carefully I dress it, a strand always breaks free,' she said, pushing that errant strand ineffectually back into place.

Emily nodded and pushed some of her own hair behind an ear. She put down her pencil, then paused. 'May I call you Connie?'

'Of course you may, if you will allow me to call you Em.' Emily said nothing, but seemed satisfied with the arrangement. 'Tell me more about your drawing? Is that what you call it? Design would be more accurate, perhaps? As I said, I could not do it.'

'I won't tell you in French though,' Emily replied.

'I am pleased to hear it. I wouldn't understand if you did.'

Constance stayed with her for another twenty minutes, exploring the requirements of seaweed collection, the best glue to use and examining Emily's portfolio of work, some of which, she noted, had started to smell faintly. Emily seemed to value the attention and seemed rather disappointed when Flora came to collect Constance for dinner.

'Are you sure you will not join us, Emily? Your father and I would very much like it.'

'No, Mamma. I have told you. I have work that I must complete for school.'

'Very well,' she said, a little too brightly. 'I am pleased that you are so studious. Mrs Morley will bring you something to eat, have no doubt. Come, Constance. The gentlemen await us.'

'Of course, Flora,' replied Constance. 'Enjoy your evening, Em. I am sure I shall enjoy mine.'

'Thank you, Connie,' said Emily as she lowered her head over her design once more.

Flora ushered Constance from the study, closed the door and then leaned on it. 'It is so difficult, Constance. I cannot remember when she spoke to me for such a length of time,' laughed Flora nervously. 'I think your conversation must have been a raging success.'

Constance soon realised that Emily was, in Flora's mind, the only possible topic of conversation. When she was back in the lounge, she could not relax, flitting around, adjusting antimacassars and nagging her husband into replenishing sherry glasses when it wasn't necessary. 'I worry so much,' she announced suddenly. 'Emily has been very withdrawn of late. She was such a lovely girl and it worries me deeply that I can no longer reach her. She seems sullen, hostile. I so wanted her to join us for dinner this evening but she refused.'

David tried what was clearly his habitual reassurance. 'Changes have come upon her in many ways, Flora. She is at a time which can be very difficult for girls. She is almost seventeen and, like all seventeen year olds she is ill. It is called being seventeen. Happens to them all, I can assure you, at least on this side of town. Over on the east they have been at work for years and already have two children.'

'Stop being silly, David.'

'I am not, Flora. This is absolutely true, is it not, Rumsey?'

'Life is very different over there,' he conceded.

'I am sure that it is, but it is so sad that the beautiful little girl, my constant companion, has gone and has been replaced by a stranger.'

'It is hard, Flora,' said Constance soothingly. 'But she will come back to you. And she is still the same person within. It is just that the future is there in front of her and it is exciting and it is frightening at the same time. The future often is. She needs you by her side whilst she grows a little more.'

Flora wasn't really listening, wrapped up as always in her own worries. 'She was a devoted church member and yet now she finds it dull and uninteresting. The boys who were once her companions at church she now finds childish and trivial. She has outgrown them, she says. And she argues all the time, about anything and everything.'

Constance wasn't listening either. It was that mention of the church that had triggered her memory. She wondered if that was where she had seen Emily before, at Our Lady of Mumbles. It couldn't have been. The light was uncertain and deceitful. Probably a young girl who looked like her, that was all; had the same long dark hair, as many young girls around Swansea did.

'Come, Flora. You worry too much,' said David, draining his glass. 'She will become a fine young woman. What do you think Rumsey? Constance?'

'I have no doubt about it. She cannot help but be a credit to her parents,' said Bucke trying to be as anodyne as possible.

'Constance, you have a daughter. Did you go through difficult times?' asked Flora.

She found a diplomatic answer. 'Of course, Don't we all?' Agnes had been her constant and only joy. More like sisters, conspirators giggling together in the kitchen, always in trouble, always together. No, Agnes and Emily were very different.

'I have told you before, Flora. All too soon we shall be arranging her wedding,' David said with a laugh.

'Please, David! Don't say such things! When that happens I shall never see her.' Flora was suddenly angry.

Constance tried to change the subject. 'Would it be possible, Flora, for me to visit Emily on occasion? My classes at Miss Higginson's School on Tuesday and Thursday have been moved to the afternoons and I could call here before going home. Emily herself should be at home by then, I am sure. She goes to Oakley House Day School doesn't she?'

'Oh, Constance I would be delighted. I am sure that her French will come on by leaps and bounds and I am so pleased that she might talk to you as well.' She crossed the room and grasped Constance's hands in gratitude. 'I am so grateful.'

*

The evening was very successful. They did enjoy a splendid roast saddle of mutton which was followed by some crystallised fruits, truly things of beauty. There was entertaining after-dinner conversation, with Rumsey telling stories about India and cobras and David relating bizarre medical stories and peculiar tales told to him by a patient who believed in the existence of feral children living in caves by the sea in Gower. Constance listened and laughed and, although she considered talking about her experience at The Chapel of Our Lady of Mumbles she felt, for some reason, that it would not be appropriate and she wasn't entirely sure why she felt like that. But she knew that the occasion was much more than food and company. It was a symbol. She felt she had been re-admitted to society. Accepted, despite her status as the Abandoned Woman who had been unable to keep a husband, no matter how unsatisfactory he had been. She could see too, how Rumsey was truly grateful for what the Beynon's had done. She left Eaton Terrace in the warm glow of happiness, uncomfortable perhaps that they were not currently in a position in which they could reciprocate such hospitality, but feeling more complete, more normal.

As they walked home, Rumsey asked her about Emily.

'A difficult young girl, I am sure of that. Wilful perhaps; difficult. Spirited would be more polite, though less accurate I would say. But she is changing, and she must be allowed to change. Flora and David must be patient, that is all, and she will grow and become a beautiful woman who they will be proud of.'

'I am sure that it must be very difficult for them, though it is sometimes for me hard to understand.' He stopped and turned to her. 'I loved my children dearly and yet for me they are frozen in time as happy little children. But I will never know what they might have become. What problems I might have had, like David and Flora, what joy they would have brought. They were beautiful, adored and I will never forget what they were, because that is what they will always be.'

She looked at him and squeezed his hand. She knew how vulnerable he could sometimes be; she knew that he still grieved and she was moved that he was prepared to talk to her about it. 'And so enjoy those memories, Rumsey,' she said gently. 'You can grieve for Anna and Charles and you always should. But remember the happy times too. Always remember those, before you try to think of anything else. And I am sure that if Anna had grown into a young woman, no matter what the difficulties, you would have dealt with it admirably.'

'It is a difficult time for boys too,' replied Rumsey, lightening the mood. 'Don't forget that.'

Constance laughed. 'Oh please Rumsey! What do boys do? They stop playing with hoops and start throwing stones and stealing door knockers and growing spots!'

'Really? What do you know, a mere woman?' Bucke replied, with a smile.

'I know about door knockers. Someone took mine last week or have you not noticed?'

'I am far too busy getting through the door to look at it. I shall pay attention shortly. It is probably the very active and very irritating Hat Stand Gang. We shall get them, never fear.'

'There are times, Rumsey when I find your duties as a police inspector most peculiar.'

They continued walking in a happy silence until they reached the bottom of Brynamor Road, when it was Constance who stopped and turned to him, still feeling the warmth of the wine she had enjoyed, which she had not experienced for a long time. She resumed their conversation.

'You see, Rumsey, I am troubled. I am sure I saw a girl who looked so much like Emily at Our Lady of Mumbles. I can't get her out of my mind. It might have been her, but I cannot be sure.'

Bucke looked thoughtful. 'You would think that would be unlikely. Flora would not go there, she has never suggested it, and Emily is hardly likely to have gone there alone.'

'I know. But it troubles me.'

They walked on, Constance not wanting to break the contented spell of their evening together but knowing that she had too. She stopped outside the door to her rooms on St Helen's Road.

'I would so love you to come inside with me tonight, Rumsey. But it might not be wise, for a moment of immaturity might come upon me and we should regret it in the morning.' She raised her hand and gently rested it upon his cheek. She smiled and then placed a finger on his lips. 'No, Rumsey, say nothing.' She kissed him hurriedly and then went inside.

As the door closed he sighed. He was able to confirm that there was no door knocker and he turned away and walked home along the deserted street to his cold room on Fisher Street. He did not see the slight figure of Baglow, who had been on the verge of giving up and going home, hiding behind a hedge. As Bucke walked away, the reporter lifted his brown tweed cap and scratched his head, grinning.

*

Baglow sat at his desk writing a brief item for the paper's gossip column. He wanted to get it finished before he went to bed but the piece wasn't quite right and he was painstakingly reviewing and polishing each word. It would be very short – a couple of sentences at most –three if the editor was feeling generous- so he needed every one to count. He looked at the opening again. '*Our fair town...*' He wasn't convinced by the use of the word *fair* so he tried '*noble*' instead but wasn't sure it gave the right impression. '*Our fair town descends daily...*' He crossed it out and wrote instead '*Our fair town daily descends into chaos and disorder.*' He quite liked that; to him it sounded much more impressive. He tried '*daily descends into chaos and madness*' and then '*into disorder and licentiousness*' but he had used *licentiousnes*s before. He should wait a bit longer before he used it again, he decided. And then suddenly, the words came into his head, as they sometimes did, and he wrote them down quickly before they disappeared again.

Our fair town daily descends into chaos and disorder. It is not the place for this august publication to name those who you will recognise all too readily, but we would be failing in our civic duty if we did not indicate that London Ways do not work in Swansea. It is evident that the Watch Committee must act before it is too late.

That would do. Everyone would know what he was talking about. It wasn't his best piece of writing. He wondered if he should use *'journal'* rather than *'publication'* but on the whole he was quite pleased. A small stone thrown into the pond – and slowly he would make bigger ripples.

He sat back in his chair and stretched his arms above his head. It would take time, he knew that, but his campaign would get him noticed, he was sure. He would make his name as the fearless journalist who uncovered corruption and held authority to account. The world needed heroes and he would be one of them. A police inspector distracted by his own immorality, allowing crime to run out of control. As he imagined his success, he saw promotion to one of the large circulation London newspapers and he could leave this forsaken, grubby town behind him. No, he was quite pleased with the piece. Don't go in too hard. He was starting off small. Setting the mood first. Soon he could throw bigger stones. You will never stop the ripples.

Chapter 9

When it all began, James Flynn was exasperated, but as the madness took hold he moved quickly from irritation and soon embraced anger, ripping up the letters he was given into increasingly smaller pieces. A 'Snowball Prayer' had suddenly taken hold. It was the sort of thing that happened occasionally, though rarely had it been so virulent - a prayer received that must be copied and passed on immediately to five other people or eternal damnation would be yours.

Many of those who received the letters were illiterate but knew enough to be truly terrified upon their receipt. What could they possibly do? They took these anonymous letters to their chapel where the minister would read them aloud and then refuse to forward them as the avoidance of unspeakable demonic torture demanded. The minister's reassurances were insufficient and so the holders of the letters ran next to the police station, asking desperately for help to write out the prayers on their behalf and so queued, often twelve deep, anxiously in front of the counter.

Inspector Flynn was angry at such cynical exploitation. How were these people to afford the writing materials or the stamps? Would it be acceptable if, once they had the five letters required to perpetuate the chain, they hand-delivered them in the dead of night to neighbours who had probably sent one out to them in the first place? Communities right across Swansea, from Winch Wen to Penlan to Dyfatty, waited in dread for their delivery.

The Inspector soon developed an effective strategy to deal with them. He would nod sagely and with a benign smile take the letters, examine them carefully, sigh at the spelling mistakes and the poorly copied nonsense, and then rip them up. He had to admit, however, that it wasn't always received with a calm acceptance. As he later explained to Inspector Bucke, 'It was Mrs Foster who pushed me over the edge, Rumsey. Wailing and sobbing, sobbing and wailing. It was more than a body could stand. I ripped up the letter then picked her up and pushed her out of the door. Those letters are wicked, troubling those who have sufficient trouble in their lives as it is. I would like to have a strong word with him who is doing all this. If it is your man Milo then he is a curse, Rumsey.'

'He is clever, James. Keeps himself at a distance. Milo will deny it. Nothing to do with him. Where is your evidence? But that is who it is, or one of his disciples. Frightening people. Recruiting people. Inciting people. And all because God has told him to do it.'

Inspector Flynn sighed. 'Mr Foster fetched up then at the counter. Told Stan that I had condemned his wife to hell by ripping up the letter, which he was not too happy about on account of him banking on going to hell himself on his own, for a bit of peace; with her destined for heaven he'd be free of her for the everlasting. I have told Stanley that, on my orders, if any more letters like that are brought in he should destroy them. Not a problem for a proper chapel man like him. Not a problem for me either. But I also told Constable Evan Davies that if he didn't show more aptitude he'd have to do it. Not happy at all. Shook him up, I think, but for how long I don't know.'

*

Of course Constance was as good as her word and called on Emily as regularly as she could when they had both put their school days behind them. They would sit in the study whilst Emily drew or doodled and as she did so she would talk, usually beginning with daily school gossip and then moving on to more personal questions. The pretence of French lessons had long-since been abandoned.

'I love Mamma, of course I do, but whenever I want to talk about anything important my mother changes the subject. There are so many things I want to know, but I have to ask the girls at school and they don't really know what they are talking about. Can you really catch a bad disease if a boy holds your hand? Jessica Friedland says you can.'

Constance smiled and shook her head. She could appreciate Emily's difficulty and her frustration. The Beynons had a maturing daughter and they were unsure how to deal with her, and whilst she did not articulate it, Emily seemed to know that they would have been much happier if she had remained a little girl. Flora wasn't natural enough; she was too formal, too anxious. Her daughter had become a young adult and she wasn't ready for it. Nothing seemed natural or inconsequential, as most conversations are. Everything was charged with hidden meaning. David Beynon too was wary of Emily, anxious not to upset her or to cause offence, for fear of making things between mother and daughter worse. So the atmosphere was a bit uncomfortable and prickly. And all Constance had to do was be herself and talk to Emily without any concern about what she might think and that is exactly what Emily needed, a woman who would talk confidently and without embarrassment about being a woman and about the complicated and confusing world she would soon enter.

Emily put her pencil down, decisively. 'Can you tell me something, Connie?' She started twisting her hair by the side of her ear. 'Do you think the world is going to end? Are we all doomed? Are these really the last days?'

Constance looked at her quizzically.

'I am just curious, that's all. It is what some of the girls are saying at school, anyway,' she said as casually as she could. 'They have heard it said. I mean, I haven't of course. But they have heard it said around the town. There's a preacher telling everyone that we are about to die. Don't know his name but Bethan Pontesbury has heard him say it. I am not lying.'

Constance looked at her carefully 'It is nonsense, Em and you should take no heed of such silly talk. No one knows what the weather is going to be tomorrow, let alone when the world is going to end.'

'But you have got to see, Connie, if that is right, if we are all going to die, then nothing is worthwhile. Is it? It is obvious, isn't it? If the world ends tomorrow then nothing matters. Everything is meaningless.' She pushed her sketch book away from her and turned slightly to look out of the window.

'It is just a story, Em. No one knows when the world will end. It might be tomorrow. It might be next week. It could be in three hundred years' time. No one knows. Perhaps we should all be kind to each other whilst we are waiting. There is nothing we can do to prevent it. I think it is just a story to frighten people, Em.'

'But you don't know that for sure, do you? He might be right. That preacher man. You say he is wrong, but how do you know, Connie? He tells everyone that God has told him. That is what the girls say. But if there is a chance for us to be saved then shouldn't we take it? Shouldn't we try to save each other? Mamma, Pappa, you. You do see that, don't you?'

'Because he tells you God has spoken to him doesn't make it true, Em. Why don't you ask Pappa about it? See what he thinks. He might see things differently.'

Emily snorted and pulled her sketch book back towards her.

*

The death of the troubled Phillip Bowen had been an upsetting business, Mrs Prosser couldn't deny it. As she told her old friend, Nelly Damms down in the market, whenever she looked round his empty room, she could still imagine him reading intently and then feverishly writing in his diary. It was marvellous how a young man could do such things, all that writing. He knew lots of clever words, there was no doubt about that. But an empty room was no good to her. Times were difficult enough as it was, without there being no money coming in from what everyone acknowledged was a very well-appointed room.

However, a chance conversation with a neighbour, Mr Caine, brought to her lodging house his nephew, George May. It was a ghastly mistake. A greater contrast with Phillip Bowen could not be imagined. George was coarse, aggressive and prone to heavy drinking and violence. His urgent need for lodgings had been prompted by his mother evicting him. She was no longer prepared to have George in the family home on Richardson Street, a short distance away. It was later agreed that it was unfortunate that no one had found the time to tell Mrs Prosser just what she was letting herself in for.

It did not take long for the full extent of her mistake to reveal itself. George spent all of Wednesday afternoon and evening in a drinking session with some of his friends. They had been unloading a consignment of flour from a ship in the South Dock and, once paid, had repaired to their favourite – and illegal - drinking den in Sandfields. His anger at his eviction sat heavily upon him and the more that he drank, the more outraged he became at such unexpected maternal rejection. He decided that it would be a good idea to discuss the issue once again with her, but when he staggered up to her house, he was shocked to discover that his mother seemed disinclined to forgive him, especially considering the state he was in. Even worse was to follow, for George was astonished when she claimed to find his obviously reasonable behaviour threatening and called for police assistance.

Constables Bingham and Francis were quickly on the scene and manfully ejected George from the house and threw him on the road, satisfied by a job well done. George May, however, made brave by beer, was keen to revenge himself on the police officers. He struck Constable Francis, kicked Constable Bingham and then, with his companions, they ran untidily to Mrs Prosser's on Nichol Street where they made a stand against the officers who had given chase, throwing stones at them from the poorly-made road which provided such a richness of material. A crowd gathered to enjoy the entertainment, whilst Mrs Prosser hid in the kitchen at the back of the house and sobbed with shame.

Baglow was quickly on the scene. For him it was the perfect commotion, a riot without a shadow of a doubt, entirely appropriate for a town with a rotten heart. When he looked around and saw that an off-duty Inspector Bucke had been alerted by the noise and was running the short distance from Constance White's rooms, he could not have been more pleased. He stepped backwards into a doorway and watched the Inspector quickly restore order. He saw him grab May and pin him to the wall, allowing Constable Francis to handcuff him, an act that caused his friends to scatter in different directions. Order had been suddenly restored and George May was dragged without ceremony to the police cells, screaming threats at his mother until he was sick in the road.

This was a good moment, Baglow decided, and he stepped back out on to the pavement.

'Good evening, Inspector. It must be disappointing to have your piano practice interfered with,' he said, shaking his head. 'I imagine you were in the middle of a very tricky arpeggio. Something like that, anyway. Any comments for the Cambrian, sir?'

'Good evening, Mr Baglow. You are not part of this gang of ruffians are you?'

Baglow decided to ignore him. 'How disappointed were you to see your constables trapped by a vicious stone-throwing mob? Do you have any thoughts about the terrible levels of lawlessness in the town?'

'For goodness sake, Mr Baglow…'

'Is that a yes or a no, Inspector? Do you have thoughts about it? Or do you not?'

'There has been a domestic incident and…'

'So you have no comment to make about the increase in crime in the town. I see. Tell me, Inspector. Some of this large crowd of youths…'

'There were four of them, Mr Baglow.'

He wasn't going to be deflected. 'Members of this large and unruly mob ran away and you did nothing to prevent it. Do you intend to continue with this new policy of allowing criminals to escape?' Do you think this might cause alarm?'

'Mr Baglow, you were here. I imagined that you might have seen what happened…'

'So you do not know whether it will cause alarm or not? Interesting. How much does the Watch Committee know about this new policy you have implemented, I wonder?' He could see that he was starting to make the Inspector flustered and angry. This was not a bad idea at all. 'Do you agree that our constables are too frightened of the criminal classes to be effective?'

'Mr Baglow. I am off-duty. If you have any questions-'

'Once again, is that a yes or a no?'

Bucke took a deep breath. 'If you have any questions relating to the nature of policing in the town, then please address them to the Chief Constable at your earliest opportunity. Thank you. As I said, I am currently off-duty.'

'And would you agree then, Inspector Bucke that your own leisure activities are more important than the maintenance of law and order in the town?'

'A ridiculous question,' said Bucke who then instantly regretted allowing Baglow to goad him. 'Good evening, Mr Baglow,' he said and then turned and walked away.

Baglow had enjoyed himself. The interview, if that is what it could be called, had gone extremely well. He knew that Bucke hadn't been ready for the questions at all. If he had been in uniform then perhaps his responses would have been more measured. But now Baglow returned as quickly as possible to his room to write down the words whilst they were still fresh in his mind.

Off-duty Inspector relaxing with his paramour allows rioters to flee unchecked. He liked it. It wasn't subtle but it would create a stir. Was he brave enough? Certainly. Baglow had a career to consider. And the editor? Well, he might not see it. But Baglow knew he had gained an advantage over the Inspector and he was determined to exploit it.

*

When he walked through the door of the police station on Saturday, Bucke could see that Sergeant Ball was anxious. He appeared consumed by troubling thoughts that he was trying to control by tearing up a copy of the Cambrian newspaper into long narrow strips.

'Good morning, Stanley. Is everything well here today? No marauding packs of dogs? No bonfire of dead rats?'

'Did you read the newspaper, Inspector Bucke, sir?' Today he had no time for niceties. He ripped another long strip aggressively then screwed it in his hands. Bucke paused at the counter and rested his forearms on it, to signal to Ball that he had his proper attention.

'Yes I have seen it, Stanley. But you shouldn't let it trouble you. I try not to.'

'That reporter man. Baglow. I mean to say, sir. It is wrong, isn't it, sir? I read it and Mrs Ball read it too and she was shocked but I have to be honest, it made me angry, Inspector.' He threw more strands of paper into the bin and then took out his handcuffs. He clicked them shut and then sprang them open with the key, repeatedly. Bucke watched him carefully. His face was fixed, his eyes glaring. He seemed to reach a decision.

'I have got to ask you, Inspector, because it is burning me up. You can tell me, sir, and I won't tell a soul, you have my word. Are you being improper, Inspector Bucke? You can tell me straight. I know I shouldn't ask…'

'Well, Stan, I can tell you that I am not being improper. Categorically. I might want to be improper and I would not deny that to you for a moment, Stan. But my relationship with Miss White is, sadly, entirely innocent. She is my most important companion and we share many moments together. But she is a married woman and, should she wish to obtain a divorce from the man who has abandoned her, as she intends to, I must not put her into a situation where her virtue might be called into question.'

'Thought so, Inspector. Thank you. You have put my mind to rest. I am much relieved. I told Mrs Ball, sir. I said to her. Inspector Bucke wouldn't do such a thing. It is that newspaper man. A proper snake by all accounts. He should not be getting away with these lies. It shouldn't be allowed.'

Bucke smiled at him and patted his arm. 'I try not to worry, Sergeant. People read the newspaper one day and then wrap their herrings in it the next. It is a temporary inconvenience, nothing more.' He could see that Ball was still agitated by the injustice of the reports and would not yet be mollified. He slammed the handcuffs on to the counter decisively.

'But he is spreading poison, sir. He should be supporting them as is trying to make the town a better place, not trying to turn people against them. It is wrong, sir and someone should stop it. It isn't fair on Miss White, neither. Her name dragged through the mud, to be scoffed at by them as should know better. There were people at the chapel yesterday talking about it, but I put them straight.'

'I am genuinely grateful for your concern. But I can assure you that Miss White has not suffered at all from his absurd allegations. Everyone who knows her realises that his words are not true. It is his own reputation that should be his concern, not Miss White's and not mine. Once he is suspected of not telling the truth, then there is no reason for anyone to buy his newspaper.'

'He needs to take special care that he don't come my way one night, that is all I got to say. Brought in drunk and disorderly and he might find himself falling down the stairs to the cells.' He looked directly at Bucke, who could see an unsettling chill in Ball's eyes.

'You must not let it bother you, Stanley, until you see it bother me. Understand?' He realised that the usually affable and dependable sergeant was not someone who you should deliberately choose to offend.

Ball took a deep breath and focused himself on his duties. 'Nothing much to report, Inspector. Usual suspects on Friday night.' He checked though the ledger. 'Margaret Mitchell, arrested again. Drunk on the Strand, Slapped Constable Bingham. He probably slapped her back. Mary Crindle. Indecent behaviour on King Street. Had a sailor against a wall.'

'How's the sailor?'

'Survived, just about. And someone has been mutilating cattle over in Cockett. Tails and ears cut off. That's about all of it, Inspector.'

'A normal Friday night then.'

'Not much different in Cardiff. Two little girls knocked down outside the market by an egg cart. One of them killed. Only seven, too.' He shook his head. 'My cousin came up from Cardiff this morning, Inspector. He's come to see the football. He is a constable, is our Lennie. Good lad all round. But you will be interested in this. Tells me they are missing a young lady. Susannah Longden from

Roath. School teacher. Went missing about three weeks ago, they say. Wanted to know if we knew anything.'

'We didn't hear anything, did we?' asked Bucke, thinking immediately about the Canal Girl.

'Not a word. He says they sent out a message but it seems to have been lost. Don't trust this telegraph thing. I am sure we never had it.'

Bucke was interested. 'Did he give you any details about her?'

'He told me what they had but, as I said to him, it might be hard to tell on account of her being so mangled, Inspector. But she was 25 years old and she was five feet two inches they say, so that just about matches. Hair brown – well why not? Her build would just be about right, too. School teacher she was. Parents say she had a broken heart. Was keeping company with a young man but then he took up with her best friend. Dirty trick. No call for that sort of thing. He has been questioned. Knows nothing. Down the pit all day when she disappeared. But our body had a train ticket – Cardiff, as you remember. Starts to add up. Lennie reckons he could get us a photo. Not that it would help much, I grant you.'

Bucke shook his head. 'A photograph might make her too real. You see, Stanley, if she wanted to take her own life, why did she come to Swansea and throw herself into a canal without any undergarments? Don't they have canals in Cardiff? That is the part that doesn't seem right. If it was her, then what was the attraction of Swansea?'

'She might have come here to meet someone, Inspector. We can't rule that out. And anyway we don't know she threw herself in, do we? Lived with her parents and they are saying that quite a sum of money has disappeared as well. As much as fifty pounds. And her jewellery.'

'And we found no trace of any money in her clothing did we, Stan? No jewels which might identify her? Just marks on her body that make it seem as if she was set upon by a pack of dogs.'

'Not a scrap, sir. And no body to identify, to speak of anyway. Nothing you would ever want to show the parents anyway. No point digging her up is there, the poor soul.'

'If it was her. We still have a piece of clothing we dragged up with her, haven't we?'

'A long jacket with embroidery, Inspector.' Ball flicked through his log book to check. 'That's right. Ripped down the back but recognisable, I would say.'

'Ask Mrs Gardner to give it a good wash. Perhaps you can ask your cousin to take it over, though perhaps it would be kinder to let her parents think she was still alive in some faraway place in Scotland. I wonder if the truth about her death would ever help them.'

Chapter 10

He had heard the commotion when someone was brought into the station about thirty minutes earlier, but he had paid it scant regard. He was in no mood to cope with petty drama. Bucke remained standing at the window of his office, looking out at seagulls fighting over a scrap of some creature's entrails that one of them had stolen from the slaughterhouse at the end of Tontine Street. He had put journalists to one side and was instead lost in different thoughts, trying to understand all these recent and unexpected events, wrapped up as they were in such inexplicable religious mania. There was so much happening that he did not understand. He needed to talk to someone about these strong beliefs about which he knew very little, but which apparently encouraged people to kill themselves. Who was the man who had written that book Constance had found? From Llangyfelach, wasn't he? Did he know about such things? There was a knock and, as he turned, Inspector Flynn came in.

'You might like to look in next door, Rumsey. I have something that may be of interest to you.'

Bucke raised his eyebrows and, bidding farewell to the seagulls, followed him into the office where Flynn had been conducting an interview with a young woman he did not recognise. He walked around to the other side of the desk and leaned against the wall, looking at her. She was mean-faced, with thin lips and cold blue eyes. Her hair was fastened in a tight bun which sat neatly on top of her head. She appraised Bucke for a moment and then peered down at her mud-stained boots, tightly laced, and picked absently at debris stuck to the top of her long grubby socks.

'Elsie, this is Inspector Bucke. He is investigating a number of incidents in the town and I thought he would be interested in what you have to say. The young lady before us, Inspector, is Elsie Smith. She lives in Mumbles with her parents. Her father is a fisherman and Elsie works in Mr Gamble's bakery on Newton Road. So tell the Inspector what happened.'

'About what, exactly?'

'About why you are here today, lass,' said Inspector Flynn gently. 'About William Bartlett.'

'Well he is dead, isn't he?'

'Yes, Elsie. He is dead. And if you are not careful you might find yourself accused of murder, so it would help us all if you were a little more amenable. Might help a great deal, I warrant. We would both be much obliged.'

She looked away.

'Tell me once again, if you please, for the benefit of Inspector Bucke, what happened this morning at Langland Bay.'

She looked up at Bucke, wrinkling her nose. 'Shot himself, didn't he? In the head.' Elsie seemed strangely detached from it. 'Dull bugger.' Elsie pulled her brown shawl more tightly around her shoulders.

'And you were there? When he shot himself?' asked Flynn patiently.

'Of course I was. I told you. He said we should meet in Langland this morning. Said it were going to be a laugh. Said we were joining the Militia or something, so I didn't have to go to Mr Gamble.'

'And that would be your work, would it? In Gamble's Bakery? On Newton Road?'

'That's right. That is where I work. Told you, didn't I?'

'Please, Elsie. Tell my friend here, Inspector Bucke, about what happened. Properly now. Or the next time you see your mother, you will be in the cells.'

Elsie sighed and looked at Bucke, who had been observing her without emotion, even though the mention of the Militia had sparked his interest.

'William thought he was my sweetheart, didn't he? He told everyone we was engaged but we wasn't. I had been walking out with him for about a month and he was a good laugh at first, but after a bit he started to get a bit boring, a bit dull, see. I was looking around for a bit of a change, if I am honest. I mean, a girl is entitled and I didn't like him that much anyway.' She paused and sniffed, wiping her nose with her sleeve.

'Go on, Elsie. I'd be obliged,' said Inspector Flynn. 'Tell Inspector Bucke how you met William.'

'It was in that place in Swansea, on Oxford Street. Where that Milo is the preacher. Him and Ada Gammon. Calls herself Deborah now, but my mam knew her when she lived in Mumbles and didn't like her. But I'd go there, even when he moved to that chapel. It were a laugh, wasn't it? Cheaper than the Star Theatre but it did get a bit samey after a while and a lot of it were too deep for me. Went over me head. But Will loved it. That is where we met and we started walking out and he would take me home on the tram but we never went into no sand dunes together, no matter what Izzy Matthews said, that were a lie. We was always proper. Most of the time anyways. Will was in the Militia see, the Swansea Militia, and he used to bring his gun home for a laugh, didn't he? Then we would go on the cliffs at Bracelet or Brandy Cove to shoot at the birds. But I didn't like Brandy Cove because it was a bit far to walk.'

She paused, and Bucke watched her eyes flicker around the dark wood of the room, avoiding the eyes of the police inspectors and looking for something a little less official and less intimidating to focus upon, but finding nothing.

'But last week he said we were going to shoot ourselves and then we would get good positions in this other Militia and then we would fight and we would live forever. Such notions he had, but he got them from Father Milo and that Deborah woman. I think she took a fancy to him, didn't she? But last night he went to see Deborah, Our Lady of Mumbles she calls herself but really her name is Ada, and give her everything he had, even his watch, and then today, like I say, we was to shoot ourselves and then everything would be alright. He had writ a letter,' she said, addressing Bucke. 'Inspector Flynn has got it, isn't that right?'

Flynn smoothed out a creased piece of paper on the desk in front of him and read. *'I shall be gone for ever with the woman I love, to fight in the Militia of Jesus. Our wish is to be buried in the same grave. Goodbye to all, William Bartlett.'* Flynn looked at her and raised his eyebrows.

'I wasn't going to shoot meself, was I? I mean, I didn't like Will that much, not to spend eternity with him at any rate, so I told him to go first, show me the way, like, and that I would catch him up when I'd had a billy-whizz in the bushes. So that is what he did. Right in the side of the head. Dull bugger, like I said. So that's it. You won't tell me Mam about this, will you? She will be dead cross if she finds out that I haven't gone to work.' She paused and, for the first time, looked concerned. 'So why did you say I might get into trouble?'

'Because,' said Flynn, 'someone might think you persuaded William to take his own life. That you incited him to do it. Or that you are lying and that you shot him yourself.'

'But I couldn't could I? I was in the bushes having a billy-whizz.'

Bucke spoke for the first time. 'Did Ada Gammon or Father Milo tell William to shoot himself? Did you hear them tell him to do it?'

'I don't know. I wasn't there but I know that Will give her everything, on account of he wouldn't need none of it when he was fighting with that Jehovah bloke or someone. He is loaded, they say.'

In spite of the re-assurances she had been offered earlier, Elsie was taken to the cells to wait for the arrival of her mother.

'Not the most pleasant young lass you are ever likely to meet,' said Flynn, shaking his head, 'but I imagine a jury will think she is telling the truth.'

'I am sure she is telling the truth.' Rumsey rubbed his fingers over his eyes and pinched the bridge of his nose, as if by doing so he could make himself see better.

'It is not for me to say, Rumsey. You know more about this business than I do. But everything that is going on in the town points only in one direction.

'Oh yes, James. Milo and Deborah or Ada, or whatever you want to call her, they are at the heart of all of this, of that there can be no argument. And it is exactly what you said to young Elsie. Is it incitement? Is this what they are doing? Inciting other people to commit crimes for them? I am sure it is. Perhaps it is more than that. But it is with the two of them that I will find the answers I need. I know it. Milo is clever, keeps his distance from all the trouble, gets others to do his dirty work in some way and he stays well away from it all. But he is at the heart of it. Do you know anything about him?'

'Not until he started to wear his robes and call himself a preacher. Never heard of him until then.'

'I think I might try the lovely Ada, see if I can get anywhere with her. Bartlett went to see her anyway.'

'Attractive looking woman, Rumsey. But that does not make her a nice person. Always in trouble when I was working down at Mumbles. Looks like she has seen the light since then, or seen something at any rate. But she is as about as trustworthy as a fox in a hen house, to my way of thinking. Except that a fox isn't quite as vicious.'

'We need to talk about Constable Plumley, James,' said Bucke, shaking his head. It wasn't a happy thought.

'Yes we do, Rumsey and soon enough too. But he can wait. The court will have all the evidence that it needs but as I see it, there is enough to ensure that he won't hang. A relief to my mind. It is bad enough what he has done, but we don't need an execution. Won't do the police force any good at all.'

'No, James. It won't. But we do need to know why he did it. Is losing his temper enough?' Bucke shook his head at the enormity of the crime. 'There is something going on in the town – suicides, religious frenzy. And the only person we have been able to arrest is a policeman.' He shook his head. 'I think it is time for me to go to Pier Street, again.'

Flynn was prevented from replying by a loud commotion outside in the lobby. Raised voices. Then sobbing, and the sound of Sergeant Ball becoming exasperated. Inspector Flynn took a deep breath and gathered his strength. 'It will be the Snowball Prayer again. If my own prayers were answered, the dreadful thing would disappear completely.'

*

When Bucke arrived on Pier Street, he was at least reassured that it didn't smell quiet as bad as it had done before. The crucifix was still standing at an angle and beneath it, knocking out his pipe against the wood, was Old Man Rosser. He waved cheerily at Bucke and he leaned over the low garden wall to speak to him. Bucke notice an alarming and distressing vacancy in his eyes.

'Morning, young man,' said Rosser. 'Oldest teetotaller in Swansea, me, you know. Not touched a drop in nigh on sixty years and that is a fact.' He nodded for emphasis. 'Everyone knows me. William Rosser.' He winked at him.

'And I am very pleased to meet you, sir,' replied Bucke. 'It is an honour to speak to you.'

'Don't mention it. Sixty years. Not touched a drop.'

'Very impressive.' Bucke decided to take a chance. 'Did you once have the keys to the chapel on Oxford Street? Do you remember who you gave them to?'

Rosser looked at him blankly, as if he had been speaking a foreign language. 'Sixty years it has been now. Not touched a drop. I needs a drop of brandy, like, of an evening, so I can drop off but I haven't touched a drop. Everyone knows. Oldest teetotaller in Swansea, me. Famous for it. What did you say your name was? Is there a privy round here?'

'My name is Police Inspector Bucke. And you don't remember anything about these keys then? You don't remember giving them to anyone, do you? The keys to the chapel on Oxford Street?'

William smiled and shook his head. 'They used to call me Enoch, first time round. I lived until I was 365. Long time that. Don't remember it, of course, but they told me so. Very kind people.' He nodded. 'Not many can match me. Oldest teetotaller in Swansea. I used to keep chickens, me.' He puffed out his cheeks with the effort of talking. 'Fought against Napoleon, I did,' he added, as he started to fumble with his trousers. 'Nasty piece of work.'

Bucke knocked at the door and turned to smile at Rosser, who waved absently at him whilst he relieved himself against the cross. As he turned back, the door was opened by Delilah.

'Good afternoon, Delilah. I am here because I should like to speak to your mistress, Ada Gammon.'

'There is no one here of that name, Inspector. My mistress would be obliged if you would continue your enquiries elsewhere,' she said emphatically and tried to close the door.

Bucke stopped her by placing his palm flat upon it. It was time that he took control. 'No, Delilah, no. I will see her, and I will see her now. You may tell her that if she will not see me, then I will arrest her on suspicion of conspiracy to murder and she will be taken to the police station before she has an opportunity to gather together a crowd.'

Delilah paused, considering her alternatives. 'I shall go to speak with her. Please remain where you are, Inspector, whilst –'

'No, Delilah. I will wait inside, and if you do not return for me immediately, I shall go looking for her myself.' He stepped through the doorway, leaving Delilah no alternative but to walk silently down the hallway in search of her mistress.

The house was shabby and uncared for and completely silent, not even the ticking of a clock that Bucke might have otherwise expected in a hallway of this size. It seemed to him that the house lacked a heart, lacked a soul. It was derelict and abandoned and yet there were people still living in it. Then Delilah appeared at an open door. She said nothing but Bucke knew that he should approach and as he did so she stepped aside to admit him.

In front of him, sitting at a simple wooden table in the same room as before, was Ada, as striking as always, her dark hair contrasting with the whiteness of the robe where it lay upon her shoulders. She invited Bucke to sit opposite her.

'Good afternoon, Ada. I need to speak to you about –'

'Please, Inspector. I am a new woman now. I am no longer Ada Gammon. You see, I am different now. I have always known that I was not what others thought I was. I am no longer the person you like to call Ada. I am Deborah, Our Lady of Mumbles. I thought for a while that I was Mary of Magdala but it was shown to me that I had a different purpose - to guide the army of God to victory, in the final battle that awaits us all on the field of Armageddon, to the final defeat of evil. You should join us and follow the Spear of Jehovah to certain triumph.'

'I see. You must have been pleased to discover that you had a choice. But, as we are both aware, you were born as Ada Gammon and until someone tells me differently, Ada Gammon is what you remain.'

'And so the Lord God does not have sufficient authority for you, then?' Ada smiled and lit a cigar, blowing the smoke straight into Bucke's face – a calculated and deliberate assault. 'Do not be so shocked, Inspector. This shows my mastery over the fires of Hell. I consume fire and it nourishes me.' She laughed.

Bucke scowled his distaste but refused to be provoked. 'I understand that you are acquainted with William Bartlett. A member of the Swansea Militia. One of your followers.'

'Ah yes, a very good looking boy. So obliging. So devoted to the cause.'

'I have to tell you that he shot himself this morning. In the side of the head.'

Ada smirked. 'Ah. So he has been called. It is not unexpected. We should rejoice.'

'Rejoice when a young man is so troubled that he takes his own life? His mother grieves for him; she has lost a son and you say that it is to be celebrated?'

'She should not grieve. She should be proud of a son ready and willing to lead the Militia of Jesus into battle against the forces of darkness.' She exhaled more smoke which seems to gather around her like a veil. Like, thought Bucke, a haze from hell.

'Is it true that you saw him yesterday, Ada?'

'Yesterday? Let me think.' She blew more smoke at him.

'I am told that he gave you all his possessions.'

She clicked her fingers, as if remembering for the first time.' Of course he did. Now I remember. A few coins. A watch, I think. He was divesting himself of his earthly possessions, I imagine. Such an appealing and thoughtful young man, who gave his meagre possessions willingly. I am so pleased that he has found his destiny.'

'And is it normal for your followers to hand over their possessions to you?' asked Bucke.

'Of course. How else are we to survive in this material world? Our followers are very generous – and grateful.'

'And it seems that you are happy to take money from those who have so very little. Is that right, do you think?'

'They are happy to do so, for they are blessed with the knowledge that Milo has given them. You would understand if you came to one of our meetings, Inspector and listened. You can still be saved. But if you continue to harry and obstruct Father Milo – and me –this will ensure your doom. Listen with an open heart and allow Milo to dispel the devils in your soul.'

'I have no concern for the devils within my soul. I am more concerned with the examples of self-destruction here in Swansea recently and I have reason to believe that they may be linked to your cult. Would that concern you?'

Ada stared at him in silence for a moment, swathed once more in smoke. 'This is not a cult, Inspector. It is the one true Church, ordained directly by God. Be careful what you say or you will assuredly suffer eternal damnation when the Lord God wipes the earth clean of evil and venality. Not even policemen will be spared. I have seen the agents of Satan who wallow in blood-soaked vengeance and I know that they are doomed. Look at the brutal murder of an old man by a policeman in Llansamlet, Inspector Bucke. One of your own men. Possessed by demons and yet you did not know. But God knows, for even in his evil, the Satanist was doing God's work.'

She sat back in her chair. Her eyes were fierce as she stamped out the cigar in a saucer. Bucke waited, saying nothing. He was puzzled. The logic of what she was saying escaped him. The world is a conflict between good and evil and yet God controls both sides? Where was the conflict? He was not at all sure that Ada knew what she was talking about. There must be simpler ways of running creation, he thought.

Finally he asked, 'Did you know that Constable Plumley attended your meetings in the chapel?'

She shrugged. 'Many people attend our meetings, Inspector. Our mission grows daily. Perhaps he was sent by Satan to spy on our solemnity.'

'And where is Milo at the moment? May I speak to him?'

'You may not speak to him. He must fast for 40 days and 40 nights and so spends his time in prayer. It has been ordained. I must support him in his devotions and protect him from those agents of Satan who oppose him. He speaks only to God. He looks into the Eye of God and is told the secrets of creation. He is the one true prophet who speaks to us directly with the authority of God himself. Those who deny this will suffer the agonies of eternal damnation. You may regard that as helpful advice, Inspector. '

'It seems to me that you label anyone who disagrees with you as an agent of Satan,' said Bucke.

'I see that you understand. Your eyes are beginning to open,' she replied, with a faint smile. 'The world is about to end and you must decide on which side you will be fighting.'

'Perhaps I shall wait for God to decide for me. I am sure he will let me know.'

Ada looked a little flustered. 'I am sure that he will tell Milo. When it is the time to do so.'

'I see. And Milo is your husband?'

'We were married before we were chosen by God, so he must have approved of our union. Father Milo is my husband, though our relationship goes far beyond the trivial priorities of this sordid world.' She leaned forward with a calculated grin. 'I must tell you, Inspector, that there is a peculiarity in my husband's manhood. It shines in the darkness of the night like a beacon, for it has been touched by God!' She laughed, challenging Bucke with her coarseness.

Bucke sensed that the more she spoke, the more uncertain she became, as if, he thought, she was playing a game which she could only sustain for short period. A useful thing to know, he thought. 'Tell me something, Ada. Why does Delilah dress as she does?'

'It represents her past, Inspector. It is a reminder of who she once was.'

'And how do you know who she once was? I am curious to know.'

'God told Father Milo.'

'I see. And no one else? Not even Delilah herself?'

Ada ploughed on, falling back upon her usual rhetoric. 'We know it for sure, because it has been shown to Father Milo that she has always been Delilah, throughout history. Her poor twisted face displays the eternal struggle between good and evil. A punishment, if you will, for those sins long ago that she has carried with her in her soul. This life now is her opportunity to seek atonement for those sins and for the death of Samson. She will be rewarded in Paradise and in her restored beauty she will then sit at God's right hand. This has been shown to Milo. Today she lives as my servant. She has served me well and I believe that she will be redeemed in the Final Battle.'

Bucke stood up, bowed very slightly and went back down the corridor. There was no one there, so he let himself out. He had seen no purpose in continuing with the conversation, but it had been very revealing. He was more convinced than ever that he was confronting a special type of madness, one where there was a simple answer to everything and an apparent belief that those in this dangerous church were entirely untouchable. All he lacked was evidence of the crimes he was sure they were committing. The evidence he did have was that there was either trickery or madness in all that they did. They seemed to exploit everyone who came near them, and it troubled him greatly.

Chapter 11

When he arrived at the rectory in Llangyfelach, he was admitted by Reverend Rogers' housekeeper, Mrs Pennock, a suitably formidable guardian for a comfortable and attractively disordered house.

He was shown into the study, a room lined with books and with a table piled high with shells, reflecting Rogers' fascination with the ocean. On one wall there was a display of maps of the southern hemisphere and the tusk of a narwal was hanging from the picture rail. It was, thought Bucke, a room in which a mind was desperately at work, trying to absorb as much as it could before it was too late.

A few moments later Rogers fell through the door, followed by the silent Mrs Pennock, carrying a tray with a battered Wedgewood teapot and cups. He was an affable-looking man, a little distracted and rather untidy, with an air of intelligence seasoned with slight bewilderment. His white hair and beard, like the mind the study reflected, was spread in so many different directions at once. His research, Bucke thought, must consume his attention, making him quite an unworldly figure, perhaps not always completely engaged with reality. He was probably more comfortable in Biblical Canaan.

'I read your book, Reverend Rogers. The book for children. I was advised that it was just right for me,' he said with a smile. 'It has been extremely useful. I am very grateful that you have agreed to see me this morning. I am intruding on your time in this way because I need help with an investigation, which is proving to be a little unexpected.'

Rogers peered anxiously over his half-moon spectacles, as if the world was moving too fast for his rheumy eyes. Bucke noticed that there was a deep ink stain on his index finger, a tattoo from incessant writing. He seemed flattered and curious. 'Why thank you, Inspector. I have always hoped that my book would help the young understand the stories and draw from them the lessons that are there for us all, if they have lessons at all. You see, Inspector, lots of them are just part of the Jewish heritage, but for some people, of course, they become a way of life. I was like that for a while, though not as smitten as some. Do you know, Inspector? The world is full of old men reading books late into the night because they are consumed by the need to find out what precisely was going on in Gomorrah.'

'All I can say, Reverend, was that the book has proved to be very instructive.'

'I would like to hope so. But a police investigation you say? How intriguing. Of course many of the stories are entertaining in themselves, but no more than that. I am curious though.' He rubbed underneath his chin vigorously with the back of his hand. 'A criminal application, you say? I suppose you can use them for any purpose.' He looked thoughtful, then whipped off his glasses decisively. 'It is the snake, you see. Garden of Eden. Evil. Always there, always around us. If it hadn't been for that snake we would all be sitting round singing hymns and looking at the flowers.' He suddenly grinned. 'Has someone been stealing animals and putting them on a boat, waiting for rain? Won't have to wait long in Swansea. Sorry, Inspector. Idea jumped into my head. I need to be more serious.'

'No, sir. Sadly, there has been a murder, you see. I think it was modelled on the story of Jezebel but there are other more confusing elements that are attached to it, for a person such as me.'

'Oh dear. Stoning was it? Or a poor soul trampled by horses? Of course if I can help in any way, please do not hesitate.'

Bucke nodded his thanks. 'I think I have a basic understanding of the Jezebel story, Reverend, thanks to your book. But the reason why I am here is to find out more about the Book of Revelation.'

'Ah. I see.' Rogers sat back in his chair and ran his hand through his beard. 'Hmm. Tricky business, the Book of Revelation.' He took his glasses off again before replacing them. 'The Bible would be much better without it, in my opinion. There seems to be no limit to the problems it causes.'

'I want to know what it is about, Reverend.'

'Don't we all, Inspector? Don't we all? But that is the problem. It is so hard to know, especially when it is used for so many different purposes. You see, it is the last book on the Bible, and for some it means that nothing comes after it, so it is all about the end of the world, of time, of everything.'

'And is it?'

'Not in any way that any of us can understand. You can make it mean whatever you want. And people do. That is the problem, you can see that, can't you?'

Bucke showed him Phillip Bowen's exercise book. 'What do you make of this?'

Rogers flicked through it, pausing occasionally to examine some pages more intently. 'Rather typical, I am afraid. Looking for secrets and hidden messages where there are none. Seeing everything as a symbol and finding obscure answers. Wonder if he is happy in the rest of his life? Probably not. All a bit unhealthy. Would be better if he took up rowing.'

'I am afraid he is dead, Reverend. He appears to have taken his own life.'

'Oh dear. I am very sorry to hear that, though I would say that his book suggests that it shouldn't be a surprise. A young man can get unhealthily obsessed about such things.' He flicked through the exercise book again. 'And all these symbols? Just drawings. No meaning to them, nothing mystical at all. No secrets. A man puts his pencil on a piece of paper and moves it around. And somehow it means more than any other piece of paper.'

'This sort of thing doesn't surprise you, it seems.'

'Not at all. Young men do get rather obsessive about the end of the world, rather hopeful that they can be part of it. Please understand. What is in this book is complete nonsense, all of it. Dangerous nonsense.' He handed Bowen's exercise book back to Bucke. 'You can spend a great deal of time searching for meaning and hidden secrets in everything. Many people do. A waste of time.' He pointed at Bucke, in emphasis. 'Did you know that letters in the Greek alphabet are used to represent certain numbers? Why should you? Why should anyone? But this is an example. If you turn the name 'Gladstone' into Greek and then add up the total of the numbers indicated, you get 666, – which just goes to show that our prime minister has been sent to us by Satan. Then, if you add up the numbers in his birth year – 1809 - you will arrive at eighteen. The same total of course as you will get if you add 6 plus 6 plus 6. Further evidence. And of what? Nothing at all. Life is full of coincidences, not secrets. Why shouldn't it be?'

Bucke smiled and shook his head.

'It is insanity, Inspector. And you can never convince such a man that he is wrong. He will know for sure that this is the Number of the Beast and that therefore Gladstone is The Beast in human form.' He sat back in his chair. 'Do you know, Inspector? My advice? Read it for yourself. Then you will have some idea of the sort of people the Book of Revelation attracts. If you were to ask me, I would say there are more revelations in a Great Western railway timetable. More mysteries too. You see, another point is that the Book might not be referring to the future; it might in fact be obscure references to things that have already happened. Or if it is about the future, then why today? Why not in a thousand years' time. Who is revelation for? St John the Divine? Someone else already dead? Or someone yet to be born. We don't know. How can we? There are other words in the Bible that are far more significant. But the Book of Revelation is important for those who go looking for things that are not there. And then they find them.'

'The alpha and the omega. What is that about?' asked Bucke.

'Quite simple, Inspector. It means the beginning and the end. Letters of the alphabet, in Greek, again. The idea that God created the world and that he will decide when it is going to end. So all these conjurers and tricksters and false prophets appear, telling anyone who will listen that they are so very important that God has been speaking to them, rather than to anyone else, and has told them we are all about to die. But of course by rights God should be speaking to everyone. That is what being a god is all about, surely? None of these prophets ever says, 'I have seen the end of the world and it happens in two thousand years.' What profit is there for a prophet if that is the case? No, they all say it is going to happen tomorrow but that they can save you. All nonsense, Inspector. Every bit of it. If God has message to us, then surely he would find no reason to disguise it so that only a few people would know?'

'So, sir,' said Bucke. 'Would you say that that those who become obsessed with the Book of Revelation are unhappy? Or are mentally disordered? Or charlatans perhaps? Out to mislead others. Or exploit them perhaps?'

Rogers looked at him intently and chewed his lip for a moment. 'There are many different kinds of people in the world, Inspector, as well you know.'

'Yes, I know. And that is one of the things that I find most difficult about this business,' Bucke paused, wondering how much he dare say. 'I have no religious faith of my own and I find these obsessions inexplicable.'

Rogers became animated again. 'Lost your faith, Inspector? Quite understand. Very difficult to maintain and, to be frank, God does make it hard for us doesn't he? Children suffer hideous diseases. Good people die. Bad ones thrive.'

'My family passed away suddenly, Reverend Rogers, over a year ago and I cannot believe in a god who kills children on a whim. It is quite simple. To be told that their deaths are God's Will has never been good enough.'

'Yes, it is difficult, isn't it? God's Will? What does that mean? That God is cruel? No, your feelings are a perfectly logical response. It is religious devotion that seems odd in those circumstances. I can offer you no words of comfort. Nothing at all that will make your anguish disappear. And empty words of re-assurance would be the greatest cruelty, as far as I can see. But you see, Inspector, religious devotion is just one enormous leap in the dark. It defies logic, of course it does. I have made that leap, and all it could mean is that I am as mad as a hatter. But it is a belief that gives me comfort. And if you are right and we live in a vast unedifying void, then at least I have enjoyed living a lie whilst I have been here. Whereas for you, your darkest suspicions will have been fulfilled. Except you will know nothing about it, because for you, after all this, there is nothing. So I am happy to live in a world of delusion, because the alternative is so much worse. I know what you feel when you lose some one dear to you but I managed to find a consolation which has been denied you.'

'In fairy stories?' asked Bucke.

'Perhaps. But if you are right and there is no after life, does it actually matter what I believe? I will have lived a lie but it will have given me comfort. Why should it trouble you? What I do regret is that it is a comfort you haven't had.'

'My children committed no crime, no sin. So why should they be punished? Because the world is cruel. That is the only explanation. And if I die and find myself in the presence of God then I shall tell him so,' Bucke said with determination.

'Good, I hope you do. He will understand. Won't condemn you for it. Won't punish you. Not his way. Should be an interesting argument. And when it does happen, at least you will be able to see them again.'

Bucke looked at him, carefully and nodded. 'Thank you, sir.' He was impressed by his humanity.

Rogers smiled at him. 'God lies within us, in the way in which we live our lives and the ways in which we treat others. Faith is less important, I think. I have little patience with devils and angels, with heaven and hell.'

'Thank you, Reverend Rogers. There is madness on the loose in the town and you have gone a considerable way to help me understand some of it, at least.' Bucke could see that Rogers appeared to be about to say something, but he seemed to think better of it.

*

After his visit to see the Reverend Rogers Bucke felt particularly anxious to speak to Constance, for that evening she and Mathilde were going to the Chapel of Our Lady of Mumbles. Everything suddenly seemed to be running out of control and he was starting to feel guilty about involving her, but he still felt he had no choice.

'Ignore the religious element of it, Constance.'

'In a chapel? How odd, Rumsey,' she teased.

'I have been assured that it is all nonsense. Devious and dishonest.'

'I have already formed that opinion.'

'I know. And you are not a policeman – '

'I am flattered that you have noticed, Inspector.'

'But I want you to think like a policeman.'

'Heaven help us all.'

'Please, Constance. Listen. Think about what they are doing, think about why they are doing it. Don't allow yourself to be drawn into their tricks.'

Constance shook her head. 'There is no danger of that, Rumsey.'

'And please be careful. They are, I know, a threat to us all. And it is my duty to root them out.'

'And you really think that they are dangerous people?'

'Without a doubt. Try and keep Mathilde safe too. She appears to be more gullible.'

'She wants to be believe, Rumsey. It is the only interesting thing in her life. She enjoys the drama and the excitement. The more threatening it is for her, the better.'

Bucke shook his head. 'Milo has gathered unhappy people around him, but he does not do so to help them.' He sighed. 'These are very unfortunate days, Constance. The town seems very unsettled at present. And it troubles me. An incident got out of hand very quickly this afternoon. For a while, it was very troubling. This sort of thing happens all the time, though it is impossible to prevent. Young boys are sent out by their parents to steal a couple of buckets of coal from the trains on the docks, especially at this time of year. The boys are very good at it and they are rarely caught and if they are, well they regard it as a necessary hazard. The constables might slap them round the head and send them home with dire warnings about the consequences of any further offences, but it doesn't make any difference. They always say it is their first offence when they are caught and the constables rarely contradict them because often they cannot identify them anyway. Sometimes one is taken to appear before the magistrates, who might have him birched and they stay away for a week or so and then try their luck at the railway station.

But soon they are back on the docks - the families need them to do it or they cannot stay warm. The problems come you see with the Hat Stand Gang.'

'The ones who stole my door knocker? ' asked Constance.

Bucke smiled. 'Probably. Our very own Hat Stand Gang. Two of them were arrested last year when they carried a hat stand out of Malachi's Old Furniture Shop in the middle of the day. Said they wanted to examine it carefully in day light before they decided to buy it. The name stuck.'

'Why on earth did they want a hat stand?'

'The only possible use they could have for a hat stand would be as firewood, I imagine. Since then they seemed to have been involved in everything. Well, today some of them seem to have gone off to the docks together. And it wasn't a boy with a bucket scraping up bits of coal. No, it was six of them, each with a sack. Quite brazen – they seem convinced that they are untouchable. Well, of course, they are seen and they swarm like mice across the sidings and the wharves. Soon there are constables in pursuit. One of the boys manages to slip away back home to Lewis Street to fetch the parents who come down in force. Constables Gill and Smith have the gang cornered and then the parents turn up and there is mayhem. Suddenly we have a riot.' He paused and shook his head.

'The constables blow their whistles but no one hears them down there and no one is willing to take a message to the police station for them. So the boys got away and the constables were lucky they weren't thrown into the dock.' Bucke scratched his head. 'A woman turned up at the police station last night at around midnight. She was bleeding quite heavily, after being thumped in the mouth by one of our new constables, someone you have never heard of called William Armstrong. Apparently he told her to clear off home and then struck her. Whilst Sergeant Ball was listening to her, three other women turned up telling a similar story. When they found Armstrong he had collapsed in a door way, blind drunk on

Orange Street and was unable to speak. So he is in the cells now and on his way to gaol I shouldn't wonder. Nothing seems right. The town is tense, aggressive, as if it is looking for a fight with itself. Two miners had a fight on The Strand yesterday. One was knocked to the floor and smashed his head. He is in the hospital, not expected to survive the night. Donkeys have been mutilated in Winch Wen. Cattle mutilated in Cockett. It is as if there is something in the air. And I am troubled by the idea that I am sending you out into it. You must be careful, Constance.' He smiled, nervously. 'Remember, I shall be waiting for you in the shadows.'

Chapter 12

Mathilde stood before her impatiently, tall and severe in her beauty, waiting for Constance. She had taken scant regard of Constance's suggestion that they should moderate their clothes to make themselves less conspicuous. Her ivory coloured dress, stylishly ruffled down the bodice, only served to draw attention to the single, large pearl drop hanging from a black velvet choker. Constance was more understated, having borrowed a faded but clean woollen shawl from her neighbour, Mrs Grove, who occasionally sold laver bread in the market and thus dressed in the traditional fashion. When she looked at herself, Constance thought that she resembled Mathilde's maid servant – though she could never aspire to being as efficient as Elodie, who had been imported from France.

It was Bonfire Night, the annual night of chaos and disorder, without a doubt the very worst night of the year. It had become, by tradition, a night of vandalism, a night when all normal rules of behaviour were abandoned. No one and nothing was safe. Bucke knew that Constable Davies was especially apprehensive. Last year, a group of beer-emboldened youths, with rags across the bottom of their faces like cowboys and whooping like Indians, had grabbed him and put him inside a barrel, rolled it across Wind Street and then set fire to it. On the Fifth of November, such a thing was regarded as acceptable. No matter what the civic authorities said or did, nothing seemed to reduce the mayhem.

This was a particular dilemma for Inspector Bucke. Whilst on the one hand he needed to be part of the force that must attempt to preserve order, it was precisely the night when he could not allow Constance (and Mathilde) to walk unescorted through the town. It was normally a night when most people- respectable or otherwise - stayed at home. It was safer.

Consequently the ladies were required to walk at a brisk pace to a point close enough to the chapel to allow Bucke to feel he could disappear into the night in response to the distant sound of a cheering mob down towards the prison, where young men gathered every year to taunt the prisoners and to throw fire crackers over the walls.

There was another large congregation that had gathered in defiance of the abuse and intimidation they would face from rowdy Bonfire revellers. Their personal salvation was far too important to be jeopardised by traditional apprehensions.

Once more, Constance led Mathilde into the gallery for a better view of the proceedings. It might be easier to collect information from up there. This time there were even more mirrors at strange angles. In one of them she caught sight of a familiar profile and then involuntarily laughed out loud, for it was a reflection of herself. Mathilde gave her a disapproving glance. She was desperate for that moment of release that the proceedings would bring and wanted nothing at all to spoil her special rapture. Once again the smoke from the incense created a heady atmosphere, slowly separating the chapel from the drab world outside and creating a claustrophobic intensity which tonight was intensified by the unpredictable bangs of the firecrackers and their flashes of bright light.

Constance looked around her. 'Look at them, Mathilde. Look at the people who surround us. This church, Our Lady of Mumbles, speaks for the lonely and the poor. Can't you see it? These are desperate people, who have so little. Now they feel they have become part of something and it makes them special. Milo gives them the hope they have always been looking for,' said Constance, thoughtfully. 'But he takes their money, too.'

Mathilde corrected her sharply. 'Milo speaks with the authority of the Lord. You would do well to heed his words.'

Constance turned away and smiled, though she did not reply. She saw in a corner at the back, embarrassed by poverty, a huddle of women who she presumed had slipped away unnoticed down Mount Pleasant Hill from the workhouse. They would soon inherit the earth, apparently, which was without doubt the best thing they had ever heard. The sooner the better, too. Her eyes flicked around the chapel, now full, seeing who she could recognise. They were Swansea faces, people she passed on the street every day. Their reflections in the deceitful, angled mirrors were like playing cards. Were these really Happy Families, like those you would find in the card game? Yet these were families happy to see other Swansea residents condemned to the everlasting flames as a final act of revenge for an impoverished life.

Once the service had started, Constance was entranced neither by the nature of the words nor by the rich cadences of Milo's voice, for no matter how seductive he might have been, she knew too much to be seduced. She could see that Mathilde, on the other hand, unhappy in her domestic life, found a release and an engagement in the passion of Milo's performance that she experienced nowhere else. She was not alone. The congregation desired fervently for his words to be true and waited desperately their triumph; the triumph of the desperate and the forgotten.

Tonight, she thought, he seemed anxious to reinforce the idea of unswerving obedience. Constance wondered if police attentions had unsettled him.

'It is through his laws that God governs the universe. Order means happiness, disorder brings misery. We must obey his laws and those of his anointed representative. I have looked into the eye of God and I know that I am his instrument upon earth; if you disobey the words of his chosen prophet, then suffering must surely follow. Where there is disobedience or revolt, then comes disorder and contradiction. You can see this around you every day, here in the town which God will shortly forsake, the town where immorality and disease brazenly stalk the streets.' He raised his voice. 'We are approaching the End of Time – I am the alpha and the omega, I was at the beginning in the Garden of Eden and now I am here at the end. Listen now to the evil upon the streets, for you cannot ignore it and know without question that death stalks the shadows. I have no need to tell you what the policemen do – they actively destroy our prayers. You know that this is true.'

'Yes, Milo!' came the reply from the gallery, just in front of Mathilde.

'They are devils!' cried another. 'Burn them!'

'All those who oppose us shall burn,' nodded Milo, holding up his hands to staunch further contributions. 'But fear not, I have spoken with God and he will protect you, just as the policemen are surely damned. We know they are placing spirits in the sky above us. Voices will travel along those wires, they say, but I know that those deceitful wires are designed to steal our prayers.'

'They shall perish!' someone shouted. 'Rip them down!'

The police were now the enemy of those chosen by God. Perhaps, Constance wondered, he had welcomed the reactions of the police to the Snowball prayer. She missed the next few sentences as she considered the idea, but it didn't seem to make much difference. 'You are sinners, and as sinners must return to a state of obedience or you will be consigned to the flames. It is vital that you renounce all wealth and possessions. They are without meaning for the Lord. They are but the ornaments of Satan and will assuredly prevent you inheriting the earth, as God most assuredly desires. Together you must, like myself and Our Lady of Mumbles, abandon all worldly goods.'

There was another loud bang outside and someone screamed involuntarily. Constance wondered if he was in some way co-ordinating these explosions.

'Listen,' Milo said, then paused for a moment. 'Listen. You can hear it. Without doubt, we are living in The End of Times. Outside in Swansea's satanic streets there are dogs, and sorcerers, and whoremongers, murderers, and idolaters. A plague of rats swarmed through the church, feasting upon the dead. A vicar was attacked by a swarm of wasps in West Cross. I see giant locusts flying high in the winter sky, spewing out the fires of hell upon the town for three nights to wipe away the foul corruption in which we must wallow.'

A voice called out. 'I am a sinner! Father Milo save me!'

'The town is in the hands of Satan, its people prostrate in vice and misery and the righteous are threatened. Our own prayers abused and destroyed. But I will protect you. And then together, beneath the Spear of Jehovah, we shall vanquish evil forever!'

The chant of 'Deb-or-ah' began softly somewhere within the chapel and the drumming and the beating of the spear upon the wooden floor soon created the immersive rhythm which Ada orchestrated, with the spear held high over her head in both hands and her head thrown back so that her black hair hung free. Milo stood motionless, his head bowed, his hands grasping the sides of the pulpit. Mathilde's hair, carefully sculptured in tight curls, shook as a spasm passed through her in visible waves.

Milo waited for silence to settle. 'You know that I have looked into the eye of God! And I know you will rise above in the midst of your enemies! You shall make them your footstool! But first you must abandon all earthly things. Do not waste your strength in tears and broken sighs. I will lead you. I am your light, I am your guide and...' He paused briefly but dramatically. 'Oh Hallelujah! The Holy Spirit is amongst us! I can feel his presence! I know, for it has been foretold, that he is here to expel the evil from your souls!' There was another flash of light outside, another small explosion close by. Milo raised his hands and threw back his head. Milo seemed to be the only visible thing in the chapel. 'He is here! Oh Lord! Make us worthy!'

The lights began to dim still further and from the gloom there emerged an outbreak of unexpected rustling. Constance saw strange shapes which seemed to be writhing about the floor. Someone screamed and then alarm and hysteria spread rapidly around the chapel.

'Do not touch them!' commanded Milo. 'These are emissaries from Almighty God! The Holy Spirit has sent them to take away the very source of evil from within your soul. Stand upon your seats. Do not step upon them! Or you will release the very worst elements of the sin trapped and confined by your faith within. If you do, it will be released into the world! Cleanse us, oh All-seeing God! Take away our corruption!'

Constance watched the congregation jump up on to their seats and benches in alarm, as the strange brown shapes twisted and moved erratically on the floor. She helped Mathilde, encumbered by her long tight dress, on to the bench and then bent down and scooped up one of the strange shapes from the floor and put it in the chatelaine bag at her waist. It seemed to be nothing more than a brown paper bag with something inside. She then climbed up on the bench next to Mathilde, so as not to look out of place, although her inability to share the delirium made her feel conspicuous enough. Amongst the consternation, a handful of people, moving efficiently, scooped up the bags and took them away.

A voice cried about above it all. 'Now I am free! Now I am Blessed!' Men dressed in their Sunday best, who nevertheless still looked shabby, ripped off their collars and threw them in the air, 'I am in the presence of the Lord!' shouted a bald man with tears streaming down his cheeks, above a cacophony of shrieks and sobs.

Milo started a new chant. 'Serve the lord and rejoice with me! Serve the Lord and rejoice with me! Serve the Lord and be set free!'

Constance could see people lost, wide eyed in wonder, mesmerised by the sheer theatricality of the show. Yes, she thought, that was the word. Mesmerised. She realised that in other circumstances it could have happened to her – the sound of his voice, the thick and perfumed air – she knew she would have struggled to fight against the slow drift into compliance that she could see in Mathilde, for whom the words that rolled around the chapel were nothing less than the words of God himself, seeping into her soul. It was rapture, but Constance was unable to share in that surrender.

Watching Milo was like watching a magician, she decided. But once you could see how it all worked, nothing could ever restore the wonder. All that remained was the artifice. She would always admire the skill, but not the intention. But she had to admit that a meeting like this had the perfect background, with the mayhem of Bonfire Night outside. There were more flames and bangs and the crackers thrown at the windows of the chapel made it feel that the congregation was under siege.

Then the lamps were turned down completely and the chapel sank into darkness, the windows lit by red-tinged, hellish light. The congregation lost its enthusiasm for their chant and its order and shape became ragged in the darkness. When the lamps restored the light, Milo was no longer there and his followers had been abandoned, the focus for their devotion and their passion taken from them. The service broke up and groups of the faithful began to leave in disappointment, dropping coins in the buckets that were rattled by the doors. Constance led Mathilde down the stairs in the crush and they paused at the bottom of the staircase, waiting for a gap in the crowd to open up for them. Suddenly Billy Evil was standing in front of them, enveloped in the scent of filth and chemicals. He stared at Mathilde, noticed the pearl drop and pulled it away from her choker with a grin. 'I'll have that. You don't need it. Earthly possessions? They will be melting soon when the fire falls from the sky. You heard what Father Milo said. World is ending. Don't want nothing to get in your way of everlasting life, now do we?'

'So what good is it to you?' asked Constance, squaring up to him. 'If it is melting soon in the flames as you say, along with you and everything else, then why is it still important?

'Wouldn't you like to know.' He put the pearl in his pocket.

'Give it back to my friend,' she said firmly.

'Don't be stupid.' He put his hand underneath Constance's chin and then lifted it up. 'A pretty one, eh? Need to crack on, don't I? See when I can fit you in. Haven't got long, have I? Before the End.' He smiled and reached out his other hand towards her.

Constance kicked him hard in the shin. Hers were substantial boots beneath the woollen skirt and he gasped and stepped backwards. With eye contact broken, she grabbed hold of Mathilde's elbow and dragged her through the crowd and outside, where they walked as quickly as their clothes would allow, away from the chapel, occasionally glancing nervously over their shoulders.

'What will your husband say about the pearl?' Constance asked, as they finally turned the corner and she searched the crowd anxiously for the Inspector.

'Louis?' There was scorn in her voice. 'He will say nothing. He will not notice and I have no intention of telling him.'

'I can ask Rumsey...'

'There is no need. I must blame myself. I should have dressed as you suggested. And are you going to tell the Inspector about your own encounter with that horrid man?'

'No, Mathilde. I will not mention him in any detail. He does not need to know, for fear that he might become a little over-excited.'

'And do you think we should come here again?' asked Mathilde apprehensively.

'But of course! What fun it is! Ah, there he is – our escort.'

Mathilde smiled faintly in relief and then, in the presence of the Inspector, Mathilde restored her demeanour and sense of social superiority. She bowed her head very slightly in greeting, as Inspector Bucke raised his hat.

'We have no time to dawdle this evening, I fear. It is a busy night, as we expected. And has your evening been -'

'Most instructive and somewhat unexpected,' Constance smirked and reached out to touch Bucke's hand in the darkness.

'It was thrilling and we were blessed, Inspector, for the Holy Spirit walked amongst us,' added Mathilde, as if correcting her.

'I suspect the Inspector would have preferred him to have assumed the shape of a firefighter, ready to lend a hand, on this night of all nights.'

Constance heard a sharp intake of breath from Mathilde Barree, though she made no comment.

'I'd be grateful, Miss White,' added the Inspector. 'There is a large bonfire on the Burrows which is barely under control and the constables are busy pursuing gangs of unruly youths through the streets.'

'Perhaps some public floggings would help those unruly youths learn a little decorum and protect the decent people of the town. We should not tolerate such disorder,' said Mathilde.

They carried on in silence along Union Street, the lights in the Six Bells on Park Street offering a haven against the cold in the air and the disorder in the town. There were the sounds of small explosions in front of them. As they stepped from the rough pavement on to the muddy road, the ladies hitching up their garments, there was a loud bang over to the left. The smell of gunpowder was in the air.

'Why do the authorities refuse to deal with this annual humiliation?' asked Mathilde irritably. 'Good people trapped in their houses? Ridiculous.'

'They are probably throwing firecrackers at the Institute for the Blind, I expect,' remarked Bucke.

'Poor mites,' sighed Constance.

'Such cruelty,' added Mathilde as they reached the stability of the pavement.

'The boys inside enjoy it, I am told. They find the unexpected bangs quite exciting,' Bucke said reassuringly, as they walked on towards the locked up Music Hall.

Suddenly a group of boys came running towards them at speed. There may have been five of them but Bucke was not sure in the dark. The one in front saw him and shouted 'Copper!' and the gang swerved to their left along Pell Street. Although Mathilde was impressed by this easy show of authority from a police officer escorting her home, she was more alarmed by a taller figure, not easily distinguishable, appearing behind the boys in the gloom, a figure who seemed to be carrying a large stick. As they got closer, the clothes suggested to Constance that the figure was a woman and Mathilde paused, her mind still over excited by mystical happenings in the chapel. 'It is a witch,' she gasped and grabbed at Constance's arm.

'*Bonsoir, Madame Barree.*' It was Elodie. 'Good evening Inspector, Mademoiselle White,' she said with a curtsey so brief, it was virtually lost in the folds of her clothes. 'There were young boys throwin' the firecrackers at the 'ouse and calling Monsieur dreadful names and offerin' 'im affronts and imprecations, so I chased them away with my broom.'

'Thank you for that, Elodie. I am sure my husband welcomed your intervention,' said Mathilde sarcastically, with ill-concealed disgust at his imagined feebleness. She turned to Constance and the Inspector. 'Thank you so much, both of you, for your attendance and protection on such an evening. Father Milo is right, of course. The town must be cleansed of its sin, and as soon as possible too.

But we are merely a few yards from my home and I am sure that Elodie will ensure my safety, particularly since the ruffians appear to have fled. It is a ridiculous evening for you, Inspector and you must first see Constance to her home, so I shall wish you both a good – and a safe – evening.' She nodded to them and followed Elodie along Cradock Street, with Bucke watching discreetly from the shadows.

They walked back towards St Helen's Road. There was a red glow in the sky, presumably from the large bonfire in the Burrows, which added a suitably apocalyptic air to Constance's report of a peculiar evening in the chapel. In the presence of the inspector, it seemed less threatening than it had when she'd been swamped by derangement in the chapel. They paused beneath the gas lamp outside her rooms on St Helen's Road whilst she told the Inspector of the visitation of the Holy Spirit. He said nothing, listening carefully to what she said and smiling, impressed at her initiative, when she told him that she had snatched up one of the shapes from the floor.

'How enterprising of you, Constance. And so far, there has been no attempt to recruit you to the Militia of Jesus? Despite your proximity to the Holy Spirit?'

'Not so far, Rumsey. At least not as far as I am aware. I have this emissary from the Lord here, in my bag. And it has been fidgeting away at my waist, ever since I picked it up. The most restless emissary you could imagine.'

She drew the chatelaine bag from her waist, its shape still shifting, and opened the clasp and offered it to the Inspector. He looked at her, raised his eyebrows and pulled out a paper bag, opened it and emptied the contents on to the floor.

Constance stepped backwards in surprise before her hand flew up to her mouth and she laughed at the absurdity of it.

On the pavement in front of her were two rather confused frogs, which collected themselves and hopped off into the gutter.

'They were in my bag? I have been carrying them through the town with Mathilde Barree? Oh my goodness! No wonder they were never still.'

'It is all a trick, Constance. You know better than I do. Everything Milo does is just part of a stage show. But a dangerous one.'

'It worries me very much, Rumsey. He gives people hope with the intention of snatching it away.' She shook her head, then smiled. 'May I offer you tea this evening, Inspector? The wind is cold.'

'Not this evening, I regret that —.' There were more bangs and then a distant police whistle. 'I fear, Constance that I am required. I imagine at St Mary's Church. It is attacked every year.'

'I understand, Rumsey. Perhaps it is for the best.' She leaned forward to kiss him but he had turned and was running off along St Helen's Road back into the town.

Chapter 13

'Bonfire! There's a fire! Bonfire! There's a fire!' The chant echoed from the bottom of High Street and two unhappy constables, Davies and Morris, standing outside the King's Arms, sighed.

'Listen, Morris. They is calling you.'

'That's enough of your cheek. Or I shall start to call you 'Mutterer', be warned.' This was a calculated insult by the older man, because since the previous November when he had been so wantonly attacked and had escaped serious injury by chance, Davies had acquired the habit of muttering to himself when on the beat, for fear, perhaps, that silence was the prelude to another attack by bored and fickle youths – and naturally those youths soon learned of his habit and shouted it after him whenever they saw him.

'No, I am telling you, mun. They is calling you. Listen. 'Bonfire' they is shouting. You're needed, like.'

Whilst Morris was convinced that Davies was always making fun of him, for he was a man easily affronted, in fact he was not. Bonfire, as everyone knew – and whether he liked it or not was immaterial – was his nickname, unfortunately acquired. He had begun his working life as a sailor on the ships in the copper trade, working between Swansea and Valparaiso in Chile. After a particularly difficult trip around Cape Horn, during which three of his colleagues had been washed overboard, he had decided to seek more stable employment as a police constable on land. 'From copper, to Copper,' he liked to say.

The ship, battered and splintered by the mountainous waves of the South Atlantic, had stopped, exhausted in Montevideo, where a drunken Morris had been inexpertly tattooed in a filthy backstreet. On the knuckles of his left hand there was the word *LOVE* and on the right *HEAT*. Who was responsible for the spelling mistake had never been established, but once the boys of St Thomas heard about the constable with *HEAT* on his hands, and once it had been confirmed by those who could read, he became known as 'Bonfire' and the more he slapped those boys who shouted it after him round the head, the more they used it.

But Constable Davies was right. That is what they were doing now. They were calling him, because there was, in fact, a fire and it was consuming the Southern Seas Shipping Agency on Castle Street and was threatening to spread to adjacent buildings. One of the boys from the Hat Stand Gang, Alfie Woods, had been sent running up High Street with the news that there was 'a building afire' but they both regarded it is a trick that would end with at least one of them in a barrel. Consequently, by the time the constables saw the column of black smoke and the red glow of the flames in the night sky, it was too late.

Baglow the reporter was there before them, of course. He seemed to have his own independent, and much more efficient, information network. More importantly though, Bucke was there too, having seen the flames from St Mary's where a group of boys had been throwing fire crackers at the vestry, and he was able to bring some authority to the incident, even though his mind was full of frogs. Sadly though, by the time Alfie took another message up to Sergeant Ball to tell him to deploy the fire engine from the stables at the police station where it was stored, and by the time they collected Mr Gibson the turncock, so that he could turn on the water supply to allow the hoses to work, it was too late. The pressure was poor, the fire engine itself was miserably under-powered, and Bucke knew that there was nothing that could be done to save the old timber building. Their attention must be focused on preventing the fire from spreading.

Plumes of sparks, shooting up into the sky and dispersing into the smoke, attracted a large crowd which gathered to enjoy the show. Older people shook their heads in wonder at the blaze, the boys threw stones at the rats that fled the building and whenever something went wrong - when a constable dropped a hose or directed the feeble water in the wrong place – Baglow wrote in his notebook.

The evacuated neighbours stood and watched their ineffectual attempts, though they took what comfort they could from the knowledge that, fortuitously, the shipping agency was not joined to the buildings on either side and hoped fervently that the gap, however small it was, would help to contain the fire. It was one of the fiercest fires that any of them could remember. Nothing would be able to diminish ferocity of that blaze.

Mr Wallage, the ironmonger with the shop to the left, wasn't sure if anyone was inside the shipping agency. No one had seen Dermot Murphy, the shipping clerk, who sometimes worked late. On the right was the shop of John Dennis, who sold biscuits. He thought he remembered seeing the dim light of a candle and he thought he might have heard something unusual but it was hard to tell amongst all the Bonfire Night noise. He had no inclination to go outside to see what it was. Anyway, he was far more concerned with the fact that the contents of his shop were not insured and would the constables please be careful with their hoses, because he'd never be able to sell wet biscuits. But if Murphy was inside, there was little they could do. The heat of the blaze was intense and the beams were starting to crack. Evan Davies, bravely, got closest to the blaze with a wet rag around his head but it could only ever be a token gesture. He came back, his eyebrows singed, claiming to have seen a shape at the heart of the blaze, standing with arms outstretched. He was adamant, though no one was inclined to believe him.

Then, the lintel over the front door fell in, to the cheers of the crowd – and allowed them to see it, too. As the entrance collapsed, there behind, for all to see, was a figure with its arms outstretched, seemingly embracing the flames which were dancing upon it. The figure seemed to move in the heat, the arms lifting and then lowering again, the head rising.

'Oh my good God!' shouted Morris. 'It is an angel!'

A gasp went through the crowd and Constable Morris, unwittingly, defined for them what they had seen. Even the raucous youths paused in their revelry to watch the figure bow its head, as if in respect. Even Bucke was momentarily shocked by what seemed to be there.

'Look at the angel!' shouted Alfie.

And then the upper floor collapsed and the angel disappeared.

The decades of accumulated dust and filth, the wet beams of the inadequate roof and the haphazard slate tiles when they collapsed, did more to suppress the flames than the constables had managed and gave them a more clearly defined area at which to point their hoses. Soon the fire was under greater control.

The Hat Stand Gang walked away, their night of misrule undoubtedly their best ever; a house burnt down, the fire engine out, constables to laugh at and an angel in Swansea. Throwing stones at the Town Hall just wasn't going to cut it in the future. It seemed so childish in comparison.

*

The next morning Bucke went back to Castle Street in the helpful rain to see what he could find. Baglow was there, of course, compiling his newspaper story in front of the charred and fallen gable, beneath the wet morning sky, though he had been denied access to the wreckage by Constable Davies, who had been guarding the site.

'Morning, Inspector. Any clues?' asked Baglow.

'I think there has been a fire, Mr Baglow.'

'Very amusing, I am sure. What caused it, do you think?'

'Hard to say, as you know. A candle, probably. After all, it was a shipping agency. It would have been full of paper.'

Baglow nodded. 'Invoices, orders, manifests. Old wooden building too. Was there anyone inside, do you know, Inspector?'

'We are not sure at the moment. We'll check when it is safe to do so. No one will have survived, Mr Baglow, as you can see.'

'So you haven't been able to find Dermot Murphy then? Are you prepared to say that he is still missing?'

'All I can say is that we haven't given up looking.'

Baglow nodded and wrote something on his pad. 'And this angel idea, Inspector. The one that is already sweeping the town. Do you really think there was an angel in the building?'

'Of course not, Mr Baglow. I am sure it was an optical illusion. Remember, as anyone who has ever visited the building will tell you, there was an old ship's figurehead. Been there for years. Large carving of an albatross, the bird from the South Seas. Wings outstretched. It was a surprise to see it in the flames, even for me. That is what they saw, I am sure.' Bucke was surprised but pleased. The reporter had been surprisingly professional this morning.

Baglow nodded. 'I am sure you are right. Makes a good story though.' He paused and then smiled. 'And how is Mrs Bristow this morning, Inspector Bucke?'

Bucke stiffened. 'As well, I hope, as she was when I last saw her.'

'Don't worry, you will be seeing her soon, I suspect. Give her my regards, won't you?' He touched the peak of his cap and walked away. Then he turned. 'If you find anything interesting in the ruins, you will let me know, won't you?'

Bucke nodded imperceptibly and watched him walk towards his office on Wind Street.

Damn the man! thought Bucke, kicking at a fragment of charred timber, then he approached Constable Davies standing at the edge of the ruins, his cape glistening in the rain.

'All quiet here, constable?' he asked.

'Not really, sir. Still a great deal of cracking and hissing, sir.'

'You are not to worry about it, constable. In the circumstances it is quite natural. You must be tired after standing here all night. I think you can be discharged.'

'Always ready to perform my duties to the best of my abilities, sir.'

'I know, Constable Davies. A quality of yours that so many of us admire.' He laid a comradely hand upon his arm. 'I think you need to go home and rest, Evan.'

He shook his head. 'If you is about to climb into the ruins, sir, then I have to insist on coming with you, on account of it still being so dangerous.'

Bucke was touched. 'Thank you, Constable Davies, but there is no need.'

'I insist, sir. If you was to fall, no one would know. But if I am by there with you, then I will know, won't I? You wouldn't let me go in all by my own, I'll be bound. So lead on, Inspector.'

Bucke was impressed and gratified both by Davies's concern and by his thinking and so together they stepped into the black smouldering ruins of the building, amongst the burnt timbers and the fallen stones, glancing anxiously at occasional glowing embers in the fire-chewed gable. There was little recognisable furniture and of the albatross there was no sign at all. He tried to recall the vaguely remembered shape of a building he had only entered rarely. He wondered if there had been an explosion, but if so, it would have been lost in the noise of Bonfire Night.

And then he saw it, in a corner. Slumped at a desk, the outline of which had been preserved by the falling roof tiles, there was a charred, blackened corpse.

They fought their way across the wreckage towards it, stumbling and sending up plumes of smoke from the smouldering wood that their boots disturbed. It was undeniably a body, though any distinguishing features which had once existed beneath this layer of charcoaled flesh had been obliterated. The most obvious feature, however, was a large knife which was still plunged almost to the hilt into the back of the body. It once had, Bucke presumed, a wooden handle that had burnt away, but there was no doubt that he had been stabbed – unless, of course, you were Constable Davies.

'Who would have thought it, eh?' Davies shook his head. 'What are the chances of a knife like that, falling from a room upstairs and landing slap-bang in the middle of a dead body? Makes you wonder, don't it, sir?'

Bucke closed his eyes momentarily, marvelling at the mental dexterity required to avoid drawing an obvious explanation. He felt he ought to say something, although he was not at all sure what, but Davies continued.

'And look 'ere, sir. There's another thing. I know what that is.' He pointed at a metal canister overturned in the ashes behind the door and moved towards it. 'Seen them plenty of times. Paraffin, that's what that is.' He rolled it with the sole of his boot and pointed at faint letters still showing in the ashes of the label. 'Here. 'P... R A F. It is from the chandlers at the end of Pier Street, Jeremiah Wharton. See, like.' He bent down and rubbed with his finger at the blistered letters that had once been painted on the side. 'Look at the letters – 'H… R T and then the last one looks like an N. Obvious to me.'

Bucke nodded his approval and looked carefully at the container. It was empty of course, blackened within, and without, from the flames. There were the remains of something that might once have been a rag or a cloth, perhaps a primitive fuse, he speculated, useful if the murderer had needed time to get away. On the other hand, he might have just splashed it everywhere. There was so much paper around there was no need for anything sophisticated. All that was needed was one match.

'Must have been refilling his lamp and it all went up, whoosh! Tricky stuff, paraffin.' Davies looked pleased with himself, proud of his incisive detective work. 'Look there on the desk,' he said. He swept aside some ashes and debris with his hand to reveal a twisted blob of metal, apparently thin shapes now fused together. 'Shows you how fierce it were.' He frowned as he studied it, unable to recognise what it once was. 'Perhaps it were keys or something. Or coins. But they melted and that is a fact.'

The post-mortem, when they had carefully removed the roasted body from the ruins, established that he had been stabbed in the back with a large butcher's knife before the fire started. If that hadn't killed him then the fire had finished the job. Dr Beynon removed the jaw of the corpse and examined the teeth. The fact that all of the teeth on the upper right were missing was taken to confirm that this was Dermot Murphy, the manager of the Southern Seas Shipping Agency, for he had been similarly afflicted.

Who would want him dead was quite another matter. A single man, living a simple life, who apparently weekly visited his aging father and sang in the choir of his local chapel. What could an unassuming, blameless man have done, what did he possess, what did he know, that meant he deserved the butcher's knife? Bucke felt that Swansea, the town it was his responsibility to protect, was slowly but inexorably slipping into chaos and madness.

The only lead he had at that moment was the paraffin from Jeremiah Wharton. Who had put it there? Murphy? His murderer? It was time to visit the chandlers.

Chapter 14

'Nothing to do with me, is it? How can it be?' Jeremiah Wharton looked contemptuously at Bucke and then spat into the sawdust behind the counter. 'Don't understand why you is here.'

'As I said, I am here to ask you about your paraffin store. Do you remember any of the customers to whom you sold paraffin recently?' Bucke could smell it in the air; it seemed to permeate everything in the chandlery. The counter on which he rested his elbows seemed to be covered in an oily, dangerous film of paraffin. The smell was seductive.

'And, as I told you, I sells it to as many as comes in here. I don't ask them why they want it. I don't need to ask them who they are. I just sells it. It is what I do. This is a ship's chandlers, sergeant. I sells the things that sailors wants.'

Bucke ignored the deliberate insult. 'And I will repeat what I said before. Who have you sold it to in the past few weeks?'

'Told you. I don't know.'

'Do you keep a record of how much you sell? In containers like this?' Bucke showed him the charred tin recovered from the shipping office. 'The ones with your name on, like this.'

Wharton turned it round in his hand, with thinly disguised contempt. 'Why do you think it is mine? It is just a can.' He stood it up on the counter.

'Those letters there. See them? *H R T N*. Could be Wharton, couldn't it?' Bucke watched him closely.

He snorted. 'Could be Hartson, too? Or Horton? A shop in Merthyr that, isn't it? That is what someone told me. Nar, not mine, copper.' He pushed it back to Bucke across the counter with the back of his hand. 'Never seen it afore.'

Bucke had already seen the identical cans on a shelf behind the counter. *Safest, Sweetest and Best* the label announced proudly. *Burns extensively in all climates.* He pointed at the shelf, though Wharton refused to turn to look at it. 'I repeat my question, Mr Wharton. Do you keep a record of how much paraffin you sell? Or who buys it?'

'As long as it gets written in the book then I know, don't I? Everyone buys paraffin, of course they do. What else is going to make light in your home, eh? But not everyone who works here writes it in the book. That can't be my fault. Gets busy just before the tide. No time to write things down. And what is it anyway? Just paraffin, isn't it? That's all. '

'And who else might be selling it then, here at the shop,' asked Bucke patiently. 'Who might not be writing down the sales?'

'You can speak to Violet. She works behind the counter most days. But this is a ship's chandler. It is a shop. People buy things. They comes off the ships, don't they? No idea who they are. Foreign, lots of them. They don't speak English. Don't even speak Welsh. They buys a barrel for their lamps. You need lamps at sea, sergeant. Did you know that?'

'And has any paraffin been stolen from your stores recently?'

'No. Always very secure here. Only three of us go into the back where it is stored. Me, the wife and her maid, Violet, sergeant. Cash in the till was a bit short last week but probably just a mistake. No thieves here. It is not a police station.'

'I would like to speak to Violet, Mr Wharton.' Bucke remained patient.

Wharton shrugged, spat once more, and called Violet out from the back. 'Don't keep her long. She is packing macaroni for one of them German ships. Can't get enough of it. So I would be obliged, sergeant, if she wasn't delayed.' He walked into the back room.

Bucke smiled thinly at Wharton's back as he departed and Violet appeared, grubby and untidy, her hair in tight, dull, dirty curls and her eyes narrow with suspicion.

'They is coming for that macaroni shortly, Vi, so crack on, for goodness sake.'

It was immediately clear to Bucke that Violet had no intention of co-operating with him.

'Customers for paraffin? I don't rightly recall no one in particular,' she shrugged. 'People are always taking it away. They take big barrels sometimes, then they sell it themselves in their own shops.'

'And how do they take them away, Violet? Some of those barrels must be heavy.'

'Carts and barrows, mostly. But most people don't want barrels in their house, if they are that size, so they buy what they need from an ironmongers or somewhere. Not news that, is it?'

'And you have no memory of anyone from the Southern Seas Shipping Agency coming here to buy paraffin?'

'Never heard of them. You can look in the book. Won't find their name in there,' she flicked casually through it at random. 'They can buy paraffin anywhere, they don't have to come here. Anyone can.'

Bucke was surprised at how certain she was. He turned the ledger around so that he could see it properly and turned the pages. There was a neat, legible hand on some of the pages that gave the impression of efficiency, for those entries appeared in substantial blocks. Other handwriting, with untidy and blotched letter formation, appeared sporadically.

'Who has written these entries?' he asked, pointing at the legible hand.

'That will be Mrs Wharton.'

'And who does this other handwriting belong to?'

'That will be me.'

'And are you supposed to write down all your sales?' asked Bucke.

'Yes, we are but Mr Wharton has told me that he would rather that I sold things. So sometimes I forget.'

He turned silently to the most recently completed pages and noticed that there was an entry for a paraffin sale in Violet's hand. 'Who bought this paraffin, Violet? I can't read what you have written.'

She looked at it and then looked away. 'Oh, that. A man from...' she paused. 'Oh yes, I remember now. From Llandeilo. Or was it Llangadog?' She ran her finger along the line. 'That's it. Had a shop in Llangadog. Called Jones.'

Bucke was sure that she was lying. 'I see. And did he say why he had come all the way down here to buy paraffin? Wonder why he didn't go to Carmarthen? If he wanted paraffin. In fact I am sure he can buy it in Llandeilo.'

'Oh, I remember now.' Violet avoided eye contact. 'Came down here to see a solicitor, that is what he said. So decided to pick up some paraffin whilst he was at it. Then he went off in his cart.'

'And I would be right to assume that he did not tell you the name of his solicitor? The one he came to see.'

'No he didn't, Inspector.' She smiled at him, with what Bucke interpreted as a look of relief. Why was she lying? What was she hiding?

'What is this about, anyway, Inspector?' she asked with more confidence.

'There's been a fire.'

'It is what you get with paraffin, if you are not careful. Can I go now? They will be wanting their macaroni.'

He avoided Pier Street, since he did not want to be distracted from his thoughts, and walked back to the police station along Somerset Place, through the dark haze of smoke spewing from the funnel of a ship in the South Dock which made him cough, wondering why Violet had found it necessary to lie about a simple paraffin sale. Wharton's hostility was tiresome: it was Violet's reaction that surprised him. That entry in the ledger – it wasn't right. What was she hiding? He looked again at the can in his hand. He was sure it was Wharton's, no matter what the chandler said. In other circumstances the simple explanation would have been that Murphy had merely refilled his paraffin lamp just before the fire started. But Murphy had been murdered and an attempt had been made to destroy the evidence in a fire. He was sure that Violet knew something. The most significant question of all, of course, was why? Why did an unassuming man have to die in this way? Who could possibly have benefitted from his death? He looked up and saw that he was at the bottom of Wind Street. It was Friday afternoon and old man Webber was standing against the wall, selling copies of the Cambrian from the pile draped over his forearm , so he bought one.

*

Inspector condemns 'hysterical' Swansea public. Belief in Angels is 'ridiculous,' says Inspector. Leading churchmen say police inspector's views 'unfortunate.' Body found in debris. Police still unwilling to confirm whereabouts of Dermot Murphy. Shipping Office completely destroyed. Small paper fire likely cause, believe police.'

Bucke threw the paper across his desk in exasperation and stamped loudly towards the front desk of the police station where

Inspector Flynn was talking to Sergeant Ball. The latter seemed especially eager to attract his attention, though Bucke was too angry to respond. Flynn held up both hands to him.

'I know, I know, Rumsey. I have seen it.'

Ball continued quietly gesturing to him with the palm of his hand, suggesting calm and reflection, and flicking his eyes towards the bench placed against the wall. Bucke eventually glanced at a couple who were sitting there, and saw the man jump up and approach him.

'Rumsey? Rumsey Bucke? The Inspector? Please forgive my intrusion, but we are sure you must have news for us.' The man grabbed his hand, squeezed and shook it. The woman followed to join him and held on to Bucke's clothes, her wet eyes shining. They both looked at him expectantly, pleadingly, and Bucke quickly realised who they were before Sergeant Ball introduced them, and realised too, that whilst they had shed a great many tears in recent weeks, there were still more to come.

'Inspector Bucke, this is Mr and Mrs Longden, from Roath. They have come about the garment we sent to the Cardiff Constabulary.'

Bucke stepped away slightly and bowed his head. 'I regret very much the circumstances in which we meet. These must be dreadful days for you both.' His previous anger ensured that his mind was working at high speed. 'Please allow me a moment to complete a vital piece of work pertinent to our current investigation, and then I shall give you my complete attention. I have some news that may be important to you.'

Mr Longden's hand squeezed his brow in an attempt to dam his emotions, and he closed his eyes as his wife led him back to the bench.

Bucke immediately abandoned his intention of looking for Dermot Murphy's acquaintances and, back in his office, he quickly wrote a note which he folded in half and took back into the lobby, handing it to Inspector Flynn. He opened the note, looked up and nodded and then left the police station. When the door closed, a silence settled upon the police station, a silence amplified by that inexorable clock. It was a moment, perhaps, for reflection and for disclosing unwelcome secrets and so Bucke invited the Longdens into his office where, with the easy authority of a uniformed police inspector, he lied.

The couple were leaning forward across the desk, Mrs Longden biting her knuckle with anxiety, and listened to the story that Bucke invented.

'Our investigations are almost complete and I will tell you as much as we have established, though I fear there is little more of substance to discover. I believe that your daughter, Susannah, came to Swansea in search of new employment. We know that she met with a teacher at Miss Higginson's Select Day School for Girls, situated in one of the better parts of the town, with the intention of taking a position there. The teacher's name is Constance White and you may speak to her if you wish. I believe she may be here shortly on another matter entirely.' He hoped that if they did meet her she would be able to improvise. 'The school is an admirable and respected establishment and they were delighted with her appointment. She told them that she had sufficient money to rent a suitable property in a respectable area close by. Susannah also told Miss White that she was coming to Swansea to start her life afresh having, I believe, been unlucky in love and that she was intent on contacting you directly by telegram to allay your certain fears at the very earliest opportunity.'

The Longdens said nothing, horrified and trapped by the finality of her death, from which they could never escape, and confronting an episode in their daughter's life about which they had no knowledge.

'On her arrival she had taken a room at one of our most prestigious hotels and on her way back there, presumably delighted by her appointment, she was knocked down by a runaway cart on a bridge, which pitched her, unseen, into the clear waters of the canal beneath. Her body was recovered some hours later but, sad to relate, the life force was extinguished.'

'Yes, Inspector, that would be right,' said Mr Longden, his hands clutching the edge of the desk. 'She is such a headstrong girl. Impulsive, of course, but sensible, Inspector. Always very sensible'

'Yes, she is,' Mrs Longden echoed, through the tears. 'We are so very proud of her.'

'I regret very much that at the time of her tragic death, we had no means of identifying her or of knowing where she had taken a room. We were all very moved by her. She was so peaceful, her face so striking, so unblemished; it was hard to believe she was not merely asleep. She appeared like an angel who had lived all too briefly amongst us, the undeserving and unworthy. She has been buried in a prominent position in St Mary's Churchyard, where I believe she should rest in peace. I will show you her grave, of course, and I assure you that it will always be properly tended and maintained by those of us who were touched by her fate.'

He had struggled to maintain eye-contact throughout his narrative, seeking security from the non-existent notes on his lap. He looked up and saw Mrs Longden studying him closely and, he feared, sceptically, though she said nothing.

'It is with regret that I must tell you that all her possessions were stolen from the hotel, the room for which she had paid in advance, remaining unoccupied for a few days. Our constables were, regrettably at first, unable to link the empty room with the beautiful young woman they recovered from the water. Hardened police officers to a man, who have seen such sights no man should see, yet they were moved beyond words by her tragic loss. In the Section House, where some of the constables lodge, there have been many quiet and painful nights as they have tried to accept her tragic loss.' On impulse, Bucke produced a necklace from the drawer of his desk, one which he had taken from Winnie's pocket. 'All we have is this, which I believe might once have been hers.'

'Yes! Yes! This is Susannah's,' said Mr Longden, desperately. 'This is what she would wear, isn't it, Clarissa? All the time. I never thought I would see it again.' Mrs Longden said nothing, unwilling, Bucke thought, to puncture her husband's desperate belief.

'There is little more that I can say. There is more that we would all like to know, though in truth we will never know enough. A beautiful young woman taken from us all too soon. And in that we can find little comfort, other than the knowledge that she led a good life in the midst of a devoted family.' Bucke stood and sighed, 'There is little I can say to ease your sorrow and I regret that bitterly. No pain matches the loss of a loved one. Shall we spend a few moments at the graveside? I am sure you would like to see it.'

Why should they know the awful details of her last hours? What good would it do? None at all. This was a story which did not pretend she was alive but which might help to salve the loss of their only child. There was no one to tell them otherwise, apart from himself. Why in God's name should he tell them the awful truth?

They passed through the lobby where was Constance was waiting, with a newspaper beneath her arm. 'Inspector,' she began with a smile, but Bucke interrupted her.

'Miss White I –'

Mr Longden rushed to her and seized her hands in her own. 'Oh, Miss White! Thank you, thank you. Clarissa and myself are so moved by the kindness that you showed Susannah when she came here to start her new life. She would have been such a success. Tragically, terribly, cut short.' His eyes leaked tears. His wife said nothing and Bucke knew she was aware that Constance was having to pick her way carefully through an unexpected and confusing conversation.

She was trying her best, looking to the Inspector for help and managed to say,' She was a delightful young woman and I was so sorry –'

'That you never had a chance to work with her? Yes, I am sure Mr and Mrs Longden understand completely, Miss White. A shocking loss to the teaching profession,' said Bucke, sombrely.

'Without doubt, Inspector,' replied Constance, clearly puzzled, knowing she had a part to play in a drama she did not understand, not knowing what it was. 'I have come here to enquire about an item of lost property, Inspector,' she said speculatively.

He nodded. 'I was informed earlier, Miss White. I am sure that Sergeant Ball will be able to assist you. If you will excuse me,' he continued, 'I must escort Mr and Mrs Longden to the cemetery at St Mary's.'

'Please allow me to say how sorry I was to hear of your terrible loss,' she guessed.

Mrs Longden held a handkerchief over a mouth and shook her head, and Bucke politely guided the grieving couple out of the police station.

When they reached the cemetery Inspector Flynn had done his work well. There was fresh wooden cross above a grave with the words 'The Girl from the Canal' written upon it. The Longden's stared at it in silence, holding on to each other, facing the final physical representation of their daughter's life.

Mr Longden released his wife and turned to Bucke. 'We must have a proper headstone.'

'Of course.'

'We shall commission one.' Mr Longden looked fervently into Bucke's eyes. 'You must understand, Inspector. She was never a disgrace to her family. Never. Not before; not now. It is no disgrace falling into a canal, is it? Is it?'

Bucke could feel the moisture gathering in the corner of his eyes. 'No, Mr Longden. It was a tragedy, but never a disgrace. There is no disgrace in a young woman trying to better herself. Tragically, she was in the wrong place, at exactly the wrong time. A terrible twist of fate.'

Longden grasped Bucke's arm, closed his eyes, tried to speak but could not and turned away to his wife. She said nothing; perhaps, thought Bucke, accepting something that she believed wasn't quite right, for the sake of her husband. Bucke was sure that it didn't matter at all that this was not Susannah's grave. So long as they believed that it was, that was all that mattered. It was more of a truth than anything Milo had ever said and brought infinitely more comfort.

He left them there alone to grieve and, blinded by unexpected tears, walked to the Cross Keys Inn where he surprised Mr Turner, the landlord, by asking first for one glass of brandy and then for another. 'Cold day today. A bitter wind. Made my eyes water,' said Bucke. Turner looked at him carefully but chose to say nothing.

Bucke went over to the window and looked up towards Castle Street where a column of thin smoke drifted up from the ruins of the shipping office. He knew that he had to find out what happened to Susannah Longden. A young woman, attractive and obviously intelligent, suddenly dead in a canal in a strange town. Why? Those marks on her body troubled him considerably. He wiped his eyes, again, his own grief re-awakened. The town had suddenly been filled with death, mania, murder and the sorrow of those bereaved parents echoed through his mind.

There were no other customers and so Turner walked over to join Bucke at the window.

'Shockin' thing, that fire. Lit up the whole sky. It were like the middle of the day in the snug. I was very sorry to hear 'bout Murphy. Shocked I was. He had been in here just the day before. Always came in after choir. Always good company, he was. Can't believe I won't see him no more. They are sayin' he were murdered.' Turner shook his head. 'Who'd want to do that? His father will find it a hard. Still, him bein' a reverend should help, I reckon.'

'Who is his father then, Mr Turner?' asked Bucke, trying – and failing – to identify a Swansea clergyman called Murphy.

'That would be Reverend Rogers, wouldn't it? Never did know why he had a different name to his old man. You know the one. Out at Llangyfelach.'

Chapter 15

The sky was grey as he approached Llangyfelach, and there was a cruel edge to the wind once again, which spoke of a bitter chill to come. If the cloud cleared there would be frost tonight. The last time Bucke had been to see Reverend Rogers he had been there to talk of the damnation and the fires of hell; now it was to talk to him about an earthly fire – and the cold embrace of death. Sergeant Ball, surprised that Bucke had not realised, confirmed that Dermot Murphy had been Rogers' son. And now he was dead, murdered whilst his father sat reading in the vicarage in Llangyfelach, oblivious to the broad-bladed knife that had sought out Dermot's heart.

Bucke had already ruled out robbery as a motive. Murphy was a man of regular habits. Every afternoon at 3.00 pm he took any money he had taken during the day to the Glamorganshire Banking Company on Temple Street. There would have been nothing in his office to steal.

As he approached through the garden, the house seemed in mourning, the windows blinded by the heavy drawn curtains. Mrs Pennock admitted him with a quiet nod of recognition. 'He has been in his study all morning, Inspector. At the moment he has little to say. Very quiet, thinking about the funeral, I imagine. I would feel happier if he had some company.' She wiped her eyes with a lace handkerchief. 'I shall bring some tea, presently.'

'Of course, Mrs Pennock. I understand how difficult these days must be for him.'

Reverend Rogers was sitting in a chair by the window, staring out into the garden, lost in his memories. He turned as Bucke closed the door.

'Please accept my sincere condolences, Reverend Rogers. I was shocked by the discovery that I made in the shipping office. I was so very sorry to discover your terrible loss.'

He nodded in response. 'A good man lost, Inspector. A good son, my only companion.'

'I didn't realise at first that he was your son, Reverend.'

'My youngest son, yes. He decided to take his mother's name. Proud of his Irish heritage, you see. I was rather moved by his decision.' Rogers paused. 'I cannot believe that I am not going to see him again, Inspector. When you opened the door just now, I thought it was him.' He tugged at his beard. His eyes seemed raw and swollen. 'Do you think he was murdered? There was a knife in his back, they say. A reporter came here. Called Baglow. Wasn't very skilled at listening, it seemed to me. Was he murdered, Inspector?'

'My enquiries are continuing, Reverend Rogers, But I fear that he had been killed before the fire started. Can you think of anyone who might have wished him harm?'

Rogers did not reply immediately and continued to stare out of the window. He took off his glasses and then picked abstractedly at his ink-stained finger.

'You're a widower, aren't you?' he asked suddenly. 'I am sure you told me so, the last time we met.'

'Yes, I am. I do understand how awful it can be,' Bucke replied gently.

'The moment when my life changed, Inspector. She was a beautiful woman, you know. And talented. A great singer. Meara Murphy, *The Irish Songbird*. She appeared on the stage, really she did. I met her when she came to church. She would sing our boys to sleep every night. We were together for five years, you know. Five wonderful years. And then I lost her and nothing could be the same again.'

Bucke waited, knowing that there was more to come. Was Rogers losing himself in anguished visions of the past? Or was he offering a convoluted answer to the question about who might want Dermot dead?

'Neglected my boys, do you see? Couldn't really function, do you understand? Once I became a widower I rather threw myself into my work. Lost myself in the past and in the ocean. Waste of time, really. I found some solace but it didn't help my boys at all.' He paused again and lowered his head to stare at his hands crossed in his lap. His mouth was hidden deep in his beard and when he spoke his voice seemed to come from deep within his soul. 'They were brought up by other people and when I turned around I found the eldest was a stranger to me. Always a difficult child. Truculent and contrary. He rejected the church because he was so keen to reject me, I believe. His mother had died and it was my fault, in his mind. He missed his mother. I missed her to, but for him I wasn't up to the mark, I am afraid. Didn't like me. Didn't like his brother either and so he walked out. Dermot on the other hand, was always a quiet, respectable young man. Worked as a shipping agent. Lived a quiet life. Sang in the choir. Did charitable works. And now he has died in a fire. Such a loss, such a waste.' Rogers shook with sorrow and then lifted his head and turned away, to look out of the window once more. 'My son, my only true friend and companion, dead,' he repeated. ' Murdered, you say?'

'And your eldest son, Reverend?' asked Bucke. 'Does he live close by? Has there been a reconciliation in these troubled times? Will he be able to support you in this time of grief? It is so hard to be alone, as I know myself.'

Rogers laughed bitterly and turned back to him, a wildness in his eyes. 'Inspector, my eldest son is called Milo.'

183

His words were a silent earthquake which shook the room. For a few moments, Bucke could not effectively process what he had heard.

'Milo?'

'Yes, Inspector. Father Milo, the prophet. God's messenger on earth. He is my son. May God forgive him.'

*

Mrs Pennock's tea tray restored some equilibrium to the room, though Bucke's mind was in a state of disorder. It was something that he had never contemplated.

'I apologise for not realising,' he began, as Mrs Pennock closed the door.

'How could you know? It must seem so unlikely,' said Rogers before taking a sip of his tea. 'I have told no one else this before, but you see, I lost my love so unexpectedly and found I had a child who was a complete stranger to me. Yes, Milo is my son. I gave him life and held him as a baby. For a while he was the light of my world. Then he rather went off the rails, as you might have realised. Now? I do not like him. Milo became a charlatan, a stage performer, a magical healer, a seller of magnetic belts, a liar and a thief. Who knows what else.'

'And was there something which happened that caused this change in him? Was there one particular incident that you remember?'

'Not entirely, Inspector. If I am honest with myself, I had worried about him for quite some time. He played games as a child on the lawn in the summer. They troubled me a great deal, I cannot lie. It was always funerals. He was always burying his toy soldiers and then crying because he couldn't remember where he had buried them. And then in his game, sometimes one of his soldiers would die and he would construct a building from sticks and leaves – a mausoleum I suppose you would call it. He would arrange a funeral procession. Incredibly detailed, and all his soldiers would be lining the route. Very patient he was. Took him hours. Then he would make the soldiers follow the coffin to the mausoleum and Milo would arrange them very precisely. Some would enter with the coffin and then he would make the mausoleum collapse, burying them all inside. I watched him from this window.'

Bucke made no reply. Rogers seemed anxious to talk and Bucke had no intention of interrupting him.

'Then he started to play this same game in his bedroom, hiding under his blankets with his toy soldiers, a Pharaoh insisting on being buried with his retainers.' He shook his head. 'A troubled boy. He took Dermot's soldiers away from him and then burnt them in a fire in the garden until they melted. Dermot kept that lump of metal on his desk as a paperweight. It is what Milo did. He seemed to spend his childhood murdering his toys or burying them, like the Pharaohs – Retainer Sacrifice it is called. Servants killed so that they would continue to serve you in the afterlife. Of course, it meant that if you were a retainer then your life was not likely to any better in the afterlife than it had been in this one. So where was the incentive?' He poured himself some more tea. 'He never tired of the game but to be perfectly honest, I wasn't sure that it was entirely healthy. Had a succession of governesses and the like, of course, but they never seemed to last very long. Then Milo disappeared and returned like a prodigal and telling me he was living in Mumbles and was about to marry.'

'And this would be Ada, would it?' asked Bucke, hoping that Rogers would keep on talking.

'I don't think his marriage has helped. Our Lady of Mumbles? She might have come from Mumbles but she has never been a lady. And now she claims she is Deborah? She should have instead have tried on the garb of the Whore of Babylon. She brought her own tragedies to the union. Her mother ran off and Ada was brought up by her grandparents - until they died. She took to the streets, they say. As far as I can see, she is a pagan woman.' He wiped his eyes and sighed. 'The worst part is that I feel responsible for all of this. If I had been a better father...' Rogers' voice trailed away.

'We were talking about Dermot, Reverend Rogers,' said Bucke gently. 'What did he think about his brother's re-appearance?'

'I am sorry?' Rogers had not been listening properly. 'Dermot? Well, yes he was very concerned. Very concerned about the corruption of the Christian message. We talked about it a lot. He wanted to do something but we were not sure what to do. I wrote some letters to the press outlining the dangers of extreme religious beliefs but they were never published. Not terribly interesting, I suppose.'

'And did Dermot do anything? Did he meet Milo, did he talk to him?'

'No. Nothing like that. They were estranged.'

'And did Dermot have any heirs? Who will inherit his property? Do you know?'

Rogers shrugged. 'He had no one else. I imagine what he had will revert to me. Not that I want any of it, you understand.'

'But Dermot was concerned about what his brother was doing? He may have told someone, do you think?'

Anger suddenly washed over Rogers again and he became agitated. 'Anyone with any sense can see what he is doing! Offering hope to those who have nothing! Their lives are difficult and unrelenting. And then a man tells them they will experience the end of the world and that only they will be saved whilst all those others, who seemed to have better lives, will burn forever in hell. They have been chosen; they are the most important people who ever lived. So they are happy to give away all that they have, because they believe they will inherit the earth. Their own death will be a liberation.' He shook his head. 'They are desperate people looking for answers, for escape. And all he gives them are his illusions. This Spear of Jehovah nonsense. It might be a mop. Probably is. But doesn't matter in the end, in a devotional sense, whether it is real or not. You see, it is all about the symbolic value of things , not what they really are. If you believe that is what it is, then that is what it becomes. The truth doesn't matter.' Rogers raised his voice still higher. 'He is my son and I created him but you need to stop him! It is your duty!'

'I can only do that when I have evidence. And that is difficult to find. Your son covers his tracks very well. And he has a devoted congregation, but we are watching him closely, I can assure you.'

Rogers sighed. 'All he offers is an illusion of salvation and revenge, nothing else. A perfect mix. But ask yourself, why should the world end now? Are we so special in our villainy? Is the world in some way worse than it has ever been before? Hardly. It will carry on as it always has and good men like Dermot will die, whilst others will prosper.' He snatched up his glasses from the desk and put them on decisively. 'Do you know something, Inspector? Perhaps hell is just another way of saying that nothing will ever change? It will never change; it will never be better. Everything will carry on as it always has. Yes, that's it. The endless hope of a salvation never to be delivered. Isn't that Hell? Must write that down. I have never thought of that before.' He began to shuffle through the mass of papers on his desk, looking for a place to write. 'Always writing things down. Always losing them.'

Bucke watched his scribble frantically on a piece of paper. He wasn't sure that Rogers was actually writing recognisable words. He seemed frenzied. 'It seems to me that your son has acquired a great deal of property, for a man who has abandoned earthly goods. He has another house now, I believe.'

Rogers wasn't listening, again. 'You see, you could argue with Milo on points of theological interpretation until your face turned blue but it would make no difference, because he knows nothing about it. Never going to admit he was wrong. Milo knows nothing about truth, he is a music hall entertainer and a fraud, that's all.' He suddenly calmed and looked reflective. 'But then perhaps that is all people want. Entertainment and simple answers. The world is changing, Inspector. You have seen those wires hanging around the town. For some, best if it all ends now, before it gets too complicated.' He took his glasses off and turned to look out of the window as he had been when Bucke first arrived.

Bucke felt that it was time to go. There was more that he wanted to ask but he knew that this was not the time. His questions would today only open up his wounds still further. He knew that Mrs Pennock would look after him, but nothing could soothe the grief in his mind. By the time that Bucke had reached Treboeth on the way back to town, he was, finally, able to identify what it was that had troubled him when he had been in the vicarage. He had asked Reverend Rogers about Dermot; he had asked about any enemies he might have. But all Rogers had wanted to talk about was Milo.

*

Violet sat up in the untidy bed and watched Billy pulling on his tight, mud-stained trousers. She saw the patch she had sewn on. It looked quite neat, she thought. Billy sat down with his back to her, lit his pipe and then pulled on his thick woollen socks. He seemed distant, disconnected, and she wondered what he felt about their relationship. She wanted him to show a bit more interest, even a bit more commitment. But perhaps that was not in his nature.

Her head was still sore where she had been struck and she could not stop herself picking at it. She pulled a piece from the crusty scab and then rubbed at the bruise on her shoulder where Billy had bitten her. She was right, she decided. She could never be sure what he really felt about her, about anything really.

'You do love me, Billy? Don't you?'

He spoke to her over his shoulder. 'Course I do.' He put down his pipe briefly and cut a piece from the cheese that was on the unsteady dressing table. He tore off a piece of bread and stuffed both into his mouth.

'Well, it is just that I don't see you as often as I used to.' Violet pulled at her ear, nervously. 'Thought you might be with someone else.' She poked at her scalp, trying to bring some shape to her stiff, disordered hair.

She was thin and dirty. To those who only occasionally visited the chandlery, she seemed unpleasantly stained by her occupation, carrying with her always a faint, but persistent, odour of paraffin. Those around her more frequently seemed not to notice.

'You worry too much. Very busy these days. Lots to do. Out in Llansamlet on a job at the moment. Lots of digging. Tell you what, though. I need gunpowder. Like the paraffin you give me the other day. Good work that was. I know you want to help. Miah does have some, don't he?'

'He is not supposed to have it. Don't have no licence. But he keeps some round the back. Some of the sea captains like to take it, don't know why. Miners come in now and again. If they use a bit of dynamite they can earn more money if they are working at the face, that is what they say anyway.'

'You will get me some, won't you? Knew you would. Knew I could rely on you. Delilah will help you. She will bring the cart round. Tea time would be good, I reckon. Old Man Miah and his missus will be too busy arguing to notice. Do you think you can manage it tomorrow, Vi? Can you?'

She gave the briefest of nods.

'Good on you. You're a good lass. They won't forget none of this when you joins the Militia, I reckon.'

'Policeman came round at dinner time yesterday,' Violet said, 'asking about paraffin. Checked the books. Wanted to know everything but I told him nothing, like.'

'Did he now?' Billy grinned. 'He needs to be careful or someone might be paying him a visit, if he likes paraffin that much.'

There was the sound of a horse and cart pulling away, down below on Pier Street. Billy looked out of the attic window. 'Looks like Our Lady is off out for the evening then.'

*

She seemed to be in some sort of carriage. She was swaying from side to side, although she could not move her hands, which was a puzzle she had no way of solving. It was dark and cold and she could hear a horse. She was very sore and could find no way of making herself comfortable, but it was being so uncomfortable that showed her that she wasn't asleep. Why couldn't she move her hands? Her chin felt wet and sore. She must have been dribbling. But she could not remember when or why. She tried really hard to put her thoughts into a logical shape but everything seemed disconnected. She knew all about Eddie, of course she did. How could she ever forget about her son? Where was he, though? She tried to call out for him but the right words were far too elusive. Why was she thinking about a train all the time? She wasn't on a train at the moment because she was sure she could hear a horse. A letter. What letter was that? Why was she thinking about a letter? And a suitcase. Did she have a suitcase? What did she use it for? She thought really hard about this but everything seemed suddenly to get darker and then the next thing she knew someone had picked her up, quite roughly, and was carrying her. She had been on a train. Alone. Going somewhere. Something about a letter. This was starting to make some sense. But then she wasn't in the cart anymore; she was standing up with something around her neck and she knew that she was in very grave danger.

He had carried her from the cart quite a distance into the wood, to a small clearing which was lit by the bright, cold, autumn moonlight. An owl hooted. He held her whilst the noose was put around her neck and then watched as the other end of the rope was thrown over a branch. He then put her to stand on a stool. He stepped back to stand with his companion to watch.

The girl was clearly disorientated and swayed around on the stool, the pressure of the rope repeatedly forcing her upright. They watched her expectantly and soon they could see her knees begin to buckle.

'Soon now. Very soon.'

'Oh yes.'

And then the stool toppled over and the woman, suspended from the rope, kicked her legs around desperately looking for purchase and finding none at all. They watched her body twitch and shudder uncontrollably as she was slowly strangled.

They stood together in silence, listening to the terrible gasps until the woman was still, swaying amongst the trees, her life departed.

He was standing behind her, pressing himself against her, his hands reaching around her, cupping her breasts. She had thrown her head backwards and so he whispered in her ear. 'And how was that, my dear?'

She breathed deeply and then relaxed. 'Quite satisfactory.'

Chapter 16

They found the body hanging from a tree some distance from the Carriage Drive. It had been there all through the cold night. She had been spotted through the trees by Mr Haynes the Baker when he made an early morning delivery and the police had been called immediately. Mr Dillwyn-Llewelyn, The High Sheriff of Glamorgan, due to return from a meeting in London, had been informed by telegraph and, inevitably, would not be best pleased to hear of another death of an intruder on his estate and would be demanding immediate action, though no one was sure what that might be. To Bucke that did not matter a great deal; a young woman swaying from a tree above an overturned stool should be afforded a moment of sympathy, rather than a rich man's complaints, he thought.

It seemed right to lower her gently, though of course it made no difference to the young woman. But she had once had hopes and dreams, and there were people somewhere who loved her, he was sure. Bucke laid her carefully on the floor. There was frost on her clothes and on the noose where it rested above her ear.

'Do you reckon this is another of them suicides then, Inspector?' asked Constable Davies.

Bucke sighed, wondering what had happened to that surprising moment of insight Davies had shown at the site of the fire. 'I don't think this is a suicide, constable. If you look carefully, you will see that the woman's hands are tied together behind her back. I can't imagine that the poor woman did that to herself.'

'Begging your pardon, Inspector, but bloody hell! So you reckon someone did it to her? Killed her, in fact. Is that what you mean?'

'I think so, constable.'

'And they brought that stool, too. I'll be bound.' Davies pointed at it and nodded wisely. 'A stool like that should be easy to trace. It's only got three legs. I shall begin my enquiries immediately we return to the town, Inspector,' he announced helpfully.

Bucke sent Davies down to the house to question the servants, who would probably be the only ones with anything sensible to say. He needed to be alone in the woods, to collect his thoughts in peace, to consider how this may or may not fit in with the other recent deaths. He looked down at her and wondered why she had been brought here to be killed. Out of the corner of his eye he saw the stool again. It was such a commonplace detail but it would now be forever linked in his mind with the ending of a life in this unexpected location.

He looked at the woman closely, trying to get some impression of what she looked like in life, trying to see beyond the contorted face which revealed nothing except fear and agony. She seemed quite slight, her black hair pulled back away from her forehead and held by a red velvet ribbon. Her hands, when he released them, were the worn and chipped hands of someone who regularly used them for work. Perhaps she did the laundry somewhere, he thought. Or she worked in domestic service. Her clothes seemed too clean and quite fashionable, her jacket particularly so, though the dark woollen skirt was badly stained. He loosened the rope around her neck, as if in some way he could set her free from death. And then he saw it, emerging from beneath the livid mark around her neck. A bite mark, like those which had covered Susannah Longden's body. He moved the neckline of her blouse slightly, noticing as he did so that it had been incorrectly buttoned, and saw more of them. He looked at the other side of her neck— there were more marks there too. David

Beynon would tell him more, but he had already realised the terrible significance of this young woman's body, which, in death, might be able to provide answers to the murder of a different young woman.

He checked her pockets. There was nothing on the left other than a lace handkerchief. On the right though there was a small bundle of neatly folded papers which Bucke placed in the breast pocket of his uniform. He would look at these later.

There was a rustling in the undergrowth and a young boy emerged, in a tight cap and shorts, his knees scratched by blackberry thorns and his long woollen socks decorated with wet grass and dried leaves. It was Richard, the young tennis-playing boy he had met when Phillip Bowen's body had been found. 'Oh I say! This is so exciting! Another body! Pappa is going to be so angry about this, you bet. He doesn't like people killing themselves on the estate. Bet this hurt. Can you imagine? Do you think that she did this to herself? Oh my! Why would anyone do such a thing? Where did she get that rope? Is that why you are here? Are you looking for clues?'

Bucke positioned himself carefully between the boy and the corpse.

'This is a moment for quiet thoughts, Master Llewelyn. It is a moment of sadness, for someone who was loved by her family has passed away.' He paused 'Does Mamma know that you are out here?' he asked and watched as the boy avoided eye contact. 'Did she tell you to stay away from this place, perhaps?'

He shrugged. 'We had a bonfire. I told her that I was going to look at the ashes. I put one of my metal dragoons in the fire and I want to see how much is left.'

'She would be upset if she knew you had disobeyed her, wouldn't she?'

'Yes. But I couldn't stay away, not when I knew.' He scratched his head through his cap. 'Do you think she has been here all night? Is she really cold?'

'Now, Master Llewelyn, I will tell you what I will do. If you go back to the house now, I will say nothing about you being here. Our secret. But if I find that you haven't gone straight back, the first thing I will do is speak to Mamma. Do you understand?'

Richard tried to look around Bucke at the body and then, reluctantly, nodded his head. 'I understand, sir.'

'Good. Well off you go. We have an agreement. We must shake hands to seal it.' He offered the boy his hand, who briefly slipped his own inside it, smiled at what he considered to be an honour, and then turned and slipped back into the undergrowth.

Something about the young boy troubled Bucke, though he couldn't say precisely what it was. Perhaps it was a consequence of a privileged background, one about which he had little understanding. Not his problem, not at the moment anyway. He leaned against a tree and looked at the papers he had found in the dead woman's pocket. There were three of them. One was a child's drawing. Beneath the painstakingly written words 'To Mammy' there was a primitive outline of a horse and cart outside a square house with four windows, a door and a smoking chimney. At the bottom there was an untidily written name – 'Eddie.' Bucke found it particularly affecting. There was a scrap of newspaper which appeared to be part of an advertisement for soap. The last was a torn fragment of a handwritten letter in a flowing script.

but it does not mean that I am immune to higher feelings. Do you know Bowood? It is a charming village and I still hope fervently to retire there soon and adopt the style of a country gentleman. The years I

He bent down and checked the woman's pockets again but found nothing more. He stood up and sighed, gently shaking his head. What a cruel waste. He heard something approaching along the drive and put the papers away once more. It was the gardener Mr Whittlestone, who had brought Constable Davies back on a cart.

He had thoughtfully brought with him a couple of sacks in which they could wrap the body to take it back to Swansea.

Whittlestone walked into the clearing and glanced down at the body. 'Found my frogs yet, Inspector?' he asked.

'Our investigations continue,' said Bucke.

'I'll wager they do. But someone takes our frogs and leaves us bodies. The High Sheriff is not going to be happy when he comes back, I can tell you that. Think on, Inspector.'

Bucke nodded, as if taking the warning seriously, and they wrapped the body and carried back to the police wagon as Constable Davies reported his findings. He confirmed that no one in the house knew anything about her— all the domestic staff were accounted for and none of those who had seen the body recognised her as coming from the village. One of the kitchen maids might have heard a carriage of some kind last night but she could not be certain. The body was a long way from the house.

On the way back to the police station, Bucke remained in silent thought whilst Constable Davies chattered on about velocipedes and telephones and other essential improvements to the service. He was sure that in the wagon with him he now had some vital pieces of evidence. But someone else had had to die for him to have it and he owed it to that poor young woman's memory to use it well.

It seemed that today at least, fate was smiling on him. Whilst waiting for Dr Beynon to turn up to confirm the cause of death, Bucke leaned on the counter and watched Sergeant Ball check through the recently received telegraph messages. They found it almost immediately.

'Here we are,' said Ball. 'A message from the police station in Bridgend. A young woman has been reported as missing. *Doris Pulverbatch. A widow. 28 years old. Five feet two inches.* Mind you, that is always a bit of guesswork as far as Bridgend is concerned, in my experience, Inspector. *Black hair. Works in a dairy. Last seen Monday afternoon. Reported by Mother.* What do you reckon? Should I send them a telegram?'

'Nothing to lose, Stan. They can come over and have a look. It isn't far.'

*

She answered the door promptly thinking perhaps that it was someone seeking piano tuition – she still had gaps in her weekly schedule. But it wasn't.

'Good morning, Mrs Bristow. My name is Baglow. I am a reporter with the Cambrian newspaper. I would be much obliged if I could have a few moments of your time.' He smiled, looked her up and down and nodded.

She had seen him watching the house on more than one occasion. He must have seen her last pupil leave.

'How may I help you? If it is musical tuition that you require –

'No, Mrs Bristow, it is not, I fear. I need to talk to you about Inspector Rumsey Bucke.'

Constance's hand fluttered up to her mouth. 'Oh my goodness, he is not hurt is he, Mr Baglow?'

'He is not harmed, Mrs Bristow, but I believe that you will be able to help him out of a particular difficulty that he finds himself in,' he said smiling faintly. 'It may be better if we continue our conversation inside, Mrs Bristow.'

She could not hide the fact that she was concerned but, as she brought him into her rooms, her suspicions began to gather. Rumsey had spoken to her about the reporter and she knew he was being deliberately targeted. She knew some of the things Baglow had written.

'Mrs Bristow, can you confirm that you meet the Inspector privately at all times of the day and night?'

'Mr Baglow, I have now reverted to my maiden name, Miss Constance White.'

'As I understand it, Mrs Bristow, there have been no legal proceedings which have changed your marital status. You are still a married woman -'

'Who has been deserted by her husband, Mr Baglow.'

The reporter shrugged. 'And you see the Inspector here in your rooms. Alone. He visits you in the night. He is seen here early in the mornings. Do you think this is acceptable for a man who is charged with the responsibility of upholding standards of behaviour in the town to be involved in an illicit relationship?'

'Mr Baglow. I take great exception to the improper and ridiculous allegations you are making and I should be very grateful if you would leave my rooms immediately. I wish to hear no more of this. I have a pupil who is already overdue and –'

'My observations of these premises tells me that this is highly unlikely. Your lessons begin on the hour.'

'You have been observing my rooms? Is this what you do? Have you nothing better to occupy –'

'Is it true, Mrs Bristow, that the Inspector has been sharing inappropriate information with you about the cases he is dealing with? It is what people are saying. That could be very serious, Mrs Bristow. You see, I am out to get your lover, the mighty Inspector – and I shall do it. I shall drag his name through the gutters of the town – and yours too, if I have to. You must never forget that I am the press in Swansea; I create public opinion – I do not follow it - and I shall destroy him, utterly. But, of course I don't have to do that. Not at all. And I can be persuaded not to do it, Mrs Bristow. And you can do that. It is your choice, entirely. You are a married woman, as we have already established, whatever lies you try to present to the rest of the world. And I am sure you know what I am talking about. Because, of course, a man will never miss a slice from a loaf that has already been started. Isn't that a fact, Mrs Bristow?' He smirked at her.

Constance said nothing, her mind racing. It was a ridiculous idea, she knew it. How would it stop? It wouldn't. She also realised immediately that she could never tell Rumsey about this conversation, that would be very foolish indeed – but perhaps she could find some way to warn him in a roundabout way about Baglow and his intentions, though she knew that he was already wary of him.

Baglow pushed Constance against the wall of her room, knocking over her pile of music manuscripts and loomed against her, his vile breath turning her stomach.

'Mr Baglow, please. You forget yourself, I think.'

'Perhaps that is what you should do, too.'

He came closer and closer and Constance decided that enough was enough. She poked him in the eyes with two fingers of her right hand. He squealed and staggered backwards, his hands clutching at his face. He banged into the door frame and, as he bounced off it, she grabbed him and twisted him towards the front door. He was unable to remove his hands from his face and Constance managed to pin him against the wall with one hand whilst she opened the front door with the other. She was surprised how strong and energised she felt and then pushed him forcibly down the steps and into the street.

Her neighbour, the portly and jovial Mrs Grove, watched Baglow tumble down on to the pavement. 'Good morning, Miss White,' she said, nodding with approval. 'I see you are busy today, removing filth from your house.'

'Indeed I am, Mrs Grove. It is a wonder how it accumulates.'

'It happens to good folk as well as bad, in my experience.' She put down her large shopping bag and nodded. 'You are a worthy example to us all, Miss White.'

'Thank you, Mrs Grove. I hope Mr Grove's piles are tolerable this morning.'

'Fair to middling, Miss White, fair to middling.' She picked up her bag and stepped around Baglow, who was still crouched on the pavement, clutching at his eyes in the belief that he could stop them falling out. 'The state of our streets is disgraceful. I have a mind to write a letter to the press. I shall be wishing you a good morning, Miss White.'

'Thank you once again, Mrs Grove,' replied Constance, closing the door and then leaning against it in relief. Perhaps hitting Baglow had been a mistake, but she didn't regret it. Who did he think she was?

Outside, Baglow staggered away after pulling himself to his feet, using the iron railings that surrounded the entrance to the unoccupied basement. The blood was roaring in his ears and he was reluctant to remove the heel of his hands from his eyes, for he was sure that they were the only things holding them in place. He felt humiliated, vengeful. What was wrong with the woman? It seemed to him to be a perfectly sensible arrangement; surely a woman should be prepared to go to any lengths to protect her lover from a mauling at the hands of the press and his subsequent dismissal? But Constance Bristow, or whatever she wanted to call herself, had made a choice and he must now ruin her too.

He was hurt and rejected and more determined than ever to bring down everyone's favourite policeman, Inspector Rumsey Bucke.

*

Baglow never managed to report effectively on the murder in Penllergare, but he picked up the news soon enough, brought to him at his lodgings by a boy, running errands for the editor. He spent the afternoon crafting the headline for his latest piece in this week's edition, dabbing frequently at his eyes which were still especially sore. This was now the time for impact, not detail. And truth could continue to wait.

Something rotten at the heart of Swansea.

Prostitution in residential areas ignored

Cruel murder stalks the streets.

Mystery woman hangs herself at Penllergare. Police baffled once again.

Chapter 17

He had been awake for most of the night thinking about the woman hanged in Penllergare. There had been a disturbance on Little Wind Street in the early evening and Bucke had not been able stay too long with Constance, who in any case had to go out to the Beynon's to attempt an improvement in Emily's French - and her own. She seemed rather distracted – which Bucke ascribed to her anxiety over her language skills - and Bucke missed the clarity that she normally brought to his thoughts. He was sure the body was that of Doris from Bridgend and that her identification was merely a formality. He was equally sure that those marks on her body linked her death, inevitably, to that of Susannah. However, even though he had spent a long time considering the papers he had found in Doris's pocket , the break-through, when it came, had been a little embarrassing. Before she left, Constance had looked at them and turned over the soap advertisement, examined the other side briefly, before returning it to him. He had been looking at the wrong side. On the reverse, circled in pencil, was a matrimonial advertisement from the Cardiff newspaper, the South Wales Daily Post.

A young man in business, aged 29, wishes to meet a Christian young lady with means, with view to early marriage. This is genuine. Replies should be sent to *Cupid* at the post office in Llandaff.

Bucke stood washing himself. He wiped his left arm with a flannel and then swished it in the bowl. He rubbed it with the carbolic soap, enjoying its refreshing scent of cleanliness and then wiped down his right arm. His mind, however, was lost in analysis.

She had come to Swansea to meet someone after replying to the advertisement. She had brought with her a drawing by her son to keep her spirits up and part of a reply she had received. Complete speculation, of course, but this was an invention which linked the three scraps of paper in a plausible narrative. Something to go on, and certainly better than nothing at all.

He wrung out the flannel, poured the dirty water in the bowl into the slops basin and replaced it from the jug of cold water he had brought upstairs last night.

And if he was right, then his story could provide a similar framework for the death of Susannah Longden. He knew that she seemed to have been disappointed in love and perhaps she was looking for a new start. This could be the reason she came to Swansea, where she met the same person as Doris, the person who had inflicted those similar wounds. Was he going too far? But the more he thought about it, the more convinced Bucke became. He was sure someone was luring young women to Swansea through that advertisement in the newspaper, and if that was the case, then he had to break into that trap somehow. He splashed water over his face again. There was an anonymity here that he had to dismantle – an unnamed advertisement, secret responses, unacknowledged death. He had to destroy it. He knew about Susannah and Doris. Perhaps there were others he had yet to uncover. Susannah seemed to have been dumped in the Swansea Canal. Where else had bodies been abandoned? Hanging Doris in the woods wasn't quite the same and didn't really fit in, but however incomplete his explanation, he felt that he was making progress.

He looked at the water in the bowl before him. It had been clear, pure, if he was lucky, when he collected it. Now, as he squeezed the flannel, the dirt that had attached itself to his skin and the soap had made it cloudy and scummy. If only he could wash away the wickedness in the town so easily, scrape it off and pour it away and then return Swansea to the pure at heart. He dipped his toothbrush into the dentifrice powder and started to brush his teeth.

As a child his mother had used soot which was cheaper and probably more effective too. He still remembered the taste and the sight of the blackened water he spat out, circulating slowly in the bowl, like a crime spreading slowly through the town.

The idea came to him suddenly, unbidden. He was always baffled by where his thoughts came from. Pure at heart. That was the key. Who was pure at heart? Reverend Rogers? Yes. Constance? Of course. Milo? Ada Gammon? Billy Evil? Of course not. But David and Flora and Emily – and, despite her profession - Sarah Rigby? A contradictory person, sullied but decent in her heart, he thought. And it seemed to him that Sarah might be able to offer him a possible solution.

He smiled, dressed and then carried the jug downstairs, together with the slop basin, which he emptied into the gutter outside.

*

In the early evening, he walked the streets in search of a woman. Down the dark alleys, outside the convivial public houses, their small windows glowing brightly, underneath the flickering gas lamps. It was close to the docks where he eventually found her, down on Quay Parade, sheltering in a doorway from a cold November wind carrying a thin penetrating rain. As he approached, she hitched up her skirt in response to the sound of his footsteps.

'Good evening sir, are you ready to oblige a young lady....Oh I do apologise, Inspector Bucke. I did not realise it was you,' she said, dropping her skirt.

'Think nothing of it, Sarah. It is a bleak night to be out seeking companionship.' He looked up and down the deserted road.

'And there are no gentlemen seeking it either, this evening. It would be better if I was at home,' she said, drawing her shawl more tightly around her shoulders.

'I am sure that you are right, Sarah. But I must tell you that have been looking for you all over the town tonight so I am pleased that you have not yet gone home. You see, I believe that you might be able to help me.'

She looked at him quizzically. 'I will always endeavour to do my best for those who uphold the law and try to protect the ladies of the night whenever they can. So how may I help you, Inspector? I am eager to learn.'

'Information, Sarah. There are things I am sure you know that would assist me greatly.' He watched her face closely in the darkness. 'I see great danger in Swansea at the moment. I fear that innocent people may be harmed.'

She returned his gaze. 'I see. Information is a valuable commodity. It does not come cheap, as well you know. There is nothing I do for which I do not accept payment, Inspector.'

'Oh, I am quite aware of that. Here, Sarah.' He pointed across the road. 'Shall we repair to the Lifeboat Coffee Tavern? We can shelter from the cold for a while whilst we take coffee and you can tell me a story. And then I will contribute willingly to the Rigby Emigration Fund.'

She raised her eyebrows and nodded. He led her across the road and into the warmth and light of the Temperance tavern. There were a couple of solitary sailors there and they had no difficulty in finding a quiet and discreet table in the corner. She removed her bonnet and put it on the chair next to her, running her hands over her hair and around the back of her neck, as if composing herself, whilst Bucke brought over two cups of coffee. She released her hair from its restraining ribbon and shook it out, saying nothing. Then she spooned excessive amounts of sugar into her cup, a luxury she indulged when someone else was paying for it. She stirred her cup steadily in an attempt to dissolve the sugar she had added.

Bucke studied her face whilst she was preoccupied. Hers was a face was lined with cynicism and regret, a face that needed to smile, but rarely did. But he did not know her well; he did not know her deepest thoughts. No one did.

Those dark nights on the streets had changed her view of human nature. She had fierce loyalties to those she believed were decent and honourable, though in her profession she came across few men who were. But Rumsey Bucke was one of them, for he never appeared to judge her. When she looked at him she knew that her life had taken the wrong path and that she could never now chose a different one. But she regarded Bucke as her lost destiny, and in the night when she could not sleep, always asked herself why fate had chosen to show him to her but then to make him unreachable.

'I don't much like coffee,' she said, 'though it does help to keep the cold out. What is it that you would like to know, Inspector?'

Bucke said nothing and pushed a half sovereign across the table. Sarah raised her eyebrows. 'You are particularly keen to learn this evening, Inspector.' She picked up the coin and pushed it into the pocket of her cardigan.

'You came to Swansea from Bristol, I believe, Sarah.'

'Yes I did. I worked as a bar maid in the Antelope, to begin with.'

'And in those days you came across Ada Gammon, did you?'

'I see. That is who this is about, is it? Our Lady of Mumbles?' Sarah lifted her cup and sipped at her coffee, never removing her eyes from Bucke.

'Tell me about Ada Gammon,' Bucke prompted.

'She is a very unusual person, Inspector. And an intelligent one too. When I first knew her she worked the streets around Mumbles. Some called her the Mumbles Donkey – that of course was before she became Our Lady of Mumbles or whatever she chooses to call herself today. She had her own particular gas lamp on Newton Road that she stood beneath. Everyone knew where to find her and no one dare encroach upon her pitch. That brother of hers watched out for her. Brought up by her grandparents, they say. Mother disappeared and she became a wild and unruly girl.' She drank more coffee, wiped her mouth with her sleeve and then pushed the empty cup away from her. 'Then Milo turned up – he'd been on the stage. A mesmerist. Did tricks. Healed people. Spoke to the dead, that sort of thing.'

'And where did he come from, do you know, Sarah?'

'I have no idea, really. I heard he was from Swansea but some said that he came from a family of toffs in Neath, as if there ever could be such a thing. Wherever he came from, it wasn't anything he wanted to parade in front of others.'

Bucke nodded. Her answer reassured him that she was telling the truth. 'Why did he come to Swansea? Have you heard anything?'

'He did something. Or something went wrong. He was a mesmerist – perhaps he hurt someone. I don't know and I've never asked. Came down to Mumbles to hide away. Met Ada. They started in a chapel off Newton Road. The League of Purity. Never going to be popular in Mumbles with a name like that, was it? They are supposed to be married but no one is sure. Some of the girls reckon he has strange appetites but I don't know what they are. I moved away and then he and Ada turned up in the Agricultural Hall, calling themselves something else. I heard that they hadn't paid their rent on their rooms for months, or so they say, but the landlord was found dead. Fell off the rocks in Bracelet Bay. Convenient, I'd call it. Ernest Palmer or something like that.'

'Elliot Palmer, as I remember.' Bucke remembered the case. 'There were no witnesses. He had gone out and left a cup of tea on the table. It had been raining and the coroner decided that he had slipped and fallen.'

'What else do I know? They have at least one house on Pier Street, just round the corner, one of which used to belong to grumpy Old Malachi, bless him. Oh, and Ada disrupted a meeting of the debating and coffee society in the Mumbles Library Reading Room, by holding a séance and declaring that Mrs Llinos Williams was possessed by Satan. Mrs Williams was outraged of course, but Satan was the one I felt sorry for. He must have had a hell of a time.' She sat back in her seat. 'That's about it, I think. If anything else occurs to me, I will let you know. Not much really.'

'Oh no, Sarah. That is really useful. It fills in a lot of background for me.'

Sarah nodded and picked up her hat, ready to leave. 'I think my night is over, Inspector Bucke and – '

'Actually there is something else you can help me with, if you are prepared to do it. A completely unrelated enquiry.' Bucke pushed two more half sovereigns across the table. 'It may not be straightforward, so if you don't want to...'

Sarah raised her eyebrows in surprise. She was undoubtedly interested. He wouldn't offer her such a sum if it wasn't very important. 'You need to tell me more.'

'I need your help. You can read and write, Sarah? That is important.'

'Of course, Inspector. What do you take me for?'

Bucke raised his hands in apology. 'I need to find out about girls who answer matrimonial advertisements in the Cardiff newspapers. I have evidence that two have died as a result – perhaps more. I need to know how they are persuaded to come to Swansea and what happens to them here. Where do they go? Who do they meet?'

'I assume you have made some investigations here in the town?'

'Limited ones so far, Sarah. If I send my heavy-footed constables making a noise around town I will drive whoever it is underground. I need rather to trap him. So it may be dangerous.'

'I see. And what would I be required to do, to earn this money?'

Bucke took from his pocket a page from the most recent edition of the South Wales Daily Post and passed it to her. 'Here. This advertisement. It appears in every edition.'

She looked at it. 'This twenty nine year old business man is destined for a bitter disappointment. I am not a Christian young lady and neither do I have means.' She laughed derisively. 'And so you would like me to reply to this, in an air of desperation, a lonely woman in pursuit of the happiness only a man can bring?'

'Yes, Sarah. You will be the bait in the trap. Once you have made contact, then you will have to arrange to meet. But I will ensure that you are carefully watched and protected.'

'And will you watch me, Inspector Bucke?'

'No, I am too well known. I shall use constables dressed as if for work, once we know where you are going. As I said, it may be dangerous.'

Sarah shrugged. 'I am able to look after myself, Inspector. I have to. It is the path I have chosen, or at least one that has been forced upon me. And my profession is a ridiculous and disgusting thing, Inspector. I know that of course, for I am the one doing it. But please understand, Inspector. I do not do what I do for trinkets and for ribbons for my hair. I do it to stay alive. I am a fallen woman, and now I am unable to be anything else. I have skivvied and cleaned in my time but now I am soiled. Who will have me, who knows anything about me? You are a clever man. Tell me that.' She paused, then without thought, spoke from the heart. 'You wouldn't would you? So I must leave, start again somewhere else. No one will make that happen for me. I have to do it for myself. And so I need money. I will be the bait in your trap, as you put it, because I need to get away.' She picked up her coffee cup and turned it around in her hands as she spoke, watching the grounds circulate slowly. 'I hate this town, life must be better elsewhere. It is a place without care or compassion. Look at Ellen Sweeney, Inspector and what do you see? A hopeless drunk or a lost soul? Tell me.'

'Poor Ellen,' replied Bucke, thinking of the notorious drunk who spent her time smashing the windows of public houses when they wouldn't serve her.

'Yes, poor Ellen. And how many times has she been arrested now? You must know.'

'155 times, I believe.'

'And it is absurd. Surely you can see that? Every time the poor woman is arrested for drunkenness she is imprisoned. But it doesn't work and yet our civic leaders wring their hands and then do exactly what they did before. It hasn't worked on 155 occasions, so it is not likely to work now, is it? But still they drag her through the courts for the entertainment, for the well-to-do to feel good about themselves.' She sighed. 'It is stupid. Everyone says how shameful it is, how she is a stain upon the respectability of the town. But no one does anything to help her. Lock her up and then wait for her to smash some more windows so that you can arrest her for being drunk once more.' She returned her cup to the table, her face flushed with frustration and anger. 'It will keep on happening because there is nothing to stop it.' It was a long time since she had been able to talk to someone like this, to voice all those feelings that she kept contained within her. Who could she talk to anyway? The men who used her? What did they care? 'You have to understand, Inspector. You need to stop chasing the poor who have committed crimes in order merely to stay alive.' She pointed her finger at him. 'Arrest those who make us poor in the first place and make us do these things.'

'These are dangerous words, Sarah.' Bucke was surprised at the ferocity of her ideas.

'But this is how the poor are treated here. Because we are poor and live on the streets, is this what we deserve? Are we really less worthy than those with money? Is a life of suffering what we deserve, simply because of how we are born?' She put her elbows on the edge of the table and pushed her hands into her hair. 'I need to get away from here. So yes, I will do as you ask. If it saves someone from more misery, then it will be worthwhile.'

Bucke was surprised at the torrent that she had unleashed. 'So write your letter, Sarah, and let me know what happens.' He handed her some sheets of writing paper and an envelope. He smiled at her. 'I hoped that you would agree.'

Sarah looked a little embarrassed at her unplanned response and she was not really sure what Bucke thought about what she had said, but she could not unsay it now. She picked up her hat. 'I will do as you ask.' She smoothed the ribbons around it with her fingers. 'Please do not misunderstand me, Inspector Bucke. I will do whatever I can do, to prevent other women from suffering. And I am flattered that you are prepared to trust me like this.'

Chapter 18

They came from Bridgend to identify the body and then to take her home. The responsibility belonged to the vicar and a police constable, for Doris' mother was too distraught to attend and, sensibly perhaps, too concerned with caring for her grandson. The vicar recognised Doris immediately, a judiciously positioned sheet obscuring the angry lesions on her neck, though her relatives would learn about her death soon enough. Bucke thought the manner of her death would be a difficult thing for them to deal with. Doris was dead, and nothing would change that for the family. Was it wrong for them to know she had been murdered, and so leave them with a need for revenge? Perhaps the truth was always better; perhaps the Longdens should have known the truth. He didn't really know what was best. Could anything, in the circumstances of your child's death ever be said to be acceptable? He told the constable how she had been found, that he believed there had been someone else involved in her death, that the inquest had suggested that she had been a victim of an outrage and that his enquiries were continuing.

The constable, in return, offered a little more information about her. She had become an unexpected widow last year and had a small son, Edward. Her husband had been crushed between two trucks in Bridgend station; she now worked in a dairy, churning butter, and her mother looked after the young boy. She had left home, telling her mother she had cause to visit a solicitor in Swansea to discuss a legacy from a long-lost aunt of her husband. She had been seen boarding a train with a small case, had smiled sweetly at the guard. And now her boy Eddie was an orphan. Her life ended; his life changed forever.

Of course, there had never been solicitor waiting to see her, but Bucke did not think it necessary at that stage to mention it to the Bridgend constable. But she had arrived in Swansea the day before she was found hanging. Where had she been? Who knew she had arrived? What had happened to her suitcase? These were his problems and Bucke felt no urgent need to share them with anyone at that moment, though there was a more professional embarrassment that required his immediate attention.

It was very hard for the visitors from Bridgend to get her coffin on to a train, even though the police station was only across the road from High Street Station. There was a huge crowd blocking their way and the whole area was in a frenzied state, the focal point for an enormous excitement that had temporarily gripped the whole of Swansea.

Mrs Theophilus had, at last, been found and everyone had rushed to the station to see her return home in disgrace. Jane Theophilus, landlady of the King's Head Inn in Oxford Street and a mother to thirteen children, had eloped with one of her lodgers, the blacksmith Andrew Seymour. They had been found in Merthyr, detained, arrested and escorted back to Swansea for their prosecution. The thrilling news had raced unchecked around the town, generating remarkable levels of excitement. A mother of thirteen? With a worn and exhausted body? With calloused hands from dragging around beer barrels? A woman ready, in a moment, to quell fights and disturbances in the King's Head Inn? And she eloped with a lodger? A blacksmith? It was the most risible news to have emerged in Swansea for quite some time. But the salacious gossip they had already generated was topped when the pair of lovers had been detained and were required to return in handcuffs to High Street Station. Obviously their relationship had been simmering over a long period of time in secret, but it had suddenly erupted and taken the town by storm. Now everyone wanted to be there to see the train pull up to the platform, to see such unlikely lovers paraded to the police station in shame. It was a free spectacle and few people wanted to miss it.

The straining crowd stood, stretching their necks to catch a glimpse, however fleeting it might prove to be. At least they would be able to say that they had been here. Those at the back were so far away they may as well have been standing outside Oystermouth Castle for all the good it did them. But they felt they were part of a drama they did not want to miss. They could see nothing, but the news was relayed to them by a system of whispers, based on rumour rather than fact. The train has arrived. They have been taken off the train. Jane Theophilus was in tears. Her lover – what was his name? – he was in handcuffs. Tried to make a break for it. Wrestled to the ground. Police constable posing for photographs. They are coming your way. They are in the police wagon. The crowd surged, there were shouts, there was pushing, people fell.

As far as Inspector Bucke was concerned, notwithstanding that the constables were trying to free a coffin trapped in the middle of the swaying crowd, it had been a successful operation. He had arranged for Theophilus and Seymour to be taken off the train, untroubled and largely unnoticed, in Landore and brought quietly up to the police station in a police wagon and on to Tontine Street behind the excited crowd, fighting to see a couple in the station who were not there.

It troubled Rumsey Bucke to see all these people pushing and shoving in a cheering mob. Mocking, laughing. And why? Because two people who loved each other had dared to make real their dream? Because they had something for which they believed it was worth risking everything? He thought back to Nancy Peters and John Rowlands– another couple striving for happiness; in their case they had been punished horribly for it. How could it be that these things were permitted?

He found Andrew Seymour very easy to talk to. He was open and honest and entirely genuine. He had nothing to hide. He had followed his heart and he would do it again. What was the crime in that? 'Do you know what, Inspector? Have you realised? You don't chose who you fall in love with. It happens. To blacksmiths, to landladies, to princes of the realm. To anyone. And when it does, you can't fight it, not to my way of thinking, any road. You can't deny it. It has happened. So what are you going to do?' Seymour was an ordinary man, a blacksmith with no home of his own, who lived in rented rooms and yet in this polished office, often a stage for confessions and lies, he spoke directly to Bucke's soul – follow your heart, he said. Be brave, he was saying and seize your chance, or forever live in the shadows.

Everything he said was reasonable and Bucke respected and admired him, for he had displayed more bravery and determination than he himself had been able to command. But he had more to say too, which once again spoke to Bucke's current concerns.

'You see, Inspector, we could have gone on as we were. We always thought we would. We were quiet about things, like. No one knew about us, leastways not that we knew of. But there was a problem and I had to get Jane away from it. That church, you see. Our Lady of Mumbles. A wicked place, Inspector, never doubt it. Twisted her mind, telling her lies about the end of the world. I mean, Inspector. Why should the end of the world happen in Swansea? Have you been to Newport?' He raised his eyebrows, as if it was impossible to argue with the point he had made. 'They started asking for money, more and more. Jane was having trouble sleeping, worrying what would happen to her kids, like. Not about looking after them or anything. Old enough to look after themselves. No, it was about them dying and the Devil taking them away. And then that Billy Gammon started sniffing round the back yard, looking to get in to the wood yard next door, asking to borrow ladders and stuff, asking me to lend him tools. So I thought, enough is enough. Got to get away, got to set Jane free first, so that is why we run when we did. Could have got away too, but they come looking sooner than I thought.'

His problem, of course, as Bucke knew well, was that they had taken property from the Kings Head, property which Jane was adamant was her own. They had fled initially to Bristol with a feather mattress and a mirror, and Bucke could only marvel at the determination and physical dexterity required to take those two items with them on the train. They were commonplace possessions which, for Bucke, brought home more than anything else the fact that these were ordinary people. But of course, a large mirror and a feather mattress would have been difficult for any couple, however devoted they might be, to hide effectively. Their flight to Bristol had been easily traced.

Jane had believed these things were hers and wished to dispose of them. But they were – like Jane herself – the property of her neglectful husband. He had been wronged. He was the victim. His property had been stolen and someone must pay a price for that.

A disproportionately heavy price too. 'They will send me inside, I know that, Inspector. But it will pass, I know that too. I have done time before,' he said with a smile. 'Thumped a copper, didn't I? In Ebbw Vale. He deserved it too. You would have hit him if he was one of yours, I'll be bound. And Jane has already promised to wait for me, like. Knew she would. But a woman might and she might not. I am not stupid. I know how these things are when a man is locked up. But I could rest proper, even then, even if she didn't wait like she says, just as long as she sets herself free of that chapel and those in it. Liars and cheats, I reckon. That is what you coppers should be dealing with, not them as wants a bit of happiness in their lives.'

Bucke knew Seymour would not be treated lightly. He had broken the taboos. Stepped outside the general acceptance of unhappiness and tried to do something about it. But it was the property that would seal his fate. Jane might have said that the property belonged to her and that she had taken those two poignant items with her as her right, but the Judge would say that they belonged to her husband, David. And so Seymour would be imprisoned for theft — a mirror, a feather mattress and a wife. Twelve months with hard labour, Bucke speculated. If they had got drunk together in the bar and he had killed David Theophilus accidentally, in a fight on the street under a guttering gas lamp, then he would have had a month inside and he and Jane would have been free. Bucke laughed to himself. It was absurd.

The crowd eventually realised that they had been outwitted and stood outside the police station baying and jeering in a generally good-natured way. They did not want summary justice as the crowd often did when there had been a killing or a murder. These people wanted their entertainment, something scandalous that could briefly light up drab lives filled with toil and smoke, nothing more than that. But perhaps there was another truth here too, that they were jealous of the bravery the couple had shown. They had shown that they were ready to sacrifice everything for love, to have the chance to experience such consuming emotion that had passed by most of the leering crowd.

What right did Andrew and Jane have to make a choice that had seemed to have been denied them? How many in that crowd would have shown the bravery to do what they did, Bucke wondered? In a dishonourable world, Andrew Seymour had tried to do the honourable thing, to rescue the woman he loved from something that might destroy her. Once he had recognised what Our Lady of Mumbles represented he had not been prepared to ignore it.

He leaned back in his chair and sighed. Andrew Seymour was an ordinary man who, on his own admission, appeared to have made mistakes in his life but Rumsey admired him greatly for what he had tried to do. There was nothing other than love, pure love, in everything he had set in motion. They had been on the run for ten days, snatching hungrily at the chance to be together, believing in an anonymous life together in a distant town, believing, foolishly it turned out, in a joyful alternative. The world's scorn, their own humiliation and punishment represented a price they were prepared to pay – neither of those things was more important than their love and the chance to dream together. It couldn't really be that simple, could it?

He tried to order his thoughts and get back to business, but the resolve was elusive. Was it any surprise that Sarah Rigby wanted to flee from this small town, which sought revenge from those who sought happiness? Isn't that what he and Constance should do? Just leave this tawdry little town behind them and flee, to start again somewhere else? They would have not committed a crime. No one would come looking for them. They could just leave and show Sarah Rigby how it was done. They could go to Portsmouth or Bristol or somewhere and get on a boat to Australia or South Africa. Ten miles offshore no one would ever know they were not married. They could start again, a new life together. He was sure he would get a job. Others did it all the time. And why wasn't it possible for them? Why was it somehow wrong?

The conversation he had had with Sarah last night chimed constantly in his head for the rest of the day. He had confronted so much sadness in recent days. It was an inevitable part of being a policeman perhaps, but he had been surrounded by those who had lives defined by pain and unhappiness. The Theophilus case hung over him like a black cloud for the rest of the afternoon, a gloom that not even supper with Constance could dispel. Bucke could see that she knew something was wrong and that she was waiting patiently for him to speak. He knew too that he would have to, that he could not keep it hidden. He had to tell her. What if he died suddenly? In a brawl, in an arrest gone wrong? It could happen, he knew that. It would be too late then, when he was bleeding to death in a filthy Swansea alley. They had to leave now, he decided, it was their chance and they had to be together. You had to seek out your happiness and seize it, for no one will ever congratulate you if you do not. His mind was racing. Don't let the moment slip away. Don't let someone else steal your happiness from you. He pushed his chop to one side and put his cutlery down.

'Constance. I have worried all day. About Jane Theophilus. I cannot get the poor woman out of my mind. It has been such a cruel day. A crowd assembled to celebrate her arrest, to mock her and Andrew Seymour.'

'It is so unkind, Rumsey. I can see no earthly reason why the world has taken her unhappiness for their entertainment. I cannot see-'

And then suddenly there was a knock at the window. It was so unexpected, so unusual. They looked at each other. It came again, insistent. Getting louder. And there was a shouting too. A male voice, filled with fear.

'Rumsey! Inspector! Where are you? This is Beynon. Are you there? I need you most urgently! It is Emily! Please!'

Constance ran to the front door and as she opened it, David Beynon fell inside, landing on his knees. He looked up at Bucke, who had followed Constance to the door. 'It is Emily,' he gasped. 'You must come! Someone has taken her! She was there and then she was gone!'

Bucke grabbed his coat and his hat from the stand and jumped down the steps, then pushed his arms quickly into his sleeves. He turned briefly, 'Constance – '

'I shall follow presently, you go on ahead. You are faster than me.' He nodded. They both realised how terrified Flora would be.

'For God's sake, Rumsey! Come on!' pleaded Beynon. Together, they ran off into the darkness.

*

Mrs Morley was walking around the drawing room sobbing and wailing 'Oh my Emily! Why? Who could do such a thing? My Emily!' Flora was in a state of complete withdrawal. Shaking, vacant, vomiting. Constance gathered her up and held her close, but she felt uninhabited, like an empty shell. David Beynon, still breathless from the race down to St Helen's Road to collect Bucke and the return up the hill, was wide-eyed with hysterical rage and terror, desperately requiring action, frustrated at the inspector's methodical assessment of what had happened. The only person who could speak to Bucke with any sense was the housemaid, Edie.

In the evening Emily had gone to the study – to draw she said, as was her habit. No one would have thought anything of it. She had been quiet at dinner, it seemed to Edie, though that too was not unusual. Nothing at all seemed amiss. Until Edie had gone to ask her if she wanted a cup of cocoa and she wasn't there. The window overlooking the garden was wide open. Her outdoor clothes had not been taken, so it seemed that she had gone into the chill evening without hat or coat or shawl. There had been no callers at the door, for Edie would have heard them - one of her duties was listening for the constables coming to fetch Dr Beynon. Tonight all had been quiet. Emily had been there and then the window was open and she had gone.

Bucke examined the study carefully and what struck him most was not what he saw but what he didn't see. There was no sketchbook on the desk, everything was neat and tidy. There was no evidence at all that she had been there. Perhaps she had taken her work with her. But why? He searched the drawers as best he could but found nothing. He needed Constance with him, since she knew the room better than he did, but she could not abandon Flora.

The door to the study was flung open. 'For Christ's sake when are you going to do something, Rumsey? Emily is out there! Somewhere! With someone! It is your job to find her! You have seen what happens to young women in this town.'

'David, calm yourself as best you can. These are terrible circumstances but I know that we will find her. But we need to think about where she might have gone and deploy ourselves accordingly. There is no point in racing around Swansea aimlessly.'

'Find my daughter, Bucke. Now! Before it is too late!'

Chapter 19

Emily had gone and had left no trace behind. Taken or run away? And why? Those were perplexing questions. But what was far more important was finding her, wherever she had gone. All of Bucke's informers had been mobilised, instructed to ask questions quietly across the town. The constables were required to stop strangers, to look in deserted buildings, to listen out for shouts and cries. It wasn't long before the town knew what had happened in Eaton Terrace.

Bucke was frustrated, for he had no clues to work on; that was the hardest part and it made him feel foolish. No one came forward to say that they had seen her; she had left no message or note. The window into the garden had been wide open and in the light of the morning Bucke could see that there was a mark on the grass beneath it to suggest that Emily had turned a heel as she had climbed out. But there was no sign of any other footprints. No suggestion at all that the window had been forced. Bucke was sure that Emily had chosen to leave. But why? There had been nothing in her behaviour in recent days to suggest that her disappearance was imminent. Her parents and Mrs Morley had noticed no change in her behaviour or attitude and neither had Edie nor Constance.

Bucke's greatest difficulties came from the parents. They had now entered a terrible world of perpetual fear and he knew that he could never fully appreciate their emotions at this awful time. But they wanted action, they wanted something done now, in the belief that by doing something – anything - it would suddenly make sense of the senseless and cause Emily to reappear at the breakfast table. David especially, regarded Bucke's careful approach as a reflection of indifference. He demanded the arrest of every male in the town and could not understand why Bucke would not do it. Vigorous questioning with an unusual array of medieval implements would guarantee a confession. His failure to do so made Bucke complicit in what the Doctor was convinced was an abduction.

Constance spent as much time as possible with Flora, who was less aggressive but equally unbalanced by the terror that consumed her. Flora, emerging briefly from her shock, had convinced herself that her daughter had been kidnapped by gypsies, a small group of whom were encamped at Killay. Their caravans should be set on fire and thus Emily would be rescued. Why had not Inspector Bucke taken this eminently reasonable course of action?

But there were no clues at all, no witnesses, no sightings. Just conjecture, based on nothing other than prejudice. But as a result, Bucke's enquiries were deemed to be ineffective and inadequate. It was easier to focus all their horror upon him and by so doing avoid the horror that was squatting in their minds. What else should you expect from an incompetent police force? Beynon let it be known that he was ready to offer a substantial reward for information about her, and arranged for handbills to be printed. It would do nothing to help, Bucke knew that. It might make the Beynon's feel they were doing something, but it would not bring her home.

*

Milo's soft voice was enticing and re-assuring and she was drawn inexorably into those wide eyes that she saw in the mirror. 'Look into the mystery, look into the eyes of God,' he whispered. His eyes were all that she was aware of and slowly she was drifting away, swaying slightly, mesmerised. He laid a gentle hand on hers.

'I can see it now. My poor child. You seem so weak. I fear that the devils within you are consuming your soul. You are being eaten alive. Here. I have a draught for you. Take this and it will ease you. The devils will no longer harm you, I promise you. You are safe here.'

Emily wasn't sure that she wanted to do it but it was so hard to resist. Just a little sip couldn't do any harm. Surely not. And she did not know how to say no, anyway. She drank it and it was sweet, like drinking a strawberry. It was probably quite pleasant but she wasn't sure. More than anything else, she wanted to be back at home.

'You will feel the strength in your veins. Can you feel it? Of course you can. Drink a little more.'

She did as she was told. Her arms no longer seemed to be part of her. Where were they? The room seemed to be revolving. She wanted to speak but she was unsure what to do to make it happen.

'I see that the evil is leaving you. I know it. This is good, Emily. Very good. This is why God told you to come to me. You must now lie down. Here. We have a bed for you. Rest yourself, for now you must be at one with the Holy Spirit who acts through me. I have been charged by God to drive away the darkness from within you, to set you free. All has been ordained by the Lord God.'

He helped her from the chair towards the bed. Her chin was wet. Her jaw felt slack. Now her legs seemed to belong to someone else who had forgotten how to make them work. Then she was lying down and she closed her eyes although even that did not stop the world from plunging into the dark centre of a swirling vortex.

Milo stood by the side of a bed, looking at her young, unsullied, vulnerable body, ready to drive out her demons. He smiled.

The door was thrown open.

'Milo. What do you think you are doing?'

'What do you think I am doing, Billy?'

'You told me that the next one would be mine. I want what is rightly mine.'

'Billy, please. Give me a few moments with her, please.'

'Ada wants you upstairs. Now. A police constable has been round Pier Street, calling at the houses. Looking for her. They knows something, I am sure of it.'

'They know nothing, Billy. Go and tell her that she will be able to take her pleasure soon enough.'

'No, Milo. Ada said. Now. Very insistent, she was.'

He sighed. 'Very well. You must keep her warm for me, Billy.'

Billy grinned. 'Don't you worry.'

'I shall be back.'

'Take your time, Milo. Do what your sister tells you.'

*

The constables had been deployed; the railway station was visited but it sadly produced no news of a young woman departing on any train in any direction; telegrams had been sent. The gypsy encampment had been visited, doors knocked upon and prostitutes questioned but no one seemed to know anything, As the news of Emily's disappearance took hold of the public consciousness, well-meaning Swansea residents asked questions of each other, checked sheds and out-houses and looked beneath market stalls. There were no clues. She seemed to have slipped completely out of sight. David Beynon's offer of a reward for information had sadly provided an unnecessary distraction, with the police station already dealing with a steady stream of chancers and fantasists, each of whom needed interviewing and then escorting back on to the streets.

Bucke knew that he needed good fortune if he was to make any real progress. He needed someone to see her – it was probably his only hope. He stood in thought outside the iron foundry on Waterloo Street, chewing his thumb nail and listening to the banging and the rattling and watching the activity within. He did not want to contemplate the emotional turmoil of finding Emily's body, but he knew that it was a real possibility. His recent days had been full of anguished parents but understanding how they felt about losing a child did not make it any easier for him. A sudden plume of flame from a furnace shone with diabolic intensity for moment. There were shouts and curses and then everything returned once more to grey in the cavernous interior. It was a cold day and Swansea, oppressed by the stained air that hung like a threat in the narrow streets, seemed to have become a reservoir of sorrow, ready to burst. Earth, water and air all poisoned and fire unable to cleanse it.

He walked up to Dermot Rogers' funeral in Llangyfelach in the late afternoon. There were many mourners, for Reverend Rogers was a notable and popular resident. Bucke watched him from a distance across the graveyard. He seemed a lost and bewildered man, unable to turn back time, unable to protect his son, unable ever to see him again. He seemed like a shadow, someone playing the role of a man at a funeral as he had done so many times before, never knowing that he would have to do so in front of a coffin containing his son.

Bucke could not hear him properly, in spite of the wind-tinged silence that enveloped the graveyard around the old picturesque church. Rogers had decided to speak – it was clear that he would not allow anyone else to carry out his duty, his final obligation to the son he loved. Mourners, their heads uncovered, stood in silence as Rogers spoke of Dermot. 'Our town is poorer without such a kind heart in its midst...our community is weaker without his conscientious care and sincerity...his neighbours have lost a genial man of common sense and ability...I am lonely without his love and companionship.'

There was no reason for him to stay any longer. He decided he would go down to Danygraig Cemetery. He could get some flowers and take them to the family grave, where Julia and Anna and Charles rested together, close to the sea. Yes, that is what he would do; he had time before it was dark, if he went now. He hadn't been to see them for a while and he needed to apologise for ever thinking that he might run away from them. Bucke looked around for the final time. There was no sign of Milo, though he never expected that there would have been.

*

In the morning Emily knew what had happened.

She screamed and screamed and screamed. She was in Hell. Where else could she be? Emily knew that what had happened would happen again and again, every day until the very end of time. She could never escape from this place. She was now Milo's familiar, his creature, his concubine. She screamed again.

She was sick, throwing her head to one side, filling her hair, for she was tied to the bed. She was sore, raw, wet. There must be blood but she couldn't see. It was a blessing that she could not remember the details. Emily cried, sobbing with guilt, shame, terror, each convulsion sending rivers of pain through her arms and legs. There was someone standing by her bed. It was a man but she couldn't recognize him and she shuddered in fear.

'You're a bit of a mess, then. If there are still devils in there ready to be driven out, you best clean yourself up first. They love mess, and sick best of all. Never get rid of the buggers,' he laughed. 'I'll go and get some help.'

'No! No!' She closed her eyes tightly, not wanting to see him or her wretched, abused body.

But then the man was gone. And then someone else was there, a gentler presence, who untied her wrists and her ankles. A hand wiped her face gently with a warm sponge.

'Come. Sit up now. The worst is over. Let me clean your hair.' Emily opened her eyes and Delilah, concerned, smiled faintly at her. 'Do you want me to wash you down below? Or do you want to do it yourself? I will leave you, if you wish.'

'No, please. Do not leave me.' Emily bit her lip and shook. 'I want my mother!' she sobbed.

'She is not here. But let me help you, please. I am called Delilah.'

Emily looked at Delilah sensing, in her desperation, that here was contact, a human decency that she must cling on to. With Delilah's help, she forced herself up with some difficulty and looked round her. It was a dismal brown room, dark and grubby. There was no window, only an oil lamp on a battered table. Hell wasn't full of raging fires, Emily thought. It is more mundane, less dramatic, but equally terrible, like a dungeon where she would be shut away from light and hope, forever.

'If you can stand up I can turn the sheet over. It won't look so bad then,' said Delilah. 'It might feel a bit better too.'

Emily looked down at the bed and saw the extensive blood stains. 'Is that mine?' she asked.

'No one else's. But it is done now. Please let me sponge your hair. Cleaning your hair will help, I know it.'

Emily turned round and put her feet on the floor, feeling giddy. Delilah knelt in front of her.

'You are Delilah?'

'That is what these people call me. My mother called me Beryl.'

'I feel sick,' groaned Emily, who started to gasp.

'Here,' said Delilah, holding out her bowl into which Emily retched, and stroked her matted hair. 'He's marked you. He always does. It will fade, do not worry.'

Emily sat back and Delilah removed the bowl and offered her a mug of water from which she sipped briefly.

'I feel awful.'

'It will pass.'

Emily wiped away new tears with the back of her hand and sniffed. She did not want to ask the question but she could not stop herself, even though she knew what the answer would be. 'Will this happen to me again, Delilah. Will it? Tell me it won't.'

Delilah looked away. 'Yes it will, until they find someone new.' Emily sobbed plaintively, shaking, crying away. 'You must not think about it. Believe when it happens that it is not happening to you, that it is happening to someone else. You can deal with it, I am sure you can. If they chose to trouble you, then take comfort, for it means you do not look like me.'

Chapter 20

It was a dispiriting morning. Beynon's desire to expedite the investigations into Emily's disappearance by offering a reward was perfectly understandable – and Bucke wondered what he might have been driven to do if his own daughter, Anna, had disappeared – but it was in fact having precisely the opposite effect. Inspector Flynn had dealt with a series of unreliable and speculative reports from hopeful Swansea residents yesterday and Bucke felt it was only right that he met some to relieve the pressure on his colleagues.

His first witness was Martha Kennedy, who he had last met when she had been arrested and fined for throwing stones in Lion Street. She said she had seen a young girl running down the High Street wearing a shawl and being chased by a man on a horse.

'Why do you think he didn't catch her, Martha, if he was on a horse?'

Martha nodded at the cleverness of the question. 'I think it went lame, to be sure, your honour.'

'And no one else saw this, Martha?

'Sure they were all drunk, sir, as I live and breathe.'

Bucke said nothing, merely raised his eyebrows and Martha left, promising to return, presumably with a better story.

Ellen Sweeney, released again from gaol on the morning of the disappearance, said she saw a girl much like Emily walking along Quay Parade at midnight but since she admitted that she was, by then, slumped in that doorway on the corner with Mount Street, it was a wonder that she could remember anything at all.

Next up was Margaret Railton, who began her statement by asking when the reward money would be paid and whether it would be notes or 'proper sovereigns.' Her reliability was called into question since on that evening she had been arrested for making indecent overtures on the Strand and she was so drunk Constable Gill had taken wheeled her to the police station in a handcart.

By the time Lionel Merriman turned up Bucke was struggling to keep his patience. Dapper as always, with his top hat and walking stick, with his carefully shaped beard and bow tie, he looked like a prosperous, recently retired solicitor. However, as every policeman knew, he was a fantasist. Bucke listened as Merriman explained that he had examined the grass at the Beynon house very carefully and seen clear evidence that Emily had been abducted by the Tylwyth Teg. He smiled indulgently when Bucke indicated that he did not understand. 'Faeries,' he said. 'Or goblins. You must act quickly, before it is too late. I fear there is disorder in the faery world.'

He thanked Merriman for his advice and escorted him down the steps on to Tontine Street to ensure that he did not engage any other busy officers in his conversation. He bid Bucke good morning and then tipped his hat politely at the woman waiting on the pavement, ready to enter the police station. 'Good morning, ma'am. It is a fine morning, a good drying morning I will venture, though we may have rain later, I shouldn't wonder.'

'Good morning to you too, sir. I shall encourage my maid servant to be vigilant, in the light of your advice,' replied Sarah Rigby. 'Her employment hangs by a thread.'

'That's the spirit, ma'am. Don't let the rascal slack,' he replied, as he walked away towards the station.

'Good morning, Sarah,'

She nodded. 'It is strange company you keep, Inspector. Lionel Merriman, the Faery Botherer.

'You know him?'

'Not personally, of course. But Lizzie Thomas tells me that he exposes his manhood beneath the trees in Cwmdonkin Park in the hope of being kidnapped by faeries.'

'Is this really true, Sarah?'

'Without a doubt, but I am not here to offer you free information. I have information that you have already paid for. I have had a reply to my letter.'

They went inside where Sarah was greeted by an old adversary.

'Well, well, well. Sarah Rigby. It has been quite a while, by my reckoning,' said Sergeant Ball warmly. 'Been a naughty girl, have we? Not customary to see you in this parts, is it? Don't worry. We have accommodation for you, never fear. Is there a particular cell that you favour?'

'Your new job suits you, Sergeant Ball. You look well behind the counter, though perhaps not as spry as you once were. But alas, I am sorry to disappoint you. My crimes remain undiscovered. I am here to assist your very own Inspector Bucke in his enquiries.'

'This is the case, sergeant,' added Bucke. 'Miss Rigby and I must talk in my office and I would be much obliged if you would ensure that we are not disturbed.'

'Of course, Inspector. But should you find yourself in difficulties then do not hesitate to call and I shall burst in with my handcuffs,' he said as Bucke closed the door.

'The letter was delivered this morning. It was forwarded to me from the post office in Pyle, the address I used in my reply to the advertisement. I gave myself the name Alice Stapleton. As you can see, my correspondent calls himself George Dorrington, Esq.'

Bucke picked up the letter and looked at it carefully. Then he read it aloud. '*Dear Miss Stapleton. It was with utmost pleasure and with a sense of relief that I received your letter early this morning. You cannot imagine how my heart soared, my trust in human nature suddenly restored when I read your letter.* Hmm. A clever start, I think.'

'Oh yes,' said Sarah. 'But read on. It gets better.'

'*You would be dismayed, I am sure, if you were to read the many letters I have received since circumstances encouraged me to place my hopes in a small advertisement. Yes, it is true that I have inherited a considerable fortune from my maiden aunt in Bowood in Gloucestershire, but it does not mean that I am immune to higher feelings.*' Bucke lowered the letter for a moment. 'He adopts an intimate style – it is as if he has known you for years.' He carried on. *Do you know Bowood? It is a charming village and I still hope, fervently, to retire there soon and adopt the style of a country gentleman. The years I have spent acquiring my own modest fortune here in Cardiff have convinced me that this is how I must spend my future. But I do not wish to live alone and my cousins, with whom my relatives are keen to make a match for me are, frankly, unappealing, their lives as milkmaids rather coarsening their hands, their hearts and their spirits.*' He paused again. 'You see, Sarah. I have seen part of this before. It was written on a scrap of paper in a pocket of a woman we found dead in Swansea. George Dorrington Esq. must write this in all his letters. I am sorry to have to tell you this, Sarah. He is not telling the truth. Oh, and Bowood is in Wiltshire, not Gloucestershire.'

'Inspector Bucke, you are the destroyer of my dreams.'

'But not only a liar. This is a hoax, of course and a cruel one too. But it is worse than that. It is a deadly deception. It leads to despair and death.' He continued to read. '*Someone as honest and unassuming as your letter indicates would be troubled considerably by the hateful messages I have received from those merely intent upon spending my fortune. I was encouraged by the sincerity of your reply at a time when I was at my lowest point.*'

Sarah interrupted him again. 'But my letter said nothing at all from which he could draw such a conclusion. I merely said that I was interested in his advertisement. Should he be telling the truth, I would marry him now, sight unseen. And the others who read it will have wanted it to be true, too. But read what he says next.'

'It would be great pleasure to meet you and by happy coincidence once I have finalised a tiresome, though profitable, business enterprise in Swansea next week I will be free, for a few hours at least, from my obligations. Perhaps you could make the short journey to Swansea so that we could meet? May I suggest that you take a room at the Gloucester Hotel? It is an entirely respectable establishment and, once you are comfortable, I will send one of my people to collect you and we will be able to acquaint ourselves away from the prying eyes of those who wish merely to dispose of my fortune. Please settle the account for the accommodation in the first instance. Such items are a trifle to me and my agent with reimburse you gladly, whether we choose to see each other again or no. But I must tell you, Alice, that I approach our meeting in an extremely positive frame of mind. Shall we say Thursday next week? Please tell me if this is not convenient.' Bucke stopped and his eyes scanned the final few lines. 'Ah. Now I understand.' He resumed his reading. *'An idea occurs to me. Perhaps you could bring with you a trifling sum of money, in cash. Shall we say £50 perhaps? £100 would be even more beneficial. I should like to repay your kindness by assisting you in making a private investment, not otherwise available, which will provide a guaranteed return six times greater than your original contribution. I do feel guilty sometimes about keeping such opportunities to myself, but such is the lot of the lonely single investor. Dearest Alice, would that it were otherwise.'* Bucke threw the latter down on the desk. 'This is very calculated, there can be no doubt, and it must be stopped. Whoever George Dorrington is he is deceitful, cruel and dangerous. And quite likely a murderer too. How many young women have received this letter, I wonder?'

'And so, Inspector, what happens next?' She looked at him, anticipating the answer.

'You must go to meet him, of course. You are the means by which we can force our way into his deception. You must take a room at the Gloucester Hotel in the name of Alice Stapleton.' Bucke paused in thought. 'The Gloucester Hotel. That is not a detail I had expected. You are not known there, are you, Sarah? You won't be recognized, will you?'

'Not to my knowledge. Fred Craven is the landlord and he is not a man to be trusted, so the other girls say. I keep away.'

'I wonder what his involvement is in this? It is a shabby place, more of a public house than a hotel, to my mind.'

Sarah shrugged. 'Perhaps so, Inspector, but remember, I have no money. Fred Craven will ask for money on arrival, you know that.'

'I will give you money, Sarah.'

'And will I be safe?'

'Of course, Sarah. A constable dressed in working clothes will be watching the hotel. When he sees that you have been collected he will follow and then raise the alarm. I shall have officers waiting.'

'And this is to offer me reassurance is it, Inspector Bucke? Constables?'

'Sarah. Your safety will be my most important concern.'

'I hope that it is. I shall do as you ask. And I do it for you. But I do it for no one else and you had better make sure that everyone knows that. Sarah Rigby is many things, but she is not a policeman's nark.'

*

In the evening Bucke and Constance went to see the Beynons. He had to bring them up to date with the case, and whilst he had little to tell them, he had to present it in the best possible light. The house was still in emotional turmoil, its heart ripped out and in its place a yawning pit of despair. For David Beynon, Bucke was a suitable target for his uncontrollable fear.

'Rumsey, it is obvious to me. Why can't you see it? Emily has been abducted by gypsies. It is the only logical explanation. I insist that you go over to their tawdry caravans now and arrest them all. Make them confess. If you won't go, then I will. I warn you, Inspector. I have friends, good friends, with guns.'

'David, please. You have no evidence that she is there. They will not take kindly to your intrusion.'

'For the love of Christ, it is obvious and yet you do nothing!' He kicked a table viciously.

'I have constables watching the encampment. There is no sign of her.'

'Damn you, Bucke! Damn you! Find her before it is too late! We have both seen what happens to young women in this town!'

Flora's sobs stopped for a brief moment then she gasped and cried out loudly in terror. Constance held her as close to her as she could, as Flora's body was wracked by shudders.

'David. Look to your wife.'

'But what are you doing? Nothing!'

Bucke remained calm, but clear. 'You will always think we are doing nothing until we find her. I do not believe she has left the town, at least not openly. No one has seen her at any of the Swansea stations or at any of the other local ones. Think again, for any information, however small, might help us. Did she have any special friends who she might have confided in? Any young men who were sweet on her, that you might know of? Has any money gone missing?'

'What are you implying about my daughter, Inspector? I have told you everything that I know already.'

'Please find her, Rumsey,' pleaded Flora, who held tightly on to Constance's hand.

'Do you think it might help, Rumsey,' asked Constance, 'if we had another look at the study? See if there is anything that we missed when you first looked? The smallest thing might help.'

'We have nothing to lose by doing so,' agreed Bucke.

'There is nothing there, Inspector. You would be wasting your time,' said David impatiently.

'Please, David. Let them look. I just want my little girl back.' Flora slumped back on the sofa and covered her eyes with her hands. 'But let me tell you,' she said, her words fractured by emotion, 'you will find nothing. My baby has no secrets from me. She has been stolen. A witch has taken her.'

'Go ahead, if you must. But please, I beg you, then get back on the streets.' David turned away from them and stared sightlessly out of the dark front window.

Once inside the study, they paused for a moment. 'I never thought that it would be easy,' said Constance. 'I cannot imagine their feelings. It is a terrible time for them.'

'Where do you think she might hide something – a letter perhaps? You spent time with her in here.'

'If she hid things, then she probably hid them from me too, don't you think? If she had a letter from a young man why would she show it to me?' Constance looked around the room. 'When you came last time, did you look inside the piano stool?' She lifted the seat but revealed nothing but sheet music. There was no false bottom, though it was unlikely that Emily could have installed one herself. Together they checked the desk drawers and examined the heavy velvet curtains for secret pockets. Nothing. They lifted rugs and looked under chairs. They moved the heavy bureau and behind it found nothing but dust. Constance sat at the piano and sighed. 'What is there to do?' She laid her hands gently upon the keys, seeking solace in the familiarity of the instrument.

There was no sound.

She looked puzzled and Bucke watched her closely, realizing that something was amiss. Constance tried the keys gently, so as not to disturb or distress the Beynon's. They sounded at either end of the keyboard but in the centre she felt unexpected resistance. 'Rumsey,' she whispered urgently. 'There is something inside the piano.'

They cleared the ornaments from the top and lifted the lid. Bucke reached inside and withdrew Emily's sketchbook. He placed it carefully on the desk. On the front, in a flowing hand was written, *Keep Out! This is the Private Property of Miss Emily Beynon, Eaton Crescent, Swansea.*

Inside there were a number of drawings, perhaps of herself, including one of the naked torso of a teenage girl. There was a passable likeness of Constance, though unfinished. A couple of elaborate tombstones, one of which carried her own name. Towards the end of the book there was one of her seaweed designs, sheltering between pieces of tissue paper. Constance and Bucke exchanged a glance and very carefully Constance lifted the paper and then nodded. The algae had been carefully pulled into letters which read *I am the Alpha and the Omega.*

Bucke closed the sketchbook and put it inside his uniform. It would not help if the Beynon's knew about it now. But he knew now who had her, he was sure of it. But where?

*

He spent a restless night, thinking through his strategy. At one o'clock, unable to still his mind he had walked down to Pier Street but the house seemed deserted. He peered through windows and eventually knocked on the door but had no response. It had been a risky thing to do, but Bucke had no information about where Emily might be and so he had returned to his room. Stay measured, stay calm, stay effective, he told himself. And think, carefully. He had certain knowledge, in his own mind as far as he was concerned, but no evidence. Raiding the house on Pier Street with limited resources at this time of night would likely be unproductive. He had to go to visit Milo himself and see how he reacted. He had no confidence that he would find anything. But he needed to increase the pressure on him – small steps, without provoking something more dramatic like a murder if, of course, Emily was still alive. He needed Milo to know that he was closing in on him, and perhaps pressure someone in the house to give him information in order to save himself. But Bucke also thought it might be worth unsettling him and he had a plan in his mind, which he churned around for a long time in his cold lonely room.

When the dawn finally broke, reluctantly defining the new day it seemed, Bucke walked through the cold and gloom to Danygraig Cemetery. He knew a man. Someone who would do the most unpleasant of jobs. He'd asked him to do things before and as long as he was paid first, there was nothing he would not do. He had once climbed down a garden privy to recover a premature baby, stillborn to a teenage mother on Odo Street, who had thought she just wanted to go to the toilet. It wasn't a task any of the constables relished but Florian did it, quietly and quickly. He was from somewhere in Central Europe and rarely spoke, though there seemed to be no deficiency in his English. He seemed to prefer to keep himself to himself, and Bucke understood that his work as a gravedigger did not require well-developed conversational skills. He always wondered what Florian did for the others who undoubtedly employed him, but decided it was probably better if he didn't know.

Bucke found him outside the cemetery about to start his work, stamping his dirty boots in an attempt to shake off yesterday's mud. Florian was a small man, dark and powerful. He had deep-set eyes beneath a low brow and his thick, untidy eyebrows made him seem threatening and unapproachable. He listened carefully to what Bucke told him, raising his eyebrows in surprise when Bucke gave him a pound.

'The important thing about this is that they must not be visibly damaged, do you understand? Trap them and kill them however you want. But no marks. That's vital. I don't want you using dogs. Is that clear?'

Florian nodded.

'When do you think it will be done, Florian?' Bucke asked.

'It is for you two days. To you I will send a word.'

'Good. I shall meet you here. And no one is to know.'

Florian shrugged, smiled and put his fee in his pocket.

*

'I am looking for a young woman who has gone missing from her home. I wonder if you could help.'

'And why would you think I could help you?' Ada looked at him coldly.

'I am asking many people across the town for information. Anything you might have noticed, however small, might be helpful to us.'

'I know nothing, Inspector,' smiled Ada. 'As Delilah told your constable when he called just recently. I do not understand why you are here. You have lost a girl and cannot find her, but why is that my concern, do you think, Inspector?'

'And your husband? Does he know anything?'

'He does not trouble himself with trivial stories. Please lower your voice. He is in a trance and waking him too soon might have terrible consequences for us all. He will return to us in his own time.'

Bucke looked at him sceptically. Milo had not moved since Delilah had shown him reluctantly into the room. She was not prepared to let him in initially when he had knocked on the door, but he had prevented her closing it with his boot and then walked straight down the hall. She had had no alternative other than to let him into the sparse room at the back of the house. Milo remained leaning back in his chair, his head tilted to the ceiling, his eyes closed.

'When do you think I will be able to talk to him, do you think, Ada?'

'Who can say?' She stared at Bucke defiantly. 'He may he receiving instructions. He may be having a vision. But you must not disturb him. I hope you understand. He is looking into the Eye of God and will stay there until he is released by the Almighty.'

Bucke paused long enough for her to realise that he did not believe her. He was sure that Milo was listening, that this was all an act. 'Is he perhaps communicating with the dead? Do you think that the dead are giving him instructions? If so, have they mentioned a girl, in her teenage years, who has recently joined your congregation? Spoken to you perhaps? Given you money, Ada?'

'Please, Inspector. How am I to know if a girl has joined our congregation? We have so many followers, more join us every day, concerned for the stench of corruption that swirls unchecked around the town, about which you seem unable to do anything. The world is coming to an end and they know that God will triumph and that they will soon rejoice in paradise.' She smiled at him, patronizing him. 'You call me Ada and you do it to provoke me, I am quite sure of that. But I am her no longer. I am Deborah and it is my destiny to lead God's anointed to victory. Those who oppose us will scream forever, beyond the end of time, in flames that will burn but will never consume. This is your inevitable destiny. Unless you decide to join us.'

Bucke looked straight into her eyes, eyes that seemed cruel and calculating. 'Ada, please, I have heard enough of your fantasies. I am looking for a seventeen year old girl.'

'Many men are, I believe.' She laughed at him. 'Listen to me, Inspector. I know nothing of your fantasy. She is not here in this house. You may search it, if you wish. I can ask Delilah to show you around, even to the rooms which we don't use.'

She could be bluffing, considered Bucke, but he was more inclined to believe that she was confident for a reason. If they had her, they were not keeping her in the house. 'If you should hear anything about her, it is your duty to report it to the police. I am sure you understand.'

'I am afraid that your investigation is likely to be overtaken by events, Inspector. The world will end very soon. It would be better for you to prepare yourself for that. I advise you to make your peace with God, through Milo, before it is too late.'

'Concern has been expressed, Ada, about the manner in which you are taking money from your congregation, many of whom can ill-afford it and live difficult lives in unfortunate circumstances, whilst you live like this.' He gestured at the large room with his hand.

'They lack chattels, of course. But they possess wisdom. And they are preparing themselves for the End of the World, as should you. All material things are worthless.'

Bucke ignored her and looked across at Milo who, it seemed, had not moved. 'Before I go, may I ask you where you obtain the paraffin for your lamps?'

Ada laughed. 'Please, Inspector. What a ridiculous question. Who do you think I am? I do not trouble myself with such details. Why should I? Speak to Delilah, if it pleases you. I am sure she can put your mind at rest. There is a chandler's close by. Perhaps that is where she goes. It is of no concern to me.'

He nodded and stood, ready to leave, looking again at Milo, eyes closed, head thrown back, hands grasping the arms of his chair.

'Listen, Inspector. We have a service tomorrow night with our followers. That is why Father Milo is preparing himself. You should come and join us. You will find it most instructive. It will change your life. It might even save it.'

'I shall waste no time in considering your invitation. If you will excuse me, I must speak to Delilah.'

Ada suddenly looked exasperated. 'Oh, I do apologise. I have just remembered. Delilah is out at the market. You can't see her. Some other time perhaps. I am so sorry.' Her insincerity was unmissable. 'Let me show you to the door, Inspector Bucke.'

They walked silently down the hallway to the door, where Bucke turned to her. 'Good day, Ada.' She made no reply and appraised him coolly and opened the door. He descended the steps and then paused. He looked at Ada, then bent down and recovered a tin from behind the crooked crucifix, which he turned round in his hand. It was a Wharton's paraffin tin. '*Safest, Sweetest and Best.*' Ada watched and shrugged then closed the door. When she got back to the room, Milo had not moved but as she sat down, he spoke.

'You should not have invited him, Ada.'

'I am Deborah, remember?'

He dismissed her correction with a languid wave of his hand. 'You should not have invited him. We don't want him prying into our business.'

'He won't come. Even if he does, he will wonder whether what he sees is the truth. Perhaps we will be putting on a show for him - he won't know. He may have informers there anyway. It might be that Satan has sent him."

'How much do you think he knows?'

'It is hard to say. He is suspicious. He has been for a while. But he obviously does not have enough evidence to arrest anyone . Billy tells me that Bucke is not to be underestimated, Milo. The constables are foolish and of no consequence. But we must take care where the inspector is concerned. '

Milo suddenly sat upright. 'We should have eliminated him sooner then, shouldn't we? The vengeance of God or the death of Satan's agent or some other such nonsense.' He sighed. 'Oh, Ada. I am bored with the religious life. It is becoming so tedious. Surely it is time for us to move on.'

Ada looked at him carefully. 'My name is Deborah, as I reminded you just now. The time is coming, Milo. Our time, our destiny.'

Chapter 21

It was late in the following afternoon when Bucke received the message. He was examining the vacuous reports from the constables which contained no news of Emily at all, neither information nor rumour, when a stone was thrown at the window of his office. Then another. He stood up and looked outside. There was Johnny, one of the Hat Stand Gang who gave him a thumbs – up sign. Bucke gestured towards the door of the police station and went into reception. He stood next to Sergeant Ball behind the counter and waited until the grubby boy appeared before them.

'Afternoon, sonny. What is it I can be doing for you?' Ball asked.

Johnny was trying his best to do things properly and so ignored Bucke who was standing right in front of him. 'I gorra message fer the Inspector, Mr Ball. I am to tell him that Florrie Ann has done it and he would be obliged if he was to come down and fetch it. I can take a message back but I don't want to be out of pocket.'

'Thank you, Johnny.' Bucke slid a penny across the counter. 'Tell Florian that I shall be down to see him when the clock strikes five. Do you understand?'

Johnny looked straight back at Bucke and said nothing.

'Well, lad. Do you understand what the Inspector has said?'

'Begging your pardon, sir, but the Inspector is a policeman, Mr Ball. I reckon he has more money than Florrie Ann. He digs graves, sir. And he is foreign. So I don't think Florrie Ann should be paying.'

Bucke smiled and put another penny on top of the first. Johnny screwed up his face but picked up the coins. 'Job's done, Mr Bucke. I'll tell him.' He turned to go.

'Johnny. Have you heard anything about the girl who has gone missing? Emily Beynon?'

'The doctor's girl? There is a reward, Inspector, so we are looking. Let you know if we find out anything.' Johnny paused and then looked slyly at Bucke. 'In Neath, they are saying.'

'Rubbish, Johnny. And you know it. You let me know when you have got anything and I will deal with the reward for you. But don't you or any of the other lads start telling me lies, or I shall come looking for you. Understand?'

Johnny held his gaze for a moment and then left. 'That group of lads is getting on my nerves, Inspector. We shall have to do something about them, soon enough. That is my opinion, any way.'

'Oh yes. I am sure of that but the Hat Stand Gang has its uses at times. They see things that our constables do not.'

Ball sighed. 'I don't like encouraging them, that's all. What has Florian done, anyway?'

'Made something for me, that's all.'

*

There was a strong wind pushing in from the bay, making the young trees around the cemetery shiver, the last of the leaves pulled from the branches and swirling across Kilvey Hill. He pulled his cape more closely around him as he watched Florian emerge from the gloom, pushing a battered but solid long-handled wheelbarrow. This was his time; he was a man made for the twilight, dark and unknowable.

'Here for you I have it.' Florian put the wheelbarrow down on its struts and waited.

Bucke reached down and pulled back the dirty blanket. There is was, exactly as he had imagined it. The Seven Headed Beast. He pulled the blanket back. 'Thank you, Florian. You have done well.'

'And now? What is you want?'

Bucke handed him a pound, once more. 'I want you to take it to an address in the town. It isn't far. This evening, in about an hour or so, as long as it is empty, I would like you to nail this to the main door.'

Florian shrugged, indifferent, unquestioning, amoral. It was a job and he would do it. 'I go now. But the address. To me, it is important.'

*

Bucke's plans however were completely derailed. When he called back into the police station, for the last time that day, there was a message for him from Captain Colquhoun. The High Sheriff of Glamorgan had recently returned from London and, still agitated by the discovery of Doris Pulverbatch's body hanging from a tree in his woodland, had demanded an immediate meeting with the Chief Constable and Bucke. He seemed to believe that unless he intervened, nothing would be done; the professionals obviously needed his forceful guidance and so they were required to attend in the drawing room at Penllergare at 7.00 pm, sharp. Once more, Constance and Mathilde would have to make their own way to Our Lady of Mumbles Chapel, although they both felt perfectly comfortable amongst the crowds that flocked there, particularly since Mathilde had promised that tonight she would ensure her clothes were modest and that her generous curls would be restrained within a bonnet. There would be no jewellery either, for which Constance was profoundly grateful. Mathilde also brought her maid Elodie with her; an additional presence on the way home, one who only the unwise would approach, would give her additional security. Sergeant Ball, naturally aware of Bucke's unexpected appointment, deployed Constable Davies outside the chapel as a reassuring reminder of the rule of law, even as some residents of Swansea awaited the end of the world, though his effectiveness, whether in normal times or when approaching the Apocalypse, was always a matter of conjecture.

There was a huge crush of people standing around the door when they arrived, unwilling to enter the chapel and craning their necks desperately to see the unexpected and unpleasant spectacle. Seven dead rats had been nailed to the door, radiating out from the centre where their tails were entwined and, it seemed, irrevocably knotted. How it had arrived there no one could be sure. A gap appeared in the crowd when the dirty little girl with the pram, who seemed to be a permanent presence at these meetings, moved away after she had seen enough and Mathilde and Constance could see it clearly, 'That is the most disgusting thing I have ever seen,' said Mathilde, turning away. 'I think I feel sick. What does it mean?'

'That there is someone in the town with a disgusting imagination? I really don't know.' Constance looked at the display and shuddered.

Elodie was not impressed either. 'Why is it that anyone would tie knots with those things, I ask you? Using their own 'ands? This is, to be sure, a ver' strange place an' these are ver' strange times.'

Why? What did it represent? That was the question that everyone was asking their neighbour and no one seemed to have an answer. It was a horrible thing to look at, nailed to a chapel door. The impenetrably plaited rat tails resembled the gross mating ritual of obscene worms, a moment of disturbing intimacy no one should ever be required to watch. There was an awful fascination about it, those vile tails, like entrails, locked forever in an indissoluble union. Then a whispered phrase began in part of the crowd which spread quickly, which for some, it seemed, explained everything. 'The Seven Headed Beast.' Suddenly, for those who knew, the Book of Revelation had been made real on the streets of Swansea, Now was the time of the Apocalypse.

Billy Evil, flustered and uncertain, forced his way through the crowd. 'You lot get inside. Milo will be starting in a minute. Best get your seats.' He pulled the rats from the door and threw them in a bucket but he did not break their horrid union.

*

The evening began in customary fashion, with lights and incense, trickery and mirrors. The large congregation embraced the disorientating experience as they always did, the magic and the performance providing an escape from grey and difficult lies. As Constance looked down upon them, it seemed to be a rag-bag army of the destitute and the lonely and the old. But as the service continued she could identify a difference in the atmosphere, a change in Milo's words and approach. When he spoke he seemed more agitated, less visionary and more vengeful. It was, she thought, the first time she had sensed that he felt threatened. He seemed angry and, at times, he rambled – though the substance of anything she ever heard him say had never been as important as the manner in which he said it.

'The town is the midden of the world. It cares not for its young; it cares not for its old; it cares only for Mammon. And so it is doomed. We shall witness the destruction of this nest of wasps, this Babylon. The Angel of the Lord appears in the very heart of the flames that threatened to engulf the town to save a venal policeman. And yet they still do not listen, for the police are the pawns of Satan, those sent here to steal your prayers, to prevent you joining the Militia of Jesus. The Lord can do no more for us. A thick poisoned cloud hangs over the river – another sign for us, for it is foretold in the Book of Revelation. *The waters turned bitter and many people died from the waters that had become bitter.* We have famine; we have pestilence; we have seen the great lights blazing like torches in the sky. The time has come. We know it now, for the Seven Headed Beast has appeared. Now you must follow me to salvation. Do you trust me?' He cried out.

'Yes!' came the response. 'Save us, Father Milo!' someone added.

Constance looked beside her. Mathilde, as always, was lost in the mesmeric atmosphere, quivering slightly, her mixed and constrained emotions finding a desperate release. Elodie however was more detached. She caught Constance's eye, puffed out her cheeks and shook her head. Down beneath them Milo seemed to be sweating more than normal, Constance thought.

'Do not be deceived. Our enemies are everywhere, even here. They move amongst us, evil without mercy. They take on shapes to confuse and destroy, to separate you from God. I know. I have been told. Satan's familiars stalk us. The police arrest me. They try to silence me but they cannot. They wallow in their own depravity, slaves to the Beast with Two Backs. They murder old men, they harry my disciples. They want nothing more than to destroy the Militia of Jesus who they must face on the Field of Armageddon, for these agents of Satan are in terror of their own doom!'

There was a commotion at the rear of the chapel, unexpected, intrusive. At first, Constance could see nothing and then an old man appeared in the aisle, waving his arms and shouting, as people tried to drag him back. He had white hair, with a long untidy white beard and seemed to have a vicar's dog-collar. She could not see his face, but she could hear him plainly. 'Stop this now! Do you hear me, Milo? Do not believe this man! He is a murderer! He murdered his own brother out of hatred and avarice! He lies to you! My son is lying to you!'

There were gasps in the silence that had suddenly descended. Milo was smiling, but Constance felt he was trying to disguise his confusion. Was this really Reverend Rogers, his father, as Rumsey had told her? For a moment Milo seemed unable to speak.

'He is abusing you and your faith. He is stealing from you. He does not speak with the authority of the Lord. He lies!'

The silence exploded into uproar. Those around Reverend Rogers turned to face him, shouting loudly and abusively at this terrible intrusion into their devotional ecstasy. Billy Evil pushed his way through the chapel from the door, still full of the rage and confusion he felt following the bewildering appearance of the Seven Headed Beast, seized hold of Rogers from behind, threw him to the ground and kicked him. He pulled him up and bundled him back down the aisle and then outside. The congregation watched the encounter, fascinated. It was a fight outside a pub which had been suddenly brought into a chapel. It was something they were familiar with and yet they did not feel that they had the right to intervene. It was so shocking, so unexpected.

Milo managed to recover his poise. 'Satan has even sent amongst us his devils in the costume of the church, did you see? Such creatures do not come from the Almighty. They lie, they are here merely to wash away the truth and then wipe away your salvation. This one was one of Satan's most important devils. But together my friends, we have defeated Beelzebub, for that is who it was, The Lord of the Flies. His beard was full of flies – I saw them.'

A gasp ran around the chapel, a mixture of horror that such a one had briefly walked amongst them in human form, and relief that Milo had saved them from him.

'The Lord God preserve us,' whispered Mathilde fervently.

Milo had recovered his poise and the drumming started, softly at first, and the incense wafted through the chapel again. 'However strong we are in our daily struggles, however devoted we are, always remember that there is a greater struggle ahead of us and only together, marching beneath the Spear of Jehovah, will we triumph!'

Ada stood beneath the pulpit and raised the spear above her head in both hands and stamped her feet in time with the loudly intoxicating drums.

Constance peered through the gloom and the thick air, trying to cling on to any shred of reality amongst the mania that surrounded her, looking in vain for the old man. Then the drumming stopped and she watched as six robed figures, their heads bowed, came forward and replaced Ada beneath the pulpit. Constance tried to make out their faces and cursed her position in the gallery, which made it almost impossible to do so. All six of them looked small, spare, vulnerable and indistinguishable. She thought that one of them was trembling.

There was silence in the chapel as they waited for what came next. To Constance the congregation seemed expectant, but also, like her, apprehensive. She watched Milo standing silently in the pupil, allowing the tension to build before he spoke.

'Here before you stand six of our most noble disciples, eager to cross over to join the Militia of Jesus, in preparation for the final conflict. They have disposed of their possessions, for they need them no more and I have prepared for them an elixir which will help them find their way to the throne of God.' There was a communal drawing-in of breath. No one had been expecting this. 'Here before us all, we will witness our disciples' selfless passion for the Almighty.'

A voice, somewhere in the darkness, called out, 'No!' Then Delilah stood before the six, holding a tray on which six goblets stood. 'Don't!' someone else shouted.

'Do not be alarmed.' Milo announced calmly. 'Rather, we should rejoice. This is what the Lord desires. It is what our disciples desire, to be at his right hand, drinking those pure waters that spring from the crystal fountains beneath his sapphire throne. And we will see those things for ourselves as The Chosen Ones, when we join them very soon.'

Constance was horrified at the prospect of seeing six people poisoning themselves in front of her. She wasn't sure that she could watch, but the drama was mesmeric. She heard Mathilde gasp, with her handkerchief crushed between her hand and her mouth. Delilah moved along the line of six, giving each of them a goblet. Some, Constance noticed, snatched at it in a determined fashion. Others were much more tentative but she could see that the carefully prepared narrative required them all to hold the goblet before them and presumably drink from them in unison. As the last figure took the goblet from the tray, the hood or cowl slipped momentarily. There was a ring of dark hair, settled around the clearly defined chin. Constance saw it briefly before the material settled once more and the face disappeared. But it was enough. She was sure that it was Emily – it had to be. And it made the ceremony all the more unspeakable, for she was powerless, trapped at the back of the gallery.

There was silence in the chapel. Milo stood above them, with his arms outstretched. On an unseen signal, the six figures raised their goblets and drank from them. How could this be real? There was a groan around the chapel and Constance found herself, involuntarily, shouting, 'No! Please, no!'

Nothing happened. One of the hooded figures called out 'Dear Lord, take me to thy bosom!' but no one staggered, no one fell. No one reacted at all. There was some confusion in the congregation, but Milo quelled it immediately.

'As I feared. We are not pure enough. That is why our friends here have not been taken. Someone in this room, here with us tonight, is not sufficiently pure. They are feeding their desire for wealth and possessions; they worship Mammon, not Almighty God. All of us need to look within ourselves for our impurities and dispose of all earthly possessions. Whatever we have left, we must surrender to the Lord. Then we can continue to fight the evil. But here, tonight, in the Chapel of our Lady of Mumbles, we have been found wanting and such shame stains our souls.' He looked around the chapel imperiously. 'We have seen the Seven Headed Beast and we know that the Final Battle is upon us. So we must purify ourselves and follow the Spear of Jehovah. Deborah who once led the army of the Israelites is now here with us again. Our Lady of Mumbles will lead you triumphantly into a new world. The shadows of the Last Days gather around us but I have seen paradise, I have seen heaven. I have looked into the Eye of God and he has shown me these things. And I shall lead you to salvation. There will be no tribulation nor distress nor persecution nor starvation nor nakedness and the sword shall sleep forever. For we shall be blessed!'

'Halleluja!' It was a single voice, but it was soon taken up around the chapel. Their relief perhaps at not witnessing a group suicide? Their determination to make themselves worthy for the Lord? It was hard to say. But the drums started again and the six robed figures followed Ada through a door and then suddenly the lights were dimmed and when they were lit again, Milo had gone.

Chapter 22

They pushed their way indecorously out of the chapel, avoiding the men with the collecting buckets. Constance did not know what to do. She knew that she had to speak to Rumsey urgently but she had no idea when he would be back from Penllergare. They had arranged to meet early in the morning but perhaps by then it would be too late. The crowd was dispersing, after an unexpected evening, and it was hard to reconcile their cheery good humour as they left, with the imminent destruction of the world.

The three women stood together for a moment, collecting themselves before they left for home. 'A most astonishing evening, I believe,' said Elodie, before she snarled at the girl with the pram who ran over her feet. 'Cheaper than the Music Hall, and I could see much better.' She turned and nodded a greeting to Mrs Wharton, hurrying past on her way home with Violet.

Constance's mind was elsewhere, her eyes darting about, in the vain hope that she might see Emily or Rogers, but of course, there was no sign. Should she go to Penllergare? How could she do that and not miss him if he had started his return? She feared very much what might happen. She would go to his room and leave him a note. Would that be enough? She couldn't leave a message with the constable. He had already disappeared, chasing a youth who had stolen a man's cap.

'You appear distracted, Constance. I am sure you share my concerns for the unhappy old man who accused Father Milo of murder. He is clearly mad.' Mathilde smiled, impressed by her own generous spirit.

She made up her mind. She would go to his room in Fisher Street. She had never been there but it couldn't be too difficult to find and she could wait for him if he hadn't arrived home. 'I am sorry, Mathilde, my mind has been elsewhere and I need to go home immediately, I fear. Such an exciting evening, quite took my breath away. There is so much to think about. If you will excuse me.'

'But of course. It may be hard to find rest after such an evening, Constance. You should not concern yourself. Elodie and I will be perfectly safe. Good night to you.'

'*Bon nuit*, Miss White,' said Elodie then she turned briefly and said softly, 'I shall get her 'ome safely, do not fear. You too must stay safe, also.'

She watched them leave and walked as if going home, then turned left down Richardson Street and left again on Madoc Street. It wasn't far and the night, though dark, was quiet. Constance was confident that she would be safe, though she did not like the two malnourished dogs shuffling around in the gutter which looked back at her maliciously as she walked past. The streets were badly lit and she remembered reading about some sort of dispute involving the lamplighters, although she hadn't paid it much attention. Now she understood why it was an issue. The town was especially dark and sinister when the clouds scudded across the moon. At those moments she became disorientated, for there was nothing to guide her. There were sudden scurrying noises around her feet; there were high-pitched animal noises. She trod in the thick water of a puddle that smelt like an emptied chamber pot and made her gag, briefly, before she walked on, the miasma clinging to her skirt like an evil cloud. Sometimes there was candlelight through a dirty, ill-fitting and uncurtained windowpane, for which she was very grateful. But her imagination lit the streets with its alarming images more profoundly than any dim lights. So it was with some relief that she turned into Fisher Street. It was, she thought, as dark as the grave – and the unbidden image made her shudder briefly. She needed to have a word with her imagination, she decided, but she still could not see anything. A brass plaque, catching a momentary flash of moonlight, showed the name *Glascodine*, the solicitor. Rumsey's room was close by, she knew that. But where? Was it above the dentist's? Is that what he said? She looked up but there was no light in any of the windows. He was not likely to be there anyway.

What was she to do? It had seemed so easy. It had been a stupid idea; she should go home, find a constable and pass him a message. Then she heard movement behind her and, in her heightened state of anxiety, turned with relief. 'Oh, Rumsey. I am so glad that it is you. Something terrible –'

It wasn't Rumsey Bucke at all; it was the wrong shape. Too short, too thin.

'Evening, Mrs Bristow.'

It was Baglow. 'Dark evening. Late for a married woman to be out and about. Still looking for love, Mrs Bristow? Even though it is so readily available?' He came closer to her.

It was too dark to see him properly, but she could smell him. 'You must have damaged your vision, Mr Baglow. Seeing things that are not here.' Frightened though she might be, she was determined not to show it.

'Your lover deserted you, has he? Or have we had a little tiff perhaps? Come back to settle things up nicely, have we?' He seemed to move closer and she stepped backwards, finding her back against the wall. She wouldn't be able to kick him, not in this skirt and petticoat. She would have to stamp on his foot.

Baglow put his arm out and rested it on the wall by the side of her head. 'You owe me an apology, Mrs Bristow. But I have a forgiving nature. Ask anyone.'

'Mr Baglow. Do not forget yourself. And do not forget what happened before,' she said to summon her courage. He was getting closer and Constance raised her right foot, trying to determine where his might be. She arranged the fingers of her right hand, ready for them to straddle his nose, but his hand reached up and grasped her wrist in anticipation.

'Mrs Bristow, I am sure you would like an opportunity to put things right between us.'

There were footsteps in the dark. Constance had to take a chance. 'Good evening, Inspector.' The footsteps stopped.

'Good evening. And who might I be speaking to?' It was, thankfully, Rumsey Bucke.

'Bugger,' muttered Baglow, who fled away down Fisher Street.

'It's me. Constance.' A sense of relief washed over her as she reached out and held on to his arm.

'Oh my goodness! What are you doing here? Was there someone with you just now?'

'Only one of your ladies of the night, Rumsey. I found her crying in the doorway here. She ran away. Too frightened to speak to you, I imagine.' She was glad it was dark and that he couldn't see the lie upon her face.

He came closer and put his arm around her waist. 'Probably Annie Taylor. There has been a falling out with Eliza Keast, I am told. But that doesn't matter. What are you doing here at this time of the night? This can be a threatening place at times.'

'Rumsey, I am so relieved to have found you.' She stretched up and kissed him. 'I think, no, I am sure. I have seen Emily.'

She outlined what had happened at the chapel. Bucke said nothing, and although his face was obscured, she could sense his attention. He was methodical, carefully assessing the information she gave him. Constance was so relieved to find him and felt proud to be playing such an important part in his work. She told him about Reverend Rogers, describing him, remembering what he had said about Milo.

'Constance, I am sure you understand. There is urgent work that I must do now, but I cannot take you home. There is danger afoot in the town tonight and I would not wish you to be a part of it. You must stay in my room here. I can see no alternative.'

'But that would not be proper.' Constance realised that she sounded foolish.

'As a responsible citizen, your first duty is to obey a police inspector.' Bucke took her arm and led her a few yards back up the street and upstairs to his bare room, where he lit a paraffin lamp.

Constance looked around at the room and was shocked by the emptiness of it. It was like a wasteland. 'Is this your home, Rumsey? Truly?'

'No, Constance. This is where I sleep.' He looked around the room, indifferent, it seemed, to its barren soullessness. 'But you must stay here for a while, until I return and can escort you home. I cannot see any alternative, so I apologise for the state of my room. But I thank you for what you have done, although I cannot say how long I am going to be.' He went through the door, but came back briefly. 'Please make yourself at home, as best you can.' He tried to hide his embarrassment behind a joke. 'I should have mentioned it sooner, Constance. You smell like a gutter.' He tried to smile, then shrugged and left, running down the stairs noisily and away into the night. She looked from the window but couldn't see him.

Constance considered the room where he had left her, a room which seemed unutterably sad. There was a washstand with a dirty bowl and a piece of carbolic soap in a chipped dish which at least gave the room a scent of cleanliness; a chair on which rested what looked like a grubby vest, some cotton drawers and socks. There was a wardrobe, the contents of which she did not think she had a right to explore; a single, untidy bed, with an empty, but soiled, chamber pot underneath. There was an old crust of bread on the small table, beneath which there was mouse trap, as if a mouse could ever find any nourishment here. This was the place to which the man she loved returned every night. She shook her head. This rented room was all he had, someone who gave so much of himself to others and yet saved nothing for himself; this was the place where the man who protected the poor of Swansea passed his quiet hours, alone. As she looked around, she realised that perhaps he had never planned to stay here. He had never turned it into anything other than what it was, because he wasn't interested. Constance wondered if he was punishing himself for the deaths of his wife and his children. He seemed to feel temporary about himself, about everything. Rumsey was a lost man, she knew it.

She dragged the rackety chair close to the window and watched the dark and empty street on to which a squall of rain suddenly fell, lost in her own thoughts in such a dismal, lonely rented room, waiting for the man she loved to return to her.

*

Bucke ran straight to the chapel, blowing his whistle as he approached, wondering who would respond, not aware of who might have been on duty. It was Constable Morris who arrived commendably quickly, together with his lamp and his staff. The chapel was dark and the doors were locked. It seemed empty. They smashed a pane of frosted glass, opened the window and then, once Morris was inside, they worked together from both sides to force open the door. There was a strong scent of incense in the air and the mirrors created unsettling reflections, but at least they magnified the light. They walked together through the rest of the chapel with the lamp held aloft, but there was no one there.

They heard another voice, Constable Crocker, who had also responded. They did not need him to deal with hostility and threats in the deserted chapel, but the additional lamp he brought was very useful. A door opened on to a dark flight of stairs. Down in the cellars beneath, they found two unpleasant rooms. In one of them there was an untidy truckle bed with filthy sheets and ropes attached to the frame at top and bottom. A bowl of dirty water was on a chair. Someone had been here recently, but when, it was hard to say.

The policemen went outside. They knew that the chapel had been used that evening but all those involved had dispersed. They stood together for a moment whilst Bucke explained what he required. Crocker was to guard the chapel and Morris would accompany him to Pier Street.

They ran steadily into blustering showers, their feet echoing along the narrow streets until Bucke stopped on the corner of Little Wind Street. He sent Morris to Somerset Place to watch the back of the house from the garden, whilst he went to the front door. There was a faint light inside and he was sure that if no one was there now, they had only just left. He could not fail to notice that the cross which had dominated the untidy front garden had gone. He banged loudly on the door and waited. He banged a second time. Nothing. Then the door opened. It was Constable Morris.

'No one here, Inspector Bucke. The back door was wide open. Sight nor sound of no one.'

The house smelt and sounded empty. Bucke found a lamp and lit it with some difficulty and then they made their way through the house, casting spectral shadows in pools of flickering light. The house was bare, cupboard doors were open, their contents removed. Attics and cellars were stripped. Milo and Ada had gone and there was nothing left behind. The trail to Emily Beynon at that moment seemed to have gone cold.

Bucke asked Morris to keep the property under surveillance and returned home. What had happened, he wondered? Had they abandoned their congregation because they had milked them of all that they had? Thoughts like that didn't help.

St Mary's had just struck 6.00 am when he opened the door to his room and saw Constance dozing in his chair by the window. Bucke smiled at the uncomplicated simplicity of the moment, a woman waiting for her husband to come home, like a sentimental illustration in a popular magazine. He closed the door and Constance woke with a start,

'Did you find her, Rumsey?' she asked, instantly awake.

'No, I am afraid I did not. The chapel and the house on Pier Street are both empty.'

Constance yawned and stretched, her body stiff from sitting. 'I had such hopes.'

'Come, Constance. Let me take you home. It has been a long night.'

She stood up. 'And no sign of her?'

'None at all.'

'I am sure I saw her there. But the lighting is so deceptive. Perhaps I was mistaken?' She sighed. 'Of course, Rumsey. You may escort me home, in the manner of a dissolute woman. I have a lesson with young George Saunders this morning – George the Piano Murderer. The lessons do not progress well. Tired though I am, I shall not sleep, through fear at what I shall hear.'

Bucke opened the door for her but as she stood up, she looked around the room once more. 'It is an empty room, Rumsey. Forlorn. Unhappy.'

He looked at the separated islands of furniture, like the scattered fragments of a broken vase. 'An empty room for an empty man perhaps, Constance. I don't belong here anymore.'

She wondered where another place might be where he deserved to belong, as he escorted her up Fisher Street, taking the outside of the pavement, protecting her from the worse of the debris in the road. On the opposite side, in a doorway in the early morning gloom, there was the shadowy figure of Baglow the reporter. He lifted his hand to the peak of his cap and pretended to raise it in respect. 'Piano lessons going well, Inspector?' he said softly.

Why was he always watching? seethed Bucke. If Constance had seen him, she did not acknowledge it and her eyes seemed intent on identifying the hazards on the uneven pavement.

Chapter 23

When they got back from the chapel, they put the bound and gagged Reverend Rogers in the attic and locked away their six young disciples in the cellar, who were each left with a piece of bread as an aid to their devotions. They were trembling with an unsettling mixture of apprehension and relief. They had failed their testing. Was this a good thing or a bad thing? Bad, probably. They were not good enough. They needed to try harder. One of the young men, Iestyn from Loughor, asked for a whip with which to scourge himself, and in this way make himself more worthy. He wailed constantly 'I have been weighed in the balance and found wanting!' until Billy Evil whispered quietly and viciously in his ear and slammed the door.

Then they gathered themselves with two jugs of beer around the kitchen table, with the Spear of Jehovah propped in the corner. It had been a long and demanding day and emptying the house and moving next door with Rosser was not something they had planned, but Milo didn't feel that they had much choice. Their concerns about the police interest in them were growing and now he wanted a meeting. They had collected a reasonable amount of money, including a gold sovereign and some jewellery, but Milo was unsettled.

'It is time to move on. Someone is on to us, I am sure. What other explanation could there be for those rats nailed to the door?'

'The Seven Headed Beast?' scoffed Billy.

'That's the one,' laughed Milo hollowly. 'Who put it there? And why?'

'There is a very simple answer, Milo,' said Ada softly. 'This was truly the Seven Headed Beast. It is a sign from God.'

Milo shook his head. 'It looked more like seven rats with their tails knotted together. It is a trick. Someone is mocking us, Ada. That is all it is. It was nailed to the door to trouble us.'

'It was a message to us that would be foolish to ignore,' insisted Ada. 'Please remember, my name is Deborah. Tell me, who would do such a thing? No, Milo it is a sign. One we must see properly for what it is. The time is coming.'

'I agree. Our time is coming. We have had a good run here but, in my opinion, it is time for us to go, to leave. There isn't much more we can do in Swansea.' Milo took a long drink and then wiped his mouth with his robe 'We have a plan. It is time for us to use it. Let's get out. Moving in here will afford us a little more time to set it in motion.'

'Listen, Milo. It is an omen. The end of the world. The Beast came to our chapel door to warn us. He did not go anywhere else. He came to us. God was speaking to us directly.'

'Come on Ada. Don't be silly. It has been a game and it is coming to an end. We always knew that it would and we have plan. You do recall it, don't you? That is why Billy has been working so hard for us. All we need to do, is to carry out what we planned. Ada! You remember, don't you?'

'Of course I do.' She did not sound convincing to Milo. Her mind seemed to be a long way away, lost in thoughts of her own.

'There we are, girl. I knew you did. It is our moment now. This is what we have planned for. We have to move away. Before this inspector gets too close. Anything we can't move we need to get up to the old woman. We can pick it up later. And the cross has been moved, Billy?'

'Of course.'

'What is the state at the pit?'

'All done,' replied Billy. 'I have tidied up the tunnel, bit cramped but safe enough. What do we do about Delilah?'

'She fights at Armageddon,' grinned Milo. 'What are you doing about Violet?'

'Don't you worry about Violet, Milo.'

'I have a piece of unfinished business, I am sure you know.'

'Happy to help.' Billy finished his beer and poured himself another mug. 'Just say the word.'

'And there is a woman coming, too. Bringing money, I hope,' Milo added.

'Ready to help there too. We deserve a spot of relaxation.'

'She comes on Thursday. So we will need train tickets for Saturday. We can lead our Army to Armageddon in the morning and take the train in the afternoon,' said Milo. 'Or Friday.'

Ada broke her silence. 'We have had a message. We should do well to heed it.'

'Seven rats? Each with their own head? Hardly a seven-headed beast,' sneered Billy. 'You worry too much.'

Much later, after they had finished counting out the money from the collection buckets and had sorted through the jewellery to pack away anything that might remotely be of value, Billy looked out of the window, alerted by footsteps. He saw Inspector Bucke going up the steps of the house next door. He heard him banging on the door. 'I shall get one of them policemen, before I leaves.'

*

To lose one policeman, imprisoned for stealing a tablecloth from a washing line in June, was bad enough. But to lose another, Constable Plumley, imprisoned for ten years penal servitude for manslaughter, within six months, was a disaster for the reputation of the Swansea force and Baglow had never been a reporter to waste such a remarkable opportunity. In his writing he raged against the police who *shamed Swansea*. The force was *poisoned by immorality at the highest level*. Emily's disappearance gave him additional material. *Doctor's daughter disappears. Inspector finds no clues. Respectable parents shocked by police incompetence.* Words like *venal, corrupt, indecent, rapacious, sinful, depraved* were now the common currency of the Cambrian. It might have sold newspapers and it certainly raised Baglow's profile in the town. But some people did not like it.

Stanley Ball was a simple, uncomplicated man. He had done well by becoming a policeman. His dependability had ensured that he had achieved far more than anyone had ever imagined possible. When he had joined the force, policemen were regarded with suspicion, an unnecessary barrier to swift, uncomplicated natural justice. He had, though, earned grudging respect on his long, circular beat around Swansea, simply by being approachable and honest. He was rarely targeted by the youths of the town, for there was nothing to abuse him for and there was no reason to mock him. His parents in Skewen, now both dead, had been especially proud of him and his (sadly childless) marriage to Lillian, who he had met in the church where they were still regular members of the congregation, was a happy one.

Without a doubt he knew his limitations, but it was also equally true that he was immensely proud of the fact that he worked with, and was respected by those who were, in his mind, much cleverer and more worthy than he was. He saw Rumsey Bucke as a paragon, as a living expression of the perfect police officer. He admired Bucke's intelligence, his authority, his integrity, his common sense. Any assault upon those virtues, Stanley Ball took as an assault upon those qualities he valued above all other things and therefore as an assault upon himself.

He arranged to meet Baglow at the Dukes Arms in Morriston – a place where he was reasonably confident that he would not be recognised. He had left a message at the Cambrian offices on Wind Street. It had taken him a long time to think of the right words, and then to write them down. In the end he decided to keep it simple. *I have some information about a police inspector in Swansea which might interest you.* That should be enough, he thought, to tempt him. *Meet me at the Duke's Arms in Morriston.* He gave him a date and a time and said that he would approach him in the saloon bar.

It was quite a brisk walk from Cockett where he lived, in clothes borrowed from his brother-in-law, but despite his early departure, when he arrived he found Baglow was already leaning against the bar, looking around him, curiously.

When Baglow saw Ball he raised his eyebrows in genuine surprise. 'Well, my-my. Good evening, Sergeant. What an unexpected pleasure.' He smiled and offered to buy Ball a drink, which he declined with a shake of the head.

'Not for me. Temperance Union. Don't touch it.'

'I see.' Baglow raised his glass to him. 'Very worthy. And am I right in believing that you sent me a note, suggesting that we meet, on account of certain issues that have been troubling you?'

'I did that.' Ball had planned carefully what he would say, anxious that he could extract maximum effect; this was the moment for which he had prepared. Baglow waited patiently whilst Ball composed himself still further. Outside, they could both hear two men arguing loudly about a lame horse.

'I have read your observations in the newspaper with particular interest, Mr Baglow. There are those who are shocked by what you have to say. But not me. I have known for some time that he is not a fit person to be a police officer.'

'I see,' replied Baglow, suspiciously. 'And shall we establish, before we go any further, exactly who this *he* might be? I am sorry to be tiresome, Sergeant. But it is important, for the sake of clarity. Who it is we are actually talking about?'

'Of course, Mr Baglow. I understand perfectly. Inspector Rumsey Bucke.'

Baglow nodded his approval. 'And what is your purpose in all of this? Why are you speaking to me in this way? Is it money you are after? Because if it is...' Baglow chose not to end his sentence.

'Money has nothing to do with it,' said Ball, bristling with sham irritation. 'Some things are either right or they are wrong, as I see it. I cannot abide the idea of the police force being shamed.'

'Well, if you want to talk to me about his relationship with the lovely Mrs Bristow, then I have nothing more that I require, unless you have a photograph of her in expensive Parisian undergarments, signed 'To Rumsey, in deep affection, Constance.' I know someone who sells pictures like that around town, but I have never seen one of a lacy Mrs Bristow.'

Ball could barely contain his distaste. 'I am not here for your smutty talk. There are other things I know. Secret things.' Baglow said nothing, but Ball could see that he had pricked his interest. 'Oh yes. I know where he hides all the property he has stolen, all the things he takes from the houses he visits, all the money. And I can show it to you.'

He could see that the reporter was sceptical but tempted. 'Doesn't he keep all this at home?'

'No. There is too much of it to keep in his room. He has his own secret place. I know where it is, because I have followed him.'

'Really? And does anyone know of these thefts?'

Ball scowled and shook his head. 'They are all at it, but he is the worst. Bucke has been accused before but he got away with it.'

'I didn't know that.'

'No one knows about it. A constable accused him and for that the constable was dismissed. Allison covered it all up.'

Baglow could hardly believe his luck. 'The Chief Constable? The one who had to resign?'

'There is a great deal that goes on that no one else knows about. But I am the Desk Sergeant. I see it all.'

Baglow smiled and took a long drink of beer, wiping his palm across his mouth, thinking. Who would have thought it? This was a gift, landing unannounced in his lap, ready to transform his future. 'And what are these items you want to show me?'

'Jewellery, gold candlesticks is one thing I remember, from a church. Box of gold sovereigns. Furniture.'

'Furniture?'

'From houses.' Ball sighed at the reporter's slowness.

'And so how does he carry it through the streets then?'

'He used to pay Daniel Guy to transport it for him. That is why Guy died in the police cells. I was there.'

'You mean that Guy was murdered? So that he could cover his tracks?' Just when Baglow thought that things could not get any better, there was this. His eyes widened with excitement.

Ball knew that he had him. 'Killed him, dead. I saw the body. He didn't kill himself. Not possible. He was handcuffed to a water pipe.'

'Where is this place, then? Where all the stolen things go?' Baglow was doing his best to sound measured and circumspect, but his mind was racing with excitement.

'In Llansamlet. I can show you. But you best crack on. I reckon he is planning to sell it all soon. He'll turn a tidy profit.'

'And this is not just police station gossip is it, Sergeant?'

Ball looked suitably insulted. 'No,' he said angrily. 'I have seen it.'

'And how did you do that?'

'I took a key, the one Bucke said was his most precious. I found it on his desk when he was out so I took it. I had it copied. Then I followed him. Here it is,' and he placed a large iron key on the table.

He had said all he had planned to say and now he waited to see if Baglow would take the bait. He knew that the journalist was watching him closely but he remained controlled, hoping that he looked irritated at the length of time he was taking to decide what to do. Baglow appeared to make up his mind. He threw back the remainder of his beer and then suppressed a belch.

'And you are sure that you don't want any money?'

Ball shook his head slowly, hoping that he looked insulted.

'Right then. 'Can you take me there?'

'About twenty minutes, if you are up for a walk.' Ball stood up and walked straight to the door. He strode on purposefully without a backward glance, walking like a professional, determined not to engage the reporter in conversation. Baglow struggled to keep up. 'Where are we going?' he called out, but Ball chose not to respond. They crossed the empty Wychtree Bridge, with the dirty river beneath, unseeable in the night, and walked on through the Worcester works. The boundary between the poisoned land and the November sky had disappeared and Baglow stumbled, occasionally unable to distinguish the dark figure of Ball, walking relentlessly. He could sense that they were approaching St Samlet's church, despite the absence of streetlights, past the small cottages wrapped in darkness, save for the glow of an occasional lamp behind a small thick window. Then they appeared to be walking through a bog, their boots squelching and occasionally sticking in the mud.

Suddenly Baglow stumbled into Ball, who had turned round to face him. He scrambled around on the floor to recover his cap.

'We are here,' said Ball tersely. 'Quiet now.'

'Where are we?' asked Baglow breathlessly.

'Tower of London,' he said, smiling in the darkness. He knew that he could tell Baglow anything he liked now, it didn't matter. The truth though, he reasoned, would be easier to sustain. 'Scott's Pit. Locked up. But as I told you, I've got the key. Stay close to me, mind. It is dangerous in there. That is why Bucke chose it. To keep out them as would be unwelcome.'

'But we won't see anything in there! We should come back in daylight.' Baglow was excited, but nervous.

Ball sighed. 'Too many people around in the daytime. Now is the time. Remember, there is never daylight in a pit. I have a lamp. Stay close to me. ' He unlocked an iron gate, which then creaked on its hinges as he opened it and they entered the entrance to a tunnel. Baglow was disorientated, then there was a sudden spark of light from a match and he could see Ball's face, set and determined and rather unwelcoming, as he lit a candle in a lantern, closed its hatch and held it aloft. 'His store is a short distance along this passage, about thirty yards, I reckon. You go first. You'll be amazed.'

'Are you sure it is safe? These places can be very dangerous.' Baglow's voice was shaking.

'Everything will be well. Lead on, Mr Baglow.'

'Let me have the lamp, Sergeant. I can't see properly.'

Ball said nothing, handed it to him and then pushed him forward.

The tunnel sloped downwards, gently at first, and the small pool of light in which they walked seemed to draw them inexorably into the mysteries of the darkness ahead. The walls were wet, with water tricking down from between the stones in the roof. It smelt of mud and moss. Baglow could see a well-worn path in the impacted earth down the centre of the tunnel, with occasional ruts and larger depressions filled with stones. Other potholes were filled with water through which he splashed in an ungainly way. If he got out of this with nothing more than a sprained ankle he would be lucky, he decided.

'How long has this been going on? How long has he been storing stolen property here? Is there anyone else that knows about this?'

'Only that devious doxy of his, but I will answer all your questions later. I should concentrate on your feet, Mr Baglow, if I were you,' answered Ball from the darkness. 'This is the edge of the Llansamlet seam and all the pits round here are wet ones. Floor is always slippery.'

Baglow turned his head but could not see Ball behind him. 'How far have we come?'

'Only a little bit further, I reckon.'

'Are you sure that this is safe?' Baglow sounded frightened now. 'Wouldn't it be better if we came back tomorrow?' The smell of the dank cold of this tunnel reminded him of attending a bleak January funeral and standing next to an open grave. 'Is there something here? Looks like a big hole to me. Is this the pit shaft? I don't know anything about mining.' He took a step back. We have come too far.' He turned to face Ball. 'Either that or we have missed it. Or you are lying? Which one is it, Sergeant?'

Ball said nothing.

'I don't know what you are playing at, Sergeant, but it is not very amusing. I have ruined my clothes on nothing more than a wild goose chase. I would be obliged if you would stand aside and allow me to leave.'

Ball removed his police truncheon that he had hidden inside his trousers and hit Baglow with considerable force on the side of the head. He staggered, shocked and bewildered, dropping the lantern which flickered out immediately. Sergeant Ball still had sufficient visual memory to know where the journalist was standing and pushed him strongly in the chest with the truncheon. He fell backwards into the shaft, silently into the impenetrable darkness. He stood motionless for a few moments, then Ball located the lantern with his feet, picked it up and lit it again, then walked back out into the night.

He locked the creaking gate and thought about what he had done. He might have heard the distant splash of Baglow's body finally reaching the cold water at the bottom of the drowned shaft, but now he wasn't sure. He noticed that the sky had cleared and saw a small new spoil heap in the distance that he hadn't seen before. It felt much colder now. He looked up and saw thousands of stars, each one perhaps an eye.

Was one of them looking at him now? At what he had done?

Chapter 24

The boot boy arrived at 7.00 am and threw his bicycle down outside the door to the police station, his hair damp from exertion and the early-morning drizzle. He had ridden on the rough roads all the way from the Penllergare Estate. He fell clumsily through the doors of the police station to the surprise of Sergeant Ball, who had only just arrived on duty and was hoping for a routine day after his meeting last night.

'Come quick! You have got to come quick! Sir said!'

'Did he now?' Ball was never inclined to accept urgent instructions from red-faced boys, especially those with boots and bare legs splattered with mud. He leaned across the counter. 'And who might sir be, exactly?'

'You've got to come straightaway. There is a man dead and it's horrible.'

'Now, sonny. Steady yourself down and tell me slowly what this is about,' said Sergeant Ball calmly. 'Take your time.'

'Mr Llewelyn sent me, sir. At Penllergare. It is shocking, sir. On the driveway, sir. He's told all the ladies to stay inside but some of them are looking out of the window. I had to come past on my bike. It is terrible, sir. Honest to God. It is like one of them books that has pictures. Honest.'

'You just sit there whilst I get myself organised, sonny. Catch your breath.' The mention of the Llewelyn name and Penllergare suddenly gave Ball's mind much greater focus than it had had when he came to work. He sent Constable Bingham, who was the next to arrive, to fetch Inspector Bucke and then instructed Constable Morris to put the boot boy's bike in the back of the police wagon and then return him to the estate. Morris would be merely a presence, but at least it would look as if they were doing something. It was highly likely, Ball considered, that Mr Llewelyn would have sent a more senior servant directly to the Chief Constable. They best look lively.

The police cart was waiting for Bucke on High Street and he received what little information they had as they travelled, but it could not, at this moment, extend beyond the simple knowledge of a dead man on an important landowner's estate - and not the first dead body in recent weeks either. But nothing could prepare Bucke for what he would find.

They took the driveway at Cadle, decorated with the last of the fallen, yellowed leaves of autumn, and entered the beautiful solitude of the estate. It wasn't far from the streets where the poor lived – perhaps five miles, Bucke speculated - but for those who lived down by the docks or amongst the factories, this place might have well have been on the far side of the moon, for all the relevance it had for their difficult lives. It was no wonder, he thought, that Sarah Rigby expressed such dangerous ideas.

When they reached the final corner before the house, Bucke saw Constable Morris standing by the side of the police wagon.

'I am telling you now, Inspector. I seen a lot in my time, and most things I will do. You know that. Give me a job and I does it. But it has been a long night, I is ready to go home and I am not going near that.'

'Really, constable?' Bucke was surprised. 'There's a problem?'

'Have a look for yourself. It is round there. Then tell me there is no problem.'

Bingham looked at Bucke and raised his eyebrows. If Bonfire Morris wouldn't deal with it, whatever it was, then why should he?

'Come on, Constable Bingham, let's go. We have a job to do,' said Bucke firmly, prompting him to act before he had too long to think about it.

Bingham looked longingly at Morris, who shook his head, before the cart moved off and turned the corner. Bucke could see distant figures looking from upstairs windows but their attention was not on him. They were looking at the man who had been crucified.

It was an arresting sight, so unexpected, so incongruous. Leaning against one of the elm trees was a simple wooden cross on which was hanging the body of an old man, naked apart from a filthy loin cloth. His crossed feet and his hands had been nailed to the cross which was stained with his blood. His wrists and ankles had also been tied to the wood with a dirty grey rope, probably before the nails were driven in. On his head was a circle of blackberry thorns. Bucke took in the oddly-familiar details. It was the body of an older man who seemed to have been whipped at some point. Bingham was staring at the scene before him, slack-jawed in shock.

They needed to be practical, active. 'Morris! Get round here now!' Bucke commanded. 'We need a hand to get him down. Now!' Bucke knew where he had seen the cross before – there was a familiar dirty stain towards the bottom. Apart from that, where else could it come from, if it hadn't come from Pier Street?

It was a difficult thing to manoeuvre but together with Mr Whittlestone, they managed to lower it slowly to the ground and then Bucke could see quite clearly who it was. The beard had been inexpertly hacked off, leaving oozing cuts and grazes all over the lower part of the face but there was no doubt that this was the body of Reverend Rogers and there could be no doubt about who had done it. But why here? Why now? Was it to connect with the previous deaths in some way? Or to repeat the desecration of an earthly paradise? And why crucify him? It looked as if Rogers had sustained a significant head wound and his body bore the marks of a terrible beating. He had been stabbed in the side and there were wounds on his head from the crown of thorns. Milo was responsible for the death of his brother and now for that of his father. But who else had he killed? Malachi? Winnie? Phillip Bowen? Had Milo carried out any of them himself? Or merely encouraged others to do them? Bucke could not be sure but what was the purpose of the stigmata, of such a deliberately staged display? A message to his followers? Or to the police? The final humiliation of his father, even in death? It seemed nothing more than a wicked insult and a vicious, sacrilegious cruelty, framed by hatred.

They untied the ropes and then managed, after some effort, to withdraw the nails from the body using a carpenter's tools from the estate workshop. For Bucke it seemed horribly wrong to use such things to work on the body of a man.

As they placed the body in a sack to take it back to town, Richard Llewelyn appeared between the trees, dodging through the undergrowth in a vain attempt to avoid the eyes of the ladies in those upstairs windows. It was inevitable that he should turn up, thought Bucke.

'Bobby the Boot Boy told me about it, Inspector. It is like a picture from the Bible, he said to me. I had to come and see for myself. It is wrong to my mind that a boot boy can see it but that I cannot.'

'I think you should go back to the house, Master Richard,' said Bucke firmly. 'It is what your Mamma would want you to do, I am sure.'

Richard did his best to ignore him. 'Was he a really terrible man? Or a good man? I mean, they did it to Jesus, didn't they. The Romans. But why did someone do it here? What has Poppa done wrong? I mean, people keep dying here – '

Whittlestone came from the far side of the wagon where he had been helping to secure the body. 'Master Richard, begging your pardon, but you know that you should not be here.'

'Cripes! I didn't know you were here, Mr Whittlestone.'

'That is clear enough, Master Richard. It is for the best that you return to the house, at a run. You know that your mother expressly forbade you to come down here this morning. She could be watching from the window, I shouldn't wonder.'

'You won't tell, Mr Whittlestone, will you? Be a sport.'

Whittlestone raised his eyebrows and the boy turned on his heels and scurried off into the bushes. 'Troubles me, that boy does. Forever talking about death. Keep waiting for him to grow out of it.' He shook his head. 'Strange for a boy who has everything, I can't help wondering. Any road, the body is on the cart. All yours. Rest assured that the High Sheriff will be taking a dim view. He usually does.' He sighed and shook his head once again. 'Best of luck with this one, Inspector. A shocking thing to do. Hope you catch the buggers, afore they do it again.'

'Let me reassure you, Mr Whittlestone. The net is closing.'

*

A cheap suitcase, a borrowed bonnet (without her distinctive ribbons) and a second-hand shawl and she was ready. Sarah was not as confident as she had been originally. Sleep had been difficult to find in recent nights as the realisation of the danger in which she was placing herself became much clearer. Inspector Bucke had made it sound all so easy, so straightforward, and she had been flattered by his request for help. But she would be alone, reliant upon her own resources and the vigilance of unreliable police constables for her own safety. It was time though that she did something for others and, after all, who would mourn her if she were to die? No one. A wasted, impoverished life, defined only by survival. And what was it actually worth? But in this way, at least she would have tried. No one else might know, but she would, and at this moment that was all that mattered. Her courage might be fragile, she realised, but her resolve to try was stronger and, for this brief moment, she could be a different person, no longer a lost soul. And so she walked, confidently she hoped, along Gloucester Place, as if arriving from the station, and up the three steps into the Gloucester Hotel. Before she opened the door, Sarah paused and looked around. Was there really a policeman here, watching her, ensuring her safety? If there wasn't, she had already decided that she wouldn't go in. Then, propped up against the corner of St Nicholas's Church she saw Constable Davies, dressed in the clothes of a seaman.

Is that the best they could do?

She composed herself. He did not have to do much. Just follow her and raise the alarm. What could go wrong? She went inside.

It smelt of stale beer and there was stained sawdust spread haphazardly across the floor. It was faded and poor and the heavily varnished wood seemed to suck from the air the little light that penetrated the thick windows. She put her suitcase down on the floor and stood before the bar, waiting, looking around her with distaste. George Dorrington had described it as 'perfectly respectable.' She wondered what sort of circles he moved in. A well-built man came in through a door behind the bar. She saw his short, dirty-brown curly hair and a generous girth tightly buttoned within a stained waistcoat. She saw his filthy moustache. He may have thought his jacket reflected his proper status as landlord, but if that was his intention then Sarah felt that it failed miserably, for it was thin and torn. This was Fred Craven, the landlord. His reputation for being surly and hostile was something that he had worked very hard to establish.

'Yes? What do you want?'

'A room would be nice. Are you the owner of this place?'

He ignored her question. 'You need to pay in advance. Now. How long?'

'May I ask, have you had other young women staying here?' Sarah thought that it was the sort of question that Alice Stapleton would ask.

'Lots of people stay here. This is a very well-run establishment, clean.' Sarah glanced at an old blood stain on the wall but decided not to comment. There seemed to be raised voices outside.

'I have to tell you that we allow no immorality here on the premises.' Craven looked at her through his screwed eyes. 'Think on. None at all. If that is your intention, then you are in the wrong place. Understand?' He spat into the haphazard sawdust and Sarah looked around contemptuously, as if such an idea was beneath her.

'So, how long? Make your mind up.'

Sarah did nothing to disguise her distaste for the place, which required little pretense. She opened her purse and placed a note on the sticky bar. 'One night would be more than enough.'

'No refund if you has to leave early, like. Got some business in town, 'ave ye? Come to see someone, then?'

Her cold stare let him know that she had no intention of replying. 'My change?' she asked.

He shrugged. 'Haven't got any. Give it to you later.'

'And may I take my suitcase to my room?'

'Not ready. I do it for thee. Here, sign the book.'

He pushed the register towards her and watched as Sarah signed it. Towards the top of the page she saw the only other female name. DORIS PULVERBATCH was written in large clumsily formed capital letters. 'Alice Stapleton, is it? Got someone waiting for you.' He leaned behind him, pushed open the door and shouted, 'She's 'ere.'

Sarah's heart skipped a beat. It really was happening now. It wasn't a game, it was real. Someone was there who was going to escort her to meet a murderer. She swallowed. '*Everything shall be fine. Everything shall be fine,* she told herself. But when the door opened she realised that it wasn't going to be. The person who had been sent to meet her was Violet Lee, Mrs Wharton's housemaid at the Chandlery. She smiled at Sarah, appearing not to recognize her. 'I have been asked to take you to the house, directly. It isn't far. The gentleman is waiting for you there. You are not to worry about your suitcase. Mr Craven here will see to it for you. This way, if you please.'

Sarah swallowed again, as if she had a mouth full of flour and water paste. What was she to do? Violet had not recognized her, but Jeremiah Wharton would know she wasn't Alice. As long as the constables acted quickly she should be safe, she reasoned. Violet opened the door and Sarah paused on the top step, arranging an umbrella over her forearm, desperately buying time, looking at the nuggets of black coal scattered on the floor outside the church. She was sure she hadn't seen them earlier. Violet waited impatiently, with her hand resting on the cold iron railing. There was no one in sight, but perhaps the constables were masters of subterfuge, ready to rescue her in a moment. It seemed unlikely but she held on to the thought all the way to the house. But nothing happened and when Violet opened the door, Sarah knew that she was trapped.

Chapter 25

Constable Davies had watched Sarah Rigby enter the hotel, leaning nonchalantly against the wall of the church. He knew Sarah; he had moved her on when she appeared to be loitering and had once threatened to arrest her – though he didn't like to think too much about that because she had laughed at him. Today though, dressed in borrowed clothes, he felt like a proper policeman. His mother had seemed very proud when he had explained that he was leading a special operation in disguise. She had kissed his cheek and said that he looked the part. And it was easy, too. Just watch, follow, blow the whistle and the constables would emerge and grab whoever it was they were supposed to grab. He wasn't quite sure about that bit, but he'd let the others work that part out.

Everything started to go wrong when the Hat Stand Gang turned up, on their way home after some pilfering around the South Dock, carrying buckets of coal. Naturally they recognized him straightaway. 'Oi! Mutterer!' shouted Alfie. 'Why you dressed like that? You look like a peddler. Is there something going on?'

'You listen to me, I shall have none of your cheek. I am carrying out very important duties for Inspector Bucke, I am. An investigation.'

The boys jeered.

'You lot clear off home, before you do some serious interference with our work.'

'And what work is that then, Mutterer?' asked one of the boys at the back.

'None of your business. Now bugger off Lenny Stretton or you will feel the back of my hand.'

'Is that a fact?' He picked a small piece of coal from his bucket and threw it at him.

'I am warning you! Don't you take no liberties with the constabulary or I shall be taking you in charge.' He sounded feeble, powerless and the gang realised this immediately. They all began to throw small pieces at coal at him as he tried to re-assert a sense of authority that sadly had never been there. Then a piece of coal hit him on the forehead and another caught him in the mouth. The boys cheered. Davies was angry, ashamed and hurt; he advanced in an attempt to grab one of the boys but they easily swerved away. Coal and stones hit him again and then the boys scattered with their buckets, back into the docks with Constable Davies in futile and humiliating pursuit. He never had a hope of finding them in such a complex environment and the boys enjoyed his impotence, hunting him down and throwing things at him from their hiding places, driving him backwards until he was trapped against the door of a timber store. When he could take no more, he blew loudly and repeatedly on his whistle. The gang scattered of course, their entertainment curtailed, but the constables arrived with expectations of their own, followed by Inspector Bucke, tired after a restless night of worry, but energized by the prospect of success. They surrounded the shed and Bucke stepped forwards and ripped the door open. It was dark, it smelt of pine, and of course there was no one there.

'Where is Sarah Rigby, Constable? Who brought her here?'

Davies nodded. 'I expect she is still in the hotel, unless she has left.'

Bucke was briefly confused.

'I was being attacked, Inspector. I feared for my life. The worst kind of villains too. Hidden.'

Bucke chewed his lip. 'Constable Davies. Where is Sarah Rigby?' Davies shrugged. 'Was she ever brought here, to this place?'

'Not whilst I was in Gloucester Place. I was very vigilant.'

'Damn you Davies! Damn you!' He grabbed him by the shoulders, shook him and then pushed him through the open door of the timber store whilst the other constables looked on.

He ran across the dock towards The Gloucester Hotel. Bucke was angry with himself for choosing to deploy Davies. He should have known it would be a disaster, even if the task had hardly been a difficult one. The operation was over, he knew that, but he had to get Sarah out of the hotel and to safety. He needed to think of a new plan – for he would effectively be exposing his suspicions about the hotel to everyone and thus might never catch the murderer. He hadn't found Emily; he might have lost Sarah; Milo and Ada seemed to have disappeared off the face of the earth. Things were not going well.

But when he walked breathlessly through the door of the hotel there was no one there. Bucke saw the hotel register on the counter and turned it around. He saw that Alice Stapleton had taken a room. Perhaps she was still playing her part in the trap they had laid, but where was she? Was she still in the hotel? He saw the printed name of Doris at the top.

'Put that down, pal. Now. If you have got any sense.'

He turned to face the man who was standing behind him, with an unpleasant pipe-stained moustache and who was pointing a gnarled and polished piece of wood – a substantial and twisted length of tree root – directly at him. 'And I would put that down too. If you have got any sense. I am Inspector Rumsey Bucke of the Swansea Constabulary and I am looking for a young woman called Alice Stapleton.'

'Why? What's she done?'

'And you are?'

'The landlord here.' He lowered the weapon slightly. He looked wary, apprehensive.

'So, Mr Craven. Where is Miss Stapleton? She has signed in. She has paid for a room.' He tapped the register. 'I am very anxious to find her.' His mind was racing. He had to stay calm, if he was going to get the information he needed, but he did not know how much time he had.

'She went out. I don't know where. Why should I?' The policeman knew his name and that unsettled him.

'Straight away? It cannot have been long since she booked in.'

Craven shrugged, wondering how much he knew. He went behind the counter and put his piece of wood out of sight. 'She has gone. Anything else I can do for you?' Bucke said nothing and held his gaze, sensing that Craven's confidence was fragile. 'Don't often have any policemen in here, Inspector. This is a respectable establishment. No short measures. No immorality of any kind.'

'I am pleased to hear it. When Alice Stapleton left did she appear concerned? Anxious? Or content, do you think?'

'I don't know. Don't know the girl. She signed the book and then she went.'

'And what about her belongings? Did she take them with her? Or did she leave anything behind. A suitcase perhaps?'

Craven looked down nervously at the bar. 'She didn't have nothing with her. She just went straight out, like I said.'

'Where is her suitcase, Mr Craven?'

'She didn't have a suitcase, Inspector.'

'You are lying, Mr Craven. Alice Stapleton brought a suitcase with her. Where is it? Did she put it in her room?'

'She never went to her room, Inspector. So it can't be there. And she didn't have one anyway. As I told you.'

'Did you take it from her? Did you offer to take it to her room for her? Did you steal it? I don't have a great deal of time, Mr Craven, and I might be inclined to invite the constables to take you to Tontine Street.' Bucke went on quickly, determined not to give Craven any time to think. 'You must understand, that I am especially concerned about the Gloucester Hotel. Young women disappear when they come here to stay. So as you can appreciate, this is no trifling concern. Far from it.'

'I don't know what you are talking about, Inspector, so if you will excuse me…'

'Look here, in the register. Top of the page. Doris Pulverbatch. You see the name? She was murdered, Mr Craven.' Bucke flicked back a few pages. 'Here, Susannah Longden. Murdered. Did you not notice? That they had gone? Didn't you think it strange that two young women should disappear like that – take a room and then not use it? Did you report them missing? What happened to their possessions, I wonder? Did you keep them in case someone came to collect them on their behalf? You didn't sell them, did you?'

'People are peculiar. Not my place. They paid, then they left.'

Bucke flicked back through the register until he found what he was looking for. 'What happened to this one? Thomasina Wenlock?'

'Never heard of her,' he said unconvincingly. 'When was that, anyway?'

'Your register says it was the end of September.'

'Don't rightly recall. People come and go. It is a hotel.'

'The day after she booked in, a young woman died beneath the London train in Hafod. A terrible mess that was. Constables had to collect the pieces. And Thomasina Wenlock has been reported missing by her family.'

'How do you know it was the same girl? If she was such a mess.'

'I don't, but I do know about these two here, Pulverbatch and Longden . They took rooms and then they died. Please don't tell me that it's a coincidence, Mr Craven. And we now have another young woman staying here, alone, and no one knows where she is. I think I have a right to be concerned. Can't help suspecting that you are somehow involved.' He pressed on, bombarding Craven, taking away from him any opportunity to consider his responses. 'Did any of these young ladies leave anything behind? Books? Letters? Any clothes?' Bucke saw how uncomfortable Craven looked.

'Not that I know of,' he replied.

'And never at any time did you think that you should inform someone about what, now, may be four women who have arrived here and then disappeared? Three of them are dead.'

Craven shrugged. 'Am I responsible for all my guests then? I didn't know they had disappeared. Why should I?' He tried to summon up his own courage. 'Wouldn't it be better if you were out looking for that doctor's daughter then, instead of wasting time in useless questions in a respectable hotel?'

Bucke leaned across the bar to him, close to his face. 'All three of those girls are dead, Mr Craven. Didn't you hear me? All three. It is murder, no question. There might be some difficult questions for you to answer. You see, at the moment, you are the only link that we have got. You and this hotel. And now another young woman has booked in and we don't know where she is. Or who she is with. Or what is happening to her.'

'You best find who is doing it then,' he replied dismissively, but Bucke could see that Craven's confidence was crumbling.

'You see, Mr Craven, I am a simple policeman and I have to start somewhere obvious. It is all I can manage. Nothing complicated. I deal with the obvious. Which in this case, means here. Means you. You might be the last person to have seen Alice Stapleton alive. You might have been the last person to have seen

Doris Pulverbatch alive. Or Susannah Longley. Or Thomasina Wenlock. Are there any more in this book of yours? After a while you see, Mr Craven, it stops being a coincidence. You understand my difficulty, I am sure you do. I will take this register with me, if you don't mind. Have a look at the names. ' Bucke smiled at him. 'My advice, for what it is worth? Have a word with a solicitor. It won't do any harm. Before things get out of hand. You see, the press is always so much happier if there is an arrest. Gives them something to get angry about. I am frequently impatient with them, my friend. They like to make things up, in order to sell newspapers, and they do like a local murder, a story they can worry at and pick apart over a few weeks. A landlord arrested on suspicion of murder? Names, addresses, illustrations, portraits, special editions? Would be very popular.' Bucke turned over the pages of the hotel register in a deliberately casual way, as if he were admiring the handwriting. Then he looked up and raised his eyebrows. 'Where did Alice go? Did she leave on her own? Did someone collect her?'

Craven stared over Bucke's head at the door. 'Perhaps it was an old friend. Same age, I thought. I didn't ask. They left together.'

'And who was it?' Craven looked uncomfortably around the bar. 'Alice Stapleton's life might depend upon your answer.' Bucke paused. 'So might yours.'

'It was Violet Lee, the housemaid at Wharton's Chandlery.'

'If you are lying you will be handcuffed and marched through the town to the cells before lunchtime.'

'It was Violet. She said she had been waiting for her.'

Bucke turned on his heel and ran from the bar, taking the three steps in one jump and ran down towards Cambrian Place. The constables, loitering outside the church, watched him idly, standing around and shaking their heads in wonder in the energy of their inspector who turned at speed towards the East Burrows. What could possibly be so important that an inspector should choose to run in that way? They followed – they thought it wise – but not quite so fast.

Bucke knew this was his only chance to redeem himself. He had asked Sarah to help him, had put her in a dangerous position and then been unable to protect her as he had promised. He hoped he wasn't too late. He paused at the door to the Chandlery, just long enough to wave at the constables to suggest a vague deployment around the building, before he crashed through the doors.

'I will be with you now, in a minute,' said Enid Wharton from behind the counter, where she was busy re-arranging bundles of candles on a shelf.

'Mrs Wharton, please…'

'She turned round. 'Why, Inspector. Please forgive me. This is an unexpected pleasure. What can I do for you? Constance well, I trust?'

'I am looking for a girl, Mrs Wharton. I believe she has been brought here.'

Her face drained of colour. 'Oh my God. What has he done now?'

'A girl, Mrs Wharton. Where is she? Her circumstances might now be extremely dangerous. She was brought here by your house maid, Violet.'

'My husband is not at home, Inspector. He is meeting with a sea captain at the South Dock. He isn't here.' Bucke saw the relief on her face when she realised that Jeremiah was not in any trouble, at the moment anyway. 'He has been gone most of the morning.'

'And he went to see the captain alone?' His mind was racing, throwing up possibilities of abduction and slavery, of girls attacked on boats and thrown into the dock. 'He did not take a young woman with him?'

'Certainly not. I would not have allowed it. No one was brought here, to my knowledge. I fear you may be mistaken, Inspector.'

'And where is Violet? I need to speak to her urgently, Mrs Wharton. Urgently.'

'Of course, Inspector. I shall call her for you.' She was clearly unsettled by Bucke's agitation. 'Violet is upstairs, resting since the shop is so quiet. She complained of a head ache and went out for a powder from Moses the Chemist. She has been back a while now. And she did not bring anyone with her. I would have known.'

Mrs Wharton called upstairs, whilst Bucke paced around the shop, unable to contain his anxieties.

'Inspector Bucke, is there anything I can do to help? You seem nervous and unsettled,' said Mrs Wharton gently.

Bucke tried to smile, but failed. 'I apologise, Mrs Wharton but...' He stopped and turned as the door to the house opened. It was Violet.

'Why are all them constables outside? They look foolish, Mrs Wharton, trying to hide in the timber yard like...' Then she noticed Inspector Bucke.

'Where is she, Violet?'

'I am still unwell, Mrs Wharton,' said Violet, shakily. 'I think I might go back upstairs.'

'Where is Alice Stapleton, Violet? Tell me.' He took a step closer.

'I don't know what you mean.' Her eyes were flickering around the shop, looking for safety, but there was none. 'I need to go back upstairs. I am going down with something.'

'Alice Stapleton, Violet. You collected her from The Gloucester Hotel. Mr Craven told me. And then you took her somewhere. Where was that? This is really important. Her life is in serious danger. Where is she?'

Violet lowered her head and screwed up her lips like a child, determined never to part them again in her life. She squashed her hands together until the knuckles turned white.

'Violet, speak to the Inspector,' said Mrs Wharton firmly. 'Did you go to the Gloucester Hotel and meet the woman? Did you take her anywhere?' There was no response. 'What have you been doing?' Still Violet said nothing.

Bucke looked across at Mrs Wharton. 'I shall have to take her to the police station for further questioning. I am wasting time here. I do not know when she will return, if at all. If we cannot find the girl, then this could become extremely serious.'

Mrs Wharton sighed. 'I understand, Inspector. I am sorry-'

'I didn't do anything,' Violet suddenly blurted out. 'I didn't do anything wrong. I just took her to the house. Like I done before. Gives me tuppence. It isn't hard.'

'And who asks you to do this, Violet? Who gives you the money?' Violet looked up and shook her head. Bucke exhaled, loudly. 'And how many times have you done this, Violet. How many times?'

She shrugged, as if it wasn't important. 'Five? Six?'

'Six!' exclaimed Bucke. 'You have taken six women from the Gloucester Hotel?'

'Can't remember, rightly.'

'Where do you take them, Violet? This is your last opportunity to tell me. Some of those women are now dead, Violet. They were murdered. Did you kill them?'

'Please, Violet,' pleaded Mrs Wharton. She laid a gentle hand on her forearm. 'Tell the Inspector the truth.'

'I take them to meet Father Milo and Billy gives me tuppence.'

'And that is where you took Alice Stapleton, is it? To see Milo and Billy?'

'Yes it is. She said she was going to see a man called Dorrington but really she was going to join the Militia of Jesus.'

'And where did you take Alice? Which house did you go to?' Bucke leaned forward expectantly.

'Not Father Milo's. Mr Rosser's house. The one next door.'

*

Once she stepped inside, the door closed behind her and she was alone. She looked around her. This was William Rosser's house, Swansea's self-proclaimed oldest teetotaler, an old man notoriously confused. The stairs to her left seemed to be leaning away from the wall and the floor of the hall was uneven, its contours inadequately covered by old rugs. There was the stale smell of fish.

The door to the left opened and Milo came out of the lounge, smiling generously at her. He was not dressed in his familiar robe; instead he was wearing a smart, dark double-breasted jacket with a silk paisley waistcoat and plain cravat. She had not anticipated that George Dorrington was a pseudonym for Father Milo. He was a man of costumes and he was murdering women, according to Inspector Bucke, this man with a shadowy past, and she was alone with him. At least he did not appear to have recognized her.

'Miss Stapleton!' He clasped her hands in his. 'George Dorrington. I am so delighted to meet you. It has been a desperately tedious morning and your visit has been my only hope of salvation. Please come in.'

He stood aside and took her into the room. It smelt musty, as if it had not been used for a while. It was crowded with furniture, claustrophobic and dark. 'Please sit down, my dear.' The antimacassar felt damp.

'How remiss of me! I do apologise. I have been abandoned by my staff today and sometimes I do not remember how to proceed. Here, let me take your coat and hat. Isn't that what is supposed to happen?' He laughed. 'To be frank, it is not something I need to do normally.' He took them and threw them on to the table. Sarah saw a mirror, resting on what appeared to be a music stand.

'Thank you for inviting me,' she said, wondering where the constables were. 'Your house here appears well appointed.'

Milo nodded. 'It has some advantages, not least because it allows me to speak directly to some of my solicitors and bankers. By the way, you did bring the money, didn't you? I am eager to enable an investment for you. But you see, as you look around the room, that it needs the touch of a woman to turn it into a home. I give it so little of my time. I should take a break from merely making money.' He paused. 'I hope you have brought cash. A bankers draft might cause an unfortunate delay.'

Sarah wasn't sure how to respond. The house was neglected and tired. Better, of course, than where she lived, but hardly appealing. 'The house has a certain charm.'

'Indeed, Alice. You don't mind me calling you Alice do you? We seem to be getting on so well. There are a number of very interesting objects here. Look at the mirror, for example. I could not help but notice that it seems to interest you.' He picked up the music stand and placed it in front of her. 'So fascinating, I find. Those symbols are cleverly etched, don't you think? Here, let me get you something to drink.' He went to the sideboard and poured a small glass of a thick red syrup. 'Here, Alice. Try this. A relaxing tincture. Entirely safe and particularly reviving. I am sure you will enjoy it. I had a glass moments before you arrived.' He smiled again. 'We are getting on so well, aren't we? Look into the mirror and admire these rather clever designs.'

Milo stood behind her and she was aware of how he focused his eyes on the reflection of her own. His eyes seemed to grow in size, drawing her in. 'How pretty you are,' he said softly. 'So lonely and so neglected. All I could ever have hoped for. Take a sip, Alice. Let the liquid warm your heart.'

She found it hard to pull away her eyes and raised the glass to her lips. Sarah knew she should not drink it, and yet it seemed impossible to resist.

There was a knock at the door.

'Damn,' muttered Milo and he turned to the door. Sarah, released from those eyes in the mirror, recovered herself and quickly tipped the liquid into the aspidistra next to her. She blinked desperately trying to clear her mind.

'Ah! I see you have enjoyed your drink. It has special properties, my dear Alice.' He laid his hand on her shoulder. 'Special properties indeed. You shall be released from the earth and soar into the air.'

There was another knock at the door and this time it opened. 'Please leave me,' said Milo. 'I am otherwise engaged.'

'Listen, Milo. Ada wants…'he paused. 'Well, well, well,' said Billy Evil. 'Sarah Rigby, as I live and breathe. And what are you doing here, my lovely?'

'Looking for a rich man stupid enough to marry me,' she said defiantly.

'No, you are not. You? Marry? Who would have you? You have been put up to this, haven't you?'

'You know her? Do you, Billy?' Milo was suddenly alert.

'Oh yes. Sarah Rigby, an old piece of mutton from Mumbles, isn't that right?' He bent down and twisted a curl of her hair and tugged it.'

'Who sent you here?' asked Milo.

'Your advertisement. You know that perfectly well, Mr Dorrington.' She desperately tried to cling on to the illusion. 'I am just a woman trying to change her life, that's all. I changed my name, for discretion.'

'You lie,' said Billy calmly. Then he slapped her across the face. 'You have been put up to this.' Sarah was determined not to flinch, but she could feel herself shaking.

'Do you think they are on to us, Billy?' asked Milo.

'Without a doubt. That is why she is here. She has been sent; the officers might be close behind. Don't think she has drunk her glass either, Most unneighbourly, I'd say.'

'That's right,' Sarah tried to defy them. 'The constables are gathering around the house now. I saw them,' she said desperately. 'You should surrender yourselves.'

Milo twitched the net curtains at the window and shook his head. 'Oh dear, Alice. How sad. No one there. You have been fooled, my dear. The police are not your protectors at all. You are lost and forgotten. Such a shame.' Milo leaned over her and ran his hand down her red cheek and then, cupping her chin, tilted it up to him. 'In the twilight I am sure you could be almost attractive.' He sighed. 'Oh well. We have to stop her going back to the police, for that is clearly who sent her to us. A clumsy deception that would have fooled no one. They have abandoned you to your fate. How cruel they can be.'

'Leave her with me, Milo.'

'Of course. But don't be too long, Billy. We need to be gone.' Milo went to the window again. 'There is no one there. But for how long? Best not take any risks, eh?'

'Don't worry so much. Billy's work, this is. What I am good at. You go and tell my sister what's going on. She wanted to see you, anyway. I will tidy up round here.' He smiled at Sarah. 'Isn't that right, my old love?'

And then she was alone, in a small room in a strange house, with a grinning Billy Evil.

Sarah's mind was racing. She knew she had one chance, but only one. Her chosen profession had always dictated that she should never take to the streets unarmed. It had become second nature to her. Expect the worst and be ready for it, and always know the best way out of anywhere. Today was no different. But she also knew that there would only ever be that one chance, and there were two closed doors between her and the street outside. She also assumed that no one knew where she was, that there would be no dramatic rescue. She had to fight on her own or surrender and wipe away all those hopes and dreams that had sustained her through all her vile nights. She wasn't going to do that. Even if she was to fail, she was determined not to go gently into the darkness. And no man ever hit her and got away with it.

Billy Evil was intending to enjoy his work, she could see that. Perhaps he would be less vigilant, she hoped. He pulled her from the armchair and began to push her around the room.

'Talk to me! Who sent you? Were you being followed?'

'Go to hell.'

'You are already there.' He pulled a knife from his belt. 'Take your dress off. Now.'

Sarah lowered her head, looking compliant. Her hands went up to her neck and she began to unfasten the buttons on the back of her dress. She glanced up beneath her hooded eyes, withdrew the hat pin that was buried in her hair and stepping forward stabbed Billy Evil in the face. He screamed and staggered backwards whilst Sarah dragged open the door, pushed passed Delilah, who did nothing to stop her, and ran the short distance down the hall. If the front door was locked then she knew she was dead, but the key was in the door and, as Milo came running down stairs, shouting, she managed to turn it and throw herself down the steps.

Chapter 26

She ran.

She knew she had to get away from the quiet streets and into the safety of a crowd and even though her mind was in turmoil and terror, part of her was quite methodical; there was an obvious place to go.

Sarah listened for running footsteps behind her but heard nothing. She ran across Adelaide Street, right in front of a horse and cart. The driver shouted at her and she heard his whip crack but she ran on, over the tramway, slipping but thankfully not falling in something unpleasant and on to Quay Parade. She turned right and moulded herself into the small crowd waiting to cross the river into St Thomas. She had no half-penny with which to pay but to be pursued by a constable for non-payment of the toll would have its advantages. She panted, catching her breath and tried to remember those terrible moments in that overcrowded lounge that had happened so quickly, She decided that her main regret would always be was that she had missed Billy Evil's eye and instead stabbed his cheek. She looked back, bravely, expecting to see a blood-spattered Billy Evil bearing down on her, but there was no sign. She shuffled forward with the crowd and then when a gap appeared in front of her she ran through it, past the collector and across the bridge, to amused laughter and cheers.

Now what?

She was sure that Billy was not behind her. But where would she be safe? She leaned against a cold brick wall at the corner of Inkerman Street, feeling drained. Could she really trust the police, for they had effectively abandoned her? Was it an accident? Or had she been tricked? What if there were men amongst the police force who were part of Milo's congregation? She had never been sure who she could trust and now she felt more vulnerable than ever. She could either go back across the bridge or walk up the valley and cross the river on the ferry boat in Hafod. Sarah spent her life alone, but this was one time when she really did need help. She needed to speak to Rumsey Bucke.

A man was walking steadily down Fabian Street. His boots were muddy and a rake and a shovel were protruding from the wheelbarrow he was pushing. He stopped in front of her. 'Hello, Sarah Rigby. It is for you unusual to be here on this side of the river.'

'You don't know how unusual it is, Florian. Are you going over the bridge, by chance?'

He looked at her, said nothing and raised his eyebrows.

'I need to get back across the river and into the town. But I do not want to be seen.'

Florian waited for a moment. 'It is that you are in trouble, Sarah Rigby?'

'Oh yes, Florian. Serious trouble. Can you help me?'

'You see, Sarah Rigby, I am needing money to help you, even if you are my friend.'

'I will give you money, Florian, when I have some. But I have none now.'

Florian's mouth moved, as if he was smiling. 'I am to trust you, Sarah Rigby. You are finding the money for me, I know that this is true. It is being too much small but it is all what I can do.'

He took the tools from his barrow and pulled out a dirty piece of oilskin. The bottom of the wheelbarrow held mud, twisted weeds, and clumps of wiry roots. Sarah looked at it with distaste and Florian shrugged. She knew she had no choice.

*

Bucke deployed the constables carefully on Pier Street with a plan to storm the house in a dramatic rescue. Every second was important but it was not something you could attempt without a plan, no matter how rudimentary it might be. He sent two constables round the back of the house and chose Morris and Gill to help him break down the door. Others would follow them in, deployed to search specific floors. He need not have bothered. As they prepared themselves for the assault, the door opened and William Rosser came out. He was initially surprised to see the police but seemed happily vacant about what any of it might mean and ready to enjoy the unexpected entertainment.

'No one here, see. All gone. Very busy here. I have seen all this before. I am 356 years old. Well, not now, but I was before. Enoch they called me, then. Our Lady told me. Knows a great deal, she does.' Bucke closed his eyes and then turned to instruct his men to search the house, though he was not hopeful. He had not found Emily and he had lost Sarah. The discovery that Milo was implicated in abduction and murder was scant consolation. The incompetence of the constables had terrible consequences. He looked up at the grey sky whilst Rosser waited empty-eyed for something to happen.

'Did Milo tell you where they were going?' Bucke asked.

'Said they were going to Judea. Said that I should stay here. Wait until they came back. Long way, Judea.'

'And has Milo been here today?'

'Oh aye. You've just missed him. Him and Billy. Be a while until we see them again, I reckon. Said he was going to Judea. Too far for me.'

'I see.'

'I mean, don't get me wrong. I used to walk there all the time. Never a problem. Can't do it anymore. Much too far.'

Bucke found Rosser's obsession with a past life rather tiresome.

'My sister lives in Judea you know. Not as old as me, of course. Has her own teeth. I've seen 'em.'

'I am sure.' Bucke turned away as Morris came out of the door, shaking his head. 'No one there. Blood on the rug in the front room. Could be anything. Nothing else to see.' Bucke turned back to Rosser. 'Has Milo been here alone, Mr Rosser?'

'Oh no, officer. Very busy here. Mind you, I haven't seen the old man for a couple of days now. Not as old as me of course. But not seen him. They put him in the attic. The others in the cellar, they went yesterday. Or the day before. Don't rightly recall. They were very irritating. A woman wailing, a young man wailing. Glad they have gone. Look, that big cross has gone. Just right for knocking out my pipe too.'

Bucke wished him good day and assembled the constables. With little hope of success he sent them off to find out whether anyone had seen Milo, but he felt deflated. He now knew that Milo was at the heart of everything but he still had to find him. He had killed before, and repeatedly too, and was quite likely to do so again; whilst he believed that Milo still had Emily, for whatever reason, he still did not know where he was. And, of course, where was Sarah?

*

She waited on the other side of the street, plucking up the courage to approach the door. It took her a long time. This wasn't her life and never had been. This was not where she belonged. Through her profession, Sarah had turned her back on this world. But she did not know what else to do or where else to go. Florian had delivered her discreetly to the back of the Argyle Street Chapel, from where, filthy and cramped, she managed to walk as unobtrusively as she could along St Helen's Road. She needed to see Bucke but had convinced herself that the police station was not safe and she expected Billy to come looking for her, so she could not go home. She knocked on the door. *I must apologise most sincerely… Please forgive me…* Word combinations formed and dissolved inside her head. *It regret my intrusion…* but when Constance answered, all those words deserted her. 'Is Inspector Bucke here? I need to see him urgently.'

'Are not you Sarah Rigby? I am so glad that you are safe. Rumsey told me all about his arrangement with you. I think you are very brave.' Constance was neat and unsullied, after a day at the piano. 'You look exhausted, Sarah. Please come in.'

'I just need to see Inspector Bucke, that is all. I shouldn't be here, I know that. This is not a place for me.'

'Rumsey isn't here at the moment. But if you are here, then he must be out somewhere looking for you. Don't you think it would be a good idea to wait for him here? I can send a message.'

'Well, perhaps I better go and look for him. I am sorry to have interrupted your afternoon.' Sarah was embarrassed. 'I should not have intruded.'

'Nonsense. Please come in, Sarah. You need to rest. Let me get you something.'

'Thank you, Miss White , but –'

'My name is Constance. Now, Sarah you must come inside.' Sarah was getting confused now. This was not at all what she expected.

'Thank you, but I must not intrude. I am not the sort of person you would wish to have in your house. And I am filthy, too.'

'Let me be the judge of that,' Constance said firmly. 'This is my home and you will come inside. I no longer care for what people think. So many of them are wrong.'

'But it might be dangerous for you.'

'And if that is the case then it will be dangerous for you to loiter in this way on the streets. If you cannot go home, for whatever reason, as I suspect, then you will come inside. We shall face danger together.'

'But I am dirty, and my clothes are torn.'

'You smell like a garden, yes I know. Please come inside, Sarah. It is a cold day and your cheek is very red.'

Sarah bit her bottom lip, for she was unaccountably on the edge of tears. She walked inside and Constance closed the door behind her. Sarah sighed with relief.

In the end they decided only a bath would do and Constance positioned it in front of the stove in the kitchen. When she had boiled copious amounts of water, using every part of the stove, she left Sarah and took away her clothes. They could probably be saved but it would be a long job for a laundry woman. She could borrow one of her dresses and then perhaps tomorrow, if it was safe, they could visit the Second Hand Clothes shop.

Rumsey Bucke turned up of course, believing when he arrived that he had come to unload his anxieties and failures on Constance, dreading tomorrow when he would see Sarah's body dredged from the dock. Instead he waited with Constance in the drawing room, whilst Sarah finished her bath. The weight of the day had lifted from him when he knew she was there and when he saw her, fresh from the bath (which he had agreed to empty) he saw a different person, someone whose face was less troubled, less angry, less wary, someone comfortable in her borrowed clothes.

They ate bread and cheese and Bucke listened carefully to her report of her day. Constable Davies was a liability as he already knew, Craven was venal, turning his head away from the fate of those young women and receiving in payment the unimportant contents of their cheap suitcases, Billy Evil was, well, just evil. But Milo was at the centre of it all and that understanding added to his anxieties about Emily. She was probably still alive he thought, but tracking down Milo was the same as finding Emily. At that moment he wasn't sure where to begin.

Sarah could not go home, that was certain. She would have to stay with Constance. She protested of course, but both Rumsey and Constance insisted. Sarah would sleep on the small threadbare sofa. It might not be so comfortable but it had the important advantage of being safe. No one knew where she was, but other people knew where she ought to be and if an injured and angry Billy Evil wanted to find her, he would easily discover where she lived. To be on the safe side, Bucke promised to position one of his more reliable constables on St Helen's Road. After all, he needed to protect an important witness.

Constance took Bucke to the door and, before she opened it, he kissed her slowly and with real tenderness. 'Thank you, Constance. Your kindness is a true blessing to all those around you and I love you, more than I ever thought possible.'

She put her finger on his lips and looked deep into his eyes, then she smiled. 'I wonder if Sarah realises how much she saves me from myself tonight.' She opened the door and the cold air of a clear, cloudless November night made both of them shiver. There was flash in the sky to the east, a long trail of light that ended in a bright ball of red fire. Perhaps there was sound too, but there on St Helen's Road they could not hear it.

'You see, Constance, the stars shine their brightest for you, and at your bidding they lighten up the sky. A shooting star, a comet, a meteorite – whatever it is, has happened because you light up the world.' Bucke's voice was trembling with emotion.

'Don't be soft, Rumsey. It was nothing more than a rocket.'

*

The brooding figure of Billy Evil walked down Kilvey Hill, his job done. It didn't really matter how many people saw it. It was a sign to those who needed it. He had other more pressing issues to address. Somewhere Sarah Rigby was hiding and the idea that she might get away with what she had done was gnawing away at him, the pain in his cheek that reached into his gum a constant reminder of what she did. He paused to look down at the town in front of him. He had looked for her in her usual places earlier but she wasn't there. He would go back and search again, but he wasn't confident. Milo had been right – they didn't have time to chase her, for the police might have been close by – and they had fled from the house. But he wished that she had not got away so easily. He was annoyed with himself, for being too lax and not locking the door properly. All that he needed to have done was to have locked the door and to have taken out the key. He touched the puncture wound on his cheek. It was sore and weeping. He did not like loose ends and Sarah Rigby was something he might not be able to tidy up. There was nothing to stop him coming back though, in disguise, in a couple of months. That thought brought him a hint of satisfaction.

 He started to walk again. He really wanted to kill a policeman, it might settle his mind, but as he stepped around the spiky strands of a gorse bush he decided that he would go to visit William Rosser instead. He had seen too much – and, more importantly, who knew what he could remember? And anyway, he had just had an amusing idea…

Chapter 27

The discovery of a crucifixion in Penllergare had failed to ignite any interest in the press, about which Inspector Bucke was surprised and puzzled. He waited for Baglow to turn up at the police station but there was no sign. It would appear that Tontine Street was not an appealing place at that moment. Understandably perhaps, David Beynon was not willing to examine the body of Reverend Rogers and had refused to attend the inquest. He was spending his days walking the streets, asking strangers if they had seen his daughter and demanding meetings with the Captain Colquhoun to rage against the incompetence of the police. Whilst he spoke in detail to Colquhoun about the progress of their investigations, Bucke was more circumspect when speaking to the doctor. He was quite likely to interfere and parade accusations around the town.

At mid-morning Bucke called the constables together in the hope that by talking together they could somehow find an unconsidered piece of information which might reveal where Milo and Ada were hiding; Swansea was a small place after all. Constable Davies was not invited. Instead Bucke sent him off to settle Sarah's debt with Florian from his own pocket. It was the least he could do.

As the rest of them began to gather, Constable Morris put his cap on the counter and leaned across it. 'Did you hear?' he asked. 'That reporter, whatsisname, he's disappeared. No one knows where. They asked me at the newspaper office when I come past. Landlady hasn't seen him either. With a tart, I expect.'

'Good riddance,' replied Sergeant Ball, shuffling papers as casually as he could manage. He had rehearsed such a conversation as this in his mind many times over the past few days. 'Something like that was always going to happen,' he added nervously.

'Something like what?' asked Morris.

'Well, if you go round upsetting people, writing lies, one day you won't be able to live with yourself. Do yourself in out of guilt. That is what I think. We'll never find the body.'

Inspector Bucke looked at him with furrowed brows. 'Why do you say that, Stanley?'

'Obvious.' Ball swallowed. 'He's realised that he has got it all wrong and...and...' He wasn't sure what to say next.

'So you reckon he has done himself in?' asked Inspector Flynn.

'Yes, that's right,' Ball said with relief. 'He will have thrown himself into the sea. Disappeared for ever. He didn't want people to know, that's all.'

'How could he plan that his body would never be recovered?' asked Bucke. Something about Ball was troubling him, but he couldn't be sure what it was.

'Clever people, newspaper men. But devious,' said Ball rather desperately. 'Always thinking ahead. We will never find him. Could have fallen anywhere. Off a cliff. Off a boat. Down a pit. Not that I think that is likely,' he added. He wished he hadn't said that, but it was too late now.

'Not like you to be so certain, Stanley,' said Bucke who looked at him curiously.

'Devious and unhelpful alive, devious and tricky when dead.' Ball was pleased with those words. He wasn't sure where they came from but they sounded good enough for him. 'He won't be missed.'

Bucke tried – and failed – to interpret what Ball was saying. 'And this is the first time anyone has reported him missing is it, Constable Morris? Do we know when he was last seen?'

'Wouldn't make any difference. As I said, devious.' Ball turned away from the counter and tidied up the desk behind, avoiding the eyes that were looking at him.

'Oh well, we best keep an eye out for him. But there is no evidence you have heard that suggests he has come to any harm, is there?' Bucke asked.

'If he had it wouldn't surprise me,' replied Ball, hastily. 'Except that I think he has done himself in. As I said.' He wished that they would talk about something else.

'You seem very hostile towards him, Stanley.'

'No more than he deserves. Just a liar and a mischief-maker and we are all better off without him.'

Inspector Flynn raised his voice a little to be heard above the conversations around him. 'Anyone heard anything about Baglow the reporter? They say he's gone missing.'

'I heard that. I did ask,' replied Constable Gill. 'Landlord said he'd been seen with an older man in the Dukes in Morriston. Left together, he says.'

'Not a man to be trusted, that landlord,' muttered Ball.

'Perhaps not,' said Bucke, assessing him carefully. 'Still, we need to keep it in mind. Probably turn up again, like a cough.'

'There are more problems with rats down at St Mary's, Inspector,' said Ball, trying to change the subject. 'We'll have to set the dogs on them again. With poison you never know what's going to eat it. Just like that poison Baglow poured into the newspaper. Never know what's going to happen, do you.' He looked slyly at Bucke and emboldened, went on. 'Let's hope the little buggers don't get their tails all tangled up, eh?'

He looked at Ball carefully, wondering what was going on in his mind. But it was time to move on, for Captain Colquhoun had arrived, who locked the door of the police station and leaned against it, whilst Flynn commanded the constables' attention. They needed a few uninterrupted moments to try to share what they knew. There didn't seem to be a great deal but Bucke hoped that if they could manage to link together some apparently trivial details, something might be revealed.

No one had heard anything about Milo and Ada. No one seemed to have seen them. The two houses on Pier Street were empty and so was the Chapel. Neighbours, the few that there were, knew nothing. Their followers had been questioned around the town but if they knew anything, they were not saying, only that there had been a sign in the sky that the end of the world was nigh.

'So the three of them, Milo, Ada Gammon, and I think I can include her brother Billy Evil, have gone. And no one knows where they are. You wonder how that is possible,' asked Bucke.

'Four of them, actually,' added Gill. 'There is Delilah. She hasn't been seen either.'

'Yes and the people they are holding, like Emily Beynon. And whoever else they've got. We know what happened to the old man,' added Bingham. 'That were shocking.'

'What about Violet Lee, the Wharton's maid? She is still around, ain't she?' asked Morris.' They say she is sweet on Billy Evil.'

Bucke was surprised. 'I didn't know that. We best pull her in then.'

Morris looked pleased with himself. 'You see, Inspector. You just has to ask the right people, that's all. Instead of listening to rubbish from that idiot, old man Rosser. Tell you something, Inspector, you were a lot more patient with him than I was. What did he say when you asked where Milo had gone? He said they had gone to Judea! He banged on and on about how he used to walk there but he can't anymore!'

The constables laughed dutifully at such idiocy. And then Sergeant Ball leaned across the counter and, once their laughter had died down said, 'I know where Judea is.'

'We all do, Stan,' replied Morris.' Its bloody Palestine isn't it? Like it was in the Bible. It hasn't moved.' He was always eager to display the geographical knowledge he had gained during his time at sea.

'That is where you are wrong, Constable Morris, and if you young 'uns had spoken to me, instead of talking to lying landlords in Morriston, I could have told you. It is in Fforestfach. Big house set back from the road. Widow woman lives there, alone. Dark it is. Locals won't go anywhere near it. They say Mrs Bromfield is a witch. But the house is called Judea.'

Bucke watched him, saying nothing, his mind working rapidly and then glanced at the Chief Constable, who raised his eyebrows to express his interest. Constable Bingham, looking exasperated, asked , 'And why hasn't you mentioned this before then, sergeant?'

'Because this is the first I have heard of it, that's why. I stand behind this counter all day and no one tells me nothing.'

'What else can you tell us, Stanley?' asked Flynn.

Ball was grateful to be the centre of attention and able to move the conversation on away from more sensitive topics. 'Not much else to say. The kids call her Fang on account of her teeth. I live down the road you see, in Cockett.' He paused dramatically, and then said, 'Oh yes, and one other thing. You know William Rosser? Who you have just been laughing about? Well that's her brother.'

A silence descended upon the constables as they considered the implications of what Ball had said. Colquhoun caught Bucke's eye and nodded very slightly in support. It was a risk of course, but it was the only lead they had and for Bucke, it was a strong one, too. 'Very well then, gentlemen. We go to Fforestfach and we shall enter the house. Stan, keep Evan Davies here when he returns in the event that there is anything else that requires attention.'

'I'll be here. I'll mind the shop, Rumsey,' said Flynn. 'I will keep him busy – and out of your hair.'

'Thank you, James. Constable Morris get the carts ready – and quickly. Bingham? Gill? On your way, but don't approach the house. Just watch it and see if anyone leaves. Stan, tell me about the house and the grounds.'

*

The Chief Constable had returned to the Town Hall to speak to the mayor and his colleagues had left for Fforestfach, energised and determined, and so Sergeant Ball was alone in the police station with his own thoughts.

He had survived the first mention of Baglow's disappearance. It hadn't been easy but he persuaded himself that he'd got through it reasonably well. He was sure that interest in Baglow would fade and that he would soon be forgotten, just as he was sure that the body would never be found. Ball now realised that it might take more mental agility than he possessed, to navigate his way through similar conversations and that the best thing he could do was to keep his mouth resolutely closed. What was done could not be undone, but he was sure that Swansea was a better place without Baglow's lies.

There were no callers and so he busied himself in tidying, organising, and checking lost property – until Constable Davies returned.

After paying the silent Florian, Davies decided to try to make amends and so he had returned to Pier Street in search of conclusive evidence which would rescue his reputation. But he did not find redemption. Instead he found a very cold and very dead body.

He had seen the front door slightly ajar and had crept tentatively into the hall where he found William Rosser lying on his back at the bottom of the stairs. He had been stabbed, his shirt covered in blood. Davies quietly backed out of the house and went to the corner of Pier Street where he blew his whistle to call for support but no one responded, for the rest of the force had gone to Fforestfach. He waited for a while and a couple of sailors watched him curiously as he went back to the house. He was not inclined to undertake any sort of search, in case the murderer was still present, so he quietly closed the door and then walked as quickly as he could back to Tontine Street, avoiding a small crowd singing hymns who seemed to be heading north along the river valley. Davies was surprised at how quiet it was in the station, for there was always seemed to be a constable hanging around. He sauntered across the polished floor and leaned casually against the counter, hoping to strike the attitude of a man of the world who had seen it all and always knew what to do, someone you could turn to for sound advice. He nodded at Sergeant Ball. 'Afternoon, Stanley. See that rocket last night?'

'Ay I did, right enough.'

'Must have come from Kilvey Hill, Stanley. What was that about? Thought we had had Bonfire Night.' He shook his head. 'A great deal that's going on that is very strange, in my opinion. Just seen lots of folk walking through town. Something to do with a church party. I sent them off with fleas in their ears, don't you worry. Disturbing the peace like that.'

Ball said nothing.

'Cold out. Winter's coming, Stanley.'

He raised his eyebrows. He wasn't sure how he felt about Davies being so familiar. 'Been busy then, Constable?'

'I should say so. Found a dead body. Murdered, no doubt.' A vivid picture of what he had seen formed itself in all its horrible detail in his mind and his confidence crumbled.

'I've got to be honest, Sergeant. I was out of there like shit from a goose. It were shocking. I mean you see all sorts in this job. I have done it all. But I ain't never seen no one dead with a rat shoved in his mouth. Tail were horrible to look at, like a worm. I thought it were eating him at first. There's a cross painted on the wall too. Looks like it were done in blood to me.'

'And where was this?' Ball was alert now.

Davies was trembling now, describing the scene made it very real and he knew that it would haunt him for a very long time.

'Where, Evan? Where was this?'

'Pier Street, Sergeant. William Rosser. He's been stabbed.'

'Inspector Flynn!' Can I see you for a moment?'

*

There was a knock at the door and Constance found Elodie, Mathilde's maid, at the bottom of the steps. 'I am begging your pardon, Miss White, but my mistress wanted ver' much that you should know.' Elodie gestured expansively with her hands. 'There 'as been a message in the sky, she says. It was last night. I did not see it. And now the congregation 'as been told to go to a coal pit in Llansamlet. It was Mrs Agar. She brought the message. It is the end of the world, she said.' She placed her hands on her cheeks and rocked her head from side to side. '*Oh mon Dieu,* we are doomed.' Elodie did not seem at all alarmed. 'Madame Barree would like it to be known that she does not frequent the east side of town under any... how you say? Cir...?'

'Circumstances?'

'Thank you, Miss White. That is the word I am forgetting. Circumstances, yes.'

'I see,' replied Constance. 'It is the end of the world and she is not going to Llansamlet?'

'I think you are understanding perfectly, Miss. *La fin du monde. Quelle horreur.*'

Sarah Rigby had appeared behind Constance, drying her hair. A proper hair wash - a bowl, a jug of warm water infused with a bunch of rosemary – luxury. 'If the world is to end, at least I shall embrace eternal damnation with clean hair.'

'Naturally, miss,' nodded Elodie seriously. 'It is an occasion when we should all try to look our best. I must return to Madame Barree. I 'ope to see you very soon.' Elodie walked away up St Helen's Road, untroubled in the face of the imminent apocalypse.

Constance grabbed her coat and hat. 'If the congregation are going to Llansamlet, then I must go too. Emily must be there amongst them, I am sure of it.'

'I won't let you go alone,' said Sarah. 'You do not know what you will find. These people are vicious.'

Constance looked at her carefully and then made an instant decision. 'Thank you, Sarah. I would be very grateful for your company.'

Sarah put down her towel and brush and took down her still-dirty coat, whilst Constance looked anxiously up and down the road, then put two fingers in her mouth and whistled loudly, just as Agnes had taught her – and she was quietly pleased that Sarah looked so surprised. 'You can never find a policeman when you want one,' she explained. She smiled and raised a hand in acknowledgement to a prosperous couple walking on the other side of St Helen's Road who were staring at her with incredulity.

It appeared as if there was no response, and then a young boy came racing around the corner with Argyle Street. He arrived at the bottom of the steps, breathless. 'Yes, mam?' he panted.

'I need an urgent message taking to Inspector Bucke.'

He looked at her, weighing up his options. He was a grubby boy, small and spare, the top of his head hidden in a cap that was much too big, his feet enclosed in different unlaced boots. He had the calculating eyes of a successful card player. 'Inspector Bucke is it?' Problem is, he might be looking for me.'

'It is really important. You have to understand. A girl's life is in danger and we have to save her.'

'My life might be in danger too, if old Rumsey finds me,' he said with a sorry shake of his head.

'I do not have a great deal of time. Do you want the job or must I find someone else?' asked Constance impatiently.

The boy paused for a moment longer, then decided. 'My name is Lyndon. Everyone knows me. Tell me something. Is it to be English or Welsh? Extra if it is Welsh. Harder to remember.'

'English, Lyndon. He has gone out to Fforestfach, one of your friends came to tell me earlier. Here's tuppence. Get it to him in thirty minutes and I will double it.'

The boy snorted. 'Mam, this is the Hat Stand Gang you are doing business with.'

'I am pleased to hear it.'

'Will there be fighting, do you think, Mam?'

'Very likely. Now get on with it.'

'If there is ructions, we will be there. We'll find him.' He set off.

'What about the message, then?'

'Calm down. Don't bust your stays.' He turned and put his hands on his narrow hips. 'Well?'

'Tell him they have gone to Calvary Pit in Llansamlet. Got it?'

'Consider it done. I will call round for the rest tomorrow.' He jogged away steadily.

Constance looked at Sarah. 'We best find a cab.'

Sarah nodded. 'Can you teach me to whistle like that, do you think?'

Chapter 28

Once those members of the congregation who had responded to the rocket stepped across the fallen gate and entered the Calvary Pit, they walked along the short and narrow tunnel in the darkness and then turned sharply to the right. Their fragile bravery soon dissipated as the tunnel became narrower, snaking around the frequently positioned pit-props supporting sagging cross-beams. The floor was wet and slippery in the dangerous gloom and everything seemed threatening and uninviting, despite the flickering lamps that Billy had installed on the walls. The children, for whom this had initially been a great adventure, were increasingly uncooperative and tearful, and their parents increasingly dubious. Surely if God, who was all-powerful, wanted them to fight for him on the Field of Armageddon, surely he would have allowed Milo to provide something a little more welcoming and comfortable?

The passage opened out into a larger chamber. There were lamps here too, but the light was meagre. Milo stood before them, looking at this motley collection of his followers. He smiled at them, but not convincingly. There were about thirty of them, largely women, with a small number of children and four old men who looked in a bewildered way at their surroundings. He had hoped for more and that would have happened if they had left the chapel in procession as planned. Relying on a rocket and word of mouth had not been entirely successful, but really, the numbers in the pit were irrelevant, other than for his pride. He knew that the press would, helpfully, inflate the number of victims of course, and it would be highly unlikely that the bodies would ever be recovered to contradict their inevitable exaggeration. Just as long as Billy's escape tunnel was clear, they would be away. Ada and himself would be assumed to have died in the roof-fall along with their followers, entombed and irrecoverable in an unsafe pit, the victims of their religious mania. But as the earth closed around the congregation and entombed them, their leaders would be over the hill and down into Neath and away on the train to a different life somewhere new. He had persuaded Billy that he knew someone to whom he could sell the properties they had acquired in Swansea. 'Easy, Billy. Find an urchin – there are plenty in London. Make him my long-lost son, in front of a lawyer. All very proper. Father Milo is dead. Urchin inherits the estate. We sell it. We get rid of the urchin. They won't find us. We start again.' Billy was sceptical and Milo could see it. 'Trust me. It will work, I promise.'

No, the numbers of the faithful ready to fight for the Militia of Jesus didn't matter, apart from the insult to his ego. Not when he had a plan.

He threw out his arms to welcome the congregation. 'My friends. We shall all rise again. There is nothing to be feared. The Lord approaches us, in the knowledge that we are his most faithful servants. God will know his own, I promise you. And so we shall be transformed. He will give us new shape, new power, new authority, new life. The righteous fire will scour evil from the face of the earth and we shall emerge in triumph, to follow Deborah and the Spear of Jehovah to victory and salvation. For it is written, my friends, it is written *And God shall wipe away all tears from our eyes; and there shall be no more death, neither sorrow, nor crying, neither shall there be any more pain: for all former things will have passed away.* So my friends, let us rejoice!'

*

Constance and Sarah travelled in silence, lost in their own apprehensions. Swansea was quiet, and they could see occasional debris left by the ragged congregation who had paraded the roads before them. The cabman deposited them at The Smith's Arms and they walked hurriedly along Church Lane towards the Calvary Pit, along a recently trodden path, through wet mud that clung to their boots. Sarah noticed that the puddles seemed to ripple as they past, as if disturbed, and as she paused and put her hand on Constance's arm to draw her attention to it, there was a small but perceptible bang and the ground shook. They could see no one else anywhere, and they hurried on, consumed by their anxiety, to the pit entrance in the side of a mound; a hole, rather like the opening to a cave. There had, at one time, been an iron gate across the entrance but now it was lying down like an inadequate duckboard above the mud.

'Neither of us knows what to expect, nor what to do. But we cannot wait for the police to arrive. We must proceed carefully.' said Constance, rather unnecessarily thought Sarah, but she too felt afraid.

A figure emerged from the pit. It was the small impoverished girl pushing a pram. She saw Sarah and, ignoring Constance, said casually, 'The people you are looking for are inside. I came out. It isn't safe in there. I need something to eat. Have you got some spare change for a bit of bread? Me and the cat ain't had nothing to eat for two days and me bowels is grutching.' She looked at them through her narrowed eyes. 'I do believe I have seen the two of you before, at one of Milo's shows. He is inside there now. World's ending in a minute, they say.' There was a terrible creak and a crack. 'The roof is going to fall in, I reckon.'

'Is there a young woman inside?' asked Constance. 'Called Emily?'

'There is a lot of people inside. If that roof goes, they is not getting out neither, and I don't know nothing about it.'

Sarah opened her purse and gave the girl two small coins. 'Here you are. Go and see if you can find a policeman.' The girl assessed the coins, scowled and then pushed away with her pram. Sarah shrugged. 'It can't do any harm.'

They stood looking at the pit entrance, from which a faint but discernible haze of dust was emerging. Constance was fearful but determined. 'I am going inside. I have to know whether Emily is there or not. If the Inspector arrives, tell him where I am.'

'I am coming with you. What have I got to lose?' asked Sarah.

'Your life?'

'Sarah shook her head. 'I have nothing to lose. I merely wish that I hadn't wasted time washing my hair this morning.' The two women looked at each other, nodded and then entered the pit.

Once they had taken two steps into the tunnel they were completely disorientated. They could see nothing and the air was full of choking dust and the terrifying sound of creaking timbers. They pulled scarves round their mouths and Constance felt their way in front, with Sarah holding on to her shawl. They could not speak but now they had come this far, there was no turning back, though they didn't know which way to go anyway. *This might be Hell,* thought Sarah and they would be lost forever in this dirty, choking, consuming blackness.

As Constance felt her way around the straining pit props, there was a fall of rocks behind. The earth seemed to be reshaping itself around them. Then the tunnel turned sharply to the right and they found themselves in a section which seemed better maintained, beneath oil lamps, occasionally struggling to stay alight in air as thick as water. The tunnel turned again and the air was a little clearer and there before them, in a large chamber, there was a group of sobbing and distressed figures, huddled together, looking at them in terror, hoping to see angels but seeing only more victims.

'Emily? Are you there?' asked Constance, before she started coughing.

'Connie?' pleaded a small voice from the shadows, a voice which not even the ominous crash of falling rocks could obscure.

*

Rumsey Bucke cursed his ill-fortune. The raid on Judea had been well-executed, based upon reliable information. But they had been too late – and bringing all his constables out to Fforestfach on an unsuccessful investigation had weakened his resources elsewhere. The old lady, Mrs Bromfield, was lying slumped at the table, a small glass containing the dregs of some kind of viscous fluid loosely in her hand. It seemed that she had been drugged. She was still breathing, but unevenly. The house was empty, the doors open, no sign of anyone. And when a member of the Hat Stand Gang, who had destroyed one police operation, ran up to him with a message, it seemed like the final insult.

'A missus says that they have gone to Calvary Pit out at Llansamlet. She hasn't paid me 'cus she had no change. It will be tuppence.'

Bucke stared at him, holding the boy's defiant eyes for a moment, whilst dragging a single penny from his pocket. He handed it over and then turned away, clapping his hands and mobilizing the constables. He was slowly tracking Milo down, he knew it, though not fast enough. He sent Bingham to find a neighbour willing to look after Mrs Bromfield before he followed them, and then the policemen set off, across the Common and down into Morriston and then over the Wychtree Bridge. It seemed to take far too long. As they approached the church in Llansamlet their cart seemed to tremble and the horse missed its stride.

'Earthquake,' said Morris, turning to Bucke. 'Or an explosion.' He paused for effect. 'Or the end of the world.'

After the vicarage, they turned right down a track. There was a shout behind them, and Bucke turned to see what it was. The police wagons had collected a pack of young boys who were running along in their wake. He felt increasingly apprehensive. One of the boys came up from the back to run alongside Morris. 'Oi! Bonfire!'

'Shut your mouth, Woods. Or you will feel the back of my hand. So scarper, you brat.'

'Pull over there, to the right. Just telling you. Can't go no further.'

The boy, Woods, was right, of course. The road became a track and then it disappeared into churned mud and weeds. To the right there was a treacherous path rising up to the entrance to the Calvary Pit. Bucke knew it had been abandoned some years ago but now it had, apparently, been re-opened. The clouds of emerging dust, billowing into the drizzle, marked their destination; many feet had pressed and torn the wet grass.

Bucke climbed down from the cart. Apart from the group of boys, waiting and watching the police, he could see no one. Then from behind the hedge a young girl emerged. He was sure that he had seen her somewhere before, but he couldn't remember when. She looked him up and down.

'Missus has gone inside. She give me pennies if I could fetch a policeman, so I suppose I can keep them now.' She pulled her pram out of the hedge and Bucke put his hand on the hood to stop her leaving.

'And who was the lady?'

The girl looked thoroughly affronted. 'Dunno. I seen her before, at one of them Milo shows, like I said to her. Then she and her friend went inside. I told her the roof was coming down but she wouldn't listen.'

'Two of them went inside? Two ladies?'

The girl sighed. 'That's what I said. Can I go now?'

'How long ago?'

'I dunno. Church clock's not done no striking though.' She looked up at the sky. 'I is getting wet here.'

Bucke removed his hand and she slid over the mud and then away up the road. He called the constables and they gathered gingerly around the pit entrance, wafting away the dust. One of them tentatively put his head inside the tunnel and then withdrew it suddenly, with exaggerated coughing. Then there was a crash, the sound of wood cracking loudly, followed by falling rocks. Moments later a thicker cloud plumed out.

'I am not going in there,' said Constable Bingham.

They needed maps of the old workings but Bucke knew they didn't have enough time to get them from the Town Hall, even if they could be found. What to do? What to do? He was trying his best to remain calm, to think carefully and logically, despite his pounding heart. Constance was in there, he knew it. There was another rock fall. How far could he go before the tunnel was blocked? Was Constance already crushed and dead? *'Think, man! Think!'* There must be another way in. mustn't there? Wouldn't there be another entrance? A second tunnel somewhere? Or was that merely wishful thinking? He looked at the apprehensive faces of the constables, fearfully waiting for instructions. They did not inspire any confidence. *'Come on! Think!'*

He walked quickly away from the entrance and back towards the horses and the carts where the boys were watching them. Alfie Woods stepped forward. Bucke knew him as a boy to whom the magistrates had instructed Sergeant Ball to administer six strokes of the birch for stealing biscuits or something. It did not seem to have had a great deal of effect.

'What you doing?' asked Woods. 'Ain't you going in then?' He sounded disappointed.

'I am looking for another way in. Do you know if there is one?'

'I know where there is another way, yes I do. A mister's been working on it. He chased me with a shovel. It will cost you. You'll never find it without me – and them coppers have got no chance.' He raised his eyebrows, seeking a deal.

Constable Morris saw the Inspector in conversation with Woods and nudged Gill, standing next to him. 'Look at him.' They watched him hand over what they presumed was money. 'Stupid bugger. Just encouraging him. Buying lies, I am sure.' Then Bucke whistled loudly and waved.

'Oh god. What has he gone and done now?'

'Bingham! Look after that entrance – don't let anyone in! The rest of you, over here! Follow the boy! Look sharp!' Bucke watched them trudge cumbersomely through wet shrubs and the unhealthy wet grass in pursuit of the agile young boy, who scurried and slipped purposefully until he reached a brittle collection of bare and poisoned bushes on the side of an embankment. Wood cleared away a lattice of brambles so that the constables could see it when they eventually caught up with him. Bucke was there before them and it was immediately clear that someone had been working here – and recently too, just as the boy had said. There were neat piles of spoil. Bucke could see that the tunnel itself had not been freshly dug but it had been recently maintained; perhaps, he thought, to make it more accessible.

Woods stepped back, his work done.

'Tell me lad,' asked Bucke. 'Have you been inside the tunnel?' Woods looked both shifty and defiant. 'You won't get into trouble. I just need the truth. There are people down there, trapped, and we have to get them out before something terrible happens. You know what is happening at the other entrance. It is collapsing. We don't have much time, I am sure of that.'

Woods turned away. *'You are not supposed to help a copper.'* And yet here he was, being asked to do so and, strangely, feeling that he did not have much choice.

Bucke knelt down and looked into his eyes. 'Tell me now, Alfie. Before I go inside.' The boy's lips were clamped shut. 'When we know inside ourselves, that something is right then that is the thing that we are supposed to do. And we don't always need money to do it.'

Woods turned his head away, as if by not looking at the copper he wasn't really doing it. 'The mister cleared it out. It's been here for as long as I can remember. He put in some new bits of wood to hold up the roof. But as fast as he dug it, more earth fell down. I don't reckon it is safe. But you have to crawl in and then there is like a step and you can stand up. It goes downhill, don't it? Then it turns a bit. Sometimes it is narrow and sometimes you have to crawl, even us boys. You will need a light. And it gets very wet. Slippy. Water comes through the roof.'

Bucke nodded.

'Me and the boys used to do it as a dare. How far you could go with no light. I won.'

'I am sure you did. And where does it lead?'

'I got as far as a wooden door. Couldn't open it. Me and the boys brought a lamp but we still couldn't open it. We reckon that it was bolted on the other side. And there is one other thing.' He looked shiftily around. 'There is a horse and cart tied to a tree at the end of the field. Don't know what it is doing there. And none of the boys have nicked nuffink from it, I swear. On my mother's life.'

'Thank you, Alfie. For the bits that were true, anyway.'

'Do you want me to come with you?' he asked, looking down at the mud once more.

'No, Alfie. You have done an excellent job already. Now it is my turn.'

Suddenly there was a distant rumble from deep within the network before them.

'You are on your own then, copper,' he said with relief. 'I am not going in there for no one.'

Chapter 29

She held on tightly as Emily sobbed without restraint. 'What he did…what he did to me, that man ….' Constance said nothing, hoping that the warmth of another body, a mother too, perhaps might fill the fearful child with love for the last time. Constance herself was full of bitter accusation. How could life be so cruel, she wondered? She was very frightened, but more than anything bitterly disappointed at the way life had offered hope and happiness and then snatched it away. And for Emily, for her life to end after what had happened? Could anything be more cruel?

Around them there was the tangible essence of madness. The triumphalism at their salvation and their imminent elevation to the right hand of God had now, amongst Milo's followers, been replaced by terror and mania. They were trapped amongst the sounds of hell, of cracks and booms— but there were no flames here, just water streaming down walls, rocks falling, the ground shaking. The words of Milo, the confident boasting of Deborah, were no longer of any importance to their followers. They had been tricked and they would die.

Emily pulled herself away from Constance for a moment. 'That man. He has destroyed me.'

'Hush, Em. He did not. You are safe. What he did matters for nothing, Em. Your body was abused and you were outraged by an evil man, but you are alive and your spirit still will shine. He touched your body but he never touched your soul.'

'Connie? Are we going to die?'

'Of course not,' she lied.

Sarah was angry too, looking around the chamber in the guttering light, listening to the entrance collapsing in stages. They had been trapped in an alien place, with no hope of rescue and with light only for a brief period before it died completely, as they would too. It had all happened so quickly. This morning she had been free – and now she was doomed.

'Afternoon, Miss Rigby,' said Delilah from the gloom. A thin fountain of water sprayed from a fissure in the wall behind her. 'I am glad to see you. I was pleased to see you escape from the house.'

'As I was myself, Delilah. Although I now appear to have found myself somewhere worse. And do you know? I bathed yesterday. For this.'

Delilah looked around and nodded. Mrs Lilley, the wife of the confectioner, screamed 'Lord help us!' Iestyn, once disappointed by his initial rejection by the Militia, responded with a desperate 'Hallelujah!' which did nothing to disguise his fear.

'Did you know this was going to happen?' asked Sarah.

'I wasn't sure they meant it. I thought for a long time that Milo was just tricking people so that they could steal from them. I didn't think we would end up here, that he wanted to kill all these people. I thought it was a game.'

'But why? What's the point?'

'So that the police will think they had died in here too. They think some of the police are on to them. And so we are all to wait here for God to arrive, whilst they run away to another town.'

'And what about you, Delilah?'

'They are happy for me to die, I believe, for Our Lady of Mumbles says that the devil lives in my face. But I think I know too much.' She protected her lamp from a fall of dust. 'But you must know something, Miss Rigby, that there is another way out. The one that Milo and Ada plan to use, the one that Billy built.'

'Where? For God's sake, Delilah. Where is it?'

Delilah pointed at the door. 'I can't open it. I have tried but it is locked and bolted. Milo and Ada are in there and that is where it is.'

'But if it is the only way out, we have to open the door!'

'I think that, too,' agreed Delilah.

There was another spout of water and it extinguished one of the lamps. But suddenly, hope had not been completely extinguished.

*

It was a small space, a room now that Billy had renovated it, even though it had been carved out of the earth many years ago for another purpose, as a place where the coal could be gathered after it had been hacked from the seam. It lay between the chamber where the wretched disciples had been abandoned and the restored escape tunnel, both of which had been blocked by newly-installed doors. The explosive charges that Billy had laid had done their job all too well and the collapse of the original tunnel was now spreading an unstoppable instability through the rest of the mine. They did not have much time; Billy knew that more than anyone. Milo had changed his clothes. Now he was an exemplary commercial traveller; Mr Dorrington was eager to return home and he waited impatiently for Ada to change from her robe. 'Let's get a move on, shall we?'

'We must speak to our people, Milo. Offer them reassurances and courage.' Ada was agitated, pacing around the enclosed space. The Spear of Jehovah was glinting in the lamplight in the thickening air of the chamber.

Milo laughed scornfully. 'For God's sake, Ada! I am not going out there again. I held them last time, they listened– I do not believe that I can do so again. Not when there is no sign of angels and trumpets, let alone God.'

Billy agreed. 'Won't be long anyway. We need to get out, now. This place has never been stable and if we don't shift ourselves, the escape tunnel will go too. It is the only way out now. So let's crack on, shall we?'

Ada grabbed hold of the spear tightly and shook it. 'We must stay. The Lord is coming and we shall be at his side.'

Milo was alarmed. 'For God's sake woman! What is wrong with you? This has been a game, you know that! Just a game! You made it up! Remember? You did this. All of it - all this Father Milo and the end of the world nonsense. Angels? Our Lady of Mumbles? It was your idea. For me it was just like being on stage but with a bigger audience. This was all your story!'

'Of course it was my idea. And I know now that Almighty God has always been speaking to me. He put the seeds in my head. I did not make any stories. I said those things because God told me to say them.' She started to sway, supporting herself with the spear. 'I can feel his presence. He comes closer to us and we shall be saved.'

'Listen to me, Ada.' Milo was becoming increasingly alarmed. 'Listen. I tried to speak to God but I had no reply. I looked into the Eye of God and it was an empty socket. He isn't there, Ada. It is just us. We are alone and we need to make the best of it. We need to look after ourselves. There isn't anything else. That is what we have been doing; offering people dreams, a show, an escape. But none of it means anything. How can it? It has always been your story!'

There was another crack; another beam.

'You try to trick me with your lies. I can see through you, whoever you are. We are here, waiting for God and all you can do is test my own faith and my devotion. You are possessed!'

A frantic, uncontrolled, hammering had started on the door between them and their ragged band of followers; 'Ada! We have got to get out – before the roof goes!' Milo took a deep breath. 'Look, you are over-wrought. You have worked hard and done well. You are excited – I understand all of that. But we did what we said we would do. We have it all. Thousands upon thousands and it is all ours. We can go and start again. We get out. We leave these people behind and then we live. Now!'

She looked at him wide-eyed. 'No, it can't be...Get thee behind me, Satan!' She pointed the spear at Milo, who took a step backwards and found himself leaning against the wet wall.

'Ada! Ada! Stop this nonsense now!' Billy moved towards her but when she switched the spear to point at his chest, he too stepped backwards and pressed himself against the wooden door he had built into the tunnel. 'Don't be such a dull bugger!' The door opposite, under ferocious assault, seemed to be splintering.

'No, Billy. Everything else I have ever done has been only a preparation of this moment. This is my destiny and I shall purify the world. This is real and this is true, I know it. And all those who stand in my way belong to Satan. You must be able to see that.'

'Including me and Milo?'

'Of course. I am a messenger from God and if you oppose me and refuse the message I bring, then you must be possessed by Satan. So you must follow me or burn for eternity.'

'Ada,' said Milo urgently. 'Let's talk about this outside, shall we?'

'You said you were the true instrument of God. But I know now that this was a lie. It was me. I was never Ada. That was a mere shell, to trick Satan. I have been Deborah all along. And I ask myself this Milo. Who are you? Who sent you here?'

'It has all been a game, Ada. You know that. I am Milo. No one else.'

'And so what about the rats?' She waved the spear from side to side. 'You did not create the seven-headed beast. I did not. Billy did not. It was a sign from God and we should have heeded it. The message was clear. The end is here and now we must live out our destiny at the right hand of God.'

Milo was extremely alarmed. 'Ada, look at me.' He grabbed the spear and tried to hold her still but she was stronger than him and he swayed, struggling to hold on. 'We just need to get out. Now. We can talk about it later if we must. But my God, we have to get out!'

Her eyes flashed. 'Now I understand. Now I know. I see it all.' She looked at him in horror – and hatred. 'You have been dissembling! You are here to sow the seeds of doubt! You truly are Satan! This is why you want to take me from here, to deny me my place at the side of God on the field of Armageddon!' The Spear of Jehovah was tense and poised. 'The greatest battle of all, the final conflict, will happen here and you have been sent to fill me with doubt, to make me question my faith!'

'Ada! Stop it,' shouted Billy, but he was too apprehensive to approach her. He would have to calm her through words. 'Deborah. Please.' A new approach occurred to him. 'Perhaps our Lord is waiting for you outside. Why don't we go and see? Show him what a devoted disciple you are.'

'You lie! This is what you have been all along. He knows how devoted I am! This is a trick. To test me! I see it all now. You have been sent here to seduce me into evil!'

'For Christ's sake, I am your brother!'

'No more!' she shouted. 'You have been possessed. You are a talking serpent sent to spread sin and corruption. The great

330

Deceiver! Beelzebub! Lord of Flies!' Her eyes were wide in the gloom, shining with madness. 'Everything finally makes sense!' She moved the spear from chest to chest and saw the two frightened men exchange a glance, as if planning to attack her together. 'Just as you have been sent here to tempt me, I am here to destroy evil in all its shapes.' She paused. 'Your eyes. Your eyes. They are not yours. I have never seen them before. They are unnatural.'

Milo made a faint move towards her and she switched the spear to point it at his chest, inching it towards him. There was a loud crack and a stream of water flowed down the wall. Billy glanced at it and his alarm increased. 'Deborah! We have to get out. Or we shall die, for Christ sake! God is outside waiting for you!'

'You lie! We are to join the Militia of Jesus! Today is the day of God's Vengeance!'

Billy stepped towards her, his hands reaching for the spear. Ada looked at him with blank eyes and pushed the spear at him with all her strength. It passed effortlessly through his torso and pinned him to the door to the escape passage. His face contorted, his breath stolen from him forever, his hands grabbing at the shaft of the spear as if somehow he could remove it from his body and live. But he could not, and thick blood bubbled from his mouth as his head fell forward and his body curled itself around the spear.

Ada gasped and looked at what she had done. Milo's hands were clamped over his mouth in horror. 'It is God's Will that his enemies are destroyed!' Then she hit Milo unexpectedly with the back of her hand, knocking him against the wall where he hit his head on a rock protruding from it. He sank to the ground.

'The Lord's people have three enemies - the world, the flesh, and the devil. And now I see that they all came together in you, Milo. My husband, but also my Deceiver. And now I must deliver you to the slaughter.'

*

Their entrance had fallen in on itself. That was obvious. They knew their only hope of escape was through that sturdy door. They attacked it in a frenzy with whatever they could find, ramming it with timber, crashing rocks into it until it fell in pieces. They were through and they had to move quickly, for the roof of the largest chamber was visibly fracturing and water was streaming in. Delilah ushered them through the shattered frame. It was far too small to accommodate all of them unless they kept moving.

As they shuffled through the room in the failing light – another lamp was extinguished forever – they could see Ada kneeling next to the body of Milo. He had been laid on the floor, his body formally straightened and she had cut open his throat. She was now cradling his head in her lap and there was a pool of blood spreading beneath her.

'Don't go. You mustn't go.' She seemed more subdued than usual. 'You must stay, the Lord God will be here now in a moment. You can hear his trumpets. Father Milo has already gone to join him, to march in triumph on the Field of Armageddon. Please wait. Together we can vanquish evil for ever. I forbid you to leave. Everlasting life awaits us all. Wait with me, I command you. Or you shall be damned for eternity.' Her conviction had gone, her burst of mania burnt out. Delilah bent down and took the knife from her and threw it back into the other chamber where there was the steady, inexorable collapse of rocks. 'Delilah. You must stay with me! I command you. God will destroy the devil in your face and you shall rejoice in paradise. You will be beautiful. Delilah? Delilah?' She received no reply.

Constance and Sarah tugged at the spear but it was not until they were joined by Mrs Lilley that they managed to release the weapon. Delilah took it from them and employed it as an additional, if fragile, support for the lintel under which they must now pass. They pulled Billy's body away. His face said he was dead but the air within the body made enough noise as they dragged it away to suggest that it had still not accepted it.

'Please do not leave me. The moment of triumph is at hand. It has been foretold.' Ada raised her blood-stained hands. 'The Lord is amongst us! I have heard the trumpets!'

Opening the door to the tunnel was much easier than the other, for they were on the right side of it. However when the rocks shifted, the frame warped and, under pressure, one side of it had started to splinter. Together they kicked at the door until they could force it open. It was low and they had to crawl through, for the ground seemed to be rising too, anxious to meet the ceiling. Beyond, another horrible scene greeted them, as if they had not already seen enough. There was a chamber into which they funnelled, where Violet Lee's body was slumped against the wall, a garrotte still tight around her neck, and she shook with each vicious shudder from the dying pit. Delilah, leading the way paused briefly and looked at her friend. 'Poor Vi.' But she had no time to grieve — she had finally discovered her own destiny. The death of anyone else would be the final triumph of Milo and she was desperate to make sure that didn't happen.

Behind them there a tremendous crash as a large part of the ceiling fell, the earth determined to take back the voids that had been created. The tunnel, however, was still passable, but only just. Billy had restored it sufficiently to help three of them to escape. Now there were ten times that number trying to use it and the floor was uneven and scarred and it was shaking. There were places where it was narrow and there were other stretches where it widened. Some places they had to crawl, in others they could crouch. But the grinding vibrations were terrifying. Children cried. Some of the older ladies would not go any further, for fear of delaying the others and begged to be left behind. Sarah and Constance helped and cajoled and pushed.

At one point the stooped procession paused, resting their skinned knees and arms and Delilah moved back down the line, to Sarah and Constance, still clutched by Emily.

'It is quite straightforward now, just follow the tunnel. It has started to go up hill now. You can feel it. I will stay here at the back and help those who drop behind. You go to the front with the children. They will trust you – they may be fearful of me.' She gestured casually at her grimy face.

'Delilah, there is no need to…' began Sarah, but she was interrupted.

'Go to the front, the two of you, please. You must lead.'

There was another tremendous fall of rock behind them and small stones crashed into their backs. Emily would not let Constance go, gripping on to her clothes, and so the three of them squeezed along the passage, taking the children with them. The dust and filth on their faces was stained with tears and their eyes seemed to have been emptied of hope by the horror of what had happened. There were five of them. A boy, who must have been about seven years old, bleeding from cuts on his legs and with a large graze across his forehead, stood in front of Sarah in the light of his mother's oil lamp and asked, 'Are we dead, missus?'

'No, of course not.' She bit her lip to hold back her tears. That a child should have such thoughts. 'Come with me, young man. Up at the front you will see the daylight sooner.' His mother looked at Sarah, nodded desperately, and pushed him forward.

They moved on, slowly, gently upwards. There were times when draughts of fresh air seemed to touch their faces and stir the haze before them but then it would disappear. Both women were working on instinct; the essential rules of survival had never been explained to them but that did not matter – they were determined that they were not going to die without a proper struggle. Emily stumbled into a deep puddle of water and screamed with the shock of it. Constance was especially exhausted, for she was almost dragging Emily with her. Then the earth shifted again. The noise and the movement were disorientating and the roof appeared to collapse a few yards in front of them, showering them with water.

They could have been crushed. Had they been lucky? How could they know? They were alive – but they were trapped.

*

Bucke entered the tunnel without any hesitation. It smelt stale and rotted, like an ancient tomb broken open in a thunderstorm. Just inside there was the sudden drop that Alfie had told him about and after that he could stand up. It appeared to have been recently maintained. The floor was clear of debris and there were signs that some potholes – though not all - had been filled in. There were new props holding up sections where the roof had previously collapsed. But there was water everywhere. It didn't seem secure or safe. He could hear the wood creak and the rocks grind. He put out a hand to support himself, which slid across the wet and treacherous walls and as he regained his balance he could see puddles glistening and rippling in the light from his lamp. Bucke slipped and fell, and he was grateful his light did not go out. This was a lethal place. Someone had set off an explosion, he was sure of it, but the consequences of that could be neither predicted nor controlled; he realised that the mine was dying.

He knew that the whole of Llansamlet was riddled with mine workings. How could he be sure that he had entered the right one? The tunnel ended in a door, Alfie said. Did anyone know for certain whether this was the only tunnel that ended in a door? Alfie was a child. Could he really rely on him? He stopped to get his breath. He knew he should not have come in here alone – but was there really room enough for an unwilling constable?

Bucke heard a cry, he was sure of it, and stopped. He turned the lamp in front of him and behind, as if it would help him to hear. What should he do? He had no experience of mines at all. Now he was underground, all he could do was carry on, in hope. He looked back, convinced he had heard something and, as he did so, there was a roof fall in front of him. He stepped backwards, slipped and sat on the floor as mud splattered him and thick dust settled upon him, forcing its way into his nose and throat. What was he to do? Turn round? But he was sure that he had heard a voice. There were many sounds in this awful place, sounds that threatened, that said that this was not a place for the living. It was a mausoleum and it smelt of death. But he was sure he heard a voice. And having heard it, he could not walk away. And anyway, what was there to walk back too? Nothing, except constables. If Constance was trapped in here, why ever would he want to leave?

He placed the lamp on the floor, still bravely flickering, and started to pull at the rocks. It seemed to him that as fast as he removed a piece of stone and put it with difficulty behind him, something fell to take its place. So he worked at the top where he seemed to have no impact all. He had no tools, no expertise. He picked up the lamp again to examine the rubble in front of him. The dust that had settled on his tongue had the gritty taste of graves. He saw that a wooden prop had collapsed, though it had not broken. Perhaps that might hold back the rocks for a while, so he started to work beneath it, shovelling out grit and rubble with his cupped hands. Slowly he made an indentation, reaching his hands further into the ground each time. How far did this fall reach anyway? Feet? Yards? Was his work futile? He dragged out a rock with difficulty, his hands battered, cut and sore, and pushed it away with his foot. That seemed to open up the hole and he thought that he was almost at the stage where he would have to put his head inside so that he could reach further. At some point he would have to stop, he knew that. But not yet. Not now. The lamp was too far behind him and he could see nothing, so he worked by touch, scratching and tugging and scooping, sometimes wasting time by withdrawing handfuls of mobile mud that slipped through his fingers. He heard the sounds of another rock fall – was it behind, in which case he would be trapped? Or was it in front and had increased the blockage to something beyond his capacity to move ? He found a large piece of embedded wood and once he had pulled it out he used it as a tool to ram and loosen the rocks in front of him. And then suddenly it seemed to go forward more than he expected. Perhaps there was a void. He pulled out the probe and crawled as far as he could into the hole. There appeared to be air flowing into his face and he reached out into the void – and his hand was grasped by another.

'Can you hear me? My name is Inspector Bucke of the Swansea Constabulary and I am here to rescue you.'

'About bloody time too. It is me, Sarah Rigby. And you can let go of my hand now, if you don't mind.'

*

The women had worked together and had made more progress than the solitary Inspector. It was Billy's fortuitously fallen pit prop that had directed them to work at the same place in the rock fall. Soon they had created a tunnel – tight and temporary, but an escape route nonetheless. The bewildered children were sent through first of all. Bucke delivered them from the tight space safely, one at a time. Then came Emily, crying, having surrendered briefly her comforting contact with Constance. She saw Bucke, a representative of her return to the life she had left behind and thought she had lost. 'Inspector Bucke, I am so sorry.' He was the first man she had spoken to for many days who was not a threat or a disciple and she was not sure what to say. 'Please forgive me, I am soiled,' she said as he helped her through the hole. She flinched at his touch.

'Escort these children from this awful place, Emily. And soon you will start your life again. But please, hurry. Follow the passage and tell one of the constables to come and join me – and tell him we do not have much time.'

'I must wait for Constance-'

'No you must not, Emily. You have a task of your own. The children. Look to it and send a constable.'

She hesitated and one of the boys took her hand as she crouched, trembling. 'Please take me out of here,' he pleaded. 'The man said.'

'Emily, do it,' said Bucke, more softly than before. 'Take the children and I promise you Constance will be with you shortly.' He hoped he was right.

Mrs Lilley as pushed through – it wasn't easy, for she filled the space and she was finding it difficult to breathe. Bucke pulled on her arms, thankful that he was at that end and not the other. With Sarah pushing they managed to unstick her hips and she emerged bruised and battered. He directed her to the end of the tunnel and, unable to speak, she leaned on the wall for a moment, panting, before turning away towards the fresh air. Then Sarah crawled through. 'Where are the children?' she asked immediately. 'They are outside, I hope.'

Good afternoon, Sarah. I hope you are well.'

Sarah shook herself. 'Never better.' She leaned forward and hugged him, pulled back and then kissed him suddenly and quickly on the lips. 'No one will know. I thought I was dead.' She turned and felt her way along the tunnel, leaving a surprised inspector behind.

The others came out fairly easily. On his release Iestyn, unaware of the considerable irony, praised the lord for his salvation. 'I am saved! God is merciful!' he cried as he staggered along the passage. There was, however, noticeably more water on the floor than there had been before and by now Constables Gill and Morris were both present with their lamps, blocking the tunnel on one side as they moved the survivors along. But the pieces falling from the roof were getting bigger and he was relieved when Constance, wrapped in mire and thick dust but with eyes shining, came out. He pulled her up and held her tight and they said nothing, for words were not important. Morris coughed. 'It is getting worse, Inspector. Not long I think. Best be going.'

'Of course, Constable. Thank you for your assistance. Is that the last of the people?'

'No. There is Delilah.'

'Delilah?'

'Yes. She saved everyone.'

'Inspector, please,' Morris anxiously interrupted.

'You take Miss White. I must look for Delilah before it is too late. You must go now.' He bent down and shouted down the tunnel. 'Delilah! Come through. You haven't much time.' He heard her sloshing through the soaking mud. There was a loud crash behind her as her head came out.

'Is everyone out, Inspector?'

'All except you. Come quickly. There is no time.' He took her hand.

'No, Inspector I shall stay, with Our Lady. Thank you for helping all those poor people.'

'You must not go back in there,' he said sharply. 'You have done more than anyone could ever have imagined. Leave it now, Delilah. Leave it and come out. You will be free. No one will ever accuse you of their terrible crimes, I promise you.' He tried to pull her out but her hand, covered in mud, slipped from his grasp.

Delilah laughed, bitterly. 'I am Delilah. Look at my face, if you can. What choice do I have? And anyway, Inspector. There is always the chance that Our Lady of Mumbles might be right. God turns up and gives me a proper face, and then you will be sorry. Why not? I do so want Our Lady of Mumbles to be right.' She slithered backwards.

'Delilah! Stop!' shouted Bucke. There was another tremendous crash, a rush of air pushed through the tunnel into his face and Delilah was gone, behind a pile of wet mud and rock. He knew it was over and he slipped backwards as quickly as he could. Whether she was beneath the last fall or beyond it made little difference now. No one, not even a restored Delilah, was ever coming out of there.

Chapter 30

'I want their bodies, Inspector. When you get them out. I want them.'

It was proving to be a difficult meeting.

'David,' pleaded Bucke.

'I want them anatomised. Don't you understand? Then every fragment of them diced and fed to rats. Every last scrap. You will do that for me, won't you, Inspector?' Doctor Beynon had the look in his eyes of a man who had not slept for weeks. Bucke knew that there was nothing he could find to soothe away that rage.

'David. We don't do that anymore, you know that.'

'I want them fed to rats and then the rats killed by dogs. I demand it, Inspector.' He banged on the desk for emphasis.

'We may never recover the bodies, David. The mine has collapsed. It is extremely unsafe.'

'Damn you, Inspector! I demand it! You know what they did to my daughter. If you won't do it I shall do it myself!'

'David, you have to look to the future, not the past,' Bucke said gently. 'The past has gone. You cannot change it; you cannot unmake it. You need to help Emily and you need to help Flora. Seeking an impossible and pointless revenge isn't going to help anyone.'

The doctor's head fell forward and Bucke watched him across the table, saw the tears dropping from his eyes. He walked around to the other side and laid a comforting hand on Beynon's shoulder. 'You still have Emily, David. You haven't lost her; she is still here and she needs the strength of her father.' *And let us hope that you never have to confront her loss*, he thought, though he didn't say it.

Beynon shuddered. 'I can't sleep. I cannot remove it from my mind. The heart of our family has been ripped in two and I want to hurt those who did this. I want to make them suffer. Help me do it.'

'They are dead, David,' said Bucke gently. 'Gone. It is Emily and Flora who need your energy and your single-mindedness, not the dead, not worms-meat. They hurt her but they didn't destroy her. You must make her whole again.'

The doctor looked up, his angry eyes red and inflamed with irrationality. 'You bastard.'

Bucke said nothing, watching a man unravelled by emotions.

'You bastard,' repeated Beynon. 'Why must you be so reasonable? I want to see their bodies rotting, pecked by crows, hanging from the Castle Walls. I want to castrate them and feed their manhood to maggots. Can't you understand?'

'I have lost too, David. You know that. I cannot help my little girl. But you can still help yours. She is hurt, not lost.'

'Oh yes! But your precious girl will remain pure forever, won't she? Whereas mine…' He stood up and pushed his chair away with such force that it toppled over. 'Will you ever understand how other people feel? Or must it always be about the poor widower Rumsey Bucke? Is that it? Jealous are you, that someone else might steal the self-righteous grief that you have claimed for yourself, alone? It isn't suffering for you; it is a badge. The reason why we should all love you. But you don't know what it is like when your girl has been…' He turned dramatically towards the door, then fumbled with the handle. He opened it and, without turning round, added, 'Ask someone else to look at your bodies, Inspector Bucke. We shall be moving away from this god-less town.'

His heavy feet rang through the police station as he left, ignoring Sergeant Ball's farewell. Bucke sat down and closed his eyes, holding his breath for a few moments and then leaning back in his chair with a prolonged sigh.

Constance met with Emily at about the same time. Since her release from the mine, Emily and Flora had followed each other around like puppies, panicking if they were out of sight of each other, but Constance needed an opportunity to speak to her, to ask the questions that her mother might not have asked. She eventually found her in the kitchen on Eaton Crescent, whilst Flora dealt with the grocer.

Constance listened to Emily for a moment and then asked, 'And why do you want to die, Emily?'

'Because after what that man did to me, no man will have me.'

'But that is nonsense, Emily. It is what happened to you and we can't take it away. But it might make you stronger.' She shook her head. 'A man will love you and he will be a special man who will hate the thing that happened to you – but he will see that it has made you the person who he loves.'

'But he won't! I shall die an unloved spinster. Pappa says.'

Constance did not think that this was helpful. 'Your father is an intelligent and caring man, Emily. But I am sure things won't be as bad. Your father is perhaps talking about his own pain, his own worries and perhaps the guilt he feels for not being able to protect you. It is what fathers are supposed to do, isn't it? But he didn't and so perhaps in his own eyes he is a failure.'

'He said that everyone will know that I have been used.' She sobbed loudly.

David Beynon's words were not what his daughter needed to hear, Constance was sure.

'I wish I was dead!'

'For goodness sake, Emily! Stop it! When has anyone ever said those words and they have led to happiness? If any man at all is important, if any man is good enough for you, anywhere, no matter who he is, then answer one of those adverts in the newspapers from the colonies! *Wife wanted.* You can become the mother of six children on a homestead somewhere you have never heard of, with a brutish, incoherent, sheep farmer as a husband. He won't care and he will show you less concern and tenderness than a rapist. Is that how you will choose to punish yourself? Listen to me Emily. Your goodness still shines within you. I know it does.' Emily refused look at her. 'Em, what happened to you is now part of what you are. It is no reason to give up.' She paused. 'You are not with child, are you, Em?'

She shook her head. 'No, Connie. I am not.'

'Are you sure?'

'Yes, Connie. I am sure. Some of the girls at school told me about it.'

Constance was silently thankful. 'You are young, Em. You will heal.' She hoped fervently that her father would too.

*

A reporter came from Cardiff to cover elements of the story and then offered a eulogy for the mysteriously disappeared Baglow. Where was he? Who could say? Reporting was such a dangerous job – and he died doing his duty, seeking the truth and giving his life. This meant of course that coverage in the Cambrian was inevitably delayed and scant, and rather lost in the normal daily concerns of a busy town.

Sergeant Ball made a conscious effort not to talk about Baglow and stayed unusually close to his wife, more attentive and caring than he had been for some time. She rather liked this unexpected change in him. Perhaps it was his age, Lillian thought. He was much more involved in the church, too. He had started teaching classes in the Sunday school. He was the same age now as his father had been when he died. That was it, Lillian was sure. Still, there was no need to question it, was there?

*

Sarah Rigby slipped quietly out of sight, back towards her old life, though she was reluctant to embrace everything that was sordid and foul. But she had no prospect of any other life, no matter how grateful people might have been for what she did, and anyway, with no reporter around to record the heroism of any of the women, the story of the collapse of old mine workings some distance out of town caused little curiosity. Sarah did go looking for the little girl with the pram. It troubled her that a little lost soul like her should be drifting untethered around town. Quite a few people had seen her but no one was quite sure who she was or how to find her.

The town dragged itself back into normality, though for most of the residents it had never wavered for a moment from its everyday tedium, and the basic concerns of warmth and shelter as autumn slipped effortlessly into cold winter, were never challenged.

The Calvary Pit was declared unsafe and fenced off, though it did not discourage the more fanciful from claiming to have heard voices and chanting emerging from deep underground. In fact, the people of Frederick Place, who were close enough as far as they were concerned, claimed to have heard rhythmic knockings in the night, as if someone was thumping the floors of houses from beneath with a broom handle. The imagination has always run unchecked in Frederick Place. When it rained heavily they were convinced they could hear female voices crying out for help, and it would be the case that for many years to come on All Hallows Eve, the people of Llansamlet would be certain to claim that they had seen Our Lady flying across the sky on a broomstick back to Mumbles from whence she came, free for one night only. But then, the sulphurous darkness of a Llansamlet night provided few distractions for those yearning residents wishing for mystery and romance.

*

And what of Constance? As far as she was concerned her life would never be the same again. Just a few short months ago she had been a victim of violence in the home, abused, ignored, the submissive wife, with no opinions and no worth. Now she was respected, involved and she had found qualities within herself that she never knew were there; she had done things she had never thought possible, like saving lives. Constance now knew that when called upon she could be brave. She should never be involved in Rumsey Bucke's work; of course she shouldn't. But it had transformed her life and the trust that he gave her was startling. The qualities for which she had previously been punished – being forthright and independent – were now the things that were valued. And it had all happened by chance, when her husband had deserted her and Rumsey Bucke had turned up to find out if he was a murderer.

But she wasn't a hidden person anymore, like so many other women. People across the town knew who she was; some knew her as Bucke's companion and some as his 'paramour' - but more usually as a piano teacher and she liked that. A person in her own right. Her greatest frustration however was that her relationship with Rumsey was incomplete and would have to remain so. Her status must remain without compromise if she was to succeed in divorcing her disappeared husband. Oh yes, life was better, she knew that, but the idea that her love was unfulfilled gnawed away at her, just as much as she knew it gnawed away at Rumsey.

And it happened one night, when a late November storm was battering Swansea and Rumsey Bucke was putting off as long as he could the act of stepping outside into the driving rain and leaving the warmth of Constance behind to return to his neglected and miserable room, that he began to pace around the kitchen. It was a small space and he could not stretch out, but he was agitated. He had seen such a deal of sorrow in recent months.

Constance sat at the table and watched him. She knew what was troubling him. 'Rumsey, I know. I understand. It is difficult for us both. We must be patient. You must know that there will never be anyone else. Everyone knows that we have an understanding.'

'We could leave. Go to another town, like Sarah always says. Did she say that to you? She always says it to me. Where no one knows us. We could live as man and wife. Other people do it all the time. It would be a new start for both of us.'

'And what would we do? How would we survive? No mother would ever trust me with their daughter. A scarlet woman teaching the piano, with a bit of dancing and deportment? It would not be acceptable anywhere. And you? What would you do, Rumsey?'

'Anything.'

'But not a policeman. An upholder of civic dignity and morals, living in a sinful condition? They would not let you feed the civic donkey. You know that.'

'Constance, I will do anything...'

'I know.' She rested her hand on his wrist as he passed and he stopped his pacing. 'And so, Rumsey, the anything that you must do is to show patience. My husband will not return. Of that I am certain. He has divorced me, informally of course, but in so many ways he has left me stranded, neither one thing nor another. I married unwisely, with no hope of a second chance. And now I have it, I shall not let it go. I could never dream of escape before, but now that it is within my grasp, I will not lose it. And then next year, when sufficient time has elapsed then...

'I can speak to Mr Glascodine, Constance. He is a solicitor.'

'He cannot change the law.' A sudden vicious squall of rain thrashed into the window.

'This is wrong.' He paced the small room again, tense, angry, distraught.

'Rumsey. Please. I love you. Of that I have no doubt. I know that we can be happy together. But we must wait. We have little choice. Please calm yourself.'

'I know, Constance.' He stopped. 'You are right.' He massaged his forehead. 'I must apologise. I am consumed by worries and confusion. I love you with all my heart and yet am denied the final expression of that love. I wish only to be with you and yet fear the betrayal of my wife. I …'

'Rumsey,' Constance said softly, but insistently. 'Rumsey. Listen to me. I never met your wife but I am sure that the love you shared was true and strong. She would not have wanted you to be sad on her account. She would only ever want you to be happy. These feelings you have, this guilt you feel, comes from inside you, not from her. You cannot harm her. You cannot change who she was or what she did. But that guilt has run its course now. You do not need it anymore. Julia is dead. And I am alive.' She took his face in her hands, looked straight into his eyes and kissed him, very gently.

Bucke realised that he had closed his eyes and opened them to hold her gaze for a long moment. 'I am so sorry…' he began but she put her finger on his lips.

'Say nothing, Rumsey. Be patient and hold on to our love.' She removed her finger. 'Be patient. All things will come to us, in good time.' She picked up his hand and, bending her head slightly, put it to her lips. She looked up at him and smiled. 'But perhaps, Rumsey, whilst we wait so very patiently on such a very stormy night, inhospitable and unpleasant, you might allow me to offer both of us a little consolation?'

Afterword

This is a work of fiction and, whilst many of the locations in the book are authentic and will be recognised by the people of Swansea, the chapel and the Calvary Pit are my creation. As far as I know, there was never a religious cult called Our Lady of Mumbles.

Most of the characters are fictional, though I have introduced people from Swansea's varied history. Captain Isaac Colquhoun was the Chief Constable of Swansea (1877 – 1913). The Theophilus elopement is true and was big news in 1872. Constable Plumley did murder Thomas Fowler, a watchman in Llansamlet, in 1880, though not for the reasons given here. Ellen Sweeney who appeared in court on 278 occasions died in 1896. The boy Richard Dillwyn Llewelyn, who is so interested in death, is based upon William Dillwyn Llewelyn who was found dead in the woods in 1893 with a gunshot wound to the chest. He was 25 years old and heir to the estate. A court decided that there had been a hunting accident. Phillip Bowen is based upon a Sunday School teacher called Phillip Guy who lodged with Mrs Prosser on Nicol Street and drowned at Penllergare in 1880. It was decided that he had fallen into the river.

The derelict Penllergare House was demolished by explosives in 1961. The estate itself has been beautifully restored.

The incident with the frogs in bags comes from a report in the Spectator Magazine in 1859 about a Mormon church meeting in Cardiff.

Constance Bristow, who in the novel has adopted her maiden name of White, was a victim of domestic violence at the hands of her husband, a headteacher, who abandoned her and emigrated to America in 1872. Her relationship with Rumsey Bucke, which began in the first novel of the series, is my invention.

And Rumsey Bucke? He was a police inspector in Swansea who was forced to resign from his post in 1872 following accusations that he had uprooted and stolen a yew tree, a charge he always denied. It remains a very peculiar incident and, convinced of his innocence as I am, I believe that we have a duty to treat him more kindly.

Read more from Geoff Brookes

If you liked this story, then you will like the next in the series of Rumsey Bucke investigations by Geoff Brookes.

For more, see next page…

A SWANSEA CHILD

By Geoff Brookes

In the next novel in the series, *A Swansea Child*, Inspector Rumsey Bucke must find a lost heiress who has been living as an orphan in Swansea.

But he is not the only person looking for her-...

Extract from the book.

Something smashed into Bucke's truncheon, knocking it from his hand. He staggered on the stairs, keeping his balance by grabbing at the steps above him, as his truncheon fell into the darkness below.

A silent figure was now standing above him at the top of the steps, striking down at him with what seemed to be a staff.

Bucke instinctively moved his head to the side and the staff caught him sharply on the shoulder. The blow knocked him off the steps and on to the ground below. The attacker ran down the stairs after him, his boots confident on the steps. Winded though he was, Bucke had to get up; he would have no chance if he was on the ground. The man swiped at him again. Bucke was able to dodge and ram himself into his attacker's chest. He could feel leather, cold against his face. It was an apron; he was sure of it.

They both fell backwards and Bucke gasped, 'You are under arrest!' The man laughed and hit him on the side of the head. Bucke reached up and tried to grab his beard, but there wasn't one. He was thin and strong and wrestled himself free of Bucke's grasp. He slid off silently into the darkness.

Look out for this gripping story from Geoff Brookes, author of '*Our Lady of Mumbles*'. Published by Cambria Publishing.